PRAISE FOR JESSICA CLARE

"Blazing hot." —*USA Today*

"Great storytelling. . . . Delightful reading. . . . It's fun and oh so hot!" —*Kirkus Reviews*

"[Clare is] a romance writing prodigy."
—Heroes and Heartbreakers

"Clare has crafted a fiery, heartfelt love story that keeps on surprising . . . matching wit and warmth with plenty of spice. . . . Not to be missed." —RT Book Reviews

"A fast, sexy read that transports you." —Fiction Vixen

"[Clare's] writing is fun and sexy and flirty."
—The Book Pushers

"Very cute and oh so sexy." —Smexy Books

"An extremely sweet and HOT romance."
—Guilty Pleasures Book Reviews

TITLES BY JESSICA CLARE

Go Hex Yourself

WYOMING COWBOYS

All I Want for Christmas Is a Cowboy
The Cowboy and His Baby
A Cowboy Under the Mistletoe
The Cowboy Meets His Match
Her Christmas Cowboy
The Bachelor Cowboy
Holly Jolly Cowboy

ROUGHNECK BILLIONAIRES

Dirty Money
Dirty Scoundrel
Dirty Bastard

THE BILLIONAIRE BOYS CLUB

Stranded with a Billionaire
Beauty and the Billionaire
The Wrong Billionaire's Bed
Once Upon a Billionaire
Romancing the Billionaire
One Night with a Billionaire
His Royal Princess
Beauty and the Billionaire: The Wedding

BILLIONAIRES AND BRIDESMAIDS

The Billionaire and the Virgin
The Taming of the Billionaire
The Billionaire Takes a Bride
The Billionaire's Favorite Mistake
Billionaire on the Loose

THE BLUEBONNET NOVELS

The Girl's Guide to (Man)Hunting
The Care and Feeding of an Alpha Male
The Expert's Guide to Driving a Man Wild
The Virgin's Guide to Misbehaving
The Billionaire of Bluebonnet

GO HEX YOURSELF

JESSICA CLARE

JOVE
NEW YORK

A JOVE BOOK
Published by Berkley
An imprint of Penguin Random House LLC
penguinrandomhouse.com

Library of Congress Cataloging-in-Publication Data

Names: Clare, Jessica, author.
Title: Go hex yourself / Jessica Clare.
Description: First Edition. | New York: Jove, 2022.
Identifiers: LCCN 2021042006 (print) | LCCN 2021042007 (ebook) |
ISBN 9780593337561 (trade paperback) | ISBN 9780593337578 (ebook)
Classification: LCC PS3603.L353 G6 2022 (print) |
LCC PS3603.L353 (ebook) | DDC 813/.6—dc23
LC record available at https://lccn.loc.gov/2021042006
LC ebook record available at https://lccn.loc.gov/2021042007

First Edition: April 2022

Printed in the United States of America
1st Printing

Book design by Daniel Brount

For Daphne, my fellow rat

GO HEX YOURSELF

REGGIE

When I pull up to the location of my job interview in Nick's borrowed car, my first thought is that I've made a mistake. I peer up at the ominous-looking building, a black-brick Victorian tucked among several more-brightly colored neighbors, and consult my phone again. No, this is the right place. After all, there's only one Hemlock Avenue in the city. With a worried look, I glance up at the building again, then find a place to park a few streets over that's not too close and not too far away. It's a corner store, and I check the parking lot lines to ensure that I'm perfectly within my space, and then repark when I'm not entirely satisfied with how close I am to the yellow line. It takes a little more time, but it's always better to be precise than to be sloppy.

Ten minutes later, I'm down the street with a freshly fed meter running, and I've got my CV in hand. Am I really going to interview at someone's house for an assistant job? I'm a little uneasy at that, but it's for a gaming company, and those sorts of people are notoriously quirky . . . I think. I check the address one more time before I move up the steps and ring the doorbell, smoothing my skirt with sweaty hands. Up close, the building seems a little more imposing, with dark burgundy curtains covering every single window and not letting in a peep of light. The stairs up to the door have an ornate black iron railing, and even the door knocker looks like something out of a horror movie, all vines and animal heads.

Someone has a goth fetish, clearly.

The door opens, and I'm startled to see a woman about my age in jeans and a T-shirt proclaiming her favorite baseball team. Her hair's pulled back into a bedraggled ponytail, and she's not wearing a stitch of makeup. She's also about twenty months pregnant, if the balloon under her shirt is any indication.

"You must be Regina," she exclaims with a warm smile, rubbing the bulge of her stomach. "Hey there! Come on in."

I'm horribly overdressed. I bite my lip as I step inside, painfully aware of the clack of my low-heeled pumps on the dark hardwood floors. I'm wearing a gray jacket over a white blouse and a gray pencil skirt, and I have to admit, the feeling that I'm in the wrong place keeps hitting me over and over again. I don't normally make these mistakes. I like for things to go perfectly. It's the control freak in me that needs that satisfaction. I researched what one wears to an assistant interview, so I don't know how I flubbed this so badly. I want to check the ad one more time, but after rereading it over and over for the last three days, I know what it says by heart.

SPELLCRAFT EXPERTISE WANTED

Assistant required. Excellent pay for familiar.

I mean, I've been a fan of the card game Spellcraft: The Magicking since I was a teenager. I have thousands of dollars of cards and even placed second in a local tournament once. Sure, I was playing an eight-year-old . . . but he had a good deck. Heck,

I've even brought my favorite deck with me in my purse, in case they think I'm bluffing about my love for the Spellcraft game.

So am I qualified? Fuck yeah, I am. I can be an assistant to someone that works for the Spellcraft: The Magicking company. It's kinda my dream job. Well . . . my dream job is actually to work on the cards themselves, but I'm not experienced enough for that, so being an assistant would be the next best thing. But I'm smart, I'm reasonably educated, I'm good with spreadsheets, and I'm excessively, excessively organized.

(Some might say "obsessively," but I ignore haters.)

I smile at the pregnant woman, suspecting she's the one I talked to on the phone. "You're Lisa?"

"That's me!"

I hold out my CV, tucked into a fancy leather-bound folder. I pray that the nice packaging will hide the fact that my detailed CV is kinda light on office jobs and heavier on things like "Burger Basket" and "Clown holding sign in front of Tax Masters." It's all about enthusiasm, though, right? I've got that in spades.

Lisa takes the folder from me with a little frown on her face, as if she's not quite sure what to do with it, and then gestures at the house. "Want me to show you around Ms. Magnus's house? She'd be the one in charge day to day."

Er, that's kind of odd. Why do I need to know about my employer's house? Maybe she's just really proud of the place? But since I'm interviewing, I paste on a bright smile. "That'd be great."

Lisa's smile brightens, and she puts her hands on her belly, waddling through the foyer. "Follow me."

I do, and I can't help but notice that the interior of the place looks much larger than the exterior suggested. Inside, the ceilings are incredibly high, and the rooms seem airy despite the dark coloring. The walls are the same burgundy red, and several of them are covered in reproductions of ancient Roman murals. "Your boss must like Roman stuff."

"Oh, she's Roman. All the big names are," she calls over her shoulder.

"Ah." Funny, I researched the game and thought the CEOs were from Seattle. Maybe she's an investor? Who just likes to talk about the game? That might be kind of fun. My enthusiasm brightens as Lisa shows me through the living room and the modern, elegant kitchen. She heads down a long hall and looks over at me again. "This way to the lab."

"Lab?" I echo. "Oh, you mean office?" I beam. "It's so charming that she calls it a lab."

"What else would she call it?" Lisa opens a large symbol-covered door, and I think Ms. Magnus must be a huge nerd to decorate her office like this. When we step inside, though, I'm a little stunned. There's a large desk, all right, but instead of a laptop and paperwork, there are beakers and bottles. An old book is spread out on the table itself, and the walls are lined with jars and more books. The ceiling is hung with what look like dried herbs.

It's an absolute nightmare. Every iota of my organization-loving heart cringes at the sight of this. It's clear that Ms. Magnus needs me. I'd never let a place of work get this disorganized. The books are all over the place, there's no computer to be seen, and I'm pretty sure under the stacks of loose paper and piles of nonsense, there's a bookshelf. Somewhere.

It all needs a guiding hand, and that's what I do best. Guide. Or . . . control. Whatever. I'm good at this kind of thing.

"So this is the lab," Lisa chirps. "I hope you're up to date on your herbs, because a lot of Dru's favorite spells are plant based. She's more of a traditionalist, unlike her nephew." Her hands go to the small of her back, and she stretches uncomfortably. "You'll see him around here from time to time, by the way. He lives in Boston, but when he's in town, he stays with Dru. And he might ask you to assist him with some minor stuff. Mostly running errands."

"Sorry, what?" I ask, peering at a jar that really looks like it's got a pickled frog in it, of all things. These props are really incredible. It looks like something out of a witchy movie, all right, except there are no cobwebs or cauldron, and I'm definitely not at the apex of some fog-covered mountain, being chased by a hero. I poke another jar, but it just looks like it has wizened berries of some kind in it. "This place is amazing. Does she use these props to help her get in the mood? Sort of like method acting?"

"Method what?"

I turn to look at Lisa, and as I do, I suck in a breath at the sight of a glowering god standing in the doorway to the room. The man there looks . . . intense. He's impossibly tall, with broad shoulders that would put a linebacker to shame. He's dressed in a black suit with a black shirt underneath, complete with black tie, and his hair is dark and just brushes his collar. The long, solemn face is unsmiling, his expression stern, but his mouth is full and pink and shocking against the paleness of his skin.

"Who are you?" he asks bluntly, ignoring Lisa and looking right at me.

"Hello," I gush, extending my hand and moving forward. "I'm Reggie Johnson, here about the job. I'm such a big fan of . . ."

The tall man gives me an up-and-down look and then dismisses me as if I'm unimportant. He turns to Lisa and holds out a piece of paper. "I need these books from the library. Today. And did you file those requests I asked for?"

"I'll get to them," Lisa says tersely. She deliberately rubs her belly and glares at the man, who glares back.

Well, this is awkward. I tuck my hands back down to my sides and glance between the two of them. I truly hope that this isn't going to be my boss, because yikes. Hot but pissy.

The man casts another imperious look in my direction and then points a finger at Lisa. "Get it done, today." He turns on his heel and leaves without acknowledging me, and then he's gone.

Lisa sticks her tongue out at his back. "Such a dick."

My mouth has gone dry. "Is that . . . Mr. Magnus?" If so, my boss has a stunningly handsome (and stunningly dickish) husband.

"Sure is."

I divert my attention to what looks like a stack of bills shoved under a book, and my hands twitch with the need to clean up. "Does Mr. Magnus work for his wife?"

Her eyes widen, and then she chuckles. "Oh no. That's *a* Mr. Magnus, but he's not married to Dru. He's her nephew and between assistants himself, so I'm having to fill in." She leans toward me confidentially. "No one likes him. Can't keep anyone in his employ."

My smile returns. "I'm good at multitasking." I'm also a huge suck-up.

Lisa snaps her fingers and then pulls out her phone. "While I'm thinking about it, I had a few questions for you."

"Oh, of course." I read a book last night on interview questions one could expect for a fast-paced job, so I'm more than ready for this. I do wonder when we're going to get to the sit-down part of the interview, but maybe Lisa's just doing introductions before I meet her boss. That makes sense, and I give her a practiced "I'm very interested" look. "Ask away."

She flicks through her phone with her thumb. "Any allergies, food or otherwise?"

"No." Weird, but maybe I'd be in charge of getting coffee or grocery shopping or something. Some assistants do that, don't they? "Do you need to write this down? Should I take notes for you?" I dig in my purse, pulling out a notepad and pen. "I'm happy to do so."

"Not necessary." Lisa taps something on her phone, and I'm pretty sure I hear game music. She stares at the screen for a moment and then looks back at me. "Star sign?"

Getting weirder. "Taurus."

"Ah, a hard worker and stubborn." She dimples, nodding. "She'll like that. Tauruses are great employees. Very easy to work with."

"Thank . . . you?"

"Too bad Mr. Magnus is a Cancer. Very moody." She makes a face, still locked onto her phone. "Here we go. Any particular crystal affinity?" She gestures at one of the shelves, and I notice for the first time that there are rows and rows of crystals of all shapes and sizes in glass containers. Not in any sort of order, of course, but I'm sure I can help with that, too.

"Um, I don't think so?" This is definitely verging on fully weird territory. I'm starting to get a little uneasy, but I glance around the office again. Maybe this woman is some kind of new-age hipster that needs inspiration to work on the game? "What do crystals have to do with the position?"

"A lot. Blood type?"

"Is that really important?" I ask finally, resisting the urge to show my frustration.

"Not necessarily," Lisa admits. "But Ms. Magnus likes to know."

"I'm an O."

"Wonderful." She types with her thumb. "Any physical ailments? Do you work out at a gym? Eat healthy?"

I'm torn between pointing out that those are extremely inappropriate questions and just answering, because I really want the job. "I count macros," I say after a long moment. "For my nutrition." And because it feeds my obsessive need for control to hit the numbers perfectly.

She tilts her head. "I guess that's pretty good. Come with me, and I'll show you into Ms. Magnus's personal offices."

I follow behind her, glancing backward at the "lab" we're leaving. If that's not the office . . . Nope, Reggie. Don't ask questions until they mention the pay. You've had weird jobs before. As long as it pays well, you can put up with weirdness. I paste a smile on my face and follow Lisa's slower steps down the hall and toward the stairs. As we cut through the house, I glance over at the kitchen. Mr. Magnus is in there, with a glass of water in front of him on the counter. He's leaning over it and staring intently in our direction, practically scowling.

I can't help but notice that the kitchen is in complete disarray, with dishes on the counter and several cabinets hanging open. Maybe he hates the mess as much as I do, and that's why he's cranky.

"Just ignore him," Lisa continues. "He doesn't like strangers. Remember. Cancer sign."

Right. Moody. That fits him. I cast a brilliant smile in his direction, and I'm pleased when he gives me a startled look and turns away. I could swear he's blushing. Suck on that, Magnus.

We walk down the hall, and it seems the house gets bigger the deeper I go into it. The hall branches off into two others, both of them lined with doors, and there's a high ceiling with a crystal-covered chandelier above the stairwell. I gaze around me in awe as Lisa leads me past a glorious-looking library filled to the gills with all kinds of old books. There are portraits on the walls, most of them old, and I realize that the Magnus family is old, old money. No wonder they're eccentric. Lisa heads toward a pair of double doors and opens them. "Just have a seat, and I'll let Ms. Magnus know that you're here."

"Thank you," I murmur and step inside.

She turns and goes to leave and then pauses in the doorway. "Actually, before I go, I should give you a bit of a warning about Ms. Magnus." Lisa gives me an apologetic little look. "She can be a bit of a . . ." She hesitates, clearly choosing her words.

Oh boy. Here it comes. "Hard-ass?"

Lisa clears her throat. "Ding-dong."

I blink.

Of all the things I expected to hear, "ding-dong" wasn't one of them. This whole place has a weird vibe, and the more Lisa talks, the more I'm not sure this is a good idea. I think about the weird nutrition questions, and my Spidey sense tingles. "You know what? Maybe I should go—"

"No! You're the only applicant so far!" A panicked look comes across her face. "You read the ad, so you're clearly more than qualified. Please, Regina, just stay a little longer. I know Ms. Magnus can be a bit eccentric, but that's why she pays her assistants so well."

I bite my lip. "Exactly how well?" I feel like a bit of a heel for asking, but since she's calling her employer a ding-dong, I guess politeness is out the window, right?

Her expression relaxes. "Twenty-five thousand."

I blanch. "A year?" I do some quick math in my head. That's a little under five hundred a week, and I'm pretty sure the local coffee shop pays more than that. Maybe I should apply there instead. Oh, but the tables there are always so damned messy. It'd drive me crazy to see customers leaving the place like that.

"Oh no." Lisa giggles. "A month. It pays twenty-five thousand a month." She leans forward and puts a hand to her mouth, whispering. "She's loaded. Absolutely no clue of what anything costs these days."

My mouth goes dry, and my knees feel weak. "A m-month?" I stammer. That's insane. That's three hundred grand a year.

"To put up with an out-of-touch ding-dong, yes." Lisa raises her eyebrows at me. "Still interested?"

I nod wordlessly. She closes the door after me, and I'm left alone in the room, trying to catch my breath. Twenty-five thousand dollars a month. Good god. The things I could do with that money. I wouldn't even have to work here long, I reason. Even if Ms. Magnus is completely unbearable, a month or two and I can pay off all my bills and get a down payment on a decent place to live. I can put up with any sort of bullshit for twenty-five grand a month.

I could . . . I could pay off some of Mom and Dad's debt.

No, I chide myself immediately, squelching that line of thinking. They are not your responsibility. They got themselves into that mess.

With a little sigh, I look around the room. It's a study, all right, with books along one wall and all kinds of creepy dead stuffed animals along another. There's a stuffed ostrichlike bird standing in the corner, and several other dead animals in various stages of taxidermy are scattered about the room. Blech. Absently, I reach out and turn what looks like a stuffed ferret on its stand so it faces the right direction. Someone likes dead critters. I wrinkle my nose as I move toward a big glass case laid out upon an antique table, and I'm not entirely surprised to see it contains hundreds of dead bugs, all neatly pinned. Because of course.

I move over to the bookcase, wondering if this lady likes the classics. The organizer in me reads the spines to see if they're in any particular sort of order, but as I try to read the lettering, it fades and I can't make it out. Odd. I pick up a book. It's written in some sort of scrawling, scribbly language I can't understand, and the binding feels cool to the touch. I put it back and glance around, and as I do, I notice the door is open. Is it the hot jackass again? As I frown at the door, an elderly woman steps in, cane in hand. She's wearing a floral muumuu and a bright purple turban on her head that looks as if it went out of date a hundred years ago, and she's so old that liver spots cover her paper-thin golden skin. She is way, way too old to be the auntie of the hot dickbag downstairs, and I smile at her.

"Hi there."

She looks up at me, and her eyes are sharp even as she sits down in one of the chairs for guests. "Far too many stairs in this house," she says disapprovingly. "Whoever made this place never had to walk a day in heels in her life."

I can't disagree. I smile, nudging a statue that looks slightly out of place. I notice that the woman's feet are bare, and her cheeks are round like a cherub's and bright pink with rouge of some kind. "Are you here for the job?" I ask.

I look around for Lisa, but she's nowhere to be found. The woman is a bit old, but she's got a sweet expression on her face, and my heart hurts at the idea that she needs to find employment at this stage in her life.

The woman nods. "I suppose I am."

"Did you . . . forget your shoes?" I smile politely. "Your feet are bare."

"Was I supposed to wear shoes?" The elderly woman looks puzzled. "Is that a requirement?"

"Perhaps not." I don't want to make her feel bad. Why is she here, though? Shouldn't the interviewers be more cognizant of this sort of thing? Maybe Lisa didn't see the woman's feet with her big pregnant belly in the way, though. I decide friendliness is the way to go. Older players of Spellcraft aren't that uncommon, though perhaps not this old. "Big fan?"

She glances up at the ceiling. "Is it big?"

I fight back a giggle and pick up another book, flipping through it. More gibberish, this one with all kinds of hideous drawings in it. Again, I can't read the spine, which is frustrating. How does anyone keep anything organized in this place? Maybe that explains some of the utter chaos. "I meant the game. Are you a big fan of the game?"

"Is it a game?" she asks, musing. "Some would say it's more of a lifestyle."

I think of the sheer dollar amounts I've spent on rare cards and the weekend conventions I used to drive to with my college friends. "Well, you're not wrong about that."

Lisa rushes in a moment later, all smiles. "Oh good, you've met." She moves to stand next to the tiny woman, and when she struggles to stand, Lisa helps her up. "That saves me some time."

Boy, this place is really unprofessional. I hesitate and then put the book down, moving over to Lisa's side. "Are we really supposed to meet if we're interviewing for the same position?" Part of me wants to leave, but the small greedy part of Reggie deep inside is screaming, *TWENTY-FIVE THOUSAND A MONTH!* "It seems . . . a little unfair to pit us against each other."

"Same position?" Lisa says blankly. She turns back to the elderly woman and helps her behind the desk. "What? No, she's the witch."

That makes me pause. Hard. That . . . seems rude. "I'm sorry. Did you say '*bitch*'?"

"WITCH," the elderly woman clearly enunciates as if I'm deaf.

"Witch," I repeat.

"Yes. This job is for a witch's familiar." Lisa rolls her eyes. "Though I suppose the modern term is more like 'executive assistant' or some such. Whatever it is, she is the witch." Lisa gestures at the wizened old woman. "This is Ms. Magnus of the House of Magnus." The door opens, and the tall, dark man steps in. "That is Ben Magnus, her nephew. Also of the House of Magnus."

"A witch house," Ms. Magnus adds brightly. "Fine, rich magical bloodlines run deep in my family. Have for millennia. Though I do like 'bitch,' too."

I make a noise that might be a protest or just kind of a squawk. Now they're all frowning in my direction. Lisa squints at me. "What exactly did you think this job was about?"

I sit down weakly in the chair across from the desk. "A card game?"

BEN

This is a bad idea. Most of my aunt's ideas are bad ones, granted, but this ranks up there with the worst of them. I glare at the woman flipping through my aunt's books as if they're not precious spell tomes. She's all wrong for the job.

This isn't a card game. This is high-stakes magic, and it's something she clearly doesn't believe in. The moment my aunt mentioned she was a witch, that knowing smile came over the girl's face. The "ah, I get it now" look that said she thought she was dealing with a senile person. The young woman applying for the job smiles at me, all bright teeth and guileless innocence, and . . . yeah. She's a bad fit for this.

She's freckled, for fuck's sake. No one is going to take my aunt seriously with a sunny, smiling, freckled familiar.

So I grab Aunt Dru by the sleeve of her very ugly, very voluminous floral robe and pull her out of her study. Her pregnant familiar follows behind us, ever the loyal shadow. Once we're far enough away that the job applicant can't hear our conversation, I lean in toward my aunt. "Send her home. She's all wrong."

"Oh, Caliban, darling, she's perfect for the job." Aunt Dru

reaches up and pats my cheek as if I'm a boy of five years instead of five hundred. "You're just being overprotective."

"I can't take the time to train her," I point out. "I'm busy."

"Then I'll train her," Drusilla says, as if it's the logical answer to everything. "I trained Lisa, and look at how wonderfully she turned out."

My lip curls as I glance at the "wonderfully" trained Lisa. The freckled woman studiously pretends to examine her nails. "Didn't she get herself pregnant through a misfired sex-magic spell?"

"Hey!" Lisa says, frowning.

Aunt Dru smacks me on my arm. "Caliban, we don't talk about that. Be polite."

"It's Ben, Auntie, and I think we should." I straighten, glaring at Lisa. "If she'd been better trained, perhaps you wouldn't be looking for a new assistant."

Lisa glares at me, all belly and outrage, but I don't care. I'm not going to mince words to spare her feelings. My aunt is in dire need of a familiar, and it's clear to me that once again, I'm going to have to step in and clean up the mess that follows in Dru's wake. "Send her away, Aunt Dru. We'll petition the Society of Familiars and see if they can send you a temporary assistant."

"Forget the society," Dru says, patting my arm. "I like this young lady. She'll do nicely. And I need an assistant, pronto-haste."

"Posthaste," I correct. "And I don't care if you like her."

"Well it's not as if you're swimming in assistants, either, Caliban." My aunt puts her hands on her hips. "So I can't borrow yours."

My nostrils flare, and I fight back the urge to lose my temper. My . . . inability to keep an assistant is a sore spot I'd prefer not to poke at right now. "Send her away."

"No."

I pinch the bridge of my nose, wondering if there's a potion I can make for the throbbing migraine building behind my eyes. "You know how this is going to turn out, Aunt Dru. Do you remember Benedict?"

"Benedict . . . Benedict . . ." My aunt flutters her lashes and pretends ignorance. "Doesn't ring a bell."

"The Puritan? The one you recruited because you liked his smile? He drove you out of Salem."

"Well, maybe I was tired of Salem," Aunt Dru says defensively. She lifts her small chin defiantly. "You don't know for sure, Caliban. Maybe I was just tired of wearing black and white."

"Ben," I say again. The name "Caliban" is as dated as my aunt's spells. "Let me remind you how this is going to turn out, then." I jab a finger at the door to my aunt's study. "That woman is going to take the job, because she's desperate. She reeks of it. You're going to bring her in. You're going to show her things that are going to blow her mortal mind, and she's going to flip her lid. She's going to run off and tell the world about what she saw, and the other houses are going to panic. We're going to have every witch and warlock on the East Coast in our hair, and all because you can't wait a few weeks to get a professional!"

My aunt scowls up at me, her mouth tight. "You're yelling, Caliban—"

"BEN!" I roar. "It's been Ben since 1807!"

"Ben is not a good Roman name," Aunt Dru says with a sniff, dismissing everything I've said. She puts a small, wrinkled hand on my sleeve. "And I do hear your concerns, darling. I do. But they're easily fixed."

"How?" I ask flatly.

"What about a spell?" she asks.

Behind her, Lisa snaps her fingers. "Or a nondisclosure."

"Perfect," Aunt Dru continues. "A nondisclosure spell."

"Actually I meant a contract," Lisa interrupts. "A nondisclosure agreement. All the big businesses use them nowadays."

"Spell, contract, same thing." Aunt Dru shrugs and then pats my arm again. "It'll be taken care of, Caliban dear. Now if you don't mind, I need to put my hair in curlers. Julia the Younger went to an antique sale this weekend and found the ugliest vase shaped like a chicken. She wants me to come see it for myself."

"We're not done here," I say wearily. "Nothing's been decided."

"It's been decided," Aunt Dru says breezily. "I like this girl. I'm hiring her."

When my aunt is like this, she's impossible. No wonder Chicago burned in 1871. She was too stubborn to put out her fire spell then, and she's too stubborn to get rid of the girl waiting in her study now. I scowl, thinking about the applicant. Her big, easy smile. Her confusion as Dru mentioned actual spellcraft.

Her freckles.

This is a fight I'm not going to win, and I have places to be tonight. I have to catch a flight to Boston for the meeting of my warlock order, and attendance is mandatory. If I had a familiar, I'd just send him, but . . . I rub a hand down my face in frustration. "Give her a week trial," I say, deciding to try to compromise with my aunt. "Teach her nothing important, nothing urgent. See if she has what it takes. If she fucks up, cast a memory-clearing spell or curse her. I don't care which. Just make it stick, and send her on her way. When I get back from Boston, I'll help you find a real familiar. All right?"

"You're so very thoughtful, Caliban." My aunt winks at me as if I'm not on the verge of losing my temper. "Always looking out for your dear old auntie." She pats her hair. "Now I really do have to get my curlers. Lisa—"

"Coming," Lisa says, waddling after my aunt.

My jaw flexes. I watch the two women depart, and I can't shake the feeling that this is a mistake. This is idiocy. You never hire off the street for a familiar. Never. Even the greenest warlock knows that. I can only imagine the shit I'm going to get at the annual week-long warlock meeting that starts this weekend, and I run my hand down my face again. When I look up, the door to my aunt's study is open. The girl stands in the doorway, frowning at me.

"Did . . . did she leave? Is the job interview done?"

"Yes," I snap, storming past her and heading for the stairs. "You didn't get the job."

REGGIE

What a diiiick.

I stare after him as he heads away. There was no need for him to be ugly like that; there really wasn't. I fight back the crushing disappointment at another job slipping through my fingers and turn back toward the small, cluttered office I've been left in. There's a stack of books on one corner of the desk, and while I should probably get going, the neat freak in me won't let me leave without trying to tidy things a little. So I go through the books, trying to alphabetize them, but when that proves futile because I can't read the writing, I organize them by color and size. I dust a little and line up the jars on the shelf, making sure they're all label out and alphabetized as well.

As I do, the door opens again and I jump. "Oh, I'm sorry—"

The small, sprightly woman in the garish robe now has an absolute mountain of haphazard curlers in her white hair. She beams at me, all apple cheeks and wrinkles. "Already getting started, I see?"

I hesitate, my hands going behind my back so I don't move

forward and straighten a curler about to slide down her forehead. "I thought I didn't get the job? The gentleman said—"

The elderly woman titters, waving a hand before thumping into the nearest seat. "That was my nephew, Caliban. He is most definitely not a gentleman. And he's just grouchy. I think all warlocks are, at heart."

Right. This magic stuff again. I eye my surroundings. The first time they threw up the whole "magic" word, I immediately wanted to leave. People that think they're truly casting magic? That's insanity, and all the trappings here just feed into it. But as I straightened up the room, I realized how disappointed I was that I didn't get the job. The money sounds amazing. Life changing. I realized I didn't care if they were a little deluded about magic being real. There are people that dress up like Victorians and live their lives, right? There are people that think they're vampires. I can go along with some Gandalf crap for twenty-five grand a freaking month. So when the older lady waves a hand in the air, I feel a stirring of hope again.

"So I'm still in the running for the job?"

"As far as I'm concerned, you can have the job," Ms. Magnus declares. "Unless you're diabetic. Wouldn't want you passing out all the time. Or anemic."

Er, okay. I'm pretty sure diabetics don't just drop in the streets, so I'm not sure why she thinks they'd pass out all the time. I chalk it up to more kookiness. "So . . . when do I start?"

"When can you move in?"

My eyebrows go up. I hadn't considered that part of the job. "Oh, am I moving in?"

"How are you going to assist me if you don't?" She looks confused. "On that World Wide Web thing?"

"The . . . internet? You want the job to be virtual?"

"Virtual?" Ms. Magnus blinks. "I don't think your virtue has anything to do with this. You can be as free as you like."

I lick my lips, pausing. "I'm . . . confused."

"Oh, darling." Ms. Magnus shakes her head. "Me too. All the time."

The pregnant woman sticks her head in. "Can I interrupt?"

"Isn't that what you're doing?" Ms. Magnus asks.

Lisa ignores her and steps inside. "I don't know if the ad mentioned it, but this is a live-in position. You won't be on call constantly, but Ms. Magnus prefers her assistants to live in the house so any odd jobs that come up can be easily handled."

Oh. That explains the money. It's a live-in position because Ms. Magnus clearly isn't in touch with reality. "Of course. That makes sense. I'd need to tell my roommate first." After we both squeal and dance about the pay, that is. Nick will be thrilled for me . . . Well, maybe not super thrilled if it means I move out, but he'll understand. I'll keep making my rent payments, too, just so he doesn't struggle. I can do this, though. I really can. "And you're certain Mr. Magnus . . ."

Ms. Magnus just snorts, and that curler dips a little lower on her forehead. "You'll just have to ignore his bad temper. We all do."

Well now, that I can do. I'm good at ignoring things that bother me. I learned that from my parents. I smile at Ms. Magnus and Lisa. "Do I need to sign a contract to start work, then?"

"A tablet," Ms. Magnus chirps.

"Oh, like an electronic one? Sure, I can do that." I watch as Lisa crosses the room and heads to the desk. I expect her to pull out an iPad or something along those lines.

Instead, she pulls out what looks like . . . a square block of a charcoal-like substance with some writing on it. And a stylus.

"A tablet," Lisa says.

REGGIE

So there's good news and bad news," I say as I breeze into the apartment I share with my best friend, Nick, a short time later. "Which do you want first?"

He's in the kitchen, putting away some canned soups and ramen—the staples of our sad, cheap diet. It's not easy being broke, but we make do. He's still wearing his work clothes, the name of the private gym emblazoned across his broad back. Nick turns, grimacing when I enter, and I'm not sure if it's because he got caught putting cans away without the labels facing out, or if it's because he's afraid of my news. "You didn't get the job?"

"I did get the job," I correct, going over to help him.

The moment I reach into the bag, he smacks my hand. "No touching," Nick tells me. "You're just going to say I'm doing it wrong, and you'll stress me out."

"Sorry," I say meekly, clasping my hands behind my back. I'll have to come through later and organize things properly. When he's not looking. "But I did get the job. And it pays an absurd amount of money."

"How much is absurd?"

"Twenty-five grand a month."

Nick's mouth falls open. He clutches one of the cans, staring at me. "You're joking."

"I'm not joking."

He doesn't look excited. If anything, he looks worried. "Reg. What's the catch?"

I cross my arms over my chest, feigning outrage. "Why does there have to be a catch?"

"Well, for starters, it's a job you found in the paper. No one advertises in the paper anymore." He stacks two different brands of soup onto one another and shoves them into the cabinet. "And two, they hired you for that kind of job without a second interview? It smells like a scam." He moves toward the fridge to put away a container of hummus (his favorite splurge).

I discreetly reopen the cabinet and shuffle the soup cans. Brands together. Expiration dates to the front. Then flavors. Then—

"Reg," Nick warns, catching me in the act.

"Sorry." I reluctantly put a can back in the wrong place, even though it wounds me, and turn to face him. "The catch is that I have to live with this kooky old lady who thinks she's a witch."

"And is she?"

I snort. "Of course not. Magic's not real." I wave a hand in the air. "She's like those people that dress up and hit each other with swords on the weekends at college."

His brows go up. "So she's LARPing?"

"It's almost the same, isn't it?" I shrug. "Look. She's got money, she wants a live-in assistant, and it sounds nutty, but if I humor her and play along, I get paid ridiculous amounts of money. Even if I work there for just a month or two, we can catch up on all the bills. You can advertise for more clients. And I'll still pay my half of the rent. You'll just have privacy for a while."

Nick hesitates. "You're positive this isn't a dangerous situation? She's not going to murder you while you sleep and you'll be in the papers?"

"Ms. Magnus? Absolutely not." I think about the small, fragile woman in the floral robe and the curlers drooping over her head. "She'd forget where she left the knife."

"Golden Girl?" he asks.

"Definitely a Rose," I reassure him. It's his favorite show, and we've often debated over what category most people fall into. Blanches are fun seekers, Roses are harmless, Sophias are know-it-alls, and Dorothys are problematic.

Nick relaxes, nodding. "That's good, then. So you'll just be working for her?"

"She does have a nephew that helps her with things, I think." I don't point out that he's absolutely a Dorothy—the negative, sour attitude and bossiness evident even in our short meeting. "But I think he's gone a lot. It won't be a problem."

"And you're fine with working for someone who thinks she's a witch?"

I chuckle. "Of course I am. If it makes her happy to pretend to live in some Wiccan fantasy, who am I to tell her no? Let her do as she likes."

My roommate is silent for a long moment as he closes the refrigerator and then leans against it, thinking. "That's a lot of money," he finally says.

"A whole lot."

"You're not going to tell your parents, are you?" He gives me a narrow-eyed look, because Nick knows me all too well.

I give him a firm shake of my head. "Didn't even cross my mind."

"Reg." The way he says my name tells me he knows I'm lying.

Busted. "Okay, maybe I thought about it just a teeny, tiny bit." At his angry look, I sigh. "It's just . . . I know it could help them.

And I can't possibly spend it all myself, especially if I'm living with my employer. That's a ton of money, and even just a slice of it could make a difference—"

"Regina Marie Johnson," Nick says in a parental voice. "We have had this discussion a hundred times."

I hunch my shoulders. "I know."

"You can't keep giving them money. They're users."

"I'm their daughter."

"They're users," Nick says firmly, and I know he's right. I know he is. It's just that the sad, lonely part of me that's desperate for approval is . . . well, still desperate for approval. "They're users, and they would bleed you dry if given half a chance. And you've given them a dozen chances."

"But—"

"Remember that time they said the IRS was coming for them, and so you took out a loan with the bank? And then they drove up in a sports car?"

Remember it? I'm still paying for that loan. I bite my lip so I don't protest. I know Nick is right. I know he's looking out for me.

"And then there's the time they opened a life insurance policy against you and reported you dead—"

"Okay, okay," I mutter. "I won't say anything." I feel stupid for even thinking about it.

"Reg," Nick says in that knowing voice of his. He puts his hands on my shoulders. "I know it's hard for you. I know you want to think the best of them. But some people aren't worth bothering with. They're a black hole, and no matter how much you put in, you're not going to get anything out. You've been down this road before."

I nod, fighting back a knot of emotion in my throat. Nick's always been there to pick up the pieces when my parents let me down again. He's helped me make payments when they've left me holding the check. He's endured endless calls from creditors because he lives with me. He's always had my back. I need to listen to him. "You're right."

He grins at me. "Of course I'm right. Now let me put away these groceries, and I'll make you a cheap-ass special for dinner and then I'll help you pack."

A chuckle escapes me, my mood lightening. Nick's just as broke as me. He changed careers a year ago to personal training, and it's been a slow climb for him to build a client base. I watch him as he puts away the last of the groceries and decide to change the subject. "So you worked today?" When he nods, I prompt, "Was Sergeant Hotness there?"

Nick's cheeks darken with a barely perceptible flush. "Maybe."

Ooh, exciting. Nick's mentioned how gorgeous he is several times, and how friendly. I'd be willing to bet that the attraction isn't just one-sided. Nick's a cutie. He's fit and loyal and fun to be around. "Did you ask him out?"

"He's military, Reg."

"That just means he's got a uniform in that closet. You could offer him some free *personal* training." I wiggle my eyebrows. "Help him fill out those tight uniform pants."

Nick groans. "You're the worst."

✴ ✴ ✴

THE NEXT DAY, Nick drops me off in front of Ms. Magnus's house with a small pack of clothes, a box of my favorite Spellcraft cards, and a boatload of worried, brotherly instructions. "If anyone seems weird, text me," he says for the seventh time that day. "I'll drop everything and come get you, no questions asked. And make sure you lock your door at night. I don't care if she's a harmless old lady. You be safe. And—"

"I'll text you when I get settled," I promise Nick and get out of the car before he can lecture me further. "It'll be fine." I blow him a kiss, shut the car door, and then bound across the street, my heart racing. I'm not sure what the daily dress code will be, so I'm wearing my favorite red cardigan over khakis and a plain T-shirt. My heart hammers as I ring the doorbell and then wait for someone to let me in. I clutch the box to my chest, anxious. What if she's changed her mind? What if she doesn't want me to be her assistant? What if she's been placed in a nursing home—

The door opens. Ms. Magnus is on the other side, wearing a glittery-looking tunic top and a long skirt. She's got glasses perched on her nose and a fringed scarf wrapped around her shoulders. Her hair is puffed up into cherubic white curls, and her lips are pink with gloss.

She's also wearing a necklace with what looks like dried chicken feet on it.

Because she's a witch. Right. "Hello, Ms. Magnus," I say cheerfully. "I'm here for my first day on the job!"

"Call me Dru, darling," she says, opening the door wider so I can come inside. "And please, make yourself at home. We're very informal here."

A good sign. I smile at her, holding my things close. "I can't wait to get started. I know this is going to be just wonderful for both of us."

She beams at me, her gaze falling to the brightly decorated box clutched to my chest, the one covered with dragons and runes. "Is that your curse kit?"

"Wh-what?" I stammer.

"What?" she echoes innocently.

"It's cards. Spellcraft? The Magicking?" I hold the branded box out. It's a little worn around the edges, but I won it in a tournament a few years ago and I'm pretty proud of it. "It's a collectible card game, and I like to play it in my downtime or craft decks.

I thought I'd bring it with me, though most of my collection is at home."

Part of me wanted to bring it to prove that I do have a reason for thinking the ad was about the card game. Part of me really just wants to shove it in that Mr. Magnus's face.

"That's nice, dear." Her expression brightens. "Let me show you to your room! Lisa cleared her stuff out this morning, and she'll be back with her husband in a few days to pick up the rest of her things."

I nod and step inside, eyeing the marble bust of a very ugly, wrinkled man that leers at me from the entryway. Was that here last time? I can't recall. "So what's a curse kit?"

"Did I say curse kit? I must have misspoken." She smiles sweetly at me, all innocence. "I thought we'd get you settled in and bake some cookies. How does that sound?"

My heart melts a little at that. Ms. Magnus—Dru—reminds me of the grandmother I never had. I always wanted grandparents, but my parents had been disowned by theirs before I was born, and I've never had anyone. That cranky guy is so lucky to have someone like this, and I feel a stab of pure envy. "I would love to make cookies with you, Dru. Lead the way and I'll drop off my things." I'll just work the sweets into my daily macros.

Dru talks happily about the weather as she leads me through the strange house, heading up the stairs and to the right. "My room is down the hall on the other side," she explains, "but yours has been spelled to notify you if I need assistance."

"Spelled?"

"Oh, right." She pauses on the stairs. "Wired?"

"Ah. Like an intercom?"

Dru smiles brightly. "Sure, we'll call it that." She gestures at the room, opening the door. "This is you. The bathroom is down the hall. I do hope that's all right. It's an older house, and I can't seem to find a good, trustworthy contractor to make the proper renovations to give you an en suite. The last one had to be cursed."

"Cursed," I echo. "Did you say cursed?"

"He cursed a lot," she amends. "That's what I meant. At any rate, it's just you and me on this floor." She points at two rooms across the hall. "Those are guest rooms and rarely used. We're not very popular with the other ranking families. The Magnus line is a little . . . eccentric." She gestures at the closed door farther down the hall. "And that, of course, is where Caliban stays if he's in town for a while."

"That's your nephew?"

"The unpleasant one, yes."

"You have a pleasant one?"

She titters, as if I've said something funny. "No, I'm afraid not. Just him."

I'm not sure if I like that I'm staying one room down from an asshole like him. "Does the door lock?" I ask mildly, because I don't want to offend her.

"Of course. And Caliban very rarely stays with me anyhow. He's in Boston most of the time. I can assure you that he won't bother you in the slightest." Dru reaches out and pats my arm. "We'll make sure you're protected, dear. And he wouldn't touch you. He knows what hell it is to try and get a new familiar. I assure you that he'll ignore you. You're not his type anyhow."

Um, okay. I'm pretty sure I don't want to be his type anyhow. "Great."

The phone rings downstairs—a landline, of all things. Dru immediately lights up. "That'd be Flavia! I have to go get it. Will you be all right unpacking? Just come find me in the kitchen when you're ready to make cookies."

"I'll be fine." I smile at her, because she really does seem sweet.

If all this job consists of is being Dru's buddy, I'll be on easy street. She heads down the stairs, and I push the door open to my new quarters, a little worried about what I might see. To my relief, the room is stunningly normal. Given the oddball decor of the rest of the house, I had my doubts. But this room has a heavy four-poster bed made of solid wood, with an ornate headboard and a fluffy floral duvet on top. Ruffled white pillows cover the head of the bed, and there's even an old-fashioned teddy bear seated atop the bedding. A large window looks out over the trees and rooftops of the neighbors, and pretty paintings hang on the sage-green walls, depicting women in floral crowns and togas in various pastoral scenes. It's all very sweet and normal, even if it reminds me a bit of a teenage girl's room instead of a grown woman's. Doesn't matter. It's better than the room I have back in my apartment, which is kind of sad. There's no television, though, nor a desk for my laptop. There's a dresser, along with what looks like an old-fashioned secretary bureau—the kind with dozens and dozens of tiny drawers. I'm fascinated at the sight of it and pull one open, curious what's stored in there.

The first drawer is pins. Sewing, then? The next drawer looks like . . . strange bits of thread. When I pull the third drawer open and see nothing but dead, dried grasshoppers, I flinch backward. Ew. Given their witch fascination, I guess I shouldn't be surprised? The next couple of drawers have nothing but blocky tablets of that heavy, almost charcoal-like substance and some styli. Another drawer has chalk, and another dried flowers.

So weird. I open the closet door, wondering if I'm going to see skeletons, but there are a few dry-cleaner bags of clothing that must be Lisa's, and the rest is empty. The room is a nice big size at least. I toss my stuff down on the corner of the bed and pull out my phone. I take a few pictures of the room and send them to Nick.

REGGIE: What do you think?

NICK: I think her and my grandma shop at the same store.

REGGIE: LOL exactly. It all looks very . . . sweet. Dru seems nice, too.

NICK: Has she cast any spells yet?

REGGIE: No, but we are going to bake some cookies together as soon as I get my stuff settled. This job is going to be a breeze, Nick. I almost feel guilty for agreeing to do it.

NICK: If you didn't, someone else would. Just take the money.

NICK: And if anyone gets weird on you, let me know. I'll show up with my trainer buddies and we'll make them regret it.

I smile down at my phone and send him an emoji of a tongue sticking out. His protectiveness makes me feel good. I'm glad someone cares at least. I try to imagine how my parents would react to this job, and then I grimace to myself. Even if it was dangerous, they'd hear the numbers and tie me to the bed before they'd let me quit.

That thought depresses me more than anything.

I pick up the teddy bear, hugging it to my chest, and the smell of dried flowers is near overwhelming. Puzzled, I run my finger along the back of it and find a zipper. Inside, it's stuffed to the gills with more dried flowers.

So damn weird. I guess it could be worse. It could be more grasshoppers.

Frowning, I get to my feet and approach the door. I shut it behind me when I came in, and I can see a series of three locks on the door itself—two dead bolts and a chain. I don't know if that's comforting or terrifying, but like Dru said, I'll be safe. At least there's that.

I suppose I should go down and check on my employer. I open the door . . . and pause.

At the entrance to the door, there's an enormous black cat. It blinks up at me with golden eyes and then meows.

I laugh. What else can you do? Of course a lady that thinks she's a witch has a black cat. "Hello there," I murmur, getting down on my knees and extending my fingers toward the creature. His coat is glossy with health, and he's a big, hefty chunk of a cat, which I love. "Aren't you handsome?"

The cat starts to purr, rubbing against my hand.

I scratch at his ears, touching the collar on his neck. The tag says "Maurice." "Hi, Maurice. You're a tubby little boy, aren't you? Dru's not shy with the food—"

Maurice bites down on my finger.

"Ow!" I pull back, my good mood spoiled. "You big meanie."

He hisses at me, tail flicking, and then wanders away.

"Well, I hope that's not a bad sign," I mutter to myself, and eyeball my bleeding finger.

4

BEN

I squint at Cicero's *De divinatione* open on my lap and realize I've been reading the same passage over and over again for the last hour. With an irritated clench of my jaw, I put the book aside and stare at the fire in my fireplace. Fine. Glare. Whatever. I drum my fingers on the armrest of my chair, unable to concentrate.

I should spy on the new familiar. Catch her in the act. If she's doing something wrong—anything at all—I can nail her ass to the wall and get her fired. Problem solved. There's no issue with the Society of Familiars, no issue with an untrained apprentice, nothing.

Well . . . there's a slight issue. My aunt would be furious if she found out I was spying on her. Aunt Dru gets sensitive when it comes to her familiars. She's very protective of them.

But as the last remaining male of House Magnus, isn't it my job to be protective of my aunt, who can be too trusting? Who has gotten herself into scrape after scrape for centuries simply because she doesn't think things through? Decided, I get to my feet and bound down the stairs into the basement of my brownstone, where my laboratory is. I head to my table and murmur through the incantations for scrying, offering the proper herbs to the gods. Clover for Jupiter, sage for Mercury, and olive leaves for Minerva. Especially olive leaves for Minerva, who will let me see clearly. My aunt still likes a crystal ball for her divination, or the reading of entrails, but I'm trying to stay with the changing times. I pull out my smartphone, scatter the herbs over it, and then pull the strand of brown hair out of the bag that I've kept.

I tell myself I'm not a creep for keeping it. It ended up on my sweater and must have come from my aunt's new familiar. I tell myself that any logical warlock would keep such a thing for a time like this, and it doesn't make me wrong . . . even if my aunt would screech about it. I gently set the hair atop my phone and flick the camera on, waiting.

It takes time for the old magic to settle into new things. I'm a patient man. Have to be after five centuries. I watch as the phone's black screen shifts to gray and then continues to sharpen, focusing in on something.

The girl.

I lean against the table, my hands propped against the edge. "Show me what she did today."

Images flicker through the screen. The girl showing up on my aunt's doorstep, clutching a garish cardboard box. Her bright, cheerful, eager smile. My aunt letting her into her room. The girl poking around, her nose wrinkling at the sight of the spell components organized in the secretary bureau in her room. Baking cookies with my aunt in the kitchen and laughing as they get flour everywhere.

Aunt Dru looks pleased. She has that smug smile on her face that says she's satisfied with her new apprentice. That she likes the girl's enthusiastic personality. I'm sure she's going to tell me all about what a good choice she made when I return, but I'm not convinced. "Show me what the girl is doing right now," I snap at the phone, as if it's somehow responsible for my foul mood.

The image shivers, distorts. It cuts to the girl in bed, her hands under the covers and her eyes open. For a moment, I hold my breath. Did I stumble into a private moment—

She frowns and gets to her feet, moves to the door, and checks the locks again. Ah. Not sleeping . . . or doing anything else. I ignore the curious stab of disappointment I feel, reminding myself that if I want to watch porn, there are dozens of available channels and I don't need to resort to scrying. The girl fiddles with the locks, dressed in an oversized T-shirt from some local gym. Once she tests them again, she returns to bed but doesn't lie down. She sits on the edge of the bed and picks up her phone, loads up a game, and then sets it aside again. Her expression is . . . lonely. Frustrated and lonely, like she knows that she has everything she wants and it's not filling the hole inside her.

Or maybe I'm projecting.

Annoyed with myself, I reach out to turn the phone camera off, but then her gaze flicks around the room. She stiffens, her brows going down, and she stares at the shadows. "Is someone there?"

I hold my breath.

Then I let it out, feeling stupid. She can't see me. I'm cities away, and she's an untrained, uneducated apprentice on her first day on the job. She continues to scowl at the shadows for a moment longer, and I finally turn the phone off, a rueful smile tugging at my lips.

If nothing else, the girl has good instincts. At least my aunt chose well in that . . . not that I plan on telling her, of course.

✶ ✶ ✶

MY ARMS CROSSED over my chest, I sit in the annual meetings and glare. The conference hotel is nice this year, but I couldn't care less. I keep thinking about the girl, even as the annual meetings drag onward and warlock after warlock discusses society rule changes that don't affect me. I pretend to listen, arms crossed, as Lucius Cassius Publius (who now goes by Luke Cassian and lives in Malibu) demands tighter spell-casting guidelines and limitations on spells taught to familiars. It's the same shit every year and has been for the last five hundred, so I think instead about my aunt's new familiar. How clueless she is. How infuriating it is that she thinks all of this is just a big joke. That my aunt lives in some sort of witch-infested dreamland and I'm just humoring her.

I want to see the look on her face when she figures out it's all real. Will she turn so pale those freckles disappear? Or will she laugh with that big, infectious smile of hers?

Not that I think her smile is infectious. Or even nice. Maybe other people do. I just find her irksome. Annoying. I nudge my foot against the hotel carpet, not seeing the toe of my leather boot. Instead, I'm thinking about the girl, whose name I can't quite remember, with that slightly lost look on her face last night . . .

A gavel bangs. "Meeting dismissed for lunch," Lucius calls out. "We'll readjourn at two and go over new membership petitions then." Everyone in the meeting room rises to their feet, and I automatically do so as well, though I can't think of a single thing that was brought up in the meeting. That's not like me. I'm normally one of the first ones to make my opinion known about the rules that Luke and the others are constantly trying to shove down our throats. Today, though, I'm just distracted.

It doesn't go unnoticed, either. A tall, lean red-haired man moves in next to me. Willem's expression is pinched with displeasure as he eyes my clothing. The meetings are considered business, and most of the warlocks are in suits. Willem is wearing a tailored suit in a deep sapphire blue that looks trendy and makes his slicked-down red hair practically garish. He gives my simple black sweater and black pants a distasteful curl of his lip. "Really, Magnus. You look like a goth. The idea is to be low-key. This isn't low-key. Why not put on a black cloak and scream you're a dark mage and be done with it?"

"Shut up, Willem." I head out into the main lobby of the hotel, filled with my peers as people make lunch plans. No one invites me, of course. Hell, no one likes me. Not that I care. They're all fools.

"You didn't protest when old Aulus proposed that the board of warlocks make backups on 'the Googles'?" He flicks his fingers to make air quotes. "I thought you'd come screaming out of your chair, Magnus. Instead, you just stared at your shoes."

"He said that?" I grimace. Getting a bunch of two-thousand-year-old warlocks to grasp the internet has been a challenge, to say the least. I'm a little surprised Aulus even knows what Google is. Then again, given that he called it "the Googles," maybe I'm giving him too much credit. "I guess I need to have a word with him after all."

Willem Sauer arches an eyebrow. He's one of the younger warlocks, like me. His family is of Prussian descent, and he's only a few centuries old. Like me, he grasps the need to stay with the changing times, and he's a fan of newer technology as well. Even though I wouldn't call us friends—I'm not sure I have any—we tend to band together at these sorts of occasions. He leans in and peers at me.

I give him a not-so-gentle nudge. "Get out of my face, Willem."

"I'm just looking for hints that you've been cursed somehow. Your eyes seem clear." He gives me another studying look. "Show me the backs of your hands so I can look for identifying marks."

I stuff them into my pockets and push past him. "I'm me, you idiot. I've just got a lot on my mind."

"Like what?" he scoffs. "You live for these meetings."

Normally I do enjoy them. I like sparring with the other warlocks. I like putting them in their places when they become too arrogant. I like showing them that I know just as much—if not more—than they do, despite being centuries younger. I'm competitive, and it comes out when I'm surrounded by my peers. Willem's no better, though. He feuded with Titus for two hundred years over a stolen apprentice. Didn't care about the apprentice. Just wanted to pick a fight.

We're warlocks. That's what we do. When there's no common enemy to fight, we get bored and attack one another. Sometimes there's a power grab or two. Actually, it's been a while since there's been a power grab. I wonder if I'm out of the loop. Hmm.

Willem snaps his fingers in my face, trying to get my attention again.

I snatch his wrist, snarling. "You're going to find a curse tablet with your name on it if you're not careful."

He shakes his head at me, incredulous. "What's gotten into you? Why so distracted?" He leans in. "Is it that business with your client?"

My insides go cold. "You know nothing about my clients."

"We've all heard about it, Magnus." Willem gives me a cool look. "That you've lost your nerve after one of your biggest accounts went and killed himself. Did you orchestrate that, by the way? I was curious. I didn't think it'd be the case, given that he was part of your bankroll, but you never know."

I stare resentfully into the icy gaze of the only person I trust even halfway at this meeting. Willem is usually on the outs with warlock society as well, but nowhere near as badly as me. I should have known that gossip would be all over this meeting, and I suddenly want to turn and leave. Just walk out the door and never come back. Of course they think I engineered my client's death. Why wouldn't they?

I should remain quiet. Let them think what they want. But . . . Willem's right. I have lost my edge. Because all I can think about is that my casting made someone so miserable that he killed himself.

I feel responsible, and I don't like it.

So I focus on something else. The girl. After all, Willem is known to be difficult and has a hard time keeping an assistant himself. He might understand the gravity of the situation. "My aunt has a new apprentice," I offer. "It's a problem."

His red brows go up. "And . . . you're jealous?"

I scowl at him, my neck uncomfortably hot. "Of course not. Don't be ridiculous." I look around to make sure no one's listening and pull Willem in closer, my voice a near whisper. "She hired her off the street."

Willem recoils as if I've said something revolting. "She *what*?"

I nod. "A girl."

"Like a pigtails girl?" He shakes his head to clear it. "Why would she want a child—"

"No, you idiot." I stare at him. "She's a *girl*. A female. I don't know how old she is." I rake my hand through my shaggy hair. "Twenty or twenty-five. Thirty. I don't know. But she's young and seems far too smiley to be a familiar . . ."

"Sounds dreadful."

I shoot him another withering look. "The girl doesn't think magic is real. That we're all just pretending."

Willem's expression turns sour. "How did your aunt manage that?"

"She put an ad in the paper that was spelled to only have an appropriate candidate be able to read it. Clearly she has the proper ancestry in her blood somewhere, but that's all I know." I think about the smiling girl and the freckles again. "She's not right for the job. I need her gone."

He shrugs, lifting one shoulder casually, and scans the lobby. "So curse her with a quick tablet and take her out. What do you feel like eating for lunch. Sushi?"

Curse her.

Defixiones—curses—are the bread and butter of our work, but somehow cursing an innocent like her seems . . . wrong. Most curses inflict negative things upon the recipient. I imagine her smile dimming because she's been cursed and bad things start happening to her. For some reason, I think about her lonely expression, and something inside me aches. "I'm not going to curse her."

"Do you need me to do it?" He pauses, adjusting one of the buttons on the front of his blazer. "I'm thinking maybe shawarma if not sushi. Preference?"

"You're not cursing her, either." I grit my teeth as we walk toward the hotel lobby doors. "She doesn't deserve it. And shawarma."

"Excellent," Willem says, and I'm not sure if he's referring to the cursing business or the food. "And she's just some chit off the street. Why do you care?"

Because she has freckles. "Because my aunt would never forgive me."

I TURN OVER Willem's suggestions for the rest of the afternoon as I sit in roundtable meeting after roundtable meeting. They should be interesting—this particular one is discussing the merits of a curse tablet created by a 3D printer—but I can't concentrate on anything but my aunt and her new familiar.

Just curse her and be done with it. Why can't I? I've cursed others for less. I've cursed strangers. I've cursed people I know. I've cursed family members. I even cursed my own parents back in the day. For our bloodline, a *defixiones* tablet is the answer to everything. Curses are what we do. We can cast minor spells and do divinations, but curses are the lifeblood of any true warlock. Someone has slighted you? Pull out a stylus and a sheet of lead and write something unpleasant on the tablet. Maybe you want your neighbor's hair to fall out. Maybe you want his garden infested with bees, or you want the dry cleaner to lose his favorite shirt. You write down your curse on a tablet, hide the tablet so no one can break the curse, and wait for the magic to unfold. Curses can be small things—hell, they used to be nothing *but* small things, petty grievances needing an outlet—but over the last hundred years or so, things have gotten vicious. Maybe it was the world wars that changed everything, and people became far less interested in being polite. Maybe it's the internet that's making everyone aggressive behind anonymity. Maybe it's global fucking warming. Who knows.

Whatever the reason, a curse is not just a curse anymore. At least, not most of the time. My kind aren't hired to make a farmer's hens stop laying eggs or to make Cousin Jimmy's beautiful head of hair suddenly fall out. Corporations have gotten involved, and now most casting requires constant phone calls and PowerPoints and projections. It involves watching the stock market and surveillance and Zoom meetings. So many damn Zoom meetings. Warlocks and witches have gone from individual, petty curses to corporate espionage.

Cursing someone isn't just part of the job. It's an art.

I've done this sort of thing so often that I already know exactly what I'd cast. I wouldn't even have to think twice. One tablet to make her have something bad happen. Not to her. Perhaps a family member in need of an immediate visit, or a spate of bad luck. A car breaking down and the part impossible to find. Something that would require her to abandon the job. Then I'd use a second curse tablet to dull the memory of it and make her forget that she ever met Aunt Drusilla. She'd remember nothing but vague details, and Aunt Dru would have to go through the Society of Familiars to get an actual familiar that truly believes in magic. Since I don't have an apprentice of my own, I'd be draining myself and out of commission for a week at the very least, but what's a week to an immortal? I'd just have to schedule accordingly.

It would be easy, too. I have the supplies in the basement of my brownstone. I could have the tablets ready and buried in my aunt's backyard, maybe under her favorite rosebush, before she even knew what was happening. And the girl would have no idea—because she didn't believe in that sort of thing. She wouldn't know to hunt down a tablet. She would simply think it a string of bad luck . . .

And maybe that's why I balk at it. She's a babe in the woods. She'd be completely unaware of what happened, and it doesn't feel right. I think about Soren. I think about Zephyr First Technologies, and a sick knot forms in my stomach. Furious with myself, I push the thought away. I really hope I'm not developing a conscience after several hundred years of the dark arts. That would be annoying.

My phone buzzes with an incoming text toward the end of the day's meetings. There's another full day of discussions planned for tomorrow—new spells, new uses, and an intriguing seminar on magic and social media by one warlock's teenaged son. But I find myself unable to concentrate. I don't want to be here.

I can't work until the situation with my aunt and her apprentice is resolved.

The text on my phone is a perfect excuse. It's one of my Silicon Valley contacts, panicking because his rival's stock has gone through the roof. He needs an emergency consultation . . . and probably a few choice curses that will turn things in his company's favor. "Work calls, gentlemen," I say as I get to my feet, interrupting the panel. I gesture at my phone. "I'm afraid I have to leave early."

No one looks disappointed. Of course not. They don't like me, and I don't like them. I give a polite surface-only smile to the gathered warlocks and ignore Willem's knowing smirk.

After all, no one needs to know that I can work remotely from my aunt's house as well as from my own personal lab. I gather up my coat and my portfolio and head for the street to get a taxi to the airport.

REGGIE

NICK: I don't know about your job, but mine is definitely looking up.

My roomie (former roomie) ends the text with an eggplant emoji and a crotch shot from the gym. I make a gagging sound in my throat at the sausage filling my screen and immediately text him back.

REGGIE: Dude, do not send me that stuff! Don't be that creep taking shots of your clients like that!

NICK: Does it help if I point out that it's Sergeant Hotness? And that he's the one that sent me that pic? I didn't take it.

REGGIE: That does change things a bit. So you two are talking?

NICK: More like sexting. But we can talk too. 😉

I make a face, tucking my phone into my back jeans pocket. I adore Nick and would jump into traffic for him, but the man loves to overshare like there's no tomorrow. I sure didn't need that photo, and I especially didn't need the up-close view it gave me, showing the blatant outline of a dick in thin gym shorts. I'm happy for Nick, though. I'm glad things are going so swimmingly for him.

I'm not sure if I can say the same for me.

It's been a few days, but . . . working for Dru is weird. Fun, but weird. I'm getting used to the big, creaky house and the peculiar assortment of things inside. I'm getting used to Dru's cat, Maurice, who insists on following me everywhere, even into the bathroom. I'm even getting used to my new room, with the scent of herbs and the princess bed and the drawers full of dead bugs that I haven't bothered to clean out yet. I actually just avoid the drawers entirely, keeping my laundry in my backpack and living out of it.

It's an old habit of mine—after years of my parents having to flee town and creditors at a moment's notice, I keep things packed and light. Just in case. It's been almost a year since I've seen them and almost seven years since I lived with them, but old habits die hard. I guess part of me still feels as if Dru's going to change her mind about the job and show me the door. It seems too good to be true.

Dru herself is actually the weirdest part of the situation.

It's not that I don't like her. I do. She's sweet and just lovely to be around. She's charming and funny and . . . and okay, she doesn't act normal. At first I chalked it up to the whole witch nonsense and the fact that everyone's been catering to her about that. Strangely enough, that's not what ends up being weird. It's that every time she sees me, she holds her breath. She squirms like a kid, and a light flashes in her eyes. If she wasn't an adult and at least eighty years old, I'd swear she's a toddler with a secret.

As it is, I have no idea what's going on, and she won't tell me.

Every time I ask, she gives me some sort of task to do and then giggles and gets strange about it again. Like yesterday, when she gave me a shopping list and then giggled like a maniac. Or when I offered to dust her library and she gave me a few books and then winked obnoxiously. Twice.

Right now, I'm doing her laundry, folding her clothing with a T-shirt board because it gets the lines the neatest. I've also arranged her dresses by color and separated the winter ones into a different part of the closet. The laundry room is across from the basement, which I've not been allowed into yet, and catty-corner from the big kitchen. It's also dusty as hell, and I don't think anyone's ever cleaned the lint trap in the dryer, so I pull it out and head toward the kitchen to wash it clean of lingering detergent.

Before I can enter the kitchen, however, I hear voices. One deep and rich, and the other Dru's softer, sweeter voice. I clutch the lint trap to my chest, not wanting to intrude. Do I wait to clean the lint trap, or do I interrupt? There's a sink in the laundry room, but there's a big note taped to it that says, "DO NOT USE—ENCHANTED," and I figure that's just another one of Dru's quirky things, so I don't touch it.

"I've returned early," comes the dark, sensuous voice. It makes a shiver go down my spine. If the word "sultry" was a voice, he'd be that voice, I decide. Decadent, slightly dark, and mysterious. The man speaks again. "The girl. Have you fired her yet?"

I freeze in place. Well, I can't walk away now. Not when they're talking about me.

"No. No one's been fired. She's an absolute delight, Caliban. Just a sheer delight." There's a clink of dishes. "I can't find my mugwort, darling. Can you help me look? I think she reorganized my kitchen and put my casting herbs in with the spices."

I wince. I might have also had a hard time sleeping last night and reorganized Dru's kitchen. It was cleaner than I expected, but she has a lot of spices. Like a *lot* of them, and some I've never heard of. Even so, I reorganized everything and put them on the spice rack, which had been holding nothing but a few empty salt canisters. Now I'm regretting my late-night cleaning frenzy. What if it's the thing that gets me fired?

No job. No piles of money. I'd have to move back in with Nick, who is clearly thriving with his privacy. He texted me yesterday and said he walked around in the nude all night and that he could get used to no roomie. I think it was a joke to make me feel better about leaving him, but now I just feel tight and anxious. Like I've got no home once again and no one to have my back.

My throat knots up as the man replies. "Fire her. Have you cast anything yet?"

"I'm not firing her, Caliban—"

"Ben," he interrupts. "My name is Ben, Auntie. You know it is."

My nostrils flare with distaste and I bite back a hiss of anger. He's still trying to get me fired? How dare he? Ben—or whatever he's called—needs to learn to mind his own damn business.

"I haven't cast anything at all," Dru says, her tone dramatic. "And it is making me *so* very twitchy. You have no idea. I can't keep living this lie, Ben. I have to be me. I have to!"

A heavy sigh. "No one's asking you to live a lie, Aunt Dru."

"But you said I can't cast around her!"

"I also said you should fire her, and you're not doing that."

"I miss my magic," Dru says woefully. "I haven't even done an entrail reading in days. How am I supposed to know if it's safe to go out?"

Another heavy sigh. "It's safe to go out. Why wouldn't it be safe to go out?"

"Well, I don't know," Dru says indignantly. "I can't read the entrails, so I can't tell you."

"Fine." The single barked-out syllable is one of complete and utter frustration. "Just . . . fine. Let her in on it, but you have to be willing to get rid of her if things don't go as planned."

"Rid of her? How?"

"You're a witch. How do you normally get rid of people? You curse them."

Curse me? What the fuck? I tilt my head. Exactly what kind of witches do these people think they are? Here I thought they were like, I don't know, pretending to be good witches or something. Nice, benign, friendly Glinda witches. Curses are . . . fucked up, and I'm not even sure I believe in them. I just know I don't want one.

I don't even know what to think about this whole "reading entrails" business. Dru seems so nice, even if her interests are a little strange. How can she talk about cursing me? Or letting her nephew fire me? I blink back tears of frustration and disappointment. I don't know why I got my hopes up. I should have known better. I should have guessed that I can't count on anyone but myself.

"Can you ease her into it for me?" I hear Dru ask her nephew. "She doesn't listen to me when I mention anything to do with magic. She just looks at me like I'm senile."

My jaw drops. I do not! I try to be understanding, even if it seems ridiculous.

"I'll talk to her," Ben says tersely. "Just let me take care of it."

"I'm so sorry to pull you away from your little warlock party, dear. Was it nice?" Dru's tone turns motherly, all the frustration disappearing instantly.

Before I can hear a response, the big black cat saunters into the hall. He sees me and pauses, and I make a shooing motion with my hand. Probably thinks he's about to be fed. Now is not the time, though. I—

Maurice opens his whiskered mouth and lets out an unearthly howl.

Shit! I clutch the lint trap to my chest even as I hear a plate rattle on the other side of the door. Maurice immediately howls again, as if he's being tortured, and I know someone's about to come out of the kitchen. So much for subterfuge. Deciding to take the bull by the horns, I push through the door, smiling brightly.

The two in the kitchen don't even look guilty. Dru is seated on a stool at the island, sipping a cup of tea. Her nephew, Ben, leans against the counter across from her, taking up half the space in the room. A small plate of cookies—the cookies we baked—is set before him. He's all long, dark limbs, dressed in a black sweater and black pants. His black hair somehow manages to look like tousled perfection and frames his striking face. Why is it always the attractive ones that are the biggest jerks?

"Hi there," I chirp happily, like a good, friendly assistant. I gesture at the lint trap in my arms. "Have you ever washed this out, Dru? Did you know dryer sheets can leave a film on the lint trap and can cause fires? I'll just give it a good soak." I move toward the sink, stepping over Ben's outstretched limbs. "I can come back for it later. I don't want to interrupt."

They exchange a look. "Were you listening in, sweetheart?" Dru asks in that high-pitched voice of hers.

"Of course not," I lie.

The door to the kitchen swings open a tiny bit, and the cat pushes inside. He hops up on one of the stools, which is pretty impressive given that he's an absolute chunk, and looks around at all of us, his tail flicking.

"Maurice, was she listening in?" Ben asks, and I resist the urge to both roll my eyes and kick him.

The cat meows.

"Mm-hmm. Naughty, naughty," Dru says, and then gives another wild giggle. "Someone's been caught red-handed."

By a cat? "Oh please," I retort, keeping my voice light and teasing as I set the lint trap down on the counter to come back to later. "He's a cat. He probably wants his food bowl filled up. I wouldn't take the word of someone who was cleaning his balls on my bed an hour ago."

Ben jumps to his feet just as Dru gasps. "He what?" The man growls, furious.

Maurice immediately jumps back down from the chair and races out of the room.

"Now you've gone and scared him," I say with a shake of my head. I leave the room, because it's a good way to end the conversation, which was getting a little too tricky. And if I'm not in the room, they can't fire me, right? Right. So I breeze out to the laundry room, pick up the basket of perfectly folded clothing, and head up the stairs to Dru's rooms.

Or at least, I try to. By the time I'm halfway up the staircase, that annoying nephew of my boss is heading up after me, taking the steps two at a time with his longer legs. "What are you doing?" he asks, his tone full of edges.

"The laundry." I keep my voice as sweet as pie. Maybe I'll suggest Dru and I make a pie later. She likes baking, or so it seems. Then again, maybe that's part of the whole "living a lie" thing she was complaining about, and my heart just feels crushed all over again. I thought I was doing a good job. I thought Dru approved. I like her, and I want her to like me back. She's like the grandmother I never had, even if she does giggle and wink a lot.

Maybe the big secret was that she was going to fire me all this time.

I enter Dru's disaster of a bedroom, which makes me twitchy, but I haven't quite gotten the nerve to ask to clean it up yet. She has piles of clothing draped across every bit of furniture, and a chaise that looks as if it was purchased specifically to hold purses and shoes, as that's all that's on it. The drapes are dusty, the unmade bed is covered in more pillows than I've ever owned in my life, and stacks of books are piled atop the nightstands, along with old tissues and curlers. If this was Lisa's job to clean up, she didn't do it, but it's not my call.

I pull my phone out of my pocket and toss it down on the corner of Dru's bed to remind myself to call Nick later and give him the bad news. That I'm going to be moving back in ASAP. He'll just give me another sad, knowing smile. An understanding look, because poor, silly, controlling Reggie has screwed up another job and is returning home with her tail tucked between her legs. Just the thought makes my chest ache.

I clench my jaw in silence when Mr. Magnus follows me into his aunt's room. I kick aside a pile of dirty laundry that's on the floor and set the basket down next to the dresser so I can carefully put things away as they should be (properly). I open up the drawer I emptied out earlier and begin to put clothes in neat, tight stacks. And I ignore Mr. Magnus. Or Ben. Or Caliban. Or whatever he's going by today.

"What are you doing?" he demands.

I glance over at him and hold up a pink shirt just as Maurice slinks in and rubs against Ben's pant leg. "Putting away laundry?"

He scowls down at the cat rubbing against his leg. "Get out of here, Maurice. I mean it. You're on thin ice."

I'm more than a little incredulous as the cat's mood changes abruptly. He stops in his tracks, flicks his tail, and then rushes right back out of the bedroom as if he understood every word. I huff a laugh at that, because if there's one thing I've learned in the days I've been here, it's that Maurice is a stubborn ass of a cat and does as he pleases. Seeing him obey is strange. "Why does he listen to you?"

"Because he knows better than to ignore me," Ben says darkly. He sits on the edge of Dru's pillow-strewn bed, his long legs extending out in front of him again. His arms cross over his chest, highlighting how broad it is. He's just a massive, intimidating man who is no doubt going to try to use that intimidation against me.

Well, it's not going to work. "If you don't mind, I'm trying to do my job. I—"

My phone buzzes on the bed. Loudly.

My gaze goes to it at the same time that Ben picks it up, and even from here, I can see what look like tanned, hairy buns covering my screen. Very, very naked buns.

I'm going to kill Nick. Not just for sending me every photo that Sergeant Hotness sexts him, but for his damned timing.

Ben clears his throat and mutely holds the phone out to me, his nostrils flaring. I could swear there's a hint of color on his high cheekbones, too.

I snatch the phone away from him and stuff it into my pocket. "Thank you."

"I think you're not qualified for the job," he finally says, voice blunt.

My heart aches. Here it is, the "we need to let you go" speech. Everything inside me hurts. I should be used to rejection by now, but every time it's a fresh pain. I continue folding as if I'm unbothered, though. I focus on the task ahead of me, making sure baby-blue shirts are directly above darker blue. "And is that what your aunt thinks? That I'm wrong for the job?"

"My aunt hasn't been having you do the actual job yet."

I turn around at that, frowning. "I'm her assistant, right?" I gesture at the laundry. "Here I am, assisting. It's all I've done for the last few days. I clean the kitchen. I do the laundry. I bake. I play crosswords with her. Last night I spent an hour helping her log into her tax website." Only to find out that the reason why her login didn't work was because she hadn't filed a tax return since 1942, but I don't bring that up. "What is assisting if not that?"

"This isn't the job she hired you for." His long face seems grim, his stance tense.

"What do you mean?"

His jaw flexes. "I mean she's coddling you."

Because of the stuff they were talking about in the kitchen? About not wanting to live a lie? I don't care if his Aunt Dru dresses up like a puppy and walks around on all fours as long as they pay me. "I took this job knowing it's an unconventional one," I say carefully. "If I'm not assisting her properly, then I need to be given direction. I can do whatever she likes. She just needs to let me know. I'm not going to give up and walk out the door just because you don't like me."

"It has nothing to do with me," Ben retorts, and the flush is back on his pale cheeks. "But fine, then. If you insist, we'll stop tiptoeing around the situation." He gets to his feet and gestures at Dru's bedroom door. "Follow me down to the kitchen."

I put down the shirt in my hands. Do I protest? Say he's not my boss and continue doing laundry? I have to admit I'm curious what he has planned, though. So I run my sweaty palms down my jeans, compose myself, and head down the stairs as regally as I possibly can. Maurice slinks past me as I head toward the kitchen once more, and it's almost as if he's going to get a seat for the show.

When I enter the kitchen, Ben leans against the counter. Dru is pretending to sip her tea, but then she lets out one of those little giggles again that ruins everything.

"All right," I say, gesturing at Ben. "What's the plan?"

Instead of looking at me, he looks over at his aunt. "I want you to have the girl help you make a potion."

"I have a name. It's Reggie," I retort. "And I'm not a girl. I'm an adult. I'm twenty-five, thank you very much."

Dru immediately spits tea all over the counter.

Ben hands her a napkin, and I could swear his mouth twitches with amusement. "Twenty-five. My apologies. I didn't realize how very ancient you were."

Dru coughs more tea everywhere, mopping up the mess. I can't tell if they're making fun of me or not. It feels like they are, and it makes it hard to keep smiling.

"Potion, Dru. Pick one. Pick your favorite." Ben just gives her a surly look. "We're done with playing around the subject."

Dru looks down at her now-empty mug with a small sigh. "I would love to, Caliban darling, but I'm fresh out of crow's foot, and you know how important it is for *veneficia*."

"*Veneficia?*" I echo.

"Herbalism." Dru beams at me as if that explains everything. "And if we're going to make a potion to improve penis potency, we'll need crow's foot."

"You'll what?" snaps Ben.

"You told me to pick my favorite!" The elderly woman gives her nephew a sidelong look and lifts her mug as if to drink from it again, despite it being empty. "So I did."

His nostrils flare and his jaw works. He looks as if he wants to argue, but that high color is flushing his cheekbones and he thinks better of it. "Fine. We can have her gather your components, then. That works, too. Make a list and we'll do that, then you can make the potion with her."

"Sounds perfect. Just let me go and get my favorite pen." She beams a smile at me. "Be right back."

Spell components. For a potion. I manage to keep smiling until Dru leaves the room, and then I turn a nasty glare toward Ben Magnus. "I just want you to know that I don't approve of this."

His dark, heavy brows knit together. "Potions?"

"Playing along with all this witch nonsense," I hiss at him, taking a step forward. My fists are clenched at my sides. "Your aunt is a vulnerable lady, and you're not doing her any favors by humoring these delusions. It's elder abuse. It's cruel, and you're heartless for choosing to play along with it."

He stares down at me with narrowed eyes. "Cruel and heartless. Yes, I suppose I am. But you're being paid to be her assistant, so I guess you'll just have to deal with all this pretend."

6

BEN

The girl—Reggie—is driving me absolutely mad.

She stands in front of me, her hands on her hips, utterly defiant. Her eyes spark with anger and indignance over my supposed neglect of my crafty aunt, who she thinks needs help around the house instead of an actual apprentice-slash-familiar. I can't help but compare Reggie to the last one—Lisa. Lisa, who is a pleasant enough sort but is also lazy and folds at the slightest hint of conflict. Who helped me out for a short while after my last apprentice quit, and who quailed with terror every time I looked in her direction.

This one's not afraid of me at all. Reggie's glare is utterly disapproving, as if I'm somehow responsible for my aunt's actions. And even though I intended to force my aunt into using Reggie as a true familiar and leave, I find that I'm suddenly very, very interested in staying.

I can't wait to see the look on her face when she realizes magic is real, my aunt is a two-thousand-year-old sorceress, and no one's been pretending anything.

Feeling smug, I lean back against the counter, my arms crossed. "Sorry to ruin your plans for the evening, but it looks like you're going to have to work some overtime. You're going to assist my aunt in making potions."

She gives me another fierce glare. "I didn't have plans, so I don't mind at all." Her tone is sugary sweet as she gives me a feral smile. "After all, it's my job to assist your aunt, even if the task is cruel and feeds into her delusions."

Her delusions? "Someone here is delusional, yes." I can't help but chuckle at the sight of her. She's bristling with indignation and protectiveness for my aunt. If it wasn't for the fact that she's not from the Society of Familiars, I'd think she's perfect for the job. She's cute and disarming in appearance, of course, which is a problem. A familiar represents their witch or warlock. Aunt Dru wears bright colors in her day-to-day business, but she's also fifteen hundred years older than me, so it's difficult to get her to listen. Reggie doesn't look like a familiar, with her hair pulled into two twists atop her head, an old, ratty sweatshirt tossed over her jeans. It's another thing she's got all wrong . . . but her fierce loyalty to my aunt is commendable.

That, and her freckles. For some reason I can't stop thinking about them. I fucked my hand last night imagining those damned freckles. Just to get it out of my system.

Didn't work.

It irritates me that I'm attracted to her. She's everything that I despise, and I've already spent too much time with her in my head. Aunt Dru will get the potion done tonight, the girl—Reggie—will realize what she's gotten into, and then she'll want out. We can make an amulet to remove her memories of this last week and start the apprentice search again.

Her phone buzzes with another incoming text, and even though she doesn't reach for it, my temper flares. I think about the picture from earlier—her boyfriend sending her lewd photographs of himself. I lift my chin, deciding to needle her a bit more. "Your boyfriend thinks you have plans, judging by the pictures he's sending you."

Reggie looks flustered, her hand fluttering to her back jeans pocket, where her phone is stored, and then away again. "I'm not . . . He's not my boyfriend."

"I don't want the details of your dating life," I say in a scathing tone. I don't. Even if I'm mentally wondering how I can get a lock of his hair to curse him with impotency.

I don't care. I don't.

Aunt Dru flutters back into the kitchen, all oversized gauzy pink robe and feather-tipped pen. She waves a sheet of paper in the air. "I changed my mind. I did make a list for the penis-prowess potion—or as I like to call it, the Triple P of Penetration. But I did promise Doris I'd make one of my healing potions. She hurt her knee stepping off a curb yesterday, and I owe her one." Her smile is bright. "And this potion doesn't require any crow's foot. Just mugwort and seed of Jupiter." She winks at me. "And a little pizzazz, of course."

A healing tonic is child's play. She's coddling the girl—Reggie—again. But at least it's progress. "Fine. Go ahead and begin." I hop up on the counter behind me, letting my legs dangle over the cabinets.

My aunt's eyes light up. "Oh, are you staying, Caliban?"

I nod. I'm not going anywhere. Not when the show's about to begin. "I want to see how your new apprentice handles things." I cast a look over at Reggie, doing my best not to smirk and failing. I can't wait to see the look on her face when she realizes it's real.

"Who's Doris?" Reggie asks, stepping in next to my aunt as she heads to the pantry. I can't help but notice the imperious look she shoots in my direction, as if daring me. As if saying, "See, I'm not going anywhere." Even though she's infuriating, I love that she's not backing down.

"One of my canasta partners. You'll meet her next Thursday. She's the one that dyes her hair and brows that gaudy chestnut color. It makes her look like a really hard thousand years old." Aunt Dru shakes her head, as if she disapproves of someone else's gaudiness. Irony. She opens the pantry door and peers inside. "You reorganized things, and I don't know where my casting components are."

I'm surprised when Reggie flushes, moving forward. "Sorry. I didn't realize I wasn't supposed to. I thought I was helping."

"Oh, it's all right, dear," Aunt Dru says. "You get as old as me, you get used to things a certain way." She heads into the pantry, and I watch as she touches a few of the jars, pulling them down and considering them before putting them back. And I also notice that Reggie moves right behind her, subtly turning the jars label out and putting them back in their original spots.

A neat freak. I think about the tightly folded clothes upstairs, the color coordination, and slowly smile as Reggie discreetly turns another label face out. She turns to look over at me—or maybe to see if she's been caught—and when she catches me staring, her expression grows both embarrassed and defiant.

I feel as if I've suddenly uncovered a cache of ammunition. Quietly, I nudge one of the kitchen canisters behind me on the countertop, turning it so it sits out of place, the strawberry-shaped lid askew. As my aunt emerges from the pantry with her arms full of spices and jars of herbs, Reggie follows a step behind her. I deliberately tweak the lid of the jar at my side so she sees what I'm doing, and her nostrils flare with anger.

I wait for her to march over to my side and fix the jar, but she doesn't. The way she keeps glancing back at it, though? She's aware of it, and it bothers her.

Good. Now I'm under her skin like she's under mine. Pleased, I watch as my aunt pulls out a bowl and begins to work. "Now,

Reggie, I'm going to start the spell, and I want you to hand me the ingredients as I ask for them."

"I can do that." She gestures at the bowl on the island countertop. "Are we making a soup of some kind?"

"A potion," my aunt says. "We'll boil it up and then run it through the blender just to get the crunchy bits handled, and then we bottle it."

"Ah." Reggie slides over to the far side of the counter and discreetly moves toward me. Toward the canister I've set askew. "Shouldn't we work over the stove if we're going to be boiling things? Won't we need a burner?"

She casually reaches for the canister without looking behind her.

I move it just out of her reach.

"Oh, we don't need a stove." Aunt Dru beams at me and her familiar. "Now, let me call down my power. Before I do, though, I need your agreement that you'll act as my conduit."

"Familiar," I murmur, practically whispering it in Reggie's ear.

She jumps, turning to glare at me. "Assistant, right?" She corrects us, as if we have no idea what we're talking about. "You want me to assist?"

"A good familiar is her witch's conduit," my aunt continues. She pulls out an ancient cuff bracelet. "If you wear this, it'll allow me to bond to you, familiar to witch."

"And if I don't?" Reggie asks, wary.

"There's the door," I say helpfully, pointing. I should not be having this much fun, but I can't seem to stop myself.

She gives me a withering look and practically snatches the bracelet out of my aunt's hands, slipping the cuff over her slender wrist. "There. Bracelet done. Now what?"

"Now you watch me combine the ingredients," Aunt Dru says. "Because you're going to want to learn this potion. It's quite a handy thing. Someone always needs a healing potion. You can make a pretty penny off something like this."

To my surprise, Reggie leans over, paying attention as my aunt takes a pinch of leaves and tosses them into the bowl. "Should I get a pen and write this down?"

Aunt Dru gasps. "Of course not! One of my enemies could steal my spells."

"Enemies," Reggie echoes.

"They're everywhere," Aunt Dru agrees, adding another pinch of herbs. "Trust me."

As if she somehow doesn't quite believe this, Reggie shoots me a look. I don't know if it's amusement or chiding—or both. I do know she doesn't believe my aunt has enemies, though. On the surface, Aunt Dru seems like a slightly dotty, harmless older woman. Of course Reggie wouldn't believe that she's Drusilla Grattidia Magnus, two-thousand-year-old sorceress, and that she has a lot of spells that other casters would definitely kill to acquire. It's one reason that it's so important she has the right apprentice.

Freckles or not.

Reggie makes a face as Aunt Dru continues adding ingredients to the bowl, her small nose wrinkling when Dru pulls out a few dried bugs and then hands Reggie a stone pestle. "Grind these up, my dear. We don't want chunks getting stuck in the throat of our poor sick patient."

"I thought you said she had an injured knee."

Aunt Dru reaches over and flicks Reggie on the nose. "A potion is for drinking. You don't rub it on your knee, dummy."

Reggie yelps and pulls back, giving me an indignant look as she rubs her nose, as if this is somehow my fault. I just smirk.

Reluctance oozes out of my aunt's familiar as she picks up the pestle and begins to grind the concoction. "So after we add all the ingredients, how does this work? Do we dance around a fire and say prayers to the four corners of the earth?"

"Of course not." Dru adds one last pinch of herbs to the bowl and then dusts off her hands. "We're not Wiccan, darling. We're Roman. *Vencficae*."

"My mistake." The contents under the pestle make a sickening crunch, and Reggie blanches, pushing the bowl away. "I think that's . . . pretty good." Her voice sounds faint. "Did I mention I'm not a great fan of bugs?"

Aunt Dru just pats her on the shoulder. "I'll allow it since this is your first potion, but you'll probably need to get over your squeamishness. Bugs are a lot easier to use than, say, lambs. It's dreadfully hard to find a nice lamb at midnight when living in the city. In my day, we'd just steal one from the nearest farmer, but that sort of thing brings all kinds of questions now, especially if you get pulled over for a speeding ticket." Dru gives the pestle a few merry whacks into the contents, her movements making Reggie's expression turn green, and then she gives the bowl a nudge. "Now we channel a bit of power and call on the gods."

"The . . . gods," Reggie echoes.

"Roman gods," I add helpfully.

My aunt closes her eyes and extends her palms outward, the picture of concentration. She's crafted this particular potion hundreds of times and has no need for the theatrics, so I'm guessing this is for Reggie's sake. Reggie, meanwhile, gives her a pitying look, as if things have gone too far.

The bowl in front of them begins to smoke. The scent of charred bugs and leaves fills the air with an acrid, familiar stink. I watch, waiting.

Reggie peers at the bowl in surprise, her brows going up. "There's a chemical reaction happening in our ingredients."

"It's not chemical," Dru says without opening her eyes or moving a muscle. "It's magic."

"Mmm." Reggie glances over at me, her expression disapproving.

The weight of the air changes, becoming heavy and redolent. I can feel the magic activating, like a caress on my skin. Reggie rubs her arm, chasing away goose bumps as she watches the smoking bowl, and again, I'm surprised at how good her instincts are. Her body reacts to the energy even if her mind won't allow her to believe it's real. The sensation of magic hangs in the air, and I can feel my aunt pulling on Reggie's reservoir of energy. A strong, hard pull of a *lot* of magic.

My aunt opens her eyes slowly and then winks at me.

"So, what now?" Reggie blinks, leaning heavily on the counter. "Oh."

"Dizzy, my dear?" Aunt Dru beams at her. "Gosh, that is weird, isn't it? The timing of it? Given that magic's not real or anything."

I look at Reggie's bleach-pale face and jump to my feet seconds before the girl's eyes roll back in her head and she collapses. I catch her in my arms before she slumps to the ground. "Drusilla! What did you do?"

My aunt studies her nails, the bowl smoking in front of her. "I just gave a little tug. A hard one. Just to wake her up a bit. She'll be fine. You know the first time is always the trickiest."

I cradle the unconscious familiar in my arms, not sure if I approve of my aunt's actions or if I should strangle her. The girl—Reggie—feels so light in my arms that it worries me. I felt that intense tug my aunt gave her, felt the surge of magic. Reggie might be untested, but she's a natural with a hefty reservoir of energy to pull from—energy that my aunt blew through in one fell swoop to teach her a lesson. I hold Reggie close as her lashes flutter, and my chest feels tight with . . . something.

"I'm taking her up to her room," I tell my aunt. "You're done for the day."

"Oh, don't be so grumpy, Caliban," my aunt says, stirring her smoking potion. "You wanted me to break her in. Consider her broken in."

I wanted Reggie to acknowledge that magic exists, not for her to be knocked out. But I keep this to myself, because my aunt wouldn't understand my odd protectiveness. I'm not sure I understand it myself. All I know is that someone needs to look after Reggie, who's far too trusting. She just put on the cuff that binds her to my aunt as if it were nothing. I shake my head at the thought. She's a little fool who's jumped into the deep end of our world, and it's not my responsibility to look after her. She's my aunt's familiar, not mine.

Even so, I lift her slight form against me and carry her through the house and up the stairs. By the time we reach Reggie's room, her lashes flutter again and she stirs. "Mmm . . . what . . ." Her voice is soft and full of exhaustion. "Did I . . ."

"My aunt drained you," I say, keeping my tone gentle. I push her door open, and I'm not surprised to see that her room is in perfect order, the bed made with sharp, tight corners, the throw pillows arranged neatly in rows based on their varying sizes. I move to the side of the bed and gently set her down.

She rubs her face, disoriented. "Low blood sugar," she murmurs. "I forgot to eat lunch. That must be it."

I roll my eyes. "If you say so."

"Shoes," Reggie says, trying to sit up. "Need to . . . take off shoes . . ."

"I'll do it. You rest."

She flops back onto the pillows, her eyes closed, and I can only imagine how drained she is. I try to remember the first time I acted as a familiar for a stranger and how I felt as if a house had fallen atop me. It took me days to recover, and I was wary of my master after that, afraid he'd tap me too hard once more and kill me.

Aunt Dru would never kill Reggie. I remind myself that as I undo the laces on her battered pink sneakers and slide them off her feet. Her bright yellow-and-orange socks have a hole, one toe sticking out, and they look threadbare. Actually, a lot of her stuff does. No wonder she's so desperate to keep the job.

"I'm sorry," she whispers. "I didn't mean to pass out."

I look up, and she's so pale and vulnerable. I reach out and brush a stray lock of hair off her face. "It's fine. You're . . . fine."

There's another buzz of her phone, and Reggie groans and pulls it out of her back pocket, tossing it down on the bed. It's another photo from her boyfriend. My protective mood sours, and I toss her shoes down on the floor, leaving her behind.

That's what I get for feeling sorry for the girl.

REGGIE

I wake up with my phone pressed against my face and my head throbbing. Somewhere outside, birds chirp, and I squint at the sunlight streaming into my room.

How is it morning?

Yawning, I sit up and wipe the drool off my phone case. Ugh, there are twenty messages from Nick. He must have gotten laid and wants back pats from his friends. I rub my eyes, because I don't know what day or time it is. Did I miss Friday-night cards? A quick check of my phone shows that it's Friday morning, so at least that's something, but I feel exhausted and weak. If I'd woken up to find out that I'd slept for a week, I wouldn't be surprised. I feel that crappy. I slept in my clothes, and as I ease out of bed, I notice my shoes tossed to the floor all haphazardly. The sight of it makes my soul ache, and I pick them up, slipping them onto my feet and tying the laces.

As I do, a vague memory flashes. Dru, going through her little song and dance about potions and magic. A chemical reaction on the mushed grasshoppers. Me getting dizzy.

Ben carrying me up the stairs to my room and touching my face, brushing his fingers over my skin in a tender caress.

I tap my cheek, heat flooding through my body. When was the last time someone touched me? *Really* touched me? That has to be why it has me in a tizzy, why my brain is short-circuiting over it and not the fact that I passed out. My parents were never touchy-feely. Nick is, but only with his boyfriends. The last time someone caressed me was . . . my last boyfriend. Three years ago. That's why I'm thinking about it. Not because I find Ben attractive. I don't. I wish he'd take a long walk off a short pier.

I wobble upright and then head for the stairs. My stomach is growling something fierce, and I could eat a horse. I make it to the kitchen, and there's no reek of dead-bug potion, no bowl of smoking herbs. The counters are clean and bare, and on a cake plate, the iced lemon muffins we made yesterday are displayed. I grab one and shove it into my mouth, devouring it. Fuck my macros.

Dru wanders into the kitchen a moment later, wearing a fluttering gown of pale yellow crepe with sheer bell sleeves. She has a jaunty matching yellow bow in her curls. "Hello, darling. How are you feeling?"

"Awful," I manage, raising a hand to my mouth to shield the flying crumbs. "I'm sorry. I guess I passed out."

"Mmm," Dru says with a nod. "Because I drained you."

"Because of low blood sugar," I correct gently and take another muffin. "I'll be fine soon. I just need to eat."

She sighs, a look of sorrow on her aged face. "Sure, darling. If you say so." She unfolds a list. "Can you do me a favor and pick these components up today? We'll be casting again later tonight, and I'll need these things."

"Of course." I force myself to walk over to her, my feet like lead. "I'll go after breakfast. Is it okay if I visit a friend tonight, Ms. Magnus? I normally play cards with him every Friday night."

"After you pick up my components, I don't see why not." Dru

beams at me. "And please call me Auntie Dru. We're not formal around here. Every time you call me Ms. Magnus, I keep looking for someone else."

I smile at her around a mouthful of lemon muffin. "All right. I'll get on your list once I've finished eating."

"Excellent." She primps her curls. "There's a few specialized things on there you won't be able to find at the grocery store, and I wrote down the name of the business you can find them at."

I nod. I can do that. I'll go all over town if she needs me to. I don't have Nick's car like I did for my job interview, so I'll just have to call an Uber or take the bus. It's not a big deal. "I'll handle it."

"I know you will, dear." Dru smiles at me. "You're just what's needed around here."

"I'm not sure your nephew would agree." I snatch up a third muffin, because I really am starving.

"He will," Dru says confidently. "Wait and see." She snaps her fingers and then moves to the counter. "Oh, and take this to my friend Doris, would you? We made the potion for her, after all." She picks up a tiny glass bottle filled with what looks like a gummy, dark substance. "It's the potion for her knee."

And now comes the hard part of the job. Do I take this mess to Doris and let her drink grasshopper guts and bay leaves? Or do I pretend to deliver it and spare the poor woman? "I'll get right on it," I lie. Hopefully it'll take me so long to get the grocery shopping done that I won't have time to deliver the grossness to poor Doris. I move forward and take the bottle from Dru's hand, and my knees get weak. I lean on the counter, panting.

Dru arches one white eyebrow. "And you're sure this is blood sugar?"

"I'm fine," I say again, though now I'm a little nervous. Is it possible that someone drugged me? I think back to what I ate yesterday. A sandwich from the local sandwich shop. An apple from the farmers' market. There's no way Dru or Ben could have drugged me, so it has to be just . . . blood sugar? "It's not magic."

"You're going to be a stubborn ass about this, aren't you?" Dru chuckles. "Fine, have it your way. Just be careful, all right? And if you get overwhelmed or need anything, I've written Caliban's phone number at the top of the list."

"Not your phone number?"

Dru titters. "Oh my goodness, no. What would I do with a cellular phone?"

Call people? But I just nod, snatch the list and the potion, and head out.

REGGIE

A short time later, it becomes obvious that Doris lives a few streets down, so I can deliver her potion last . . . or not at all. The shop listed on the paper is across town, according to my map app, so I call an Uber and study the contents of the list in the back seat. I didn't even glance at it earlier, too rattled by the big phone number scrawled across the top, as if Dru is just dying for me to call her nephew.

I mean, if I do, it's going to be for a prank phone call, nothing else. He can fall off a cliff for all I care.

Even if I do think about the way he brushed his fingers gently over my skin last night.

With a little shake of my head, I force myself to concentrate. Lemon, fine. Sugar. Vanilla . . .

I squint. These are the ingredients for the lemon muffins I was eating just this morning. Seriously? She's not casting spells with that. At the very bottom of the page, she has a few new things written, at least.

- *Dried horse scrotum*
- *Gecko tails (dried)*

- *Honey-milk (dried)*
- *Baboon hair*
- *Mugwort*
- *Crow's foot*
- *Debris from a shipwreck*
- *Myrrh*

There's even more on the list, all the weirdness continuing down the page. I flip the list over again, my lip slightly curled with confusion. I can figure out what honey-milk is and the herbs, but how the hell am I supposed to get debris from a shipwreck? Or a freaking dried horse scrotum? Am I being sent on a fool's errand?

Is this all designed to get me to call Ben? His number is the biggest thing on the page. Or to get me to admit defeat? To say I'm all wrong to be Dru's assistant? Well, I'm not going to give up. I'm being paid like it's a difficult job, so I'm going to treat it like one. Whatever she wants me to do, I'll do it. If that means racing all over town looking for a dried horse scrotum, I guess I'll do that.

For a moment, I want to text Nick and complain about my weird job. He's on cloud nine with the new guy, though, and for some reason, it makes me sad. Not because I'm jealous. I'm truly happy for him. It's just that Nick's my fallback. If this job doesn't work out, I know Nick will always let me move back in . . . even if he wants to live alone. Even if he'd rather Sergeant Hotness move in than me. Which, of course, wouldn't happen for a while. But that's the part that bothers me—that I'd be crapping on my best friend's happiness because I can't get my life together.

It also makes me feel alone all over again.

The Uber pulls up in front of a tiny shop sandwiched between a juice bar and a dry cleaner. It's called CBD Whee! and there are crystals and all kinds of dream catchers hanging in the windows. I check the address one more time, because there's no name listed on my sheet, and then send the Uber driver on his way. He'll be in the area if I have to turn right around again, after all.

I head into the store, and when I open the door, mellifluous chimes tinkle. There's a heavy scent of incense and patchouli in the air, which makes me gag. This is like every bad cliché come to life. "Hello?"

There's a small woman about my age behind the counter, her hair pulled into two small black pigtails that bounce against her neck. She takes off a white apron and sets it down behind the counter. "Hey there! How can I help you today? Are you looking for CBD?"

"Um, actually . . ." I stare down at the list again, feeling foolish.

"Ooh," the woman squeals. "Is that a familiar cuff on you?" She bounds to my side, and she's shorter than I thought. "Who's your warlock? Or witch?"

I blink. "Not you, too?"

"Not me, what?" She looks down at her clothes—a baby-pink sundress with a pale, ruffled shrug over it—and then touches her name badge, as if checking she has everything. There's a recognizable-looking cuff on her wrist, too.

I'd actually forgotten about mine, which is weird, given that it looks heavy and thick. Wearing it, though, it feels light. I absently touch the cuff. "You've got a cuff?"

"Oh, yes, but mine is for the Society of Familiars." She beams at me. "I'm not assigned to anyone specific just yet. Fingers crossed, though!" She twines her fingers together and holds them up.

Oh no. "You're not into this witch and warlock pretend stuff, too, are you? Are you all part of some live role play that I've stumbled into?" A horrible realization hits me. "Is this some reality TV show I'm unaware of? Am I being filmed?"

"You are?" She blinks at me.

"I don't know, am I?"

We blink at each other in confusion for a moment, and then she gives herself a little shake. "Are you one of those nonbelievers that landed here somehow?" She wags a finger at me, chuckling. "You had me going for a moment."

"I'm here on behalf of Dru—"

"Oh em gee," she shrieks, grabbing my hands. "You're Dru's new familiar?"

Her enthusiasm is infectious. She just seems so happy about everything. "I guess so? I'm her assistant. She sent me here for some shopping . . . ?"

"That's awesome!" She practically bounces again. "My name is Penny. I'm with the Society of Familiars!"

That's the second time she's brought them up. "I'm sorry, I don't know what that is."

Her jaw drops. "You . . . you're not with the society?"

"Um, should I be?"

"Yes," she cries, all excitement. "You absolutely should be!" Penny's eyes go wide. "This is so exciting. You're a rogue familiar! How on earth did you get the job if not through the society?"

Penny's enthusiasm is warm and sincere, and even if she's buying into this weirdness, I can't help but like her. I think it might be impossible not to. She seems so full of joy. She watches me with a bright expression, and it makes it easier to answer. "I replied to an ad in the paper."

"Shut *up*!" she shrieks. "You did not!"

"I really, really did."

Her expression grows wistful, and she clasps her hands under her chin. "I've been waiting to get assigned to someone for ages. Is it a dream? Is she teaching you so much? Dru's so respected!"

"Um." I lean in. "Just between you and me, I'm not really sure I believe in all this stuff." It's starting to weird me out, how a perfect stranger is totally into this witchcraft stuff. "You do know magic's not real, right?"

She looks around the empty shop, then grabs my hand and drags me with her. "Come on. The door will chime if someone comes in. It's spelled."

"It has a bell on it," I point out. "Right against the door. I saw it when I came in."

"And a spell," Penny agrees, undeterred. "We can talk in the back, where it's safe."

I glance around, but the rest of the small shop is empty. There's a counter with a few glass containers inside it, but it looks pretty empty. The walls are fairly bare, too, the only things hanging for decoration a poster with a kitten on a branch (*Hang in there!*) and a large advertisement for a CBD company. And a few dream catchers, of course.

Penny drags me to the door behind the counter, knocks on the door three times. "To activate the spell," Penny says, and then opens the door and steps aside so I can go in first.

My jaw drops as I enter the second room of the shop. I thought she was leading me toward the storeroom, where I'd see boxes of CBD supplies, shipping containers, and maybe a fridge for employee lunches. This is an entire laboratory. There's a table in the center of the large room, with a pair of hot plates. Beakers bubble atop them, letting off plumes of coiled smoke. Ingredients—and more mortars and pestles—are scattered all over the table in various piles. The wall behind Penny is nothing but endless row after endless row of tight cubbyholes. I walk toward it and take a small plastic bag from one of the cubbies. There are a few dots of something in the bag, and a white label on it reads "Excrement of Field Mouse." I quickly put it back. "You guys really . . . cater to this sort of thing?"

"Of course we do." Penny blinks at me. "Why wouldn't we? Witchcraft is a good business, and we ship all over the country for those that aren't local. Now, what's on your list?"

I can't stop staring at the walls of components, the sheer number of things here, hidden behind a perfectly normal storefront. I force myself to glance down at the list, and Ben's number glares at me as if to mock me. I put my finger on the page to train my eyes away from it. "Um . . . debris from a shipwreck?"

Penny moves to the far end of the wall and pulls out a small bag from one of the cubbies. "This for necromancy or something else?"

"I—I don't know." I give her an overwhelmed look. "Do you get a lot of necromancy requests?"

"We're not supposed to, but yes?" Penny shrugs. "It's not my job to ask, just to supply." She holds the bag out to me.

I take it from her and give it a little shake, stirring the contents. It looks like . . . splinters from a piece of aged wood. "How do I know this is from a shipwreck?"

Penny giggles. "I asked the same thing, and I'll tell you what my boss said to me. You can tell by the price tag."

I look at the sticker on the bag and nearly faint at the price. Five hundred bucks? For a bag of splinters? "Jesus Christ. I hope Dru has an account here, because that's out of my price range."

"Oh, of course she does." Penny picks up a small shopping basket and holds it out to me. "Drop that in here, and I'll get everything else. Also, you don't have to worry about whether or not it's legit. The owner of this store has pickers that acquire things all over the globe, and he double-checks everything before it enters the store. No one wants to defraud a witch or a warlock, trust me."

Excellent point. If these people really do think all this crap is real, they don't want to fuck around.

I mean . . . not that it's real.

I put the bag of splinters in the basket and glance at my list again. "Um . . . dried horse balls."

"Testicles or scrotum?" Penny asks without blinking an eye. "They're two very different components."

"Scrotum." This is the weirdest conversation ever.

She bends over to glance at my list. "Is that Ben Magnus's number at the top of the page? Are you guys friends?"

"Absolutely, positively not friends."

Penny nods, a knowing expression on her face. "He's a dick, isn't he? Most warlocks are asses, but he really takes the cake. I've heard *nothing* but awful things about Ben Magnus. No one likes him."

For some reason, that almost makes me feel sorry for him. Almost.

REGGIE

I really like Penny. Her personality is all bright sunshine, and I sit on the stool in the back room of the shop for nearly two hours while she chatters my ear off. She gathers all the components I need, then makes us coffees and tells me all about herself and asks about me. I manage to deflect most of the questions, but it doesn't stop Penny. She continues talking, oblivious to my reticence.

Penny tells me she comes from a long line of familiars—always the familiar, never the witch, she says. She's been in the Society of Familiars since she came of age, and is still waiting for her first assignment to a witch or warlock. "Sometimes you have to wait a while," she explains. "Most *veneficae* are long lived, so it's a buyer's market, so to speak." Her expression turns wistful. "Which is why you're so lucky."

I suddenly feel guilty. Penny is all in on this witch stuff. She should have my job, not me. I should offer it to her, let her be Dru's assistant . . . but the thought of all that money keeps me silent. That, and the thought of crawling back to Nick and proclaiming I've lost another job. He'd just smile and shake his head, but we'd both know it's because I'm controlling. I clasp my hands in my lap, because I've been quietly arranging things on the table while Penny talks. "I'll ask Dru if she has any friends that need a familiar. Maybe I can put in a good word for you."

Her hands fly to her mouth, and her eyes fill with tears. "You'd do that for me?"

"Of course." It feels like the very least I can do. I'm actually tempted to invite her to card night tonight, but something inside me holds back. I want to talk to Nick. I want to tell him all about my job's weirdness. How everyone truly does think they're witches.

And I'm starting to grow concerned. Because it's one thing to dismiss Dru as a nutty old auntie. It's one thing to ignore Ben, who I could totally see doubling down just to make me feel stupid. But Penny seems sincere, and this shop . . . I look around. Penny's been filling orders as we talk, stuffing most of them into mailing envelopes. If everyone's in on this charade, there's a lot of people involved, and that seems like too much work for a joke.

So I don't know what to think.

We exchange phone numbers with a promise to get together for coffee to talk about the "familiar life" and witchcraft. There's something about Penny that's so very disarming that I find myself saying yes, despite the fact that she's part of this charade that I'm no longer certain is a charade. It's hard for me to make friends sometimes, and I like that talking with Penny feels . . . normal. Natural. Maybe I'll invite her next week.

I call another Uber and study the small bottle of sludge that Dru gave me. If witchcraft is real, is she going to know that I didn't deliver this? If it's not real, am I going to feed an old lady a slurry of bugs and leaves? Ugh. I don't know what the right answer is, but I do know I want to keep my job, so I end up having the driver take me to the grocery store to finish shopping, then on to the woman's house. I leave the potion with the housekeeper that answers the door, along with a hasty explanation.

Guilt riding me, I take the Uber to Nick's apartment, the bag of spell components in my arms. I head up, and even though I lived there as of last week, I can hear male voices inside. I knock, and my heart sinks a bit. Nick isn't alone. Something tells me this isn't going to be a regular Friday night round of cards.

Nick opens the door a moment later, his short, kinky curls mussed and his shirt untucked. "Reg! You're early!" His eyes swim with gratitude that I knocked first, and he clears his throat, hovering in the doorway and blocking my sight inside. "Guess what? My friend from the gym wants to learn how to play, so he's coming with us tonight."

I force a surprised smile onto my face. "How lovely. Fresh blood is always welcome. Is he here?"

Another person appears behind Nick. It's Sergeant Hotness, all right. I'd recognize that tan and those bedroom eyes anywhere. Nick moves to the side, and I can't help but notice the other guy's collar is open and he looks flushed. "Hey there. I'm Diego."

"It's nice to meet you, Diego," I say, juggling the bag in my arms and sticking out my hand. "I'm Reggie, former roommate."

He shakes my hand, his grip strong and firm, and I decide I like him for Nick. Diego glances at my bag. "Did you bring dinner?"

I shake my head, juggling the bulky bag against my hip. "Trust me, you do not want to eat these groceries. I had to run an errand for my boss."

"Not more of this witchcraft crap, is it?" Nick peeks into the top of the bag. "Good god, what the fuck is that?"

I peer in after him. "The horse scrotum, the dried crab eyes, or something else?"

Diego just laughs. "They really think they're witches?"

"They really, really do." I'm starting to wonder myself, given everything that's happened in the last twenty-four hours. "But they're nice people and the pay is excellent."

Nick picks up one of the small plastic bags—dried gecko tails—and stares at the contents. With a shudder, he puts it back. "I'm a little worried for you, Reg. Maybe you should quit. If they're crazy enough to be lying about being witches, they're crazy enough to be lying about the money, too. I don't feel like you're safe."

"It's fine," I promise him, and change my voice to teasing. "You don't really want me back anyhow."

Instead of protesting heavily, Nick just glances at Diego, and they share a secret smile. My heart sinks at that. Now that Nick's love interest is returning his affection, a roommate would just get in the way. I'm happy for him, but a little sad for me. It feels a bit like I don't have anywhere to go except to live with some crazy wannabe witches. "Of course I want you back," Nick finally says, slinging his arm over my shoulders. "Don't be ridiculous."

"Oh please, we all know the truth here." I roll my eyes, smiling despite the hollow ache in my chest. "Are we going to play cards or not?"

Nick's eyes light up. He likes the game Spellcraft as much as I do. "A small change tonight, though. I thought we'd skip heading down to the card shop and play up here instead. Just us . . . and Diego."

"Sounds great." Because what else can I say?

AFTER A FEW hours, it becomes obvious that Nick's attention isn't on Spellcraft: The Magicking. He walks Diego through the complex rules, then sits next to him, his chin on Diego's broad shoulder, helping him with his cards. I'm the opponent, and even though I win each round, it's a hollow victory when the person you're playing against doesn't know how to play properly. I like a challenge, and Diego and Nick are so wrapped up in each other that it's easy to see that I'm overstaying my welcome.

Even though Nick and I normally play cards until well past midnight, I affect a yawn shortly after ten and make my excuses. I'd been planning on staying in my old room tonight, just crashing out after a satisfying evening of cards and friendship, but it's pretty clear that Diego is also staying the night, and I don't want to be around to hear everything. I pack up my cards, hug my friend and his new boyfriend, and then get into my Uber with the bag of spell components.

I'm almost relieved to return to Dru's place.

The moment I step inside the kitchen, however, I nearly turn and run right back out again. Ben Magnus is at the kitchen table, his long legs sprawled out under the furniture. A wealth of paper and notebooks are spread out before him. He looks up when I enter, one black lock of hair dropping over his forehead, and his dark eyes study me. "Date night?" he asks, his voice low and sinful and as attractive as he is obnoxious . . . which is pretty obnoxious.

I force a light shrug, even though that lonely hole inside me feels like it's yawning wider by the moment. "I could ask the same of you. Hot Friday night?"

To my surprise, he chuckles. Ben leans back in his chair and scrubs a hand over his face. "My aunt mentioned earlier today she hasn't done her taxes in quite some time. I'm trying to get things together to send to my accountant, hoping he can stem the damage."

Yeah, I knew that. I give him a faint smile. "Ouch."

A weird silence falls between us. It's not quite comfortable, as if we're both suddenly remembering that he's been trying to get me fired. I avert my gaze because it feels like too much to look at him. He's too much. Too much everything.

"Your boyfriend dropped you off at the curb? It's late. He should have at least seen you to the door."

I think about Nick and Diego, and how they were all over each other all night in subtle ways. It simultaneously made me happy for Nick, a little jealous, and a lot lonely. "I took an Uber here, thank you very much."

"You could have asked me for a ride," Ben suddenly volunteers.

I glance over at him, surprised. He looks uncomfortable, the expression on his face slightly challenging, as if daring me to mock him. An awkward silence falls. I unpack some of the goods I picked up for Dru, hesitating. I don't know why I'm lingering in the kitchen. I should hurry up to my room, pull the covers over my head, and forget this awful day just happened. I don't want to feel jealous or miserable just because Nick is happy—I want to be happy for him. But that loneliness keeps building inside me, and I can't bring myself to leave the kitchen, even if it's Ben Magnus sitting a few feet away, doing Dru's taxes on a Friday night instead of whatever it is he normally does. I finger one of the small envelopes Penny packed away earlier, idly sorting them alphabetically as thoughts race through my mind.

What if Nick is right? What if they're lying to me about the job and there's no money? If they're lying about witchcraft—or delusional enough to think they're really casting spells—how do I know this is legit? I gnaw on my lower lip, thinking.

"Spit it out," Ben says.

I carefully slide a packet of "Roots from Sage Plant Harvested at Midnight" under the packet of "Pearl, Dissolved." Or should it be under *S* for "sage"?

"Spit what out?"

"Whatever's bothering you. That look on your face." He gets to his feet, and as he unfolds, I'm reminded just how very tall and menacing Ben Magnus is. He's wearing all black again today—I'm not sure if the man owns clothing in another color—and he crosses the kitchen to come and stand directly in front of me, as if that will somehow force me to answer.

I school my features into a mask of neutrality. "What look on my face?"

"Like something is bothering you deeply. Spit it out. I assure you, I am impossible to offend."

Somehow I doubt that. I nudge the packets again, forcing my gaze back to them instead of looking at my boss's nephew, who's much taller standing next to me than I remember, and who smells quite nice . . . for an ass who thinks he's a wizard. "I just . . ."

"Just?" he prompts, reaching over and pushing the packets out of my reach as I obsessively organize them.

I turn and scowl at him, because now he's gone from being slightly pushy to really pushy. I rest my hand on the counter, my other on my hip, and give him a defiant look. "Just tell me if this is real, all right? If it's all one big joke, it's past time to let me in on it. I don't like people laughing at me behind my back, so just tell me, okay? Is this real?"

"Is what real?"

I wave a hand in the air. "All this magic crapola you two are constantly spouting. I went to a magic store today, and she believed in this nonsense, too, and it's starting to get to me."

"It's real," Ben says, voice solemn.

I roll my eyes. "Of course you'd say that. I don't know why I asked—"

He leans forward, just slightly, his gaze meeting mine. "I wouldn't lie to you, Reggie."

Ben's stare is so intense that I freeze in place. Not intense in a bad way. Intense in a way that doesn't seem to jibe properly with my brain. His eyes are dark and smoky, and he's got the longest, most ridiculous lashes. His gaze flicks over my face, and I wonder if he's staring at my mouth. I look at his, and okay, that was a mistake. How did I not notice before that Ben Magnus has the most full, most decadent mouth I've ever seen on a man? I knew he looked intense, like all his features were too much all at once, but each one separately is . . . really nice. Kissably nice.

Oh god, what is wrong with me? I jerk away, flushing uncomfortably, and cross the kitchen, pretending I'm thirsty. I pull a carton of milk out of the fridge and pour myself a glass, my back to him. What were we even talking about? I can't think. All that's in my head is irritating Ben Magnus's full, pouty mouth. *Think*, I tell myself as I chug milk. Ubers and magic. Right. I take the now empty glass to the sink. "If you say magic is real, then cast something. Show me something. Anything. Make me believe."

He moves, and I can feel his presence behind me, looming. "What do you want to see?"

"I don't know." I wave a hand at the kitchen counter, where I've laid out the strange ingredients I purchased earlier today. "Make them float in the air or dance or something."

Ben snorts. "You've been watching too many cartoon movies. That's not how our magic works."

"Of course not." I suddenly feel stupid for asking. Of course he's going to agree to show me something, just not anything I want to see. Not anything tangible. He'll probably pull a quarter out of my ear and call it a day. But for me to believe, I need to see something real. I need to be convinced.

And I don't know that he can convince me.

I turn and give him a tight smile. "You know what? Never mind. Forget I asked."

Ben leans in, and for a moment, I think he's going to kiss me.

My eyes go wide in alarm . . . but he only leans in and plucks a stray piece of lint off my sweater. "Oh, I won't forget."

I roll my eyes. "Give it up already. I'm not buying what you're selling."

"Too late." He smirks at me. "The next time we meet, you'll be on your knees, begging . . . for forgiveness."

On my knees, begging? That sounds dirty and wrong. I mumble something and flee upstairs.

BEN

You'll be on your knees, begging. By all the gods, what's wrong with me to blurt something like that out? Why don't I just pull my dick out and slap her with it? Get rid of all the subterfuge? I press my hand to my forehead and groan inwardly.

I have made it painfully obvious that I am somehow, someway, attracted to my aunt's useless apprentice. This is bad. This is very bad.

But she just looked so damned sad tonight. Lonely. As if she was lost and didn't know how to find herself. And I know how that feels. I know what it feels like to see the world moving around you and to feel like you're not part of it. Like you don't belong to anything.

Maybe that's the part that calls me to her.

She needs to catch on to what's going on around her. I think she's starting to figure it out. She no longer wears the look of derision on her face when someone mentions magic. Not tonight. Tonight, she looked thoughtful. Tired.

Tonight, she asked me to show her a spell . . . and I somehow made it into innuendo.

I scrub my hand down my face again and study my surroundings. I should go back to my aunt's taxes. Drusilla gets so lost in witch society that she forgets she has to pay attention to mundane world issues. I should help her with those. Instead, I turn and glance down at the hair on the counter.

The hair I pulled from her sweater.

It's habit. After years—centuries—of casting, of spells that need personal components, I've become adept at acquiring these sorts of things. It's second nature to pluck a hair casually from someone's sweater and keep it, just in case I need to cast something. How many times have I traveled to a foreign country just to follow some rich, powerful fool's assistant to the dry cleaner to get a few stray hairs off their clothing for a spell?

I should throw it away. It no doubt belongs to the boyfriend that doesn't deserve her. The boyfriend that let her move in with strangers for a job with witches. The boyfriend that didn't bother to drive her home, just made her get a ride with someone else. I pick it up thoughtfully.

She wanted to see a spell, after all . . .

REGGIE

I wake up the next morning to the sound of my phone buzzing and Maurice rubbing against my shoulder. I roll over in bed, yawning, and Maurice immediately snuggles against my breasts, rubbing his head against the low neckline of my nightgown. Scratching his ears, I reach for my phone and flick through the messages from Nick. If he's telling me more about Diego's prowess in bed, I'm going to have to shut him down. I love Nick like a brother, but there are some things a girl just doesn't want to know.

> **NICK**: Two things.
>
> **NICK**: Okay, three things. First of all, Diego is AMAZING and I need to know if you liked him. He's kind of insane in bed and I'm obsessed. Is it bad to be this obsessed so quickly?
>
> **NICK**: Second thing. Your parents called this morning. I swear, they're like bloodhounds. They scent a bit of money and come out of the woodwork.

I jerk upright, staring down at my phone in horror. Maurice makes a grumpy noise of protest, then settles himself on my bed again. I scroll back, reading Nick's message again just to make sure that I read it correctly.

My parents. Ugh.

I think of the people I should be closest to in the world, but a sour taste fills my mouth. I think of the times they lied and stole from everyone around us. The checking accounts and credit cards they opened in my name. The scams they ran, convinced they were just temporarily impoverished millionaires waiting for their number to come up. Nick calls them users, and they are. They'll sob and guilt-trip me and make it seem like the most dire thing in the world has happened, just so I will open my checkbook and give them what little money I have.

Every time, I tell myself I'm not going to fall for it. Every time, they come up with something new to suck me back in. They sweep back into my life for a few weeks, leave again just as quickly. I end up with a wake of new debts in my name and all kinds of guilt and issues.

Trembling with dread, I text Nick back.

REGGIE: What did you tell them?

NICK: That you were unavailable. At the unemployment office.

I breathe a little easier at that.

REGGIE: Thank you. 🙂

NICK: You know they'll call back. They always do.

REGGIE: I know.

NICK: I'm not going to give them your number. I don't want you calling them, either.

REGGIE: Did they say it was urgent?

NICK: Reg . . .

REGGIE: They did, didn't they?

NICK: Of course they did. That's how they sucker you in.

He's not wrong, and yet . . . I know I'm going to stress about it. What if I don't call and it's something terrible this time? What if someone's been in an accident? Or jail?

NICK: Reggie

NICK: I know you.

NICK: Do NOT call them.

NICK: If it truly is urgent, not only will they call back, but they'll leave contact information of a hospital or some such. You know that.

NICK: You also know there's no hospital involved, and they're just trying to get you on the phone so they can shake you down again.

NICK: I know it's hard, but don't fall for it.

REGGIE: I know. 🙁 Thanks for being a buffer for me, like always.

REGGIE: I really do appreciate you.

REGGIE: What was item #3?

NICK: Oh, right.

NICK: You didn't happen to eat or touch shellfish last night did you? Before you came over?

REGGIE: Uh, no, why?

NICK: Because poor Diego's face puffed up like a balloon. He's allergic. His beautiful eyes are still swollen this morning. He's taking medication, but I feel so bad for him. We can't figure out what happened. He just broke out in hives about an hour after you left and his face got all red and bloated.

NICK: We still fucked like animals, but it's weird.

REGGIE: I promise I didn't touch any sort of shellfish or eat any. You know I don't like them.

NICK: I know. I just thought it was weird. 🙂

NICK: So . . . Do you want deets? How many inches? How many times?

REGGIE: I love you, but no and NO GOD NO.

NICK: Lol

I clutch my phone to my chest, sighing as I stew over the new development with my parents. It's not like I have money. I haven't gotten my first paycheck from Dru yet, and even if I had, I'd have passed anything extra to Nick to pay for my half of the rent and utilities. I hate that they're back, though. I should be excited to hear from my parents. It's been a while since I last talked to them, but there's only a gnawing sense of discomfort and worry instead of love.

Maurice rubs up against my chest again, pawing at the neck of my nightgown, and I absently scratch his ears again before getting up and changing into jeans and an old T-shirt. I pull my hair back into a messy knot atop my head and throw on my sneakers, then grab my phone, shoving it into my pocket. It's so odd that Diego had an allergic reaction on their date night. What a piece of bad luck . . .

Almost as if Diego were *cursed.*

Oh.

Oh no.

Show me something. Anything.

Oh no, no, no.

Make them float in the air or dance or something.

That's not how our magic works.

You have to be willing to get rid of her if things don't go as planned.

No fucking way. There's no way Diego's shellfish reaction has anything to do with Ben.

You'll be on your knees, begging . . . for forgiveness.

With a whimper of anger and frustration, I storm down the stairs and slam into the kitchen. Sure enough, Dru is seated at her table near the window, a cup of coffee in her hands. Her white hair is still in curlers, even though she's put on lipstick and a pretty gown of royal blue with sheer, billowy sleeves.

Across from her, sprawled like he owns the place, is the bane of my existence. Ben drags a spoon through a bowl of cereal, doing his best to look bored. He's not fooling me, though. I march right up to him, practically trembling with fury. "Did you curse someone?"

He arches one of those dark brows at me. "Why would I do that? Magic isn't real, remember?"

Aunt Dru lifts her coffee cup to her lips. "Uh-oh."

I clench my hands into fists, fighting the urge to smack that smirk off Ben's face. "You son of a bitch, that's my best friend's new boyfriend!"

He tilts his head. "Not your boyfriend?"

"I don't have a boyfriend!" I shout.

"Oh my," Aunt Dru says. "I do believe she's telling you that she's available, Caliban darling."

"Not for him," I snarl. I'm so mad I'm shaking. "He needs to fall off a fucking cliff. How dare you? How'd you do it? How'd you know to target him?"

Ben gets to his feet, and his large body looms over mine. I continue scowling up at him, unafraid. He's trying to intimidate me, and it's not working. He reaches forward and I jerk backward, but he only picks at my shirt. "You have a piece of lint."

What does lint have to do with anything? Confused, I gaze up at him . . . only to see a smug expression on his face. Is he . . . is he taking a stray bit of lint off my shirt and using it as a spell component? Like a forensic analyst would capture DNA on clothing?

Because as I stand there, I remember Ben did that last night, too. Plucked a hair off my shirt. Either he has a lint obsession, or he's using those hairs against me. A sound of pure animal rage escapes me. "You didn't."

"You asked me last night to show you something," he says in that silky, too-reasonable tone. "You didn't say what. Don't get mad at me."

"MAGIC ISN'T REAL," I bellow, and I don't know if I'm trying to convince him or myself.

"If not, then what's the problem?" Ben's eyes are dark slits, his expression impossible to read.

"I don't understand this nonsense," Dru chimes in. "Of course magic is real. How else do you think you got the job when no one else applied, darling?" She looks at me with innocent eyes. "The ad you answered was bespelled so only someone qualified to be a familiar could actually read it."

"Bullshit," I say automatically, and then wince when Dru's eyes widen. "I didn't mean it like that. I just . . . I . . ."

"She doesn't believe you," Ben points out helpfully to his aunt.

"It was just an ad in the paper," I say, trying to keep calm.

"Mm-hmm" is all Dru says, the look on her face pitying. As if I'm the crazy one.

I'm starting to feel crazy. Does magic exist or not? Even entertaining the thought feels utterly ridiculous, and yet . . . I'm starting to have doubts. Yesterday, Penny had been so confident (and logical), convinced that I'd somehow lucked into a secret society of some kind that she was still on the waiting list for. But . . . you can't put a magical ad in the paper.

Can you?

Scowling at both of their smirking faces, I turn and stomp back out, whipping my phone out of my pocket again. I frantically search through my photos, finding the ad I'd made a screen capture of a few weeks ago. The ad that I thought was for a freaking card game. I quickly send the picture to Nick. I'm going to call them on their crap, and then I'm going to quit because they're gaslighting me.

REGGIE: You can read this, right?

I move to the foot of the stairs and sit on the bottom step as I wait for his response. As if he can't resist tormenting me, Ben saunters into the doorway and leans against it, watching me. "So what's the plan, then? Are you going to quit?"

"You'd love that, wouldn't you?" I mutter.

"Yes, actually. It would solve a lot of problems."

"I'll just bet." I don't point out that I was considering that very thing—that I should quit and just walk out the door and not look back. I don't need this crap, and my parents can't con me for money I don't have, after all.

But it would mean walking away from an obscene amount of money. It would mean walking away from another job, one that doesn't involve wearing a uniform, cleaning fry grease, or twirling a sign on a street corner. I'd be crazy to walk away from a high-paying job that gives me room and board just because my boss is delusional.

"Well?" Ben prompts.

"I'm ignoring you."

"And doing such a good job of it, too."

I do ignore that. My phone pings with an incoming text, and I suck in a breath as I scan Nick's response.

NICK: The ad about the Persian rugs?

I grit my teeth in frustration and type a response.

REGGIE: No, the one above that.

REGGIE: Please don't joke around, I'm very serious here.

NICK: I . . . don't see anything.

NICK: Did you send the right file?

REGGIE: Never mind!

This proves nothing. Nothing at all. Nick just isn't looking in the right spot. I look up at Ben and glare at him with all my might. He only smiles and walks away, as if he knows he was right, and it makes me absolutely crazy. Doesn't he have a home somewhere else? I could have sworn that Dru said he didn't live here.

Maybe if I hint heavily enough, he'll leave. Probably not, though. He's going to wait and see if I quit, and . . . I don't think I will. Because I keep coming back to that dollar amount, over and over, and it trumps everything. Even witchcraft.

Turns out I have a price, after all. That's depressing.

Dru enters the foyer, regal despite her long, swishing dress and curlers. She eyes me, studying my spot on the base of the stairs, then clasps her hands in front of her. "If you're done having a hissy fit, do you want to do the job you're being paid for?"

Hot guilt rushes through me. I jump to my feet. As frustrating as I find Ben Magnus, I like Dru and I don't want her to get rid of me, even after all of this. "I'm sorry," I say quickly. "I just have a hard time with a lot of this."

The elderly woman shakes her head, and one of the curlers goes pinging to the ground and slides across the tile floor, right to the base of one of the ancient marble busts along the hall. "It's perfectly all right to have questions, darling. I'd be worried if you didn't." She comes to my side and takes my hand in hers, patting it. As she does, another curler tries to make an escape and falls directly in front of her eyes. Dru ignores it, continuing. "I don't want Caliban to chase you off, you know. You just have to understand him."

I'm not sure I want to. He's an arrogant ass and a half, and he seems to delight in making my job harder. "He's your nephew—"

"You have to understand him," Dru says again for emphasis. "He's really quite smart and lovely. He's just lonely. He's not good with people. Never has been. His parents are to blame for that." She gives my hand another pat, as if unwilling to release it. "They weren't ready to be parents, and so they left him with nannies and friends as often as possible. Our family is notorious for feuding, too, so it wasn't like he could have many peers or even companions.

Someone that's been hired to look after you isn't a friend. They're a keeper." She smiles gently at me. "He could use a friend."

She imbues that statement with so much meaning that I know what she's aiming at, and I want no part of it. That curler in front of her eyes is bothering me, though, so I extricate myself from her grip and fix it for her. "He needs to get a familiar of his own, then."

Dru's expression brightens. "I've said the same, but he has a dreadful time keeping one. He's very exacting and controlling. If only I knew someone like that . . ." She clucks her tongue.

I purse my lips. Well, that was a very pointed jab. "I'm not going to be his friend, Dru."

"Aunt Dru," she corrects. "And you don't have to be his friend, but maybe you two could court. Or fig."

"Fig?" I choke.

"That's what they call it now, right?" She looks confused for a moment. "Some sweet, dried thing."

"Date?"

Dru brightens. "Yes, that's it. A date. Strange name, but whatever. You can date my nephew. I give you permission. Just don't get pregnant, at least not right away. It puts an awful wrench in things."

"I am absolutely, positively not going to date your nephew! I can't stand the man! He—" A door slams somewhere in the kitchen, and I realize Ben has overheard all of it—Dru's awkward matchmaking, my loathing—and I feel a tendril of guilt. "I'm just not," I finish lamely. "Sorry."

"Yes, well, that's too bad." Dru shrugs. "Do you still want to work for me?"

I nod.

"Even though Ben might have cursed your boyfriend?"

"Not my boyfriend, and he'll be fine." Which is more than I can say for me if I lose this job. I think of my credit-card bills, the rent that's due, the debt collectors that find my phone number no matter how many times I change it. If I could be free of all of that . . . Yeah, I'm willing to put up with a little witchcraft to have a future, to be able to breathe easier.

Dru looks delighted. "Wonderful. How are you with makeup? I have a ladies' luncheon, and I need to look my best so they can all be horribly jealous of me."

"I can do an excellent winged eye," I brag.

"Oh, no wings, just eye makeup," Aunt Dru tells me.

Oh boy.

REGGIE

A few hours later, I follow Dru into one of the ritziest places I've ever seen. I feel entirely out of my depth, though I should have guessed something like this would happen when Dru insisted that I wear my nicest dress. Turns out I have only one nice dress, since I'm broke as a joke, so I'm wearing an A-line black sleeveless dress that I also wore to my boss's funeral three jobs ago. I might be wearing brown loafers with it, but I figure no one's looking at me. When a black sedan with a driver shows up to take us to lunch, though, and Dru is wearing a silk jacket over a pleated accordion skirt and tons of jewelry, I start to get the idea that this is a fancy place.

I put on a little more lipstick in the car, just in case, and powder my freckles in another attempt to hide them. My hair's pulled back in a tight bun atop my head (mostly because it's been years since I've had my hair cut and styled and this is my go-to), so there's not a lot I can do with it. I feel terribly underdressed as we head downtown, and it doesn't let up as we arrive and I notice valet parking. It only grows worse as we step inside.

The restaurant has marble floors and delicate plants in every corner. Large, lofting windows let in a ton of natural light, and there's a fountain in the corner. Classical music plays, and the waitstaff are dressed in black . . . like me. I look like a waitress. My insides shrivel just a little, and I lean down toward Dru. "Should I go wait outside?"

"No, darling, it's fine. You look lovely." Dru scans the dining room, as if searching for familiar faces. "It's just lunch, after all."

So she says. I rub my arms, clutching my beat-up purse against my side. It's times like this I'm extremely aware of just how little money I have. I watch as someone brings a bucket with ice to one of the tables and there's a bottle in it, just like in the movies. Another table has a three-tier display of what look like cookies and sandwiches. Every table has a fancy white tablecloth on it, and I don't think anyone here has ever heard the word "drive-through." "Just so you know," I murmur, "I'm absolutely going to be using the wrong fork. That's a thing, right?"

Dru titters. "It doesn't matter. I grew up without forks. It took me forever to figure them out myself."

Er, okay. I'm not going to touch that one. I bite my lip, remembering too late that I have lipstick on, and then hastily scrub at my teeth with a finger. The host (in a tuxedo, because of course) gives me an odd look and points at one of his canines helpfully. I give him a smile of gratitude and rub my teeth again. "Do you see your friends, Dru?"

"Oh, I didn't say they were my friends," Dru tells me brightly. She clutches a spangled purse to her chest and peers at the tables. "I said they were acquaintances. We are enemies, actually."

The host stares in confusion, obviously eavesdropping.

I try not to, even though I know just how he feels. "I see. So this is an enemy luncheon?"

"Rivals," she agrees. "Friends close, enemies closer, yada yada. Oh, I see Livia! I'd recognize that dreadful mole anywhere." She raises a hand in the air, waving. "Come on, Reggie darling. Let's go introduce you!"

The host shoots me a look of pure sympathy as Dru tugs me forward into the dining room. "Enjoy your lunch, ladies."

I follow my boss inside, and sure enough, it's easy to pick out Livia. That is definitely one hell of a mole, right in the center of her forehead, like a unicorn's horn. I do my best not to stare, because it's not as if she can help it. Instead I smile brightly and avoid direct eye contact with anyone.

"Livia! Julia! I told you I'd find a new familiar," Dru crows as we approach the table. "You two bitches can suck it!"

"Dru!" I gasp, shocked. "Oh my god." I give the women an apologetic smile. "I'm so sorry—"

They stare at me with narrowed eyes. "Why is she talking to us?" one asks, her tone utterly polite as she leans over to her friend. The other shrugs.

Ooookay.

"My new familiar," Dru tells them. "Her name is Reginald."

"Reggie," I correct gently. "Regina if you have to."

"Regina," Dru continues in a lofty tone. "I'm going to teach her everything I know."

Livia just smirks at the two of us. "That won't take long."

As if oblivious to the insult, Dru turns to me and gestures. "Well, darling, you can go sit with the other familiars now. We've got some big-girl things to discuss." She makes a shooing motion. "Go have fun. Tell them that your tab is on me. Drink yourself silly if you feel like it."

The only thing I feel like drinking is a gallon of antacid. I glance around, looking for the "other familiars," as if I'm supposed to recognize them by sight. The restaurant is half-full, most of the tables with well-dressed couples of varying ages. As I scan the room, a man lifts one finger in the air, and the sleeve of his suit falls back to reveal a thick silver cuff identical to the one I'm wearing.

A familiar cuff. Right. I keep forgetting to take mine off. I touch it briefly, then look to Dru, but she's being seated by a hovering waiter and doesn't seem to care what I do. All right, then. I head over to the other table, a bright smile on my face. "Hi there! My name is Reggie, and I'm Dru's new assistant." I stick my hand out, remembering Penny's joyous enthusiasm at my employment. "It's lovely to meet you."

The man just looks me up and down. He's fairly nondescript, with a flat, sour mouth and really nice clothes. The woman seated across from him is gorgeous, wearing a tight wrap dress with a designer logo printed all over it. Her hair has been slicked down into a high bun like mine, but she's got big, expensive-looking earrings hanging from her lobes and a flower tucked behind one ear. She gives me a dismissive look and goes back to her phone.

I pull my hand back, painfully aware that my brown loafers don't match my dress. I sit down at the empty chair. "I'm new."

"Oh, we know." The man gives me a petty smile. "Everyone's heard about Dru's new mongrel familiar."

It takes everything I have not to flinch. "What makes me a mongrel?" I ask politely, putting my napkin in my lap. I don't want him to see how his words hurt me. "I'm her assistant."

"You're not with the Society of Familiars." The beautiful woman sneers. She doesn't look up from her phone, just keeps typing. "All of the esteemed familiars are. People wait decades for a chance to serve."

Penny sure was a lot nicer about it. "I see. And how long have you two worked for your employers?"

They exchange a look. "Employers?" The man titters, as if I've said something hilarious. "That's cute." A waiter arrives and pours iced tea into an empty stemmed glass in front of me, then sets down a tray of cookies and sandwich triangles. My stomach growls, but I'm afraid to reach for anything in front of these two asses. "We've been working for our employers," the man continues, "ever since the war."

"Afghanistan?" I ask.

They smirk again. "The *Great* War," the man says loftily.

As in . . . World War One? Two? I pick up my drink and sip it, even though it splatters condensation all over my dress. They don't look old. Is this more of the "let's play pretend" stuff, or are they really that old? I don't have the heart to ask, because they're so unpleasant. I miss Penny.

Shit, I almost miss Ben. If this is how everyone in their little society acts, no wonder he doesn't want anything to do with anyone.

"One, James. I believe they call it One now," the woman says in a sultry voice. She types away, her long fingernails dark red and dancing over her phone. "She probably hasn't had a single bit of training."

"No, she hasn't," I interrupt brightly. "I thought that was the point? To be a familiar with an eye on learning?"

"Indeed," the one called James says.

"Well, you must be really slow learners, then." I keep my voice achingly sweet.

They both look at me with narrowed eyes.

I touch the cuff on my wrist and glance over at Dru. She's chatting happily to the two sour-faced old women seated with her, so I suspect this lunch is going to go on for a while. Fine, then. I reach over, grab a handful of cookies, and pull out my phone. Ignoring the two of them, I shove one cookie into my mouth and text with my thumb, deciding to reach out to Penny.

REGGIE: Hi there, it's Reggie from the store the other day. Dru is at lunch with two other ladies and I'm having to sit with some guy named James and a lady with talons for fingernails. Do you know them?

PENNY: OMG HI!!!!

PENNY: IT'S SO GOOD TO HEAR FROM YOU!

PENNY: Also that is probably James and Edwina, and they're both assholes. Their witches tend to go everywhere together.

PENNY: I'm sorry you have to sit with them! Are they giving you a hard time?

REGGIE: It's all good. They're just being their charming selves, I think. One of them mentioned WWI though. How old are they? Because they look like they're in their 30s.

PENNY: That's magic for ya. I don't know how old exactly, but I do know they've been familiars since before I was born. Why?

REGGIE: Just curious.

REGGIE: We still on for coffee later this week?

PENNY: OMG YES!!

PENNY: I would love to meet up!!! Do you know the little coffee shop around the corner? They have the best lattes!

Penny's enthusiasm makes me feel a little better. I guess for every James and Edwina, there's a Penny or two out there. I just have to look for them.

I glance over at Dru, but she's got her head together with the other women at the table. As if they can feel me looking, all three turn and stare in my direction. Well, that's creepy. I give them a benign smile, shove another cookie into my mouth, and turn back to my phone screen. James and Edwina have gone silent, so there's that, at least.

I flick around on my phone while I think of something to text back to Penny, and for some reason, Ben's number stares out at me from my contact list. I added him in case it would be necessary for my job, but seeing him there sandwiched in the middle of my short friends list feels odd. I think about the conversation earlier, and how I fiercely declared to Dru that I loathed Ben, and how he'd overheard it. I feel . . . guilty. I'm not the kind of person that likes to make enemies, present company excluded. I'm going to have to get along with Ben, especially if he's Dru's beloved nephew and he's part of her day-to-day life.

I wonder if I should apologize. I don't need more enemies. If anything, I need Ben to be on my side. Sometimes I wonder . . .

"You swine-loving whore!" Dru's voice rises above the soft background noise of the restaurant.

Everything goes quiet. The cookie in my mouth turns to dust, dry enough to make me cough.

"Here we go," James mutters, then sighs heavily.

I shove my phone into my purse, jumping to my feet as Dru stands up and points a finger at Livia, who looks bored and unamused. "You, Livia, are a terrible person and an even worse witch."

"You take that back," Livia says in a singsong voice.

"No!" thunders Dru. She picks up one of the finger sandwiches and flings it. It smacks Livia in the face, and the other woman gets to her feet. A dangerous tension fills the air, and I could swear I hear the crackle of thunder.

Livia looks as if she wants to rip Dru's carefully piled curls off her head. "How *dare* you?"

"How dare *you*!" Dru picks up another sandwich.

I lurch forward. Oh boy. "Dru, Dru," I call out. "Let's calm down now." I reach her side and pluck the sandwich out of her trembling hand. "They're very tasty sandwiches not meant for launching at people's faces."

"I was trying to hit her mole," Dru bellows loud enough for the entire dining room to hear. "I don't know how I missed, seeing as it covers half her face."

Livia gasps and I wince. "Now that's a low blow. Of course, I should expect such things from House Magnus. You've always been low-account trash, though, haven't you?" She gives Dru an arch smirk. "You can take the girl out of the slums, but you can't take the slum out of the girl."

To my shock, Dru snarls and lurches for Livia, as if she's going to climb across the table and go for her throat. With a yelp, I push myself in front of Dru, blocking the other woman from my boss.

Someone pushes me, and it's not Dru, but James. He gives me a dirty look. "Get your old hag off my witch."

My temper sparks. "Get *your* old hag off mine!"

"Just you wait," Dru yells. "You're going to get a curse doll with your name on it, bitch. A dozen curse dolls!" She grabs another handful of sandwiches and tosses them in Livia's direction.

"I'm not afraid of you," Livia sneers. "I've got an evil-eye amulet waiting for just this sort of occasion. You'll be sorry, Drusilla Magnus. Wait and see."

A fleet of waiters heads in our direction, and I decide it's time to extricate us from the situation. "Okey dokey," I say, grabbing Dru's hand before she can fling another round of sandwiches at her rival. "I think it's time for us to head home. We're leaving," I say to the waiter nearest us before he can call the police. "We're leaving right now, I swear."

"Filth," Dru shrieks at the top of her lungs as I escort her toward the exit, followed by a half dozen frowning waiters. "You're nothing but filth, Livia Germanicus! FILTH!" The tirades continue until we make it outside, and immediately, Dru straightens. She fixes her mussed clothing, adjusts her hair, and then pulls out her wallet and hands a wad of bills to the nearest waiter. "I apologize for my outburst. Please share this with your fellow waitstaff and let them know I appreciate them, even if they have to serve that pile of vomit named Livia."

"I'll call you a car, Ms. Magnus," the closest waiter says, his expression unruffled. "Please don't reenter the restaurant."

"Of course not," Dru says with a sniff. "She's still in there."

The moment we're left alone, I just shake my head at Dru. "Why did I think this would be a friendly lunch?"

"Eh. We always start off cordial and end up . . . here." She waves her hand back and forth, her expression calm. "Tossing food at each other's faces."

"And you have lunch with them? Often?"

"Often enough."

"Do all of the lunches end up like that?"

I could swear Dru's eyes twinkle with amusement. "Often enough."

12

BEN

Aunt Dru's library is bigger than mine. It makes sense, of course. She's been alive for two thousand years, so of course she'd have time to acquire many more books and scrolls. It's one reason why I spend so much time at her house instead of mine. In addition to her robust library, she also tends to have a familiar to do the grunt work for her, whereas I go without one for very long periods of time. Even though her last familiar, Lisa, didn't care for me much, if I gave her a task list, she always finished it, even if she was a bit lazy. Lisa also hinted that when she returned from maternity leave, if I didn't have a familiar, she'd be interested in tackling the job, but I don't plan on taking her up on it. As far as I'm concerned, her loyalty would always be first and foremost to my aunt. And while that's commendable, there are also certain things one doesn't want a parent or guardian knowing about them.

I tell myself it's for convenience's sake that I decide to stay at my aunt's for a while longer instead of returning home to Boston. It has nothing to do with her familiar. I truly should leave, because Reggie loathes me and has made that quite clear. Maybe that's the reason I decide to work on my next project at my aunt's house instead of my own. There's an almost sinful pleasure in needling Reggie, watching her flush with anger.

I'm used to people hating me. It doesn't bother me that she does.

Much.

So I find myself in the city for a few more days. Since I am, I visit my favorite rare bookseller. I flip through the books piled on the table set aside for me. He's found a few rare tomes for me that I need to peruse before I decide to purchase them or not. I've barely opened the first one when my phone buzzes with a text. I'm waiting to hear back from my Silicon Valley contact, so I glance over at the screen.

W S: Your aunt is out of control.

Willem.

I pick the phone up and stare at the screen, wondering if I should answer. If I even want to know. With a weary sigh, I close the three-hundred-year-old transcription of Greek medical papyri and text Willem back.

B. MAGNUS: Dare I ask?

W S: She picked a fight with Livia at lunch. Is she insane?

B. MAGNUS: You have to ask?

W S: You're right. I already know the answer to that. Livia has been holed up in her laboratory for hours. I'm afraid whatever she does to get revenge on Drusilla is going to be extremely unpleasant. Consider yourself warned.

B. MAGNUS: Noted. Thank you for the heads-up.

So much for a relaxing afternoon of study. I gesture at the books I haven't had a chance to look through. "I'll take all of them." If nothing else, I suppose I can have them shipped to Boston to build my library.

A short time later, I return to my aunt's house, my arms full of the carefully packaged rare tomes. The vacuum is roaring in the library, and Aunt Dru is nowhere to be found. Maurice is on the bottom step of the stairs, regarding me.

"Is it bad?" I ask the cat.

His tail flicks once.

I nod. That's bad. I set the books down on the nearest table and head for the library. I should probably find my aunt first and get her side of the story, but I find myself pulled toward the library by the sound of vacuuming. I know it has to be Reggie. Aunt Dru has never cleaned a thing in her life. I'm surprised she even owns a vacuum. Following the noise, I open the library double doors.

And stop, horrified.

My aunt's library is a thing of beauty. Two floors deep, it's wall-to-wall books, with elegant wooden ladders to assist in reaching the higher-up shelves. Magical items are artfully sandwiched between the books here and there, and scrolls are shoved into every single extra space. There are a few chairs for seating and a table by the window, but other than that, there are books on every surface possible. Is it messy? Yes. Dusty? Absolutely. But it's also a treasure trove of objects, and half of the beauty is wandering through the shelves, hunting for old treatises or pharmacology sourcebooks. I'm a warlock. Dust is part of the job.

Reggie stands in the middle of the library, the vacuum racing and blaring. She has her back to me, her hair pulled up in a messy knot, and she has on a pair of tight nylon men's shorts and another one of those gym shirts, with NICK'S PERSONAL FITNESS emblazoned across the shoulders. Around her are stacks of books and papyri, scrolls and artifacts, all pulled from their homes on the shelves. The shelves themselves are emptied of their contents, the mountain in the center of the room surprisingly small considering how much reading material is stuffed in here.

She keeps vacuuming, moving in quick, brisk motions, as if unaware of my presence.

"Reggie," I call out.

My aunt's familiar keeps on vacuuming.

"Reggie," I say again, louder, as she runs the vacuum over a priceless fourteenth-century rug that's probably being held together by dust mites. She continues to ignore me, so I move to the light switch and flick the power off.

She screams, nearly making me jump out of my skin. When I turn the lights on again, she shuts the vacuum off and pulls two earbuds out of her ears. "What the fuck, Magnus?"

I gesture at the stacks of books, letting my horror show. "What is this?"

Reggie lifts her chin at me, ever defiant. "Your aunt wants me to assist her, right? I can assist her a lot easier if everything is located in its proper place. This library is a mess and needs organizing, so that's what I'm doing."

"This library has been organized like this for nearly a hundred years. No one is going to be able to find anything if you move it all."

She hesitates, her gaze sliding to the stacks on the floor. I can see the reluctance move over her face, and then it quickly disappears. "It's a mess in here," she continues, though her tone is less brave. "It's going to be helpful to have things organized. You'll see. My way is better."

"Did anyone ask you to do this?"

Reggie's expression turns utterly crestfallen. "No." When the silence stretches between us, she bites her lip. "Do you think Aunt Dru is going to be mad? I was . . . I was just trying to help." She wrings her hands, all anxiety. "When I get upset, I organize. And today . . ." She trails off. "Never mind about today."

She doesn't need to tell me about today. I know everything that happened already, thanks to Willem. I glance around the destroyed library. "I suppose it's dusty."

"Very," Reggie admits in a small voice. "And Aunt Dru is elderly, and I wasn't sure if all this dust was healthy for her."

I'm pretty sure it would take more than a cloud of dust to take down my aunt, but I say nothing. For some reason, it bothers me that Reggie's now looking so uncertain, as if she has screwed up. I'd intended on coming in here to pick at her about the cleaning, expecting a fight. I much prefer a fighting Reggie to a worried one.

A worried one makes me feel like an utter ass.

I remain where I am, trying to think of something to say. My gaze falls to the stacks of books again. "Is this everything?"

"No." Reggie's tone is more miserable. "I put a lot of the contents temporarily into the music room, since it's almost as dirty as this one."

I grunt. "Aunt Dru's not into music, no."

She takes a shuddering breath and says in a quiet voice, "I really need this job."

And she feels I might snatch it away from her? I'm offended . . . but then, isn't that how I've been acting? Determined to get rid of her? Telling her she's all wrong at every turn? And . . . she is. But I feel like an ass for being the one to make her so miserable. My aunt likes her. She's loyal and hardworking and didn't run her mouth about this afternoon, which shows she can be discreet. I suppose everything else can be learned.

I try to think of something to make that crushed expression

leave her face. I clear my throat. "I have a list of components I need rounded up and a few books I'd like retrieved. When I stayed with my aunt before, Lisa would get them for me . . ."

Reggie nods. "Give me the list. I'll have it to you by the morning, if that's all right." She gestures at the library. "It might take me a while to find something in all this."

"I . . . Thank you." I pull the list out of my pocket, handing it over to her. She still looks miserable, and for some reason, I can't find it in me to leave just yet. "You seem like you're having a bad day."

She manages a forced smile, but it doesn't reach her eyes. "Just envisioning what a day in jail would be like."

"Jail? What happened?"

Reggie bites her lip again. "I shouldn't discuss it."

"Your loyalty is commendable, but I've already heard plenty through the grapevine."

"Your aunt threw a sandwich at another woman's mole," she blurts out. "In public. I thought we were going to get arrested."

"Ah."

"That's all you have to say?" Reggie seems surprised. She folds the list I handed her and remains standing close to me, her face tilted up to mine. "Just 'ah'?"

I shrug. "Aunt Dru is . . . volatile at the best of times."

The familiar is much taller than Aunt Dru, who has shrunk with age, but I don't think Reggie has ever stood this close to me before. I can't help but notice that her height makes her perfect to nestle in my arms . . . and now I'm disgusted with myself. First the obsession with her freckles, and now her height. I swallow hard, aware of her nearness. How she's slightly sweaty, with tendrils of hair sticking to her forehead, her lips parted as she gazes up at me.

Desire stirs inside me, unwanted and surprising. This is worse than the freckles infatuation. When she looks at my mouth, her gaze pausing there, I feel . . . hungry.

And that's wrong, because she's my aunt's new familiar. It's hard enough to get one familiar, and my aunt just lost Lisa. I can't take another familiar out of play. She's forbidden.

She drags her gaze away from my mouth and looks up at me. "I'm going to clean the guest bedrooms next, by the way. There's something in there that smells sour, and you'll probably hear me knocking around if you're staying for a few more days. Or should I wait until you leave?"

"You're not a housekeeper," I say softly, because she's still standing close to me and my hand is twitching with the need to touch her.

Her gaze darts to the mess of the library as she considers my words. "It helps me focus. Makes me feel a little more in control of my situation. I don't . . . I don't like feeling out of control."

I understand that all too well. I nod once, then turn to leave.

"Ben," she calls softly, and it's like electricity racing through my veins. Not Caliban. Not Magnus. Ben.

Even though I know it's a mistake, I turn to look at her. Turn to see her soft expression as she gazes up at me. "I'm sorry about what I said earlier. About hating you. You're just being protective of your aunt, and I can't dislike you for that."

Her words are gentle, filled with apology. There's a hint of a smile on her face that's utterly lovely, her eyes shining as she looks at me. She's beautiful. And she's forbidden.

So I ruin it, like I ruin all nice things. "Are you saying this because you're afraid I'll cost you your job?" I make my tone deliberately cold, harsh. "Because the timing is awfully suspect."

Reggie's expression shutters, grows cold. She flinches and then forces a smile to her face to hide her feelings. "I was trying to be polite. You should give it a whirl."

I can't, because being polite to her leads me into dangerous territory. Far better off to remain as enemies. I just grunt. "See that you have that list done by the morning."

And I turn around and leave, because if I stay, I'm going to lose my mind. Instead, I head out, down the hall, looking for my aunt. Her house is much larger than my brownstone back in Boston, and she's got several secret rooms squirreled here and there. Dru might play at the feeble old woman, but she's sharp as a tack and as sly as they come, and I wouldn't be surprised if every room in her house had secret walls or hidden passages. I decide to check the basement first, since that's where her working laboratory is. Apparently the one upstairs is "just for show." The door leading to the basement is in the hall outside the kitchen, and I set my palm over the wards painted on the wood, letting the spell know that it's me. There's a pause, and then the door opens.

I head down the stairs. "Aunt Dru?"

"In here, darling."

I find her in the laboratory, not at her potions table, but reading a magazine in a chair by the fireplace. I study the surroundings, because her laboratory hasn't changed in the five hundred years since I've known her, despite the fact that she's had many different houses and lived in multiple countries since then. There are always dusty shelves full of components, a few animal skulls (for "color," my aunt says when asked about them), a few amulets hanging from the walls, a marble bust of her first husband leering down from one of the top shelves, and a big, heavy stone fireplace so she can employ a cauldron, if needed. A large wooden table covered in old potion stains dominates the room, and clusters of dried herbs hang from the ceiling. It's a chaotic place, but familiar to me. I eye the magazine she's reading—*Better Homes and Gardens.* It's probably the neighbor's. "Are you hiding down here?"

"Me? I would never." She licks a finger and flicks a page.

"You're hiding," I decide.

Dru shakes her head. "The girl really does love to clean, doesn't she? What a strange little creature."

"She's doing it because she's upset. Apparently someone got into a fight at lunch?" I wait for the explanation.

My aunt lifts one of the pages to her face and sniffs it, then rubs it all over her neck. "Perfume samples are so fun. Do you remember when they used to send out those tiny little plastic vials? I used to keep them all and make my apprentices wash them, because they were perfect for a good snort of crushed mummy powder." She gives the magazine another stroke down her neck. "Times sure have changed, haven't they?"

"A fight?" I prompt. "At lunch?"

"I might have had a tiny spat with Livia." Dru smiles to herself, the look mischievous. "I might have tossed egg salad at that mole of hers." She looks unrepentant. "I know you're going to say I shouldn't have, but it did get her attention."

"You shouldn't have."

"No, probably not." She looks sad. "Now I can't go back to that restaurant for a while. But it really was fun, and Livia can sometimes be such a snot." Dru flips through the magazine again. "Reggie needs to get broken in anyhow. Best to throw her in to drown, or whatever the saying is."

"I believe it's 'throw her in the deep end.'"

She waves her fingers in the air. "Same difference."

REGGIE

Dru has a lot of books. Like, an absolutely enormous amount of books. Most of them are terribly old, smell like mildew and dust, and have faded covers, the titles illegible on the old, dark spines. It makes reorganizing things slow going, because in addition to the books, she has scattered papers shoved in between many of the pages. Sometimes the books have flowers or herbs pressed inside them. I found a long lock of hair in one, even, and I'm not sure if it needs to stay or go. Then there are also the scrolls and a few clay tablets and . . .

Basically I've taken on an enormous job, and it's not going to be done anytime soon.

I straighten one pile of books, wishing that I'd managed to put together one shelf's worth of tomes, at least, but no dice. Instead, all I've created is a mess. I've started tagging books with Post-its based on author, topic, and language, since Dru has books in multiple languages here. It's going to take me days—if not weeks—to get everything straightened out for her, and I worry she's going to get mad at me.

Ben was pissy enough, that's for sure. I tried apologizing, and he slapped me in the face (at least with words). That's the last time

I extend an olive branch to him. I've got to get his components together tonight, too. I consider tossing the entire list in the trash, but I'm already on precarious ground with Dru. I don't want to lose my job before I get my first paycheck.

When *is* my first paycheck? I don't have the stones to ask.

There's a knock at the door to the library. "Reggie darling, how's it coming in there?"

I freeze in place, terrified. Dru's going to see this and fire me. She's going to freak out and get upset. She's going to—

The door opens. As I stand there, utterly ashamed in the piles of books, Dru takes a look around, her eyes wide. "Oh my. I sure do have a lot of books, don't I?"

"It's all under control," I promise, clutching the duster to my chest. I cough a moment later, because, well, dust. "It might take a little bit longer than anticipated, though. I hope that's all right."

Dru waves a hand, dismissing the situation. "It's fine. I know most of the good stuff by heart at this point anyhow. Just do what you can. You're the only one that's wanted to tackle this, so it's all yours!" She steps around a pile of books, smiling brightly at me. "But you can do that later. For now, I need your assistance."

"Oh?" I step over a pile of scrolls clustered together on the floor. "What for?"

"We are going to get my scrying orb out, and we're going to spy on Livia, darling." She claps her hands, excited, and her jewelry jingles.

She can't be serious. "Um . . . we're what?"

"Spying on Livia. Come on. It's familiar time!" She trots out of the room before I can protest again.

With a twinge of worry, I follow her out the door. She did hire me to be her familiar, so I guess I need to do my job. I search through the house, looking for where Dru ran off to, when I spot the cellar door open at the far end of the kitchen. I peer inside. "Dru?"

"Down here! Come on down. This is my laboratory."

Oh boy. I can just imagine. I head down and . . . yup. It looks exactly how I pictured, except there are even more books and scrolls, and dust on everything. My fingers twitch at the sight of a pile of magazines next to a chair, with a wadded paper towel next to them. There's clutter on every surface, and I inwardly cringe as Dru pushes all the crap on the big table to one end, piling it up on top of itself. "What is all this?" I reach out and touch one heap of junk on the far end of the table, because it looks like a stone tablet of some kind and a writing utensil. "What—"

Dru slaps my hand. "This is my laboratory. You touch only what I allow you to touch, all right? And no cleaning down here."

I draw back, stung. I guess she minds my cleaning a little more than she lets on. "Fine."

The older woman ferrets around under the table, shoving things about, and I wince every time there's a tinkle of broken glass or the sound of paper ripping. "Here we go!" Dru finally says, and promptly bumps her head under the table. "Ow!"

"Are you okay?" I drop to my knees, peering under the table. Oh my god, it looks like a *Hoarders* convention under there.

Dru stumbles backward, clutching what looks like a crystal ball. "Just fine! Had a little boop to the noggin but otherwise unscathed." She rubs her head as she stands, and then displays her prize. "Ta-da! Our scrying orb!"

I gesture at the thing in her hands. "Can I just point out that that looks like a crystal ball?"

"Well I would hope so, seeing as how it is a crystal ball," Dru says, dusting herself off. "How else would you spy on your enemies?"

I open my mouth to protest, and then snap it closed again. I don't really have a good answer for that, do I? I want to say I don't have any enemies, but the truth is that I've been fired from enough jobs for my obsessive cleaning and organizing that I'm sure there are a few bosses out there that loathe me. My parents probably don't *hate me* hate me, but I definitely can't count them as friends, and they would absolutely spy on me.

And then there's Ben.

"I guess the question I have," I say slowly, "is why are we spying on her again? Can't you two just avoid each other for a while?" That'd be my preference, given that I already despise her familiar. Chalk another into the enemies column for me, because I am sure it's mutual.

Dru ignores me, kicking the clutter back under the table and then setting the crystal ball onto a tiny stand that's appeared out of nowhere. "As much as I would love to just leave Livia alone, she won't return the favor. That tart is going to put a curse on me, and we need to scry and see where she's hiding her tablets."

"A curse?" I blurt out. "What the fuck is with you people and curses?"

Dru blinks up at me, as if seeing me for the first time. "Reggie, my dear, we're witches. Cursing people is what we do. At least . . . the ones in my bloodline. Yours, too." She digs around on the messy table. "You haven't seen a polishing cloth, have you?"

"Wait, what do you mean, my bloodline?" I pick up a few old envelopes and help her look for the cloth, but it takes everything I have not to start organizing them by size. "I'm not related to you."

"Somewhere down the line you are. My guess is that it's very, very far down the line. All the way back to the Roman Empire." She tosses a few magazines down on the floor behind us. "That's how you have magic, darling."

I give in to temptation and get down on my knees on the old

stone flooring, picking up stacks of yellowed newspapers. "What do you mean, I have magic? I don't have magic."

"Of course you have magic. How else were you able to answer that ad I put in the paper?"

"With a phone call?"

Dru snorts. "Very funny. You were able to read the ad, and no one else was. It means that somewhere along the way, someone in your family fucked one of the gods."

This time, I'm the one that bangs my head underneath the table. With a yelp, I scuttle out from under the table, holding my stinging scalp. "*What?*"

She catches the crystal ball before it can roll off the table and puts it back in its place. "The bloodline, darling. The ancient gods are full of magic. And that Jupiter is a randy son of a bitch, so he spread his godly ambrosia"—she gives me a lewd wink that makes me want to crawl back under the table again—"all over the realm. His descendants are the ones that have magic."

It sounds . . . nuts. "Uh-huh."

Dru wags a finger in my face. "I can tell you don't believe me still. It doesn't matter how much proof I put in your face—you are determined not to believe. So that's fine, missy. You keep right on not believing, but as long as you're a good familiar to me, that's all that matters. Now, did you want to help me cast this spell or not?"

My lower lip trembles just a little. "You don't want to fire me? Even though I've made a mess of your library?"

"Gracious me, no." She reaches out and grasps my hands in hers. "You'll be just fine, Regina my darling. It'll all become clear very soon." She pats my hand affectionately. "Don't lose faith. Just like I have faith that you'll get my library back in order."

"Of course I will." I smile at her, my heart brimming with affection. Dru's a little strange, but she wants to give me another try. She doesn't care about my past or my obsessive cleaning. She's willing to give me a chance to prove myself. "I'm going to be a wonderful assistant to you, just you wait."

"Familiar."

"Apprentice?" I compromise.

"Let's get started, shall we?" she asks, ignoring my question. "Time's a-wasting, and Livia's not going to hold back in her casting." Dru releases my hands and turns back to the table. "All right, now, where were we?" She glances up at me. "I know you say you're not magical, but did you want me to teach you how to scry?"

I mean, what's the right answer for that? I want her to be happy with my performance, so I nod. I am absolutely not asking about my check, either. The rent's due in another day or two, but I'll tell Nick it'll have to wait until I get paid. "I would love to learn. I admit I'm curious."

"You mean you want to prove me wrong," Dru corrects, eyes twinkling.

"I didn't say that."

"You didn't learn your lesson from the other day?" Her gaze is all innocence. "You think I've got jokers?"

"Jokes," I correct. "And no, I don't think you've got jokes. It's just . . ." I rub my forehead, thinking about Diego's timely shellfish reaction. On one hand, it's damned convenient timing, and it plays into Ben's claims of magic. On the other hand . . . it's a shellfish reaction. That sort of thing happens all the time.

I'm starting to have doubts, but I've spent over two decades not believing in magic, and it's going to take more than one allergic reaction to make me truly believe.

Dru giggles, patting my arm. "It's all right, sweetie. I want to prove me *right*. Wait and see, you'll learn that magic is real tonight, I promise you. Then we can get on with the good stuff."

She's so very confident that she's going to make a believer out of me. I gesture at the orb. "Show me what you've got, then."

Dru rubs her hands together, studying the small area she's cleared off on her table, the crystal ball in the center of it. "Okay, the first thing we do is we make an offering to the gods." She looks over at me. "The Roman gods, of course."

That's the second time she's mentioned Roman gods. "You're a pagan, then?"

"Just because people don't believe in them anymore doesn't mean they don't exist." She lifts one shoulder in a light shrug and then digs around in some of the cluttered junk. "We need some olives or possibly olive leaves to get their attention."

"There's a jar of olives in the fridge."

"That'll work. I can't seem to find my packet of olive leaves from Mount Olympus." She tsks as she digs around in the mess. "And again, no, I don't want you to clean up in here."

With a chuckle, I head up to the kitchen and return a short time later with a jar of pimento-stuffed olives. I hand it over to her. "Will this do?"

"It won't be perfect, but it'll do for now." Dru pulls out a small bowl and shakes several olives and their juice into it. "The gods always request an offering every time you work magic. It's to show you mean business and to target who you're directing your request for magic to. Think of it like an address on a letter. If you just throw it into the mailbox, the postman has no idea who to deliver it to. But if you make an offering and invoke the gods, they know who needs to answer."

I nod as if this all makes perfect sense. I mean, they've certainly thought out all this magic stuff. "Is it going to be a problem that I don't believe in the Roman gods?"

Dru caps the jar again and shakes it at me. "Do you believe in this jar?"

"Pardon?" I give her a puzzled look.

"Do you worship this jar?"

"No . . ."

"But it still exists, doesn't it? Just because you aren't sending prayers up to it, it doesn't wink out of existence, does it? It's still here in my hand, full of delicious olives."

"You do realize this is a very weird analogy?"

Dru laughs. "Only to you, darling. Makes perfect sense in my head. Now, let's see." She sets the jar down and moves the bowl toward the center of the table, off to one side of the crystal ball. "All right. Give me your finger."

I automatically hold my hand out.

Before I can see the knife in her hand, Dru jabs my finger, hard, and blood wells up.

"Ow! What the fuck?" I try to draw back, but her hand is like steel around my familiar cuff.

"Over the bowl, please, or we'll have to do it again." She drags me toward the bowl, holding my finger over it and squeezing my blood over the olives. "Now we invoke Mercury, the patron of gossips everywhere, to aid us in our quest to spy on Livia." She closes her eyes, still clutching my hand, and begins to whisper the name "Mercury" over and over again.

I watch as she squeezes my finger until the blood slows and the olives are obscenely splashed with my blood. That is bizarre and creepy, and I'm not sure I'm into this level of pretend. I glance at the crystal ball, but it looks just like some sort of costume prop. There is zero cool stuff happening inside it.

Dru drops my hand and opens one eye, glancing at the crystal ball. "Well, shit."

"Didn't work?" I ask.

"Nope. That bitch is blocking us already." Dru sighs, her hands going to her hips. "It figures. I really thought this would work, though."

"Maybe it didn't because—"

Dru glares at me. "Don't say it."

"Magic isn't real," I continue. "Dru, I really like you and I'm not trying to rain on your parade, but have you really cast anything that works? Truly? Because if so, I haven't seen it."

"What about the other day?" Dru challenges.

"You mean when I passed out because of low blood sugar?" I didn't see magic then, and I don't see it now. I'm just further convinced this is all a big delusion that they've bought into, and it hurts me a little that Dru is so miserable with her life that not only does she have to playact, but she has to drag others into it. "It wasn't magic, Dru. It was just bad luck."

The older woman makes a strangled noise. "You are very, very stubborn, Regina. Fine. This calls for the big guns." She casts one last disgusted look at the crystal ball (which might have been purchased from a crafts store for all I know) and then moves toward one of the shelves in the back. Instead of her usual rummaging, she heads right for a small box and pulls it out. "I want you to go to Livia's place and spy on her directly, since our scrying is blocked."

I can feel my eyebrows go up. "Uh . . . how?"

"This will help you." She holds the small box out to me. "But I don't want you to open it until you get there, understand?"

I hesitate. "Dru, I don't want to trespass on someone's private property."

"You absolutely will not be trespassing, I promise." Dru pushes the box into my hand and then covers her fingers with mine. "Like I said, it'll all become clear once you open the box. Just trust me. You will be breaking no laws." Her smile is bright. "And since you don't believe in magic anyhow, what's the big deal?"

✳ ✳ ✳

TWO HOURS LATER, it's near midnight and I have a Superman Band-Aid on my finger, and the tiny box in my pocket, and I've paid an Uber to drop me a block away from the address I've been given.

This is such a mistake, seriously. I'm not breaking into anyone's house, not for any job. But the receipt for the Uber will prove to Dru that I at least attempted it, and as long as I don't get arrested, I figure it can't hurt to go look at Livia's house. So I walk over, clutching the worn hoodie I stole from Nick against my body. The neighborhood is a fancy one, each house bigger than the last, with manicured shrubs and high, ornate steel fences protecting the residents from outsiders. I am definitely not getting in, even if I wanted to.

My phone buzzes, and I yelp in surprise. I guess I'm more on edge than I thought. Hands shaking, I grab it and check the texts.

NICK: Are you awake?

NICK: Me and Diego are heading out to a midnight matinee. Want to come with? He's got a straight friend.

NICK: Also a soldier. Two men in uniform. 🤤

Ugh. Even if I wasn't busy, I wouldn't want to go. Nick set me up with my last boyfriend, who was an utter mess. He has great taste in gay men, terrible taste in straight ones.

REGGIE: Working late, I'm sorry!

NICK: It's midnight. What are you doing exactly?

I look around at the posh houses lining the street. Even the mailboxes look expensive as hell.

REGGIE: I'm on an errand for my boss.

NICK: I worry about you in that job. They still haven't paid you, have they? You should come home . . .

NICK: Don't worry about the rent. We'll figure it out. ♥

I smile at my phone like a loon. Nick is the sweetest. I love that he's so protective of me, the family I never had. Even so, I'm not quitting. Not when this job has the potential to pay through the roof.

REGGIE: I ♥ you but I swear I'm fine. Go have fun at the movies!

NICK: Will do!

I shove my phone into my back pocket once more and then cross the street, heading for the address that Dru gave me. It's the biggest house in the neighborhood, because of course it is. A massive, cold-looking modern house with a tile roof looms over well-manicured bushes and what looks like acres of lush green lawn. There's a double-door gate made of steel at the street entrance, and I wander past it, pausing only to note that the bars are not nearly wide enough for me to slip through.

Not that I'm going to break in.

There are no lights on at Livia's house, from what I can tell. I gaze at it, seeing nothing but windows after endless windows and pale white stucco. Square walls frame a large portico, and I could swear a chandelier hangs from the entrance. An outside chandelier, of all things. I guess that's when you know you have too much money. I snort to myself with amusement. At least now I can identify the house. I can just tell Dru that the place was locked down tight and I couldn't get in. Piece of cake.

Satisfied, I glance around to make sure no one thinks I'm casing the joint, and then start to head back the way I came. I'll wait a few minutes, then call another Uber, so it seems like I tried harder. As I head down the street, I pull out the tiny box Dru gave me. It's made entirely of metal, the quarter-sized lid hinged with a clasp at the front. Probably has a dried roach or something equally strange in it. I shake the tiny box. There's something inside, but I can't make it out.

With a flick of my thumbnail, I open the clasp and move the lid back, revealing what looks like a small wad of fabric. Weird. I pull it out, and to my surprise, there's a large ring inside the fabric, plain and black. Hematite, maybe? The fabric has something written on it, and I clutch the ring in my hand as I read the lettering.

WEAR ME

Well, this is all very *Alice in Wonderland*, isn't it? And it turned out shitty for her. I sigh, throwing my head back and groaning in frustration. Dru probably thinks it's a magic ring. I study the plain band, and it's cool in my hand. Why am I hesitating? I've been telling everyone for days that magic isn't real, right? So if it's not real, why do I not want to put the damn thing on? I frown at the ring, trying to convince myself. Dru will never know if I don't put it on.

But magic isn't real.

It's not.

It's just a bullshit story made up by a bunch of people that are doing their best to feel special. I haven't seen anything that has convinced me that magic is real. Not the supposed healing potion, not the crystal ball, nothing. It doesn't matter that Ben and Penny and Dru are convinced it's real. There are people that are convinced the earth is flat, after all. People are allowed to believe what they want as long as it doesn't hurt anyone else, I suppose.

Me, I don't believe.

So I take the ring and slide it over my thumb.

My stomach immediately cramps, making me double over. Panting, I hunch on the street, shocked. Food poisoning? What—

My skin shivers, and in the next moment, the world gets blurry and tilts. My eyes go black for just a brief second, and when the world rights itself, I'm . . . shorter.

I'm crouched on the sidewalk on all fours.

I lift one hand . . . but it's not a hand. It's a paw. A black paw, the large ring neatly slid over my foreleg. My tail flicks, and to my surprise, I realize I've been turned into a black cat.

All right. I definitely did not see that one coming.

REGGIE

Magic is real.

Magic is real, or I'm having a mental breakdown. I'm pretty sure it's the former at this point, because that's the only thing that can explain the fact that I now have whiskers and a tail. I stretch my feline body and notice that my shoes—and the rest of my clothing—are piled on the pavement. They didn't change with me, and in this form, I can smell the laundry soap and dryer sheets I used. Everything around me smells different, from the thick, damp aroma of the freshly watered grass to a musty scent that I can't quite place.

I look around in amazement. I can see really well in the dark, too. Sure, everything's in black and white, but didn't I read somewhere that cats don't see color much? I sidle back up the street, hopping onto a low stone wall and prowling toward Livia's house.

No wonder Dru said I'd be able to get in and spy. She was planning on turning me into a cat. I should be furious, but I'm too fascinated by the realization that I'm wearing a magic ring, I'm a cat, and everything I've thought in the past was a lie. I mean . . . holy shit. Dru really is a witch, and that means Ben is a warlock.

Penny was right. I'd text her to tell her, except my phone is in the pocket of my discarded jeans, and I currently have paws.

Fascinated by my cat body, I swish my tail back and forth and look around. The gates of Livia's mansion are still nearby, and I'm small enough to slip through them. Unable to resist—because curiosity and cats and all that—I slink toward them, heading for the entrance. I'm a little worried to leave my clothes on the ground, but no one's come up or down this street in the last ten minutes, so I figure I should be all right for a little while. I creep toward the gates, rub my side along the bars, trying to be as cat-like as possible. When no alarms go off, I slide through the bars and head for the house.

There are scents everywhere, including that weird, gross, musty one that I can't identify. Is it a spell component of some kind? A rotting plant? I head for the house, jumping up onto the ledge of one of the massive windows, and peer inside. Everything's dark, and I can just make out a sitting room in all the shadows. There's a baby grand piano in one corner, underneath a massive oil painting of a young woman who has to be Livia, judging by the mole on her forehead. She has a ruff around her neck, and she's wearing a big, fluffy dress, Queen Elizabeth–style. Huh.

I press my wet nose to the glass, but I don't see or smell anyone.

Then I hear it.

A low murmur of voices. It's coming from somewhere inside, but I'm not entirely sure where. I wonder if I can get in. This seems like a good idea to my cat brain, so I jump down from the window and circle around the house, keeping to the trimmed hedges to hide. There's a wonderful scent here, something delicious that makes my stomach growl, and when a tiny mouse scurries past the bushes, I drop to a crouch, instantly ready to hunt. God, it smells *so* good, but I force myself to focus.

Spying, I remind myself. *You're spying. Snack later.*

I tiptoe around to the back of the house, and that musty smell is stronger. I can hear voices here, too—a man and a woman. That must be Livia and her familiar. I spot a pet door with a plastic flap, a small functional square in the otherwise gorgeous white door at the back of the house, and I head toward it. Sneak in, I decide, do a little spying, sneak back out. No one will know. I sidle up to the door, push my head in past the plastic flap, and sink my paws onto the checkered tile floor—

Something stirs. A low growl begins, and then I see it.

A dog.

A really fucking big-ass dog with a spiked collar. A Rottweiler. It spots me at the same time that I spot it, and all the fur on my back stands straight up, my tail puffing like a feather duster.

It growls louder and then races for me, nails clacking on the tile.

With a yowl, I race back out the pet door and across the yard. The dog is tight on my heels, chasing me, and the hot, musty smell fills my senses. He's the thing I've been smelling, but I didn't know enough about dogs to realize it. If he catches me, he's going to eat me. Blistering fear races through my body, and I run as fast as I can, looking for the nearest tree.

There are no trees. Livia's lawn is bare of everything but topiaries and sculpted bushes.

I veer along the fence, racing for the gates. *Where are they, where are they, where are they—*

The dog barks wildly, lunging for my tail, and catches a tuft of my fur in his mouth. I feel the fur being yanked from my skin, and I let out another cat yowl of pure terror. Adrenaline makes me move faster, and I race for those double gates as I've never raced before. The dog is so close that I can smell nothing but his gross, slobbery breath.

I'm dead, I'm dead, I'm dead—

I slam through the bars, my shoulder hitting one side, and wriggle my way through just as the dog catches my tail again. With a hiss, I roll frantically, getting away before he can get a better grip, and then arch my back, my fur sticking up on end as I spit fury at him.

The dog barks again, so loud and furious his slobber is going everywhere. I swipe at him with my claws, and then I see it.

The ring.

The fucking ring. Of course.

Scuttling away, I race back toward my clothing as the lights at Livia's house come on and the sounds grow louder. "Go check and see who's here, James," I hear a voice call out. "If that Dru's sent someone, capture them. I want to know what they're up to."

I make it to my clothes, a short distance away from Livia's house, and the dog keeps barking and barking, setting my nerves on edge. I curl up on top of my jeans, trying to get the ring off my foreleg, but it doesn't want to move. Fuck, fuck, fuck. I bite at it, scratching and clawing, until it moves. Just a little.

Then it practically falls off my foot and onto the ground.

The moment it does, my belly cramps and my back tightens. I hunch over, the urge to vomit moving over me, and then I'm human again, my cheek pressed to my shoe and my naked ass in the air.

A flashlight clicks on down the street. "If you're out here, you little bitch, I'm going to find you." It's James, his voice cold and nasty. "Xerxes, sniff her out, boy."

Fuck.

Sweaty with terror, I scoop up my clothes and my shoes and race down the street. I'm naked as could be, but there's no time to stop and put my clothing on, no time to do anything except run. If Livia catches me and she really is a witch, I don't want to know what she's going to do to me. I choke back my fear until I turn the corner and find a house without a fence, a house with what looks like a small pool house in the back, and I press against the cold bricks, letting them scratch my naked ass.

A sob chokes out of me.

I nearly died tonight. I have no doubt that if that dog had caught me, he would have killed me. Strewn my cat parts all over Livia's lawn, and that would have been the end of Reggie Johnson.

Shaking with terror, I collapse against the wall of the house, more tears rushing down my face. I struggle to put my T-shirt on, but I'm frozen with fear. I can still smell the hot, musty stink of the dog, still feel his breath too close to my neck . . .

I can't stop trembling. I can't function.

Weeping, distraught, I fumble for my phone and nearly drop it. I can't hold it steady, and it takes me far too long to unlock it. Once I do, I stare at my contact list, trying to figure out who to call.

Not Nick—he'll make me quit. He'll lecture me like an older brother, and I don't want that right now. I don't want to have to explain anything. I just want to be safe. If James finds me . . .

I choke back another terrified sob and clutch my phone tighter.

Penny? No, Penny would be excited. She wouldn't understand my terror, and I don't want to answer her excited questions right now.

That leaves Ben.

The moment I settle upon his name, it feels right. I pull up his number before I can think twice, and text him.

REGGIE: Ben

REGGIE: Help

BEN

My phone pings with an incoming text, and I glance over just as I light the eighty-second candle atop the kitchen table. Aunt Dru has holed herself up in her lab with instructions not to bother her, so I've taken over the kitchen. One of my corporate accounts wants an unlikely stock of his to increase gradually without making it seem obvious, so I'm starting with low-level bad-luck spells—minor curses—on all the competitors and adjacent markets. I have two more candles to light, and then I can invoke Fortuna and start the casting properly.

Immediately, a second text pings right after the first.

Whoever it is, they're impatient. I scowl at my candles and then quickly move over to the counter to check my phone. If it's Willem, I'm going to add a candle to curse him while I'm at it, because he needs to know that midnight is prime casting time and—

REGGIE: Ben

REGGIE: Help

My heart thunders in my chest. She's not here? She's not in the library shelving books? My mouth is dry, and I turn to the mass of candles covering every inch of the massive wooden table. I crafted each one specifically for the spell, and once it's been lit, it can't be reused. It'll mean starting over again.

I consider for a moment, eyeing the hours and hours of work down the drain. But Reggie wouldn't ask for help unless she was in trouble.

I text her quickly.

B. MAGNUS: What's wrong?

B. MAGNUS: Where are you?

There's no answer. I wait impatiently, watching my candles sputter, the specially made wicks of twine woven with my hair and rubbed with marjoram cut with dirt unearthed under a full moon to nullify luck. If I leave now . . .

My phone is silent, taunting me.

Shit.

I grab a heavy blanket from the nearby laundry room and toss it over the myriad candles, using my weight to smother the flames quickly. I head over to the cellar door, but Aunt Dru has music on to drown out sounds. She does this when she wants privacy, as casting can sometimes get loud, and some spells are personal. I check my phone again, but there's no reply from Reggie.

I race across the kitchen to find a knife, stab my finger, and offer blood to Mercury in my offering bowl, even as I drag my phone forward. "Show me Reggie," I demand. "I'll do a complete offering later," I bargain. "Just show me the girl. It's urgent."

At first I think the gods won't answer. They're prickly and capricious at best, and more often than not, how well your spell is received depends on the quality of your offering. To my relief, though, my phone's map app opens up and zooms in on a particular street.

Livia's street.

"Fuck," I snarl. Is Aunt Dru having Reggie do something dangerous? And Reggie would fall right into danger because she doesn't believe any of this is real. With a growl of frustration, I lick the blood off my finger and say a silent thanks to Mercury. I'm going to give him the best offering possible in thanks the moment I return home.

I grab the keys to my car—the one I keep here for when I'm in town—and race through the streets as quickly as possible, throwing charms and amulets of nondetection on the dashboard so no cops will pull me over for speeding. Luckily, Livia is not too far across town, so it doesn't take long to careen through the streets and make my way into her neighborhood. In the distance, I see James in front of her house with a flashlight, so I drive to the next street over and park, looking around.

"Reggie?" I check my phone again, but there hasn't been another text. "Reggie?" I hiss again, taking a few steps forward. "I can't help you if you don't answer."

Frustrated, I open the map app again and check it one more time. It's zoomed in a few houses away from Livia's austere palace, so I head in that direction after shoving a charm of nondetection in my pocket. I jog through the neighborhood, looking for a slim figure, and I'm just about to give up hope when I hear a choked sob.

"Reggie?" I slow my steps, moving toward what looks like the pool house for some rich person. I circle around the building, and huddled in one corner, next to a rosebush, I spot my aunt's missing familiar.

She's naked. Completely naked. Reggie's hair is a tousled mess that hangs around her wan cheeks and she clutches her clothing and shoes to her chest, her legs sprawled out in front of her. She's weeping and shaking so hard that her entire form trembles as she looks up at me.

"D-dog," she manages to choke out.

My chest aches at the sight of her. She looks so damned vulnerable and fragile. I shrug off my black sweater and carefully lay it over her, determined not to look at her naked body. "Are you all right, Reggie?" I keep my tone gentle as I crouch next to her. "Can you stand up?"

She blinks up at me, her eyes huge. "C-can't stop sh-shaking."

I lean in, peering, and her pupils are dilated. They're enormous, dark rings in her too-pale face. I touch her hand and it's clammy, her skin ice cold. They're all the signs of a familiar's body going into shock after a particularly harrowing spell. "It's all right," I murmur, my voice soothing. "I've got you now. I won't let anything happen to you."

"J-James—"

I shake my head. "He won't dare approach me. Come on. My car is parked around the corner."

Reggie nods jerkily and tries to stand up, only to collapse at my feet like a newborn fawn. I should have guessed. Awkwardly, I pick up my sweater and tug it over her head until it hangs over her like a sack. "Put your arms through the sleeves," I guide, and with my help, she does so. The moment I release her, she lists to one side, about to collapse again. "Here," I say, and hand her the shoes and clothing she was clutching, and then I heft her into my arms. "Your system is stressed. You'll be fine in a little bit. You just need some hot food."

She whimpers and tucks her face into my neck, as if seeking comfort.

It throws me, that small gesture of trust. For centuries, I've been one of those "untrustworthy warlocks from House Magnus," a dark spellcaster from a line of questionable history. I have many enemies and few friends, and no one has ever nuzzled up against me like Reggie is right now. It makes my body react in uncomfortable ways, ways that are completely unsuitable considering the girl in my arms is shaking with shock and half-naked. I can dwell on those emotions later, I decide, in private.

For now, I won't notice how her cold nose is pressed against my neck, or how her breath tickles at my collar. I won't notice how perfectly she fits in my arms or how long her legs are.

That would be inappropriate.

"Sorry," she breathes against my skin, making my *very* inappropriate cock react.

"There's nothing to be sorry over," I say, my tone a little more brusque than it probably should be. "You're in shock because of whatever my aunt cast. It's her fault, not yours. You'll be fine once we get some coffee and food into you. I'm going to drive you to a nearby all-night diner, all right? We'll get you something hot to eat. Do you think you can dress in the car?"

She manages to nod. "Thank you, Ben. Sorry I'm being . . . such a baby."

"Again, this is all perfectly natural," I say, but I'm a little mystified by her shame at needing help. Has no one ever helped her before? Does no one look after her? The thought sends my protective instincts roaring. "Your system can't handle magic of that intensity, so it struggles to right itself after a big shock. We'll get you some food and you'll feel better, I promise. I won't let anything happen to you."

Reggie swallows, giving another jerky nod.

I start the car, pulling out into the street. As I do, a half dozen amulets fall from the dashboard and pour into Reggie's lap. She makes a small sound of surprise.

"Sorry," I say. "Those are to ward off speeding tickets."

"I didn't think you were the type to have a messy car," she manages, and her tone sounds better than it did. She picks one up and studies it before putting it back onto the dashboard. "Thank you," she says. "You didn't have to come. I know it's late . . ."

"If you apologize one more time," I warn, "I'm going to stop the car."

I don't mean it, of course. The protective side I didn't know I had is roaring at the thought of Reggie alone and untried, finding herself at the mercy of a powerful spell and not sure how to progress. Aunt Dru is a very big fan of the sink-or-swim mentality when it comes to learning, so I can only imagine how terrified Reggie must have felt . . . and it gnaws at me. I can't change what she went through, but at least I can help her recover.

To my relief, Reggie gives a little laugh. "I won't apologize anymore, then." She picks up her jeans and lifts one leg, sliding them on as I drive.

I very pointedly do not look over, even though my cock stiffens further in response. She doesn't need me leering at her naked body when she's vulnerable. I might be an impossible ass, but I'm not a monster.

"I hope you like waffles," I say, heading for the nearest truck-stop diner. It's just off the highway and it looks greasy as hell, but I know from my own experience that the coffee is good and the food is abundant. That, and no one comes to bother you when you show up at three in the morning with an armful of books. These are all good things as far as I'm concerned.

"I could eat a dozen waffles," Reggie admits, and judging from the movements I see out of the corner of my eye, she's sliding her shirt on with some maneuvering under my sweater.

Idly, I wonder if my bare-chested appearance is bothering her. I didn't stop to think about that; I just gave her my sweater because she looked so fragile. "Are you hurt?" I ask, now that she's hopefully feeling a little less disoriented. "Do we need to head straight home for a potion?"

"I'm okay," Reggie says in a small voice. "Just . . . shaken. And now that you've mentioned waffles, I'm starving."

I nod, relieved. "Food first, then."

Silence falls between us, broken only by the rustle of fabric as Reggie finishes getting dressed. I pull up to the small diner and glance over at her. Her hair is messy and her eyes are still glassy, her pupils dilated. No one will ask questions at this place, though. She offers me a brave smile and holds out my neatly folded sweater.

With a grunt, I take it. "Wait there. Don't get out of the car."

I get out on my side and tug my sweater over my head. Her scent blooms through the fabric, light and sweet, and my half-mast cock stiffens a little more. I jerk the sweater down farther, hoping it hides the parts of me that are at attention, and move to the other side of the car. I open her door and offer her my hand. "You're going to be a little wobbly for a while yet."

"Thank you" is all Reggie says, and she puts her smaller hand in mine.

I help her out of the car, and as she stands, her breasts sway under her hoodie in a way that makes it obvious she's not wearing a bra. My mouth goes dry at the sight of her undergarments in the seat she just vacated. Of course she didn't put on a bra and panties. She's still not thinking clearly. Her pupils are still dilated and dark, and I need to get her inside and get some food in her. I ignore my body's response to her nearness and concentrate on the diner. "This place is quiet in the middle of the night."

She leans against me, and I automatically put an arm around her waist. "Do you . . . frequent a lot of diners . . . in the middle of the night?"

"Sometimes," I admit. "I don't sleep well when a particular project is upon me. I have to think it through before I can move on. This place has good coffee and very greasy sausage."

"That sounds like heaven," Reggie admits.

I open the door for her, and the waitress who is usually here on overnights nods at me. If she's surprised to see me with someone, she doesn't say. My normal table at the back is empty, so I steer Reggie in that direction. The table is filthy, so while she sits in the booth, I get some napkins and wipe it down. A glance over at Reggie shows that she's still wan, her skin pale and her eyes too big in her face. Her freckles stand out like splatters of paint, and she looks very, very young.

Far too young for me, and the thought is a grimly ironic one. It's not like I could entertain thoughts of her as anything but my aunt's familiar. Poaching familiars is bad taste. Poaching my aunt's familiar just to fuck her would be egregious.

The waitress arrives and sets two empty cups down in front of us. She pours coffee into them without asking and glances over at Reggie, then at me. Her lips purse, and I can only imagine what she's thinking. "What'll it be, sweetheart?"

"My usual," I say. I nod at Reggie. "She's going to need a lot of food. Her blood sugar's dropped."

The waitress's expression immediately goes from judging to sympathetic. "You want a menu, sweetie? Or do you want breakfast? Dinner? I can have the cook get right on it."

"Breakfast," Reggie manages with a small smile. "Thank you."

She disappears, and I watch as Reggie takes the small square container holding a variety of sugar packets and begins to quietly organize them. She doesn't touch her coffee, and I can tell from her expression that she's rattled.

"If you don't drink that coffee, I'm going to forcefully pour it down your throat," I say in a low tone. "The sugar can be organized later."

Reggie looks up at me, startled, and then one of those broad, sunny grins crosses her face. She laughs and picks up her cup, taking a sip. "Better, Your Majesty?"

"It'll help you recover quicker," I point out, but I'm secretly pleased that she wasn't offended by my words. That she's not afraid of me. That even after all she's been through tonight, I'm somehow "safe" for her.

I like that idea more than I should.

Reggie takes another sip of black coffee and then cradles the cup in her hands. "So . . ."

"So . . . ?"

She looks up at me from under her lashes. "Magic is real?"

I do my best not to smirk. "I've been saying that for a while now, haven't I?"

Her expression changes to a scowl. "I'm supposed to just believe everything you spout at me? What next? The tooth fairy? Santa Claus?"

"I don't know either of them."

She lets out a shaky laugh, and when she touches her face, I can see her hands are still trembling. "It's just a lot, you know? All my life, I've been told one thing, and then you come along, all self-assured and confident that this make-believe stuff is real. Of course I don't believe you." Her gaze strays to the sugar packets, and I can see her mentally sorting them by color and brand, as if straightening things up is somehow soothing to her. "I just needed that concrete proof, and every time I asked for it, I never got it."

"Most magic doesn't work that way," I tell her, taking a sip of my coffee to encourage her to do the same. "Most of it is subtle nudges, things that happen in the background."

"Unless you've been turned into a cat."

Ah. So that's the spell that made her body shut down. I nod. "It's why your system is having such a hard time. Most spells are just a drain on energy. That one is a strong temporary curse. Your thinking process is affected as you start to take on feline attributes. You lose a lot of your sense of fear, and your curiosity grows. You find yourself hunting things you wouldn't normally have interest in. If you stay in that form too long, it can tamper with your sense of being long-term. I know one warlock that was stuck in that form for a week. He still gets cravings for rat from time to time."

Reggie shudders, her eyes going wide. "I kept smelling something that was so delicious. I'm afraid to think of what it was."

"Probably best not to think about it too hard."

She licks her lips, glancing up at me. "So you . . . Have you ever . . . ?"

"Turned into a cat? Once or twice. I didn't enjoy the experience. Have I ever turned someone into one? No. There's already a shining example of why that's a terrible idea right in my aunt's house."

Reggie straightens and goes utterly pale, her mouth gaping open. "You mean Maurice?"

I take another sip of my coffee. "You didn't think he was a normal cat, did you?"

She clutches a hand to the neckline of her hoodie. "He . . . he sleeps in my bed at night," she says in a strangled tone. "He cuddles, too. And I'm pretty sure he's watched me shower."

I scowl at the thought. "I told him to stay away from you."

Her eyes are wide. Before she can say anything else, the waitress arrives with plates of food. Mine is a simple burger and fries, but she piles a plate of eggs, bacon, and toast in front of Reggie, along with another plate of biscuits and hash browns, and one more of pancakes. The woman smiles at us. "Figured she could use everything we had."

"Excellent. Thank you." I make a mental note to give her an enormous tip.

Reggie is momentarily distracted by the food in front of her. She picks up a piece of bacon and shoves it into her mouth, licking her fingers, and then grabs one of the pancakes off the stack and does the same. I watch her eat with a mixture of amusement and disdain. I'm not sure if manners have gotten worse in modern times or if this is particularly a Reggie trait.

She notices me staring and gives me a sheepish look, a smile curving around stuffed cheeks. "Didn't realize how hungry I was until now." She takes another bite of the pancake she's holding in her hand and nods at me. "Tell me more about Maurice?"

I say nothing as the waitress refills our coffees and then saunters away. Once she's gone, I shrug. "He was my aunt's familiar at the turn of the century. A bit of an idiot, I suppose, but very devoted." I put a little salt on my fries and eat one, but I'm not really hungry. I mostly ordered so Reggie wouldn't feel awkward eating all the food I plan on shoving into her. "Maurice also fancied himself a bit of a ladies' man and tended to bed-hop, even when it wasn't appropriate. He slept with the wrong witch, and when she found out he was fooling around on her, she cursed him."

Reggie swallows hard, then washes her food down with a swig of coffee. "So why doesn't he change back?"

"No one can find his tablet."

"Tablet?" Her eyes are wide. "What tablet? Like a computer tablet?"

She's chewing with her mouth open. Normally I'd find this horrific, but on Reggie, it manages to somehow be slightly charming. Only slightly, though. I nod in her direction. "You have butter on your chin." When she mops it up with a chuckle, I look at her eyes. They don't seem nearly as dark, which means her pupils are probably retracting. Her hands are shaking slightly less, too. Good. "Curse tablet," I explain. "They're the medium for most of our spells."

"What's a—" she begins, shoving more food into her mouth even as she talks.

I interrupt, because I already knew this question was coming. "Have you seen the lead bricks at my aunt's house?" I gesture with my hands. "About the size of a cell phone, maybe? Those are the basis of a curse tablet. You make a thin sheet, and you inscribe it with the curse you want to befall someone. The spell can be broken if the tablet is found and destroyed, so most witches hide theirs away in secret locations. A long time ago, many people used to just toss them down wells, but we've had to become more creative since you want to keep the tablets hidden."

"Lead in your drinking water?" She gives me an incredulous look. "What dummy's doing that?"

"Most of ancient Rome," I admit. "No one realized it was a problem until much, much later."

She makes a noise of agreement and then reaches out to steal one of my fries. I arch an eyebrow at her, but she just grins at me and goes right on eating, and I don't have the heart to move my plate away. Something about feeding her is stoking that protective feeling inside me. I like it when Reggie smiles at me. I like sharing this moment with her.

Willem would laugh his ass off if he heard how soft my thoughts were in this moment. He'd mock me for all eternity for having a stupid infatuation with my aunt's "mongrel" familiar.

"What does ancient Rome have to do with anything?" Reggie asks, stealing another fry. "How did you guys get into that shit?"

I blink, because the question comes out of nowhere. She really has no idea who we are? Of course not, I realize a moment later. She didn't believe magic was real. Why would anyone stop to explain to her that Dru is two thousand years old or that I'm five hundred? She wouldn't have believed a word of it. I drum my fingers on the countertop, trying to figure out the best way to point this out to her. She's already been hit with a lot tonight. "How old do you think I am?"

Reggie straightens, a confused look on her face. She takes a fork and pokes at her eggs. "What does that have to do with magic?"

"Everything. Nothing. Just guess."

She shrugs, and for some reason, color flushes her cheeks. "Thirty? Thirty-five?" She stabs at her scrambled eggs and points the fork at me. "I know you're a Cancer sign because Lisa told me, but she didn't say how old."

"I'm five hundred and ten."

Reggie chokes on the mouthful of eggs. She coughs, then spits the food into her napkin, giving me an incredulous look. "You're what?"

I lower my voice. "Five hundred and ten. I was born in the year 1512, in London. Henry the Eighth was in power, the Spanish were exploring the New World, and the Medicis were struggling to keep control of the Mediterranean."

She stares at me. Just stares.

"My aunt is even older," I admit. "Her full name is Drusilla Grattidia Magnus the Elder of House Magnus, and she's two thousand years old, though she won't tell me the exact dates. Just that she was born sometime in Augustus's reign, which puts her somewhere between two thousand and eight years old and two thousand forty-nine."

Reggie's nostrils flare, her only physical response. The rest of her is completely still. She watches me for a moment longer and then shakes her head. "You're joking."

"I'm not. The bloodline is very long lived. Once you access the part of your system that houses magic, everything else slows down. You stop aging at the same speed as everyone else. It's why most witches and warlocks won't let their children practice magic until the age of twenty-one. You don't want someone to get locked in at fourteen and have it take seven hundred years for them to come of age."

She pokes at her eggs, her expression unreadable.

"You think I'm lying," I say, and I'm disappointed in her. After all she's been through tonight, I thought she'd be more open minded than this.

Reggie glances up, an apologetic look on her face. "I don't, actually. I just don't know what to make of all this." Her expression grows shy. "You both must think I'm a baby compared to you. Worse than a baby. A zygote." She wrinkles her nose. "No wonder you both laughed at me that first day when I told you how old I was."

"We weren't laughing at you. We were laughing at the situation." I shake my head. "I wouldn't laugh at you."

She nudges me under the table with her foot, and it makes my cock respond again. Her smile blossoms once more. "Thank you, Ben."

I nod, because I don't know what else to say. I'm not good with touchy-feely shit. For centuries, I've had a reputation as a ruthless, unlikable warlock, and it's served me well. My enemies live in fear of me, which means they won't cast against me. And if it means I don't have friends, well then, I don't have friends. I don't care. Success is all that matters to me, and everyone knows I'm at the top of my game.

But Reggie's expression is soft as she looks at me, and I find myself thinking about other things. Things that aren't about magic. Things like waking up with Reggie in bed beside me, seeing that bright, sunny smile first thing in the morning. Sharing a day with her. Sharing an evening with her. Companionable, cozy meals like this throughout eternity . . . And I feel achingly empty in my solitude.

Which is stupid. My jaw flexes, and I'm mad at myself for being dissatisfied with the life I've carefully built up over centuries.

"Why are you being so nice to me tonight?" Reggie asks in a soft voice. Her tone is secretive and low, perfect for pillow talk, and that mental image of her in bed with me, her form tucked against mine, hits me like a brick. I'm filled with that hot yearning all over again, like a schoolboy.

"Because I'm the only one around," I say coldly. "You needed a rescue and no one else answered."

"I don't think that's it," she says, chuckling. "Nice try, though." She points her fork at me. "You can try to be mean and cold, Ben Magnus, but I suspect you're secretly a softie."

I arch a brow at her. "I am not."

"We'll see," she tells me, and keeps on eating. "So have you ever cursed someone?"

"Of course."

"Into a cat?"

"No. Most human-focused spells are far too messy. For the last while, I've focused on corporate magic." At her confused look, I continue. "Corporate espionage. I'm hired by mega-companies for sabotage. I ensure that their launches go well and the rivals' do not. I nudge the stock market one way or another. I hex a particular corporation's new campaign that threatens my client. And then there's the far more nefarious stuff."

Her eyes are wide, and she chews slowly. "It gets more nefarious than that?"

I chuckle. "I've been known to use some of the obfuscation charms on corporate tax accounts, among other things."

"Do you take out rival CEOs?" she asks, her expression dubious. "Like murder?"

My amusement dies. For a moment, I wonder what she's heard, and my hackles go up. I want to lash out at her for even asking, but I see her wide-eyed, guileless expression in front of me and know she means nothing by it. She's not aware of my past. She's not aware of Soren Jeffries or his suicide.

She's not aware that someone killed himself because of my spells. It doesn't matter that Soren asked me to cast those spells. It doesn't matter that I haven't been able to sleep with the guilt of it all. It doesn't matter that my entire body clenches up every time I get a meeting request.

I'm a ruthless, evil warlock. Casting spells that ruin lives is what I do. Reggie doesn't know that, though. She's not aware of my reputation. "I do not murder for hire, no."

She nods as if satisfied with my answer. "But you're still a bad guy, right?"

I don't know the answer to that anymore. Once I would have sneered at Reggie's question. There is no morality when it comes to magic. But sitting in front of her, seeing her vulnerable like this, it makes me tired. It makes me want something different.

And I'm not entirely sure what that is anymore.

I just lift my chin, indicating her dinner. "Eat your food."

And because she's Reggie, she reaches over, snags one of my fries, and gives me a defiant smile.

REGGIE

My brain feels like mush with everything I've absorbed tonight. I'm not entirely sure what to think anymore. Everything feels like a lie.

Ben Magnus is a warlock. A bona fide warlock. Sweet, unassuming, slightly nutty Aunt Dru is a two-thousand-year-old Roman witch.

Magic? Real.

Maurice? Asshole.

Me? A real familiar. A legit, genuine familiar who somehow read an ad in the paper. All that crap that Dru was spouting about a bloodline must be real, then. Penny's belief in witches and warlocks is legit. It's Nick and I that are somehow the ones that are wrong in all of this.

Oh god, Nick. I can't tell Nick any of this. I feel full to bursting with everything I've learned, everything I've fought against learning for the last week or two, and I desperately need someone to talk to about all of this. I want to go back to Ben and ask him a million more questions, but it's late and I've already been enough trouble. He took me home to Dru's and guided me up the stairs, making sure I was fine before turning and shutting the door behind him. I'm in my nightgown in my bed, but I can't sleep.

I can't go keep Ben up all night, either. He's made it clear he's got work I'm keeping him from, and when I saw the mess of candles on the table, the wax stuck to the blanket, I felt guilty. I'd interrupted some heavy-duty work of his, and yet he'd still come to rescue me.

Only Nick has ever truly had my back like that, and I can't tell him about any of this. It'd be a breach of the trust both Ben and Dru have shown me.

And if Nick ever mentioned it to anyone . . .

I hate that I have to keep a secret from my best friend, but Nick loves to talk, and I know he blurts out everything when his clients are training. He has a heart of gold and zero filter.

Penny. I could talk to Penny. Schedule that coffee a little earlier than I planned. Penny will be able to give me all the gossip. Excited, I pick my phone up to text her and then look at the time. Shit. Okay, that'll have to wait until morning. I toss my phone back down on the blankets.

There's a scratch at the door.

I get to my feet, because I know who it is before I even undo all the locks and open my door. Maurice looks up at me and meows pitifully.

I put a hand on my hip. "Don't try that shit with me, buddy. Your secret's out. I know you're a guy under all that fur."

He sidles into my room and rubs against my leg, purring.

"Uh-huh. Were you watching me change all those times I went into the bathroom and you followed me? Or was that just normal cat nonsense?"

Maurice gives the tiniest, cutest, most innocent little meow.

"I'm calling bullshit on that," I tell him. "You can sleep on the bed still, but no rubbing against my boobs or I'm going to make sure that someone puts you on a kitty diet and your litter isn't changed for a month. You catch my drift?"

If a fat black cat could pout, Maurice would be giving me a sulky look right about now. He twitches his tail once and then hops up on the bed, then very deliberately moves to the corner of it.

Seems like we have an understanding.

Even as Maurice settles in on my bed, I can't bring myself to lie back down. I'm too wired, too wide awake, too buzzing with everything that's slid into place. So many things that seemed a little odd or off have suddenly clicked in my head. Of course Dru has all kinds of Roman art in her house. Of course she gets modern sayings mixed up. Of course they talk to Maurice like he's a real person.

I slide out into the hall, glancing toward Ben's door. It's closed, of course. It's very late and I imagine he's tired. He's probably going to have to work all day tomorrow on all those candles that were ruined on my behalf. Maybe he'll let me help him. I head down toward the kitchen, wondering if he's left the candles on the table. If so, maybe I can get a good look at them, see where I can help him.

The kitchen's exactly as it was earlier, and Ben has left his mess everywhere. The control freak inside me trembles in horror, and I immediately start straightening up. I rinse out bowls and return herbs to their jars and clean the tables free of dusty markings. Ben mentioned he'd have to start over, after all. I'm not sabotaging things.

I'm helping.

I might be organizing his things more to my liking, but sure, I'm helping, too.

There's a jar of something sludgy on the counter, and I don't know if it's supposed to be refrigerated or not. I sniff it, then cough as it burns my nostrils. Oof. Maybe I'll put it in the fridge anyhow. I pick up a lid and then pause, because on the counter is the jar of olives I got out for Dru earlier, the ones she used as an offering.

And next to it is the crystal ball.

I hesitate. Did Dru leave this out deliberately, or did she simply forget to put it away? I gravitate toward the thing, my fingers grazing the olive jar's shiny label. I study the crystal ball. Dru said it'd work. What did she do? Pray to Mercury? And it doesn't matter if I believe in him or not . . .

Before I can think twice about it, I shake a few olives into a bowl. I find a sharp kitchen knife and prick my finger, letting the blood drip over the olives. If this is real . . . I should be able to do it, right? "Mercury," I whisper, closing my eyes. "Mercury, help me see."

When I open them again, the olives have a curl of smoke rising from them. A tiny thrill shoots through me. Magic is real—of course it's real, I chide myself. I was a cat earlier, after all. It's still new and exciting to me, though. I peer at the crystal ball, but it's cloudy inside. Oh. I peer at it, but nothing shows up. It's like the television is on, but I haven't picked a channel. Do I need to be more specific? Do I need to focus on *someone* specific?

I think about my parents, but I don't really want to see them. If I see them in jail or in the hospital, I'll be devastated. Better to just assume they're fine. I don't want to see Nick, either—it's late and he's probably doing unspeakable things to hot Diego. A name comes to mind, and before I can overthink it, I whisper it aloud. "Show me Ben Magnus."

The crystal ball swirls, as if considering my request.

"Please?" Maybe it wants me to ask nicely.

The mist inside the ball clears, and movement stirs inside. I can't quite make it out, but I remember those Magic Eye posters and this reminds me of them. I unfocus my eyes and everything comes into sharp, crisp view.

It's Ben's shirtless back. He's wearing nothing but a pair of pants that are barely clinging to his butt, they're so low. He's got a big hand on the wall, and his broad, pale shoulders are tense. Wow. It looks so real that he could be standing in front of me, if it weren't for the fact that the vision's a little smaller than the reality of Ben's gargantuan frame. I watch as he stands there, and his body makes a tight, abrupt motion, then another. What's he doing? I squint, tilting my head to the side as if trying to see more, and the crystal ball obliges, swinging the vision around to the side and—

I yelp, because Ben Magnus, powerful five-hundred-year-old warlock, is jerking off.

My hands fly to my mouth, quieting my noises of surprise. I watch in horrified fascination as Ben strokes a really, really impressive cock with short, quick bursts of motion, his face full of tension. *This isn't right*, I tell myself even as I stare. *This is a private moment. This is naughty, and he was so, so good to me earlier.*

But he's just . . . beautiful. For a five-hundred-year-old warlock who spends most of his time in front of books, his body is gorgeous. His arm is corded with muscle, taut as he works his length. His chest is broad, and his entire body is tense as he builds up toward a quick, brutal climax. I stare at the big hand on the wall, clenched there for support, and I wonder what it'd be like for him to touch me with that big hand.

I wonder what he'd think if I was the one touching him.

With a horrified squeal at the line of my thoughts, I turn away from the crystal ball. It seems even more intrusive to watch him finish, and I press my fists against my mouth, my mind racing. Where are these dirty, filthy thoughts coming from? Is it because Ben rescued me earlier tonight? Carried me in his arms and promised me he'd look after me? That he'd take care of me?

Or is it because I'm just now realizing that he's completely gorgeous to boot?

"Please turn it off," I whisper aloud to Mercury or whoever might be listening. I wait long minutes, my back to the crystal ball so if I turn around, I don't see an O-face. I'm not ready for the O-face. I'm not even sure I was ready for the jerking off, but here we are.

A worried thought hits me. What if the crystal ball doesn't turn off, ever, and everyone knows I was watching Ben stroke one out? Oh god. With a whimper of distress, I turn around—

The ball is quiet, the image and mist gone. The olives in the offering bowl are nothing but ash now, the only clue that I used the scrying orb at all. Hastily, I clean the dish out, dumping the ash into the garbage and washing the offering bowl before putting it back in its place. The olive jar is missing quite a few of its tenants, so I lid it and shove it into the back of the fridge, hoping that no one notices.

My cheeks burning, I race back upstairs, and once I get into my room, I pick up Maurice and plop him outside my door. "Plans changed, buddy," I say, shutting him out before he has a chance to slink back in. I flip the three locks, then dive back under the blankets like a child and stare up at the ceiling.

I just saw a five-hundred-year-old hot warlock masturbate through a crystal ball. I don't know what to do with this information. I can't stop thinking about the mental image of him stroking his cock with the same grim determination that he rescued me with earlier . . .

I pull the blankets over my head, as if the world can somehow see my embarrassment.

I'm not embarrassed that I caught him. I'm embarrassed that I watched and I liked it. I'm embarrassed that it's made me realize that after tonight, I no longer see Ben as the grouchy, horrid nephew of my boss.

After tonight, I might be nursing the tiniest crush on him, and watching him like that? Stroking the most perfect dick I've ever seen? It did not help matters at all. I don't have to put a hand between my thighs to know that I'm flushed with arousal. I can feel my pulse beating, centered at my core.

Even so, I feel guilty that I watched him without him knowing. He rescued me tonight, put aside his own plans and hard work to come and save me. He took care of me, and I repaid him by watching him jerk off.

I'm going to have to tell him, I realize. We can't be friends and be around each other daily with a secret like that between us.

And I groan at the thought. Tomorrow, over breakfast, I decide. I'll get it out in the open.

BEN

I set up my candle-making workstation in the kitchen again the next morning. It's a multistep process, so I have all the ingredients shoved onto the kitchen island so they're in easy reach as I work. There's an even larger table in the private office I have connected to my room upstairs, but I find that I don't want to spend the day in solitude. For some reason, I'm looking forward to seeing my aunt's familiar, to hearing her tart takes on everything.

Part of me wonders if she'll be back to the whole "magic isn't real" argument this morning, and then I'll really have to show her some things. Nothing dangerous like what my aunt put her through last night, just some flashy stuff to convince her.

Showing off, a little voice inside my head says. I squash it. I'm not going to get involved with my aunt's familiar. That's bad news all around. I know better. Besides, she needs someone around today after last night.

Reggie heads into the kitchen at a surprisingly early hour, her hair freshly washed. She's wearing another gym sweatshirt and a pair of tiny shorts that accentuate long tanned legs, and I wonder if she's got freckles everywhere. I should have looked last night.

I clench my jaw at the thought, because that is *not* the thinking of a mentor. "Good morning," I say evenly. "If you're looking for Aunt Dru, she's gone."

"Gone?" Reggie asks, confused. She moves to my side, watching as I drag my specialized wicks through the hot wax trays in front of me. "She left so early?"

I nod. "Said she wanted some time away from things."

"Oh." Reggie fidgets next to me. "Did—did I do something wrong? I didn't get to tell her about my spying mission."

"You did nothing wrong," I reassure her. "And I suspect Aunt Dru sent you on that mission less to have you spy and more to teach you that magic exists. Did she cast the cat spell on you? Was it an amulet?" I carefully drag the wicks back and forth in the wax, watching as the layers thicken with every pull through the gluey material.

"A ring," Reggie admits.

"I know that ring," I say. "It packs quite a punch. I stole it when I was a young idiot of eighteen and wanted to learn but no one would teach me. I think I vomited for two days once I managed to get the damned thing off."

She rubs her arms, offering me a small smile. "Glad to know it's not just me that had a bad reaction."

"Most magic is cast despite the effects on the caster. You usually know what you're getting into, though." I'm still slightly pissed that my aunt threw Reggie out into that situation. It's probably why Aunt Dru has decided to make herself scarce today. She's waiting for my mood to blow over. I glance over at Reggie. "If you wanted to quit now, I'm sure she'd understand."

Her eyes widen. "Oh, I'm not quitting." She chuckles. "Not with the amount that your aunt has promised to pay me. It's going to be life changing."

I can imagine. "You'll have the money to spend on whatever

you choose." I wait for her to volunteer what she's going to spend it on, but she just watches as I hang the newly crafted candle up so it can dry fully. "Anyhow, you have the day free."

"Mmm. I guess I could work on the study some more. I do need to get it done." She hesitates, though, leaning on the counter. "But I'm aware I ruined your work last night, and I was wondering if maybe you needed some help? I'd be happy to assist."

I grunt an acknowledgment. "If you like."

"I'll feel better helping you after knowing you helped me," Reggie confesses, moving to sit directly across from me on the opposite side of the kitchen island. As I watch, she immediately begins to straighten my components, lining them up and nudging the pile of long, newly crafted wicks into straight lines.

I resist the urge to point out her compulsive straightening, instead gesturing at the wicks. "You can dip the candles for me."

"Is this like they teach you in grade school?" she asks, picking up a two-foot-long length of wick. "I hold it in the center and drag both ends through the wax?"

"I didn't go to grade school, so I don't know. But yes, drag both ends. Once it's dry, I cut the middle and then I have two candles."

Reggie dips it, gliding it through the wax as I nudge the spell components closer to me and begin to assemble another wick.

"You should really put everything in order," she tells me. "So you can have an assembly line."

"Do you manage everyone?" I ask, ignoring her suggestion.

"Most of the time, yes," Reggie tells me, her voice sunny. "So you never went to grade school? How did you learn?"

"Self-taught. My parents left me with a tutor that was responsible for my upbringing, most of the time. When he wasn't around, I read books. After I grew of an age to cast, Aunt Dru took over my education." I don't like to think about those times very much, the years of loneliness, of no one to talk to but a few servants and a tutor who thought that children should be seen and not heard. The endless years at the country estate, forgotten and resentful.

"Where are your parents now?" Reggie asks.

"Dead." My tone conveys that I do not wish to discuss it.

"I see." She goes quiet, and there's no sound except for the slight noises of my fingers as I pick through the components, adding a lock of hair here, a brushing of marigold there. She drags the wicks through the wax over and over, and I wonder how long she's going to be silent. Not long, it seems, because she speaks again. "Thank you again for last night."

"You would have done the same for me."

She tilts her head, her wet hair sliding over her shoulders. "What, take my shirt off and try to cover your naked body? Not likely."

I look up at her in surprise, and she flushes, her cheeks pink, her freckles standing out. Her eyes are sparkling, though. Is she . . . teasing me? "Your shirts won't fit," I tell her. "Not that they fit you, either." I nod at the sweatshirt she's wearing. It's huge, with a hole at the neck against the collar, and the logo is faded. For all that she's an average height, Reggie is slender and wiry. Delicate.

Which is why she fits in my arms so very perfectly. Not that I'm thinking about that.

Her chuckle fills the kitchen. "I snatched this from Nick. He had a bunch made up when he started his personal-training gig, and a few of them came through with askew logos or the collar slightly off-center, so I stole them." She shrugs. "Cheaper than buying my own clothes."

I'm dying to ask about Nick. She brings him up a lot, and I'm curious to know more about the man that has Reggie's affection but that she's not intimate with. If I do, though, I suspect it'll shine a spotlight on my not-so-innocent obsession with her. I don't plan on doing anything about my obsession. Just like a moth and a candle flame, I'm going to get close enough to burn myself, simply because I can't resist.

I turn the conversation in a different direction instead. "I've been meaning to ask you—what made you end up here? Answering an ad in the paper about spellcrafting?"

"Oh, that." She chuckles again, sliding the long strands of wick through the wax with a swirl. "I told Dru already. I thought it was my favorite card game."

"A card game?"

She nods, and when I reach over one component to get to another, she leans over and rearranges them so I can grab things in order. "See? Better." With a defiant wink at me, she continues. "Spellcraft: The Magicking is a collectible card game. You buy a few packs of cards and you get random spells, or mana pools for energy, or treasure items. You make a deck featuring these items, and when you play, the object is to defeat the other person with your deck of cards. It's a game that actually requires a lot of strategy, because a lot of the cards can be used in very different ways, and you have to know when to cast the appropriate spells on your opponent. Because it's collectible, no two decks are ever the same. I've played it hundreds of times, and it's like new every single time." She lets out a little sigh. "Some games are short, but some last for hours. Those are the best ones, I think. When you go head-to-head with someone that's a match for you. It's no fun beating the stuffing out of someone that never stood a chance. There has to be a challenge."

I like the enthusiasm in her voice. "So you're a good player?"

"Well, I don't like to brag," she teases. "But you're looking at the local champion." Reggie lifts her chin. "Well, almost. I'm officially the adult local champion. I lost to an eight-year-old in three out of five games at the last tournament. Won a fancy card box, though."

I look up in astonishment. She's bragging about playing an eight-year-old at cards? But her eyes are twinkling with amusement, and when our gazes meet, she breaks out into laughter.

"You played an eight-year-old? At a tournament?" This seems so bizarre to me.

"He won, too. Vicious kid." She shakes her head. "He wanted to trade me for my Sun-Phoenix but I was kind of pissed about losing, so I refused." Reggie pauses. "He cried."

"You absolute monster," I tease, grinning.

"I felt so rotten about it, too," she giggles. "But he was the worst winner. Absolutely terrible. His father was quite embarrassed. Nick came in third that day, and he's vowed vengeance on me, so I have to be ready." Her grin fades a little. "The only time I get to play now is Friday nights, though. That's our regular card night. Back when I wasn't working, Nick and I would play every night instead of watching television. I'm going to be positively rusty by the time the next tourney comes around."

She sounds so very sad, and it's clear it's something she loves. "Maybe you could show me sometime—"

Reggie gasps with excitement, reaching out to touch my hand as I twine another wick. "Are you serious?" Her eyes are wide. "You want to learn how to play?"

I shrug, more focused on that hand touching mine than on cards. "If you wouldn't mind showing me."

"I would love to," she gushes, and then straightens, pulling her hand away. "But you're going to have to eventually buy your own cards. I don't have a lot of them, because I never have much money."

She's hinted at financial troubles before, and her clothing is all castoffs. I wonder just how badly she's in debt, but it seems a rude thing to ask and I don't want to ruin the moment. I'm going to have to find out where these cards are sold and purchase some just so I can learn how to play. Just so she can reach over and touch my hand again.

Forbidden fruit, thy name is Reggie.

I force myself to concentrate on the wick in my hands, the careful braiding so the hair entwined burns evenly. "I haven't played cards in a very long time."

"No one to play with? Even back home? What about your friends?"

Her question is innocent, but it makes something sour inside me anyhow. "I'm a warlock, Reggie, of House Magnus. I don't have friends."

"Oh." Reggie pauses, her hands going still. "That makes me sad, Ben. Everyone should have friends."

I shrug. "Don't be. I gladly chose power over friendships a long time ago. I'd choose it again today." Especially if it meant being bosom buddies with people like Aulus or Titus. The only one I can tolerate is Willem, and that's for short periods of time.

Reggie makes a sympathetic noise. "Well, everyone needs friends. You're welcome to play cards with me at any time. You're even welcome to come to the next Friday-night cards, but you're going to have to endure Nick and Diego all over each other all night." She makes a face. "I'm happy he's happy, but I could do with a little less PDA."

"Nick is your roommate, yes?" I pounce on the opportunity since she brought him up.

"Yes, and before you ask, we're like brother and sister." A wry smile curves her mouth as she maneuvers her fresh candles over to the wire rack and hangs them. "Nick has never been interested in girls, and I have never been interested in Nick. But I love him like a brother, absolutely."

For some reason, I feel a strong surge of satisfaction at hearing that. "And how did you two meet?"

"We worked together at a gym for about three months. I got fired, Nick did not. We remained friends and eventually moved in together when he needed a roommate and my parents left town."

"Left town" seems like an odd way of mentioning family leaving, but I don't ask. She looks as reluctant to talk about her family as I am to talk about mine. "Why did you get fired? You seem a very . . . enthusiastic employee, let's just say."

Another blinding, sunny smile creases Reggie's face. "Well," she announces. "I couldn't help but notice that the gym had very little workflow."

"Oh no."

"Oh yes," Reggie says. "I spent all night one night rearranging extremely heavy treadmills and stair-climbers and anything I could move with a dolly. I was positive my boss would love my changes, since they just made more sense, you know? Instead, I came in to work, and he handed me my check and told me to get out."

I don't laugh. She's smiling brightly, but I just imagine her disappointment. How many times had I worked tirelessly on something to impress my parents when they returned, only to find out that they weren't coming home at all? I remember that bitter disappointment as if it were yesterday and not five hundred years ago, and it sours my mood. "Why do you meddle in things like that? Why do you rearrange everything?"

"Because it's better," Reggie says stubbornly.

"Obviously. The library is *clearly* better right now." I nod.

"Well done. I particularly love the ambiance of having all the books in piles on the floor. Very convenient."

She stiffens, but when our eyes meet, another smile cracks her face. "You're teasing me! You bastard."

I find myself smiling. "Maybe a little."

She throws her head back and laughs, full of delight, and that hot yearning rushes through me again. What would it be like to have someone like Reggie at my side, as my familiar? Someone unafraid to needle me? Someone who enjoyed spending time with me?

Or maybe not just as a familiar . . . I clamp that thought down before it gets away from me.

Reggie's laughter dies and she goes quiet. She stares at the tray of wax in front of her. "Ben, I have a confession to make."

My curiosity is piqued. "Go on."

She doesn't look me in the eye. Doesn't reach for another candle. Just nudges the tray with her finger over and over again. "I . . ." Hesitates, then continues. "I used the crystal ball last night."

I wait for her to continue. When she doesn't, I prompt her. "And . . . ?"

Her expression is pure mortification, her cheeks pink. "I watched you. I didn't think it would work, though," she blurts quickly. "Until, well, it did."

I frown, trying to follow along with what she's not saying aloud. She watched me? She watched me what? And then I remember that after rescuing Reggie, my mind was still full of her smile, the way she nestled against me, her long, bare legs . . . I jerked off before bed.

Hard.

And it was thoroughly unsatisfying. It did nothing to take the edge off wanting her. Wanting to walk down that hall, use magic to bust open the locks, and sweep her into my arms again. But I will not, because she's my aunt's familiar. She's young. Most of all, she just deserves better than to get caught up with someone like me.

Even so, I can't resist the uncomfortable expression on her face. Reggie is a unique sort of person if she spied me self-pleasuring and decided to tell me about it.

My silence apparently distresses her, because she picks up another wick and drags it through the wax. "I didn't realize what I'd be seeing. I think it was just bad timing, and you know, I wasn't sure it would work, and . . . yeah."

I put down the wick in my hands and lean on the counter, fascinated by her reaction. She's squirming in her seat, her cheeks bright red. If she thought of me like she thought of this Nick guy, her reaction would be different, wouldn't it? She rolled her eyes earlier at the mention of Nick's PDA, but when she talks about me touching myself, she turns into a schoolgirl.

I can't resist pricking at her. "And what did you think?"

Reggie's gaze jerks up to mine, her eyes wide. Her lips part. "Wh-what do you mean?"

I lift my chin in her direction. "Did you find it pleasing?"

Her mouth opens, and a wordless sound comes out of her. She recovers and then shakes her head, chuckling. "I'm not going to tell you and feed that enormous ego of yours."

So she liked it, then. The forbidden lust for her roars through my system. I should turn around and walk away. Turn and pretend we never had this conversation. Instead, I saunter around to her side of the kitchen island, and I laugh. "I have had hundreds of years to get over any sort of modesty I might have had."

And then I lean over her so I can whisper in her ear.

"I know I have a big cock."

I saunter away as she makes another incoherent noise. "W-wait," she calls out. "Where are you going?"

"You finish those candles for me. I am overdue on a very big offering I need to make to Mercury." Plus, I need an excuse to get out of the room, because if I stay next to her for much longer, I'm going to steal my aunt's familiar, and I have enough scandal following me around.

REGGIE

Ben's bold words turn circles in my head for the rest of the day. He doesn't come back to the kitchen, so I finish dipping the candles and leave them hanging. I twitch with the need to organize the components he's left out, but I also don't want to piss him off. For some reason, our developing friendship matters to me. Maybe it's because he saved me and that places him ahead of most people. Whatever it is, I don't want to ruin this strange, fragile thing between us.

So I head to the library and begin the process of organizing books. I've made a spreadsheet of all the titles and the colors of the spines, along with a brief description of what each book is about, and what shelf I'm placing it on. I'm not sure why I can read the titles now when they were blurs before, but I try not to think about that too hard. I figure I can email it to all of us and we can have a quick reference to find books easily. I'm a little more concerned about what I need to do with the scrolls, given that I can't read the languages they're written in, so I make careful note of the appearance of each one in my spreadsheet, copy the first few words (if the characters are on the keyboard), and categorize them that way. All the categorizing soothes the restless part of me that desperately needs control, and by the time I've returned a few more books to their places in the library, it's getting late and I haven't eaten a thing since breakfast.

Stomach growling, I return to the kitchen just in time to see Dru pouring tea leaves into the Keurig's water reservoir. "Wait! What are you doing?"

Dru turns and beams at me. "Hello, darling. Do you want some tea? I'm just about to make some."

"But . . . that's not where the tea leaves go."

She gives me a blank look. "Where do they go, then?"

"In the cup?"

"Well, then what's the point of this idiot machine?" She puts her hands on her hips. "Ben gave it to me last solstice, and I swear I can't figure it out. You don't put leaves in it, you don't put honey into it—what's the point?"

My eyes want to cross at the thought of Dru putting honey somewhere inside the Keurig. "It heats the water for you. If you have a K-Cup, you can use it to make tea. Otherwise, you heat the water and put your flavorings and everything in your cup."

"Why wouldn't I just use a kettle?" She looks utterly indignant. "Kettles have been perfectly fine for two thousand years."

"You can totally use a kettle," I reassure her, making a mental note to hide the poor Keurig before she breaks it. "I'll put some water on for you right now."

"You're a sweet child," she says, patting my arm. "Thank you."

I fill the kettle with water and then set it atop the stove. As I do, Dru hums to herself and gives a fresh bouquet of flowers a sniff. She must have brought those in with her when she returned. I want to ask how her day was, but I wonder if she'll see that as too nosy.

"Where's my nephew at?" Dru asks suddenly.

I can feel my face heating with a blush, because my mind immediately goes to that naughty, naughty crystal-ball image. I look around the kitchen, but it's been cleared of all of Ben's spell components. "I think he's avoiding me," I joke. "He's holed up in his rooms, probably working."

"Hmph," Dru says. "Did you piss him off?"

"Not that I'm aware of." I watch the kettle and then glance over at her. "I'm still working on the library, by the way."

She waves a hand in the air. "That's fine."

I should probably confess how badly I failed at spying, too. "And as for last night's mission—"

Dru jumps to her feet. "Old news. I don't need to spy on Livia anymore. Want to make a curse tablet? I can show you how."

I blink, more than a little confused at the sudden change in topic. "But I thought you needed me to spy on her. You said it was urgent last night. I put my life in danger to spy on her. Her dog almost ate me."

She rolls her eyes. "Don't be so dramatic. You weren't in danger. You would have figured a way out. You're smart and capable. Don't sell yourself short." The old woman fixes her expression on me. "So . . . curse tablets? Or are you too busy?"

Her strange, jumpy, almost brusque attitude is throwing me off. "Are you mad at me, Dru? Did I do something wrong?" Am I about to get fired?

Dru's expression softens. She approaches me and puts her hands on my arms. "I'm sorry, dear. I'm in a strange mood today. Things aren't quite working out how I planned, and I'm trying to think of new approaches. If I seem like I'm surly, it's not you." Her smile brightens. "I bet that bitch Livia cursed me to make me like this, don't you think? We should curse her back."

"Should we?" It seems a little petty to me, but she's also my boss and rather moody today. I don't want to get fired, not while I'm still new to everything.

"Well, we won't really curse her back," Dru admits. "Livia is an old friend-slash-rival. But maybe we curse her dog so he doesn't like the taste of cats."

I actually don't mind that thought. "We can curse a dog?"

"We can curse anything we want," she says with a chuckle. "Curse tablets are the basic blocks of our particular talent. It's why it's so important to show you how to create one. Especially now that you know magic is real." She pauses. "You do believe magic is real, right? We're still on the same page?"

"Oh, yeah. I'm a believer now."

"Thank goodness." She smiles brightly. "I was getting tired of going back and forth with you. Short of having a unicorn show up, I wasn't sure what else to do to get you to open your eyes."

"If we're voting on things to happen in the future, I would absolutely pick a unicorn over being turned into a cat again."

She giggles. "Come on. Let's go down to my lab so you can learn how to make tablets. It's such a handy skill to know. Given time, you might be able to make them on your own! Won't that be exciting?"

The way she describes it with such enthusiasm, she makes it sound like we're making a pie and not bringing ill upon someone's dog. "Thrilling," I agree, amused.

When we're situated down in her messy study, I watch as she pulls out a large lead bar. "I once went to pencil factories to get lead in bulk," Dru tells me. "And did you know that pencil leads aren't even made with lead? The nerve! So I get my lead bricks through Amazon. Now when I get them, I have my apprentices melt them down and pour them into these sheet molds." She points at a few thin pans hanging from a spot on the wall. "You'll learn how to do it, and Caliban can help you if you need assistance. My eyes are getting too bad for the detail work."

I nod slowly.

"Lucky for you, I already have a few sheets made from when

Lisa was here." She pauses, sighing. "I do miss Lisa. Such a sweet girl and chatty as could be. Always had the best gossip. Wasn't afraid to sleep with anyone to get a bit of good information."

I don't know if I'm supposed to be offended by that or not. "Um, is sleeping with people part of the job? Because I don't think I can do that."

Dru waves a hand. "It's not at all. Lisa's just . . . dedicated, you know?"

Her clear adoration for Lisa makes me feel awful, like this is just another job I'll never quite get the hang of. Like I don't belong. Square peg in round hole. It's the story of my life, and it makes me ache inside. I can't be Lisa, but I can at least be the best familiar that Reggie can be.

"Tablets?" I prompt. "How many do we need?"

She pulls one square of dull metal out. "Just one. You can use multiple sorts of mediums for this kind of thing—pewter, silver, copper, papyrus, paper, whatever. But your curse only lasts as long as your tablet is intact, so I like something long lasting." She lightly strokes the blank front of the metal square. "I spent weeks making papyrus curses, only for them to get destroyed at the first good rain. Such a waste of time and energy. And if you make a lot of tablets out of silver or precious metals? They tend to get stolen. So . . . lead is the best. It's cheap and it's hard, much like my first husband." She barks a laugh.

This is the first time Dru has mentioned marriage of any kind. "Oh, were you married?"

"I've been married six times," Dru confirms. "Most of them were quite lovely gentlemen, but my first husband was a real piece of shit. He didn't like magic and broke my fingers when I tried to cast."

My jaw drops and I gasp. "What the fuck?"

"I mean, to be fair, I was trying to curse him." She shrugs.

My jaw drops again.

"But he did try to have my sister burned at the stake," she continues. "So I can't say he didn't deserve it."

I can't believe what I'm hearing. "Dru, what the hell?"

"Ancient Rome, darling. It was a very rowdy sort of place compared to now. All a girl had was some witchcraft to defend herself." She strokes the tablet again. "People pay you to cast curses with one hand, and then burn you as a witch with the other. So fickle. But at least back then we were needed. Now I mostly cast just to entertain myself." She looks up at me. "It's a dying art, witchcraft."

I think about Ben. "Your nephew casts for investors, doesn't he?"

Dru nods. "He does, but for me, it's just not as fun. I'd much rather have a good, meaty curse on someone to sink my teeth into rather than tooting around in the bull market."

"Bull market?"

She blinks at me. "Bear market?"

"Stock market?"

"Whatever you want to call it." She taps the blank tablet. "Okay. So, we have our tablet here. Lisa really was the best at making tablets, you know." Her expression grows wistful. "One of the best, really."

It seems less like Dru wants to cast magic and more like she just wants to talk. Her mood seems sad tonight. "How many familiars have you had?"

She lifts her chin, thinking, and then shrugs. "More than I can count. The good ones go on to practice magic on their own, like my Caliban, but the bad ones flit in and out of your life quickly. Most apprentices don't last nearly as long as you want them to. Some get married, some have babies. Some just aren't up to being a power conduit."

I think about how I passed out that one time. "I'm your power conduit?"

Dru nods. "Some spells don't work with offerings. They require something a little more intense. With some spells—like the scrying one—you are asking the gods to show you something. With a power conduit, you're trying to imbue that power permanently onto an object, and it takes a lot more out of you." She reaches over and pats my arm. "And by 'taking a lot out of you,' I mean you specifically. Most familiars serve to channel their energy to their master so the master can cast the big spells, and in exchange, the master teaches the familiar."

"So I'm your battery."

"Yes. I'm afraid I don't have the energy I used to. I'm getting old." Her expression grows melancholy again. "My days are numbered."

"Don't talk like that," I tell her. "You're probably going to be casting curses and scrying long after we're all dead and gone."

Her expression brightens. "I can show you how to scry after this. We can have a one-two punch. Unless you already figured that one out on your own?"

Dru's face is completely innocent, but that's the second time she's brought up scrying, and I wonder if she knows I gave it a try. Oh god, I wonder if she knows I was creeping on her hot nephew? Or did he tell her? My face burns. "Let's just stick with the curse tablet for now."

"All right, then. Let me show you how this works," Dru says, gesturing for me to lean in. "Pay close attention."

REGGIE

For the next week, my life revolves around naps.

Now that Dru has decided that I'm going to be her familiar in all ways, she's not holding back on the spellcasting. It means there's a lot for me to learn, since this is all new. It also means a lot of naps, since Dru is always imbuing objects and making potions to help out those around her. We curse Livia's dog to avoid cats. We create a fertility potion for Dru's driver's daughter, who is struggling to get pregnant. A small business that Dru likes is in danger of going under, so we cast two days' worth of luck spells to try to bring business in to them.

"I don't like taking money for witchcraft," Dru tells me. "I did for a time, but there's just something so dirty about it. I can't shrug it off like Caliban does. I only cast when I want to help someone. It's far more fulfilling."

Judging by how much we've cast in this last week, Dru wants to help everyone. There's the grocer at the store who mentions having trouble paying the rent, so Dru casts a financial-windfall spell. There's the pizza guy that has car trouble. There's the book club at the library that hasn't had as many attendees as of late.

And I'm the battery for all of them.

I know some of it is because Dru's trying to teach me, but each spell sucks the energy right out of my system. I spend most of every afternoon asleep, with Maurice curled at my side. Nights are for Dru's spellcasting, which means I have mornings to work on the library or to run errands. I have lunch with Penny twice, just because she's such fun to be around.

Well, most of the time. The last time we had lunch, Penny touched my hand and gave me a worried look. "If no one has told you, remember to stay away from Caliban Magnus. He's bad news."

"How is he bad?" I asked.

Penny didn't have anything concrete, of course. "I've heard he eats bats and drinks blood, but he's a warlock, so that's not entirely weird? It just means he's casting a spell or two. Either that, or someone mixed him up with Ozzy Osbourne." She shrugged. "Lots of rumors and whispers. I'm trying to get specifics, but a lot of people won't tell me anything, because I've never been a familiar." She twisted her trainee cuff. "Just be on your guard, Reggie. There's a whole lot going on in warlock and witch society that you and I aren't privy to."

The week passes quickly, though, and I'm surprised to receive my paycheck on Friday morning. My first paycheck.

It's enormous. It's five figures, all of them before the decimal.

I might have cried a little. I might have also bought pizza and a box of Spellcraft: The Magicking cards and brought them over to Nick's to celebrate.

He pauses as I appear on his doorstep, his eyes wide. "Reggie! Cards isn't until tonight!"

"I know," I tell him. "I can't make it. Dru needs me tonight." Apparently she wants to work another spell involving the evil eye (I didn't ask). "Next week?"

Nick looks disappointed. "All right. I guess I'll see if Diego wants to go out or something." He wrinkles his nose at the pizza. "You know this isn't healthy, right?"

"It has mushrooms."

"Still not healthy."

"And olives. And tomato sauce. It's practically a salad, really."

Nick just shakes his head at me. "You're insane, you know that?"

I just breeze inside, grinning. I set the pizza down on the counter, opening it up and taking a slice. "You'll work it off. So how's things?" I glance around the apartment. It's a little messy, which makes me twitch, but I also notice a few things that aren't Nick's. There's a mug on the counter with an air-force logo on it, plus a big khaki-green bag hanging from a hook by the door. There's a Vitamix by the fridge, along with a couple of containers of protein powder, which I know Nick abhors. Even though I already know the answer, I ask, "Diego been around much?"

"Most nights," Nick admits, picking a mushroom off the pizza and eating it. "If this works out for you long-term, we might . . . move in together."

I can't believe they talked about it already and it's only been two weeks. I fight back my wounded feelings and pull out the check I wrote earlier. "Speaking of roommates—ta-da!"

His eyes widen. "Oh, shit, Reg. You really are going to pay me rent?"

"I really am," I retort, stung. Did he think I wouldn't? "Just because I had to move out quickly for this job doesn't mean I want to screw you over."

"It's been two weeks now?" Nick asks, grinning as he tucks the check into his pocket. "That's amazing. I'm so proud of you. Are you resisting the urge to reorganize the entire house?"

I think about the library, which is still in shambles. "Uh-huh."

"Awesome," Nick gushes. "And you even brought cards." He moves behind me and wraps me in a bear hug, squeezing me tight. "Everything's coming our way, Reg. Things are finally looking up. Business is good, you've got a job, and I've got Diego. We just need to find you a man or a woman and make you happy."

For some reason, I think of Ben. Ben, who I haven't seen all week and I suspect is deliberately ignoring me after my spying on him. "For now, let's stick with the employment," I tell Nick.

AFTER I RETURN home, Dru makes a few potions with my assistance. One's for healing—several of her friends are older, she says, and need pick-me-ups. The other is an infatuation potion for a bingo buddy. Dru decided to save her evil eye spell for tomorrow, so I'm free. Unfortunately, I'm also utterly wiped. I don't pass out, but I find that there's no strength left in me to do more than lounge around. I lie flat on the sofa in her living room and stare at the wall, contemplating crossing the room and picking up a book. I don't even have the ability to dial up an Uber for Friday-night cards over at Nick's. I'm too tired. Even if I did, I'd just fall asleep the moment I got there.

No wonder witches go through their familiars so quickly. This heavy casting takes its toll on me.

Just as I yawn again, the front door opens. I don't bother to get up, because if it's a burglar, well, I'm sure they'll be turned into a rat or something before I can even defend the place. Not that I have the energy to defend the place.

Big feet appear in my line of vision. Black pants. Black shoes. I crane my neck and see Ben Magnus peering down at me, dressed all in black as usual, with a shopping bag in his arms.

He frowns at the sight of me. "It's Friday night. I didn't think you'd be here."

"Does this confirm that you're avoiding me, then?" I roll onto my back, but I still don't have the energy to stand up.

Ben gazes at me loafing on his aunt's sofa. "You look like a turtle on its back."

"Don't change the subject. You're avoiding me, yes?" I try to give him my best evil glare, but I ruin it by yawning again. "Did I say something to piss you off?"

Instead of answering me, Ben sits on the end of the couch, forcing me to lift my legs halfway. I raise up my knees, but that's the only concession I make to his large form. I was here first, after all. He sets his bag down on the ground and then leans on my knees, gazing down at me. "You look pathetic."

"I might look pathetic, but you're still avoiding the question."

His face splits into a grin. "I wasn't ignoring you, Reggie. Or avoiding you. I had a few spells ongoing that took up my time, and you're supposed to be focusing on your job with my aunt right now, anyhow."

"Well, she went to bingo," I grumble. "And I'm lying here waiting for my strength to return."

Ben pats my knee in sympathy. "What'd she cast today?"

"A couple potions."

"That's not too bad, then. You'll perk up in a few hours."

I stick my tongue out at him. He makes it sound so simple. Like I'm somehow going to make a miraculous recovery when I feel like death warmed over.

"You forget, I've been where you are right now. I know what it's like. It's rough at first, but it gets easier, trust me. Just hang in there." He rubs my knee.

I let out a pitiful groan. "It's just hard," I whine. "I'm used to having a lot more energy. Now I don't even have the ability to get an Uber and go hang out with my friend. I'm just depleted."

"Do you want me to drive you?" His hand slides to my calf,

comforting in its presence despite my thick sweatpants. "I can take you over there. I don't mind."

I consider his offer, then shake my head. "No, I'm just going to lie here on this couch like a pile of pudding," I say dramatically. "So much pudding."

"Odd place to store your pudding."

"It's a figure of speech, warlock."

He chuckles. That's the second time tonight he's smiled at me, and I don't hate it. My heart pitter-pats, and I think about the crystal ball and him stroking himself. *I know I have a big cock.*

Good lord, I'm in danger of developing a massive crush on this strangely attractive man.

"Well," Ben says after a moment. "I was going to spend all night doing warlocky things like gathering eye of newt and playing with dried chicken feet, but since you're here, maybe you can help me with something else."

"What is it?" I ask, frowning. "If it's a spell, I don't have the energy. Literally."

"Nope. Be right back." He heads for the stairs, jogging up them with noisy thumps of his feet that echo even into the living area.

I force myself to sit up, my head slightly woozy. I do feel better, though, after lying down for a short while. Maybe some coffee will help me perk up enough to be human tonight. I peer down at the bag he left near my feet, because I'm nosy.

Books and what looks like some rolled-up parchment. Nothing nefarious. I think about what Penny said. How Ben is dangerous. Funny, he doesn't seem dangerous. Then again, neither does Dru, and she turned me into a cat. But there's something about Ben that I find appealing and trustworthy. The rumors are probably just that—rumors.

He returns a few moments later, a shoebox in his arms. This time, he sits next to me on the couch. "I purchased these, and I've been trying to learn the rules online, but it's a little complicated. I was wondering if you could show me."

Ben pulls the lid off the box, and inside are several packs of unopened Spellcraft: The Magicking cards.

I let out a squeal of surprised delight. "Ben! You bought cards?"

His face is alternately shy and pleased. "Yeah. You mentioned how much you enjoyed the game and how you didn't get to play much anymore, and it sounded like something I'd be into. So I bought some, but like I said, the rules are throwing me for a loop. If you don't have the energy, though, I understand—"

I squeeze his arm excitedly. There's nothing I love more than ushering a new player into the joy that is Spellcraft: The Magicking. "Put on some coffee, my friend. You are about to experience card-game nirvana."

"Is that so?" he says, but the smile is back on his face.

BEN

I know it's a mistake to be around Reggie. I just can't stay away from her.

Among warlocks and witches, it's considered bad form to prey on another's familiar. Familiars are our lifeblood. They're the power that enables us to cast bigger, trickier spells without leaving ourselves vulnerable and useless when an enemy might be coming for us. As a result, familiars are considered off-limits. Despite Reggie's scare the other day, had Livia caught her, she would have done nothing more than chastise Reggie and send her back to Dru.

To court someone else's familiar is akin to cuckolding a man in front of his face.

So I should stay away from Reggie. She's right that I've been avoiding her. I recognize that ache inside myself, that yearning, that covetous need for more of her, and I've been fighting it. I've done other things to keep me busy, had remote meetings with clients, researched spells, and even organized my private study, all to keep away from her. Even so, she's been on my mind. That shy yet radiant smile when she's happy, as if she's not sure that happiness will last. Her obsessive need to organize because she's positive her way is better. Her sweet laughter. Her damned freckles. Her stubborn belief up until the last minute that we were all playing pretend and magic wasn't real.

I force myself to stay away, and it's the most difficult thing I've done in a very, very long time, because I know she's just down the hall. Sometimes I hear her moving around. I smell her freshly used shampoo in the bathroom. I wander into the kitchen and see the dishwasher going and know that it's Reggie, because my aunt has never washed a dish in her long, long life.

And because I think about her obsessively, I buy Spellcraft: The Magicking cards and try to teach myself how to play, just to have another thing to discuss with her. Not that I should be having discussions with her. If I were wise, I'd return to Boston and my quiet, empty home and remain there. I'd get far away from freckled, stubborn familiars.

But I'm a fool. When I see her sprawled on that couch that night, exhausted and alone, I'm drawn to her. I sit next to her. I touch her legs. She smiles at me and teases me as if I'm not Ben Magnus, one of the Magnus warlocks, a family with a terrible past and a worse reputation. As if I'm not a five-hundred-year-old spellcaster who grew sour on life decades ago. She smiles at me and . . . I smile back.

I'm lost after that. I bring out my cards, and we have coffee and Reggie shows me the basics of the card game. It's more complicated than I expected, with one card changing the rules of another, and it's clear Reggie's mind is sharp. She can see combinations the moment a card is laid down, knows how to counter my spells and what to cast of her own that would stop me in my tracks. She wins every round with ease, and I don't mind in the slightest. I just like seeing her mind work.

I contemplate stealing Reggie away from Aunt Dru. Just sliding the magical cuff that brands her as Dru's personal familiar off her wrist and tossing it to the ground. Replacing it with my own. But Reggie's met other familiars at this point. If she became mine, others would suspect I'd stolen her from my aunt . . . and they would be right. I would be even more of a pariah than I already am. And while I don't care, Reggie would. And Aunt Dru would be hurt. She's the one that taught me magic. She's the one that picked me up off the ground when my parents died. She's been there for me, and we're the only family each other has left.

She needs Reggie's strength, because she's getting older and more forgetful. So no. I can't have Reggie.

But nothing says I can't play cards with her.

20

REGGIE

Two Months Later

I hum a song as I scrape wax off the countertops in the kitchen with a putty knife. I should be thinking about ways to get Dru to use dripless candles, or perhaps putting paper down over the counter before we cast another spell involving thirty candles, but instead, I'm thinking about Spellcraft: The Magicking.

More specifically, I'm thinking about a deck I can create to beat Ben.

He's taken to the card game as quickly as I expected and enjoys it as much as I do. Every day, he seems to have crafted a brand-new deck with a new strategy to it and offers to test it against mine. We play cards most nights, when I'm not passed out from another one of Dru's spells. Ben's got an amazingly sharp mind—not surprising given his age and profession—and it's become a real challenge to beat him. So I turn over my cards in my head, trying to think up combinations that will surprise him and put a smile on his face when he realizes he's losing.

I do love making him smile, I think with a silly grin of my own.

Maybe a flying-walls deck to counter all those vampire bats he's been throwing at me—

"Oh, there you are," Dru says from directly behind me.

I yelp, jumping in surprise. "Oh good god! You scared the shit out of me!" I toss the putty knife down and clutch the counter, my heart racing. For all that she wears flowing, ridiculous dresses and loves jewelry (the more the merrier), Aunt Dru can move with the stealth of a ninja. "Don't sneak up on me like that."

"I said your name twice," Dru tells me, blinking innocently. "Didn't you hear me?"

"Did you? Oh. I was just lost in thought, I guess." About Ben's smile, the one that creases his entire face and makes my heart pound. Stupid, stupid crush on a five-hundred-year-old warlock. I'm such an idiot. I turn around and face my boss. "What's up?"

"It's Lisa," Dru says. "I just wanted to give you head."

I pause, not entirely sure I heard her correctly. "I'm . . . sorry?"

"Head," she says again. "Give you notice."

"A heads-up?" I correct.

"Whatever." She shrugs. "Same thing."

Not the same thing at all. "Did she have the baby?"

"No, she's been cursed." Dru smiles brightly. "Okay, I'm going to bingo with Julia! See you!"

"Wait, *what*?" The witch is already wandering back out of the room, though. I trail after her, unwilling to let her walk away without explaining more. "What do you mean, Lisa's been cursed?"

Dru picks up her sequined and glitter-covered bag that holds her bingo bottles. "I'm not entirely sure what part of that wasn't clear, darling. Lisa called me. She said she's been cursed. She can't open a single door without getting intense pain. I wasn't sure if it was just one of those pregnant-lady things, so I did a quick divination and sure enough, she's been cursed. Now, I really must go. I'm always luckiest with the early-bird sets, and Julia wants to split nachos with me." She smiles at me. "You're on your own for food, by the way. See if dear Caliban can take you somewhere if you need anything."

I shake my head, still focused on the whole "cursed" thing. "When did you do a divination? I didn't feel anything."

"You were probably asleep. Did you sleep for longer than normal?"

I might have? I shrug. "She really is cursed, then? Who would curse a poor pregnant woman?"

Dru sighs. "Probably the same person that's been cursing all of my familiars." Outside, a car honks. "That'd be Julia. I really have to go, darling! We'll talk more later."

"You're just . . . leaving?" I gape after her. After she dropped that on me? "What do you mean your other familiars have been cursed?"

"If you're worried, stay close to Ben. Bye! Kisses!" Dru blows kisses over her shoulder, hurrying out the door.

"Dru," I call out, following her toward the porch, but I swear that woman can motor when she doesn't want to talk about something. She races across the front lawn, practically jumps into the car idling at the curb, and then gives me a cheerful wave before she disappears from sight.

Well, fuck.

Lisa is cursed. Lisa—the prior familiar and the one Dru adores—has been cursed by whoever has cursed more than one of Dru's apprentices. Why does Dru not seem to care? I sure as fuck care.

Anxious, I pace through the house. I can't call Dru. She doesn't have a cell phone. Or rather, she did, but she left it somewhere and never remembered where. I found the bill the other day, and it seemed she'd been paying for it for years. So that's out of the question. Ben? I bite my lip, hesitating. I worry I'm already spending too much time with Ben. He's going to think I'm just being clingy and needy. I'm doing my best not to pounce on him the moment I see him, because my crush has only deepened with playing cards with him. It was a lot easier when I thought he was still a big, arrogant jerk.

I certainly can't tell Nick. He still doesn't know magic is real. He thinks Dru is a rich old lady being humored by people.

By the time I retrieve my phone in the kitchen, I know who to text.

REGGIE: Penny, are you busy?

PENNY: Hey friend!!! Never busy! I have all my orders here, just waiting for the delivery guy to come pick them up.

PENNY: What's shaking today?

PENNY: Oooh, wanna go for coffee in the AM? They have a new honey foam latte!

REGGIE: Sure, but I need help. Dru's gone to bingo and she told me that her last apprentice just contacted her and that she's been cursed.

PENNY: Dru's been cursed?!!??

REGGIE: No, Lisa has been cursed. The last familiar Dru had.

PENNY: Wait, the pregnant lady? Seriously?

REGGIE: And that's not all—Dru said it was probably the same person that's been cursing all her familiars.

REGGIE: And now I'm a little freaked out. Have you heard about this?

PENNY: OH EM GEE

PENNY: No!!!

PENNY: Do you think it's . . . you know who?

REGGIE: Penny, I don't know who at all. That's why I'm asking. I'm worried.

PENNY: I meant . . . Ben? Caliban? Whatever name he's going by? He's supposed to be into dark stuff.

I clutch the phone to my chest, frowning. Penny has said that about Ben many times. She's a sweetheart, but her Golden Girl is absolutely Rose. She believes everything anyone tells her, and she's trusting and sweet and guileless to a fault. So Penny is great, but she's not much help when it comes to most gossip. And because she works at the components store, she hears a lot of gossip . . . none of it good, and a lot of it about Ben Magnus.

Penny has told me in the past that she's heard all kinds of ugly rumors about him, but she hasn't been able to find anything concrete. He's very private, and so that doesn't help matters, she says. A lot of it is speculation, and it's fueled by his appearance. Whereas other warlocks do their best to blend in with modern society, Ben wears his wavy black hair deliberately longer than is fashionable, so long that it brushes against his collar. He wears black at all times, and along with his pale skin and huge frame, he looks menacing and unrelenting.

And maybe he is, but he's also wonderfully protective and smart. He has a great sense of humor.

And maybe I *like* his long, floppy hair.

I stare down at my phone's screen, feeling a bit like I'm betraying Ben just for entertaining the idea. I mean, Ben is around all of Dru's familiars. He'd know if they were cursed or not. He's commented before on how difficult it is for Dru and himself to keep familiars, so I can't imagine him cursing them.

Unless I've been in a house full of evil witches all this time and been completely unaware of it. But if that was the case, why would they be teaching me magic? Why would all of Dru's potions be to help friends? Heck, we spent hours the other day making a healing concoction for a squirrel that the neighbor kid ran over with his bike and left in the street. Last I saw, that squirrel was completely better thanks to the potion (which gave me a migraine that day) and was living in the tree in the front yard.

If I'm surrounded by evil, it doesn't feel like it.

I text Penny back, worried.

REGGIE: I don't think it's Ben? He's complained a few times that Dru can't hold onto a familiar.

PENNY: Of course she can't if he's cursing them all!!

PENNY: I don't know him, so I trust you, but he seems like the most natural suspect.

PENNY: But I will put on my detective hat and ask around!

REGGIE: Thank you. Do you know what I can do?

PENNY: Where is Dru? Did she leave you?

REGGIE: She went to bingo.

PENNY: Oh. Well, I mean, if she's not worried, then I wouldn't be worried either.

PENNY: You still want to get together for coffee in the AM?

REGGIE: Yes? I think so? I'll text you if it changes.

Penny sends me a string of emojis that makes no sense, but she's just an excitable sort, so I send a smiley face back and end the text chain. I don't know what to do. Dru wasn't worried, but Dru is Dru. Just because she's not freaking out doesn't mean I shouldn't. Doesn't mean that Lisa's not panicking, either.

Poor Lisa.

Poor me, considering I'm the current familiar and next in the line of people to get zapped with a hex.

The thought makes me vaguely panicky. Wringing my hands, I race back to the kitchen and open the pantry, tweaking cans and touching their labels to make sure they're face out. It's already organized, so it doesn't fill that need inside me. Frustrated, I head over to the library, pulling out a stack of books. The "simple" reorganization of the library has been a never-ending task. It's been over two months now, and I'm still piecing the endless pile of books together. I pick one up, and then another, but they don't help ease my nervousness. They're all about magic and filled with spells, and, well, spells are what have put me in danger. Lisa freaking retired months ago because she was pregnant, and someone still cursed her.

And this happens to all of Dru's familiars, and no one told me. It feels like a betrayal. I set down the book in my hands, glancing back at the door. Lisa can't open any of them. It's a peculiar sort of curse, but an invasive one. Someone would have to follow her around at all times, or else she could get trapped anywhere, even the bathroom. I shake my head, full of sympathy for the woman I barely know. The worst is that Dru just doesn't care. Has she had so many familiars that we're disposable to her now?

My jaw clenches at the thought, and I pick up another book, this time fighting the urge to throw it across the room. I stare down at it, my insides practically boiling with a mixture of anger and terror. I thought this job was too good to be true. Seems like it is, because—

"Reggie?"

I jump, a choked scream rising in my throat. With the book clutched to my chest, I turn around to face Ben, panting. "Don't sneak up on me!"

His brow furrows. "I didn't. In fact, I knocked before I came in the room. Did you not hear me?"

I glance at the door, then back at him. "I—oh."

Ben looks good tonight, I decide. He's dressed in all black, but he always is. Today it's a heavy, thick sweater with a black cowl-neck that somehow makes him look broad-shouldered and appealing as well as vaguely menacing. But the look he's giving me is one of concern as he moves forward, sidestepping a stack of books written in some sort of Greek dialect. "Is something wrong? You look pale."

I touch my cheek, fighting the urge to burst into tears. I don't cry. I don't. Tears don't solve anything. I hate the gentle tone he uses with me, as if we're truly friends. My crush on Ben is just like the rest of this job—a mistake. "At what point were you planning on telling me that all of Dru's familiars are cursed? Because that's a shitty thing to keep to yourself. Is that why the pay for this job is so high?"

He tilts his head slightly, confusion on his face. "What are you talking about?"

"I'm talking about Lisa," I hiss, holding the book against my chest as if it's a shield. "Even though she's so pregnant she freaking waddles, someone cursed her. And when I talked to Dru about it, she told me that all of her familiars get cursed." I throw a hand out, palm up, demanding an explanation. "So?"

Ben blinks. Twice. "Wait . . . All of her familiars get cursed?"

"Don't play dumb with me, Magnus—"

He puts a hand up, cutting me off. "This is news to me, Reggie, especially considering I was one of her familiars at some point. Exactly what did she say?"

Some of my rage bubbles away. "You don't know about this?"

Ben's expression is starting to mirror mine in its confusion and frustration. "How could I? I'm normally in Boston all the time. I knew my aunt had difficulty keeping familiars, but most of us do. It's a high-turnover sort of position, because anyone halfway decent goes on to become a witch or warlock themselves, and anyone that's wrong for the job doesn't stick around." He shakes his head. "But this is the first I've heard of her familiars being cursed."

I set the book I'm clutching down on top of the stack once more. "Other than Maurice, you mean?"

"Maurice is a special case."

"Well apparently not," I snap. "Apparently all of Dru's familiars get cursed, and she doesn't care! She fucking went to bingo!" I wrap my arms around my chest, hugging myself. "Am I going to end up like Maurice, Ben? Because I don't think I can be a cat for all eternity. I was a cat for ten minutes and I hated it."

Something hardens on Ben's face. He takes a step toward me, offering his hand. "I'm not going to let anything happen to you, Reggie. I promise. And a warlock takes their promises seriously."

I swallow hard, fighting the feelings of panic inside me. I stare at that outstretched, oversized hand. Do I trust Ben? Or is this just another way to get me to let my guard down? After a moment's hesitation, I take his hand. I need to trust someone.

For some reason, I really do trust Ben. Even though we started out as enemies, we're friends now . . . and maybe even something more than friends.

My fingers rest lightly against his, and I'm surprised to feel that his fingertips are warm and strong. I mean, of course they are. I'm not sure what I was expecting. But all my senses suddenly lock in on his hand touching mine, and a shiver runs through me.

"Come on," Ben murmurs. He runs his thumb across my knuckles. "Come sit with me in the living room, and we'll figure this out."

I nod.

BEN

I'm going to kill my aunt.

Just murder her outright. This isn't the first time I've run across Reggie being completely panicked because of Aunt Dru's actions. Last time, I thought I understood Aunt Dru's reasoning—that she was pushing Reggie into magic, whether Reggie wanted to believe or not, by tricking her into putting on a cursed ring. But this is something so callous that for a moment, I can't even believe it's my aunt involved.

As Reggie speaks, though, it *sounds* like Aunt Dru. She tends to make decisions and act upon them in her own time. And she does love bingo.

Reggie's seated next to me on the couch, her knees tucked against her chest, and she bites at her nails anxiously as she tells me what Dru mentioned in their brief passing. It's not nearly enough to go on, but I have to believe Reggie. It doesn't make sense, though. Familiars are workhorses and witches in training. No one attacks them. It's akin to attacking the helpless. There's a code of honor among warlocks and witches, and this goes against all of it. But Reggie's no liar.

"And now I don't know what to do," Reggie confesses in a tiny voice, chewing on her nails. "I don't want to become cursed. She says Lisa can't open any doors and—"

"Meow?"

Maurice wanders in, his tail upright, and jumps onto the sofa next to Reggie. As I watch, her face grows paler at the sight of him.

He is definitely not helping the situation. "Not now, Maurice." I get to my feet and offer Reggie my hand again—a selfish move, just because I like the feel of her fingers against mine. "Come on. Let's work some divination and see if we can determine who is behind this."

Reggie immediately puts her hand in mine again, something that will never cease to give me a sense of pleasure. She hesitates, then reaches out and scratches Maurice's head, right behind the ears. "It's not you, buddy. It's me. I'm sorry. We'll hang out later."

Maurice just swishes his tail and settles in on the spot Reggie vacated.

"Come on," I say, tugging her by her small hand. "Let's go up to my private lab." She follows behind me wordlessly, and even though I could let her hand go as we climb the stairs, something tells me she needs the contact. She needs someone to hold on to. I suspect Reggie has never had enough people hold on to her in her life, because she's clinging to my hand right now.

And I don't plan on ever letting go.

At some point in all of this, I stopped loathing the sight of Reggie and started actively looking forward to seeing her. To hearing her laughter, to experiencing her smile. I've started to live for the moments when she gets close enough for me to breathe in the fresh scent of soap and vanilla that she wears like most women wear perfume. I'm obsessed with her, and the obsession has been growing deeper by the day.

The thought's a vaguely disturbing one. I can't be this possessive of my aunt's familiar. I can't. She's off-limits to me. But . . . I also can't just walk away, especially when Reggie's in distress.

We head down the second-floor hall, past Reggie's room and toward my suite of rooms. I open my door with a hand on the ward, and if Reggie notices the spell, she doesn't say anything. Inside, my room is slightly messy. Old clothes hang out of the hamper, and I have piles of books scattered on the nightstands. My bed hasn't been made. I glance back at Reggie to see if she's going to comment on my mess or if she'll pull her hand free and start straightening up, but she just clings to my hand, her gaze tight on me.

I give her a little nod, as if reassuring her that I've got her. That everything is all right. "This way."

I open the closet door and push the hanging clothing aside. It's all black, just because I can't be bothered to match up colors and patterns when clothing should just be serviceable at best. Black hides stains and potion spills, so black it is. Once the clothing is pushed aside, the rune on the wall is revealed. "This is my laboratory," I tell her. "Spelled only to me, but you can enter since you're with me. Just don't try to come in on your own, or you might not like what happens."

Her hand squeezes mine, and a tiny smile curves her mouth. "I won't like what happens? What, is it going to curse me, too?"

My heart aches. She's acting as if she's already cursed. As if it's just a matter of time. "Rashes," I tease, to lighten her mood. "Rashes for days."

"You monster," she teases back. She's still smiling, though, and it makes me feel better.

The door slides back, revealing my lab to her eyes. There are no windows, no doors except the one we came through. Wall-to-wall bookshelves and a massive rack of components dominate the room, and my enormous wooden worktable takes up most of the floor space. It's not the best laboratory—my one at home has a sink nearby and windows to add ventilation—but it'll do.

Reggie's mouth opens in surprise. "I had no idea this was here. This is between our rooms?"

I nod, moving to the far side of my table. I head for the components rack, pulling out the stronger herbs for divining. "Yes. It used to be a guest room once upon a time, but I spent several weeks here when Aunt Dru hurt her ankle a few decades ago, and so I had the door to the hall sealed, and repurposed this room for myself. It's not perfect, but we'll have privacy here."

Reggie immediately moves to my side, as if my presence comforts her. "So . . . what are we going to do, then? Do we need a crystal ball?"

For some reason, that makes my body respond. I think about how she watched me in the crystal ball and confessed it to me. She didn't act upon it. Didn't confess a second time, so I know she's never done it again, and I find that oddly disappointing. With every day that passes, I find it harder and harder to resist her, and it'd be easier if I knew how she felt about me.

Reggie's in her twenties, though. She probably thinks I'm far too old for her, far too dour, too unappealing. And I'm a warlock, and right now she's stressing about a spell, so I'm surprised she's even talking to me.

I toss handfuls of herbs into my offering bowl and add a dried chicken's foot for good measure. Some gold leaf. Saffron. I pull out a jar I have set aside for such occasions, open it, and dump the contents into the bowl.

Reggie's chin pushes against my arm, and I realize she's trying to peer over my shoulder to see what I'm doing, but she's too short. Her breast presses against me, and my fingers tremble for a moment. "Is that caviar? You're offering caviar?"

"The gods take you more seriously based on your offering," I tell her. "If you want to get their attention, you offer expensive things or you make a flashy statement."

"Flashy statement?" she asks.

I purse my lips, wondering if I should mention animal sacrifices. They were common in the past, but thankfully not any longer. "Let's just say they involve entrails."

"Oof, okay, yeah, I don't think I want to know." Her hand grazes my sleeve, and I wonder if she has any idea of what she's doing to me. "Are we asking Mercury to step in again?"

I nod. I've considered approaching Egeria or Minerva, but Egeria likes to answer in riddles and Minerva doesn't tend to answer me at all. Mercury is easily swayed with pricey gifts, so Mercury it is. I prep the components and then pause. "Reggie, I'm going to use my blood, but I'll need yours, too, since it'll give us a better chance of getting the god's attention. Are you all right with that?"

She immediately holds her hand out to me, fingers curled up. "All yours."

That should not be nearly as erotic as it is. I take her wrist carefully and pull out the small silver knife I keep for such occasions. I rest it over the pad of her forefinger, letting her get used to the idea before I actually stab.

"Be gentle," Reggie whispers.

My cock twitches in response. Does she realize how flirty that sounds? I don't look over at her, because I'm afraid she's going to see the blatant lust on my face and run away. I force myself to focus, and when I gently prick her and the blood wells up, I resist the urge to put her finger to my mouth and suck on it. Reluctantly, I release her to do the same to my finger. "Hold that over the offering bowl until the blood flow stops."

We bleed together in silence until her finger dries, and then mine does, too. I lick my fingertip automatically and then pull out my phone. Reggie twitches in surprise but remains silent. I flick the camera on, then close my eyes. "Mercury, patron of divination, show us who has cursed Lisa . . ." I pause, because I don't know her last name. I glance over at Reggie, who shrugs helplessly. "Lisa," I continue, "the former apprentice of my aunt. She has been cursed. We want to see who is behind this."

The picture on my phone changes, turning gray and shimmering before sliding back to a dull, ugly black.

"What does that mean?" Reggie whispers.

I repeat my request, and again, my phone reacts the same way. So it wasn't a coincidence or a software mishap. "Thank you, Mercury," I murmur, and close the camera app on my phone. "We're being blocked. Mercury answered us, but he has nothing to show us."

Reggie gives me a wide-eyed look. "Because we don't know Lisa's last name?"

I shake my head. I've had less information on a topic and gotten better results in the past. I glance over at the offering bowl, watching as it smokes and the contents turn quickly to ash. "No, we did everything fine. Mercury accepted our offering. He just can't show us. It's likely that someone has cast an obfuscation spell to prevent others from doing as we have."

"Well, of course they would," Reggie says with a frown on her face. "They're witches. Or warlocks. Of course they'd hide their tracks."

"Some don't. Some leave their names as a calling card, of sorts. Or as a dare." The good news is that we don't have to deal with that. Only the strongest of warlocks and witches deliberately leave their signatures all over their curses, hoping for a confrontation and a chance to take out an enemy (or just feed a bit of bloodthirstiness). The fact that this spell has been hidden tells us that it's someone with less power than me . . . but I don't like that they're targeting my aunt or her familiars.

Why has Aunt Dru never brought this up to me? The moment she gets home, I'm going to lay into her. I'm half tempted to drive up to the bingo hall and yank her out, but Dru has never responded well to being rushed. The only thing we can do is wait.

So I turn to Reggie and force a casual smile to my lips. "My aunt will be home shortly. We'll talk to her then."

She nods, frustration apparent on her face. "Thank you for your help, at least. I was just so panicky I wasn't sure what to do . . ." She trails off, then shrugs. "Nothing to do but wait. I guess I should go back to work in the library."

"I'll join you."

That makes her pause. She gives me a puzzled look. "Why? It's just cataloging and sorting."

"Someone needs to be with you at all times," I point out. "Most spells cast against someone—a curse, an evil eye, a hex—involve using an object from the person being cursed. It could be a sock, or a lock of hair, or something along those lines. You need someone at your side constantly to ensure you don't leave behind anything that could be used against you."

I expect her to protest, to say I'm being silly. Overprotective. I expect her to say that she knows better than to leave her things out, that she won't shed, that we're not in public and that she's safe. That I'm overbearing and obnoxious. Maybe I am. I just know I don't want to leave Reggie alone for a moment, not when she's so damned miserable. Not when she could be in danger.

But her expression grows soft, vulnerable. "You'd . . . wait with me?"

I hate that aching note of hope in her voice. It makes me wonder if anyone has ever been there for her—her parents, that fool Nick, anyone at all. "Of course."

She smiles softly at me, and I know I'm in such danger. Not from hexes or spells, but from becoming entirely besotted with my aunt's familiar.

I might already be there.

BEN

We clean up my lab (without Reggie being, well, Reggie) and head back downstairs. She sighs as she looks toward the wrecked library, and another idea hits me.

"Why don't we play cards instead of you working tonight?" I suggest. "You need to get your mind off of things."

Her face lights up. She loves that card game more than anything. I've never seen someone so into a game, but Reggie's also incredibly good at it. She can see combinations that aren't obvious and can assess the gameplay at a glance. I love watching her mind work, and I have to admit I'm getting fairly addicted to the game myself. "Do you think we should?" Reggie finally asks. "Shouldn't we be working on something to help Lisa?"

"If she called my aunt instead of coming over, she's not that worried about it," I point out. "And if Aunt Dru went to bingo instead of working on fixing this for Lisa, it means she's not worried about it, either." That, or she has no idea how to fix it, but I don't say that aloud. "All we can do is wait on Aunt Dru, and until then, you might as well enjoy yourself."

It doesn't take more convincing than that. "All right," Reggie agrees, and the twinkle in her eyes is back. "I'll put on some coffee. But you're going down, Magnus."

Damn it all, why is everything she says today innuendo? I pretend to ignore it, and head toward the living room, where we normally play at the coffee table, and retrieve my cards. They're still here from when we played last night, and I pull out my latest deck, shuffling as I wait.

She returns a few minutes later with two cups of coffee and a sunny smile on her face. "Can I just say thank you, Ben?"

I arch a brow at her. "For?"

"For being my friend." She smiles sweetly at me.

It almost makes me want to throw my cards down. I don't want to be her friend. I want to grab her and kiss the hell out of her . . . but I know that's wrong. I absolutely know it is. Friends is all we can be. "Don't try to make me regret the trouncing I'm about to give you."

Reggie laughs with sheer delight, setting down the coffee mugs and then bounding into her seat across from me. "Ante tonight?"

"Of course." Since I know the rules now, we've started playing for an ante card. We both draw the first card in our decks and set them aside. Whoever wins the match wins the card. Most of the time, it just adds a bit of an edge to the play, knowing that you're going to win something of your opponent's and then you can promptly rub it in their face.

When we pull ante tonight, though, I pull from Reggie's deck as she pulls from mine. She pulls a cauldron—an energy source—and makes a face. I pull her favorite card, Brilliant Sun-Phoenix.

Before I can set it down atop my ante, Reggie reaches for it. "Wait, Ben, no."

I hold it in the air, giving her a look. "It's the ante, Reggie. You set the rules yourself."

"But that's my Sun-Phoenix!"

"So?"

"So it's worth fifty dollars! I can't just go out and buy another!"

For all that Reggie's being paid well by my aunt, she still has the mentality of someone that eats instant ramen and shops at Goodwill. She can buy a dozen of these cards now. I shake my head. "Those are the rules, I'm afraid." She's fun to tease, and I hold the card higher in the air. "I look forward to winning this one—"

Before I can complete my sentence, Reggie crawls the short distance across the couch and reaches for the card. I automatically hold it higher, and then she's in my face, and our noses are an inch away from each other.

I can see every freckle on her face. I can see her dark eyes as her gaze focuses on me, and I watch as her breathing speeds up. I'm suddenly no longer thinking about cards, and neither is she. Her expression grows soft, her gaze flicking to my mouth.

I've never wanted anyone more than I want Reggie now in this moment. "Reggie," I groan.

"I'm sorry," she breathes. "I'm all over you, aren't I?"

But she doesn't move away. She doesn't move at all. She just hovers, as if waiting, and I can feel her breath on my face.

I know she's my aunt's familiar. In this moment, I don't care. "Can I kiss you?" I ask, voice hoarse.

"Please" is all she says.

I close that brief distance between us, flicking the Sun-Phoenix down to the coffee table. The moment my lips brush Reggie's, her arms go around my neck, as if she was simply waiting for me to make the first move. Her mouth is soft and sweet, and there's just a hint of sugary coffee on her lips. I kiss her like an explorer, with small, brief kisses, as I learn the layout of her mouth and how she responds. I press my mouth to hers over and over again, paying attention to her upper lip, the freckle at the corner of her mouth, her full lower lip. Then I brush my tongue against the waiting part of her mouth.

Reggie moans.

My entire body reacts to that wordless sound. My sac tightens and my cock throbs. I flick my eyes open to watch her face, and notice that hers are closed, an expression of pure bliss on her as I kiss her. I hold back a groan of my own and nip at her lower lip before dipping into her mouth again. She feels so good in my arms. Like bliss. Perfection.

In five hundred years, nothing has felt so right.

My arms are around her waist, and I lick into her mouth, loving that she kisses me back, loving that her tongue brushes against mine. She tastes good, but she feels even better, and when she shifts her weight, I realize she's climbing into my lap instead of sliding away from me. She wants the kiss to keep going.

Fuck, so do I.

Holding her tightly, I kiss her harder, our mouths melding in a steady stream of flirty movements, of lips brushing against one another, of tongues teasing back and forth. I'm lost in the heaven that's Reggie's mouth when her backside vibrates.

She stiffens, pulling away from me. Giggles. "That's my phone."

"Ah." I lean forward, wanting to kiss her again. Her eyes are dark, her lids heavy, and her mouth is pink and swollen from our kissing, and it's just making me want her even more. She leans in, her gaze going to my mouth, her fingers grazing my neck.

Her backside buzzes again.

With a groan, Reggie gives me one last nipping kiss. "I should get that. What if it's Dru?"

"It's not Dru," I promise her, stealing another kiss. Now that I have her, I don't want to let her go.

"It could be important," she murmurs, and kisses me again. "It could be Nick."

Nick's not important, I want to say, but I know he's her friend. I kiss her one more time and then reluctantly pull away. "See who it is, then."

She gives me an almost-shy look of apology, then pulls her phone out of her pocket. She's wearing a plain white shirt today, and as she leans back against the couch and pulls up her phone messages, I can see her nipples outlined against her clothing, another sign of her arousal.

I wonder if it'd be too much if I dropped to my knees in front of her and licked her pussy?

Probably. I've been accused of being too intense in the past. I rub my mouth, thinking. It's difficult for me to make that kind of judgment call. After five hundred years, I tend to know what I want, and instead of making me more patient, it's made me less. I see no point in waiting on something when it's everything I need.

And right now I need Reggie. Desperately. I'll work something out with Aunt Dru. I'll have to stay here for a while, and the thought doesn't irk me like it normally does. I can share Reggie with Dru for a while. I won't steal her apprentice, but there's no reason Reggie and I can't explore this thing, see where it goes . . .

Reggie's face drains of color. She stares at her phone screen, her gaze darting as if she can't quite believe what she's reading.

"What?" I have to ask. My protective side is getting the better of me, and I don't like seeing that fear on her face. "What is it?"

She clicks her phone off and holds it to her chest, but she doesn't return to my arms. Instead, she's gazing at me with wariness. I wonder what it is she's just learned and why it's changed the expression on her face from arousal to uncertainty. "Ben, can I ask you something?" When I nod, she licks her lips—those perfect pink lips—and continues in a small voice. "Did you murder your parents?"

Murder. Such an intense, accusing word.

Yet a correct one. The old darkness threatens to flood through me, the bitterness, the anger I thought I was past. So Reggie's been gossiping about me, has she? And now someone's warning her off by telling her all the things I'd like to forget.

"Yes," I say flatly. I don't elaborate.

She flinches. Just once, but it's enough to kill the mood. To kill everything inside me.

"I see," Reggie whispers. She remains where she is, clutching her phone. "Ben. Maybe this isn't such a good idea between us . . ."

Because I'm a murderer. Because I'm a warlock and a bad guy and a monster. Because I'm one of those wretched Magnuses and our reputations are as foul as our magic. I can just imagine what they're telling her. I should have known I wouldn't be allowed to touch someone like Reggie, even for a short period of time.

I'm not good for her.

So I just shrug. "You should probably go up to your room. Don't worry. I'll keep a lookout."

Part of me wishes she'd say something. That she'd tell me we're still going to be friends, that I must have had my reasons. That what others say about me isn't possibly true. She doesn't, however. Reggie silently gets to her feet and goes upstairs.

And there's nothing left to say.

22

REGGIE

Holy fuck.

I lean against the door in my bedroom, breathing hard. My body's still singing, my nipples tight and aching, and the taste of Ben Magnus lingers on my mouth.

I wasn't expecting that. Sure, I've been nursing a crush on Ben for weeks now. All that initial hatred turned into a raging lust-bomb far too quickly, only heightened by the fact that he plays a mean game of cards. I never expected to do anything with it, though. He's just kind and caring and gentle, and so I might have said a few suggestive things or might have skipped wearing a bra when we're together, just to see if he'd notice.

The card incident happened purely by accident, though. Maybe I've been too casual with him, too friendly. Maybe I've made my crush far too obvious. Whatever it was, I didn't intend to kiss Ben. It was amazing, though. He kissed like . . . like he wanted to devour me. To savor me with tiny little bites. As if I was a delicious dessert he couldn't get enough of. Even thinking about it right now makes my toes curl.

Penny's text messages changed everything, though. I read

through them again, just because my mind still hasn't processed the gravity of them.

> **PENNY:** Reggie, I just found out something terrible. Are you there?
>
> **PENNY:** My sister's friend Marissa is a familiar for an elderly warlock in California who knows the Magnus family. She asked him about Ben and he said the reason why everyone is so frightened of him is because he MURDERED HIS OWN PARENTS. Horrifying! And the source I have is credible. Maybe you should get out while you can. I'm worried about you.
>
> **PENNY:** I'm sorry if this seems gossipy but I'd want to know if I was under the same roof as a murderer!
>
> **PENNY:** I hope you're okay! Call me! We're still on for coffee tomorrow AM right?

I've known from chatting with Dru that not all witches and warlocks use their magic for good. That morals get grayer and grayer the older the witch gets. Ben has mentioned it, too. That with the ability to curse, a lot of people use their power for darker things. I just didn't think Ben would be one of them.

Ben, who laughs when I outplay him in Spellcraft.

Ben, who tenderly picked me up when I couldn't walk straight after being turned into a cat.

Ben, who kisses like I'm the most precious being in the universe and all he wants to do is worship me.

I touch my mouth, remembering the feel of his kisses. I don't know if I'm horrified that I kissed a murderer or horrified that it was the best kissing experience I've ever had and that I want more of it. I can't believe I'm mooning over a murderer. Not just any murderer, but someone who killed his parents and openly admitted to it. I'd hoped he'd explain, that something was just a misunderstanding.

Nope. He'd given me a defiant look, as if daring me to comment on it. Ben is the bad guy everyone thinks he is, and I don't know what to do with that.

I made out with an evil warlock.

I shudder, and I don't know if it's because I'm still turned on or appalled at myself. All I know is that I can't stay in this environment. I can't live under the same roof as Ben, down the hall from a man who casually murdered the two people that are supposed to mean the most to him in the world.

Maybe they were users, my brain supplies. *Maybe they were like your parents.*

Even if they were . . . I didn't murder mine. I wouldn't. Part of me still wants their love and approval, even though I know that's fucked up in the head. I know they're toxic.

Maybe I just have a thing for toxic people . . . like Ben. It's clear my own judgment is impaired. Maybe Dru is just as bad, and I've been blinded to it because of the money. Ugh. My stomach churns at the thought. I turn and flip the three locks on the door, bolting myself inside. When I turn around, I see Maurice crawling out from under the bed. He gives me a tiny, gentle meow and then hops up onto the corner of the bed, his tail twitching.

"Are you asking me what's wrong?" I bite my lip, then lean in to whisper to the cat. "I just made out with Ben and found out he murdered his parents after we lip-locked. I have a lot of feelings about that."

Maurice blinks. Twice.

"Are you trying to tell me something?"

He blinks. Slowly. Then he begins to clean his paws.

"Maurice, do you know anything about this curse business?"

His tail twitches. If a cat could give me a look that said, "Obviously," it would be the look he's giving me right now.

Right. I guess that was a dumb question. "I just need to know if you understand me. Can you blink once for yes and twice for no?"

He blinks once.

"Is that a legit blink for yes, or is that you just blinking because you're a cat?"

He blinks once again, slow and unhurried.

I don't know if we're really communicating or if I'm losing my damn mind. When he starts to groom himself again, I suspect the latter. "Maurice, help me. I'm freaking out. Am I in danger here?"

He looks up. Blinks twice. Then he goes to curl up next to my pillows.

I guess . . . that's a good sign? "So I'm not going to get cursed?"

He opens his eyes, flicks his tail once at me, and then closes his eyes again, settling in for a nap. I don't know if that means yes, I'm going to get cursed, or yes, I'm not going to get cursed. I need to be clearer when talking to a magical cat, I guess.

I rub a hand down my face. There's something I never thought I'd tell myself. Doesn't matter. Maurice is clearly done with the conversation.

Just like I'm done with this situation. Witches or not, money or not, I know when to cut my losses. I grab my bag and begin to pack my clothes into it.

✳ ✳ ✳

IT'S LATE WHEN I hear someone coming up the stairs. I put my ear to the door, listening to the footsteps. Dru's are always small and light, whereas Ben's footsteps are heavy and the footfalls spaced far apart. When it becomes clear that the person coming up the stairs is Dru, I open my door.

She smiles brightly at me. "Oh, hello, darling! Do you know, I won on pull tabs? Twice! It's my lucky night." She waves a hand in the air. "Well, other than I sat next to a chain-smoker all night. But really, it wasn't so bad. Did you have a nice evening? I didn't see my darling Caliban tonight. Have you seen him?"

"Not since earlier," I say, and bite my lip. "Dru, we need to talk."

Her eyes widen, and she takes a step backward, as if wanting to flee me. "Oh no. You can't quit, Reggie! We're just getting used to each other!"

How did she know I was going to quit? It doesn't matter. I shake my head, keeping my voice gentle. "Dru, I'm sorry—"

She races toward me, putting her small, cold hands over mine. Her clothes reek of cigarettes and fried food, and she's got bingo-bottle ink all over her hands. "Is this about Lisa? Has something else happened?"

"You mean other than her being cursed and all of your other familiars being cursed?" When Dru doesn't blink, I give her hands a squeeze. "That's exactly why I need to leave, Dru. I can't be cursed. I don't want to end up a cat."

"Oh, don't be silly. No one ends up a cat but Maurice."

I scowl down at her lined, cherub-cheeked face. "But they all get cursed, don't they?"

She rubs my fingers, her rings cutting into my skin. "Please, Reggie. Do you need a raise? Is that what's wrong? I can give you a raise. Name your amount."

God, she's hitting me right where it hurts. I wince, because money is always the kicker. I can't ignore that I made out with her nephew the evil warlock, though . . . or that I'd probably do it again given half the chance. I can't trust myself in these situations, so time to get out of the situation. "It's not you, Dru. It's me. I can't stay. I just—"

She shakes her head, putting a hand up. “Did Caliban say something? Did he offend you with naughty words? I thought he liked you.” Her expression grows sad. “I thought he was kind of sweet on you, actually.”

Great, the evil warlock is sweet on me. I pull my hands out of her clingy grip. “No—”

“I can’t think straight right now,” Dru tells me dramatically. “My head hurts from all that smoke, and I have a migraine. It’s far too late at night, and I have a lot going on. So much going on. Can’t we discuss this in the morning over coffee? We’ll go over what kind of raise you need to stay, and take it from there.” She nods, as if it’s all been solved, and then puts a hand to her brow.

“No, Dru—”

Rubbing her temples, Dru ignores me and heads for her bedroom. “Tomorrow morning, first thing, Reggie dear. We’ll get whatever you’re unhappy about sorted away. I just can’t think straight right now.”

I sigh, my head pounding, too. I should just go ahead and leave tonight. I really should. But I’m exhausted, and Dru deserves to have a real conversation with me at least. It wouldn’t be fair to sneak out late at night just because I’m afraid to face Ben. I should have a logical, normal conversation with Dru, express why I’m leaving, and get my final check from her. Then I’ll move back in with Nick, lick my wounds, try not to think about how I found a deadly warlock incredibly hot, and get on with my life.

It’ll all be handled in the morning. I shut the door, lock it, and push Maurice aside so I can sleep.

23

BEN

My mood's as black as my coffee the next morning as I sit, alone, in Aunt Dru's kitchen.

It grows even darker when Reggie shows up, wearing jeans and a hoodie over her T-shirt, her bag slung over her shoulder. Hot, frustrated anger rushes through me. It's not like Reggie to be a coward, and yet here she is, thinking she has all the answers now and has to run away from them. "You're leaving," I sneer. "I like how the threat of a curse or the existence of magic doesn't scare you off, but one kiss and you race for the hills."

Her cheeks redden and she looks away from me, setting her bag down near the door. "I can't stay." She moves to the coffeepot and pours herself a cup, shoveling sugar and creamer into it. "It's complicated."

"Is it?" I don't think it is. She liked kissing me until someone texted her about my past and ruined it. I'm not surprised, but I am disappointed. I let myself hope that Reggie would be different. That she'd ask questions. That she'd wonder why. That she'd see the real me past the dark reputation and rumors, but I guess it's not to be. I should know better by now.

Never hope.

Reggie doesn't face me. She just stirs her coffee vigorously. "Something's come up."

I snort. "You're a terrible liar, Reggie. We both know the truth. You're leaving because you kissed a murderous warlock and you hate that you liked it."

She's silent.

"Do you deny it?" I needle, getting to my feet. "Because until your phone buzzed, you seemed to be enjoying my kisses. You seemed to like my touch."

Reggie stops stirring her coffee. "I—" She swallows hard. "No, I don't deny it."

I'm surprised that she admits it. "So you're running because you're afraid."

She turns around, clutching her coffee mug to her chest as if it's going to shield her somehow. "I just . . . I don't make good decisions when it comes to people, Ben. You and I are from very different worlds. I thought I could make this whole apprenticing thing work, but I think I'm in over my head." Her gaze flicks briefly to my face and then lowers. "I'm sorry. We shouldn't have kissed."

I can't let it go at that. "Why?"

She licks her lips, looking flustered and helpless. "I can't be with someone that's so . . . so . . ."

"Evil?" I supply.

"Wrong for me." Reggie looks up at me again, her eyes dark and full of emotion. "I don't think you're evil, Ben. Why would you think that?"

"Because everyone else thinks I'm evil? That I've done evil things?" I think of Soren Jeffries, the head of Zephyr First Tech. I think of the bleak look in his eyes during our last video call.

I didn't realize what I was asking for, Soren had said.

He'd been found the next morning, dead by his own hand . . .

and it was all because of my actions. All because I'd cast ruthless spells and hadn't bothered to stop and ask if I should have.

That's evil, isn't it? Bleak despair crawls through my veins.

"Well, they're wrong," she says, lifting her chin. "You're not evil, as far as I'm concerned. Perhaps . . . misguided?"

I snort at that. Misguided. There's a word that's been thrown into my face for centuries. I take a step toward Reggie and stop when she flinches backward. "Might I remind you that I asked for permission to kiss you, and you said, 'Please.' You could have stopped me at any time, misguided or not." I lean against the counter, because I want to stalk forward and trap her between my body and the door so she's forced to answer me, but I don't like her fear. In fact, I fucking hate that she's afraid of me now. "You didn't stop me. You kissed me back, and you liked it. Just like you enjoyed watching me in the crystal ball when I stroked myself."

She swallows hard, hanging her head, and I feel like I won a little ground. It's something, at least. Reggie doesn't want to admit that she likes kissing me or that she's attracted to me, and it's all because of my past rearing itself up again. She doesn't understand, but she's not even willing to, so I don't know why I bother. "This is hard for me, Ben. I like you, I do. But I can't do this." She raises her mug and holds it to her lips, as if she wants to say something else. Instead, she slips past me, crossing over to the kitchen table, which is normally littered with spell components and various tomes. "Where's Dru this morning?"

"Still upstairs." I want to keep pushing at her. To keep picking at her reasons. To dare her to ask me *why* I killed my parents. *Why* I am who I am. She doesn't, though, and I think that's more disappointing than anything.

I should have known that she wouldn't understand. No one ever does. The thought feels like lead in my gut. I swig my coffee in silence, remaining in the kitchen just in case Reggie wants to speak up again, to say something else. She's silent, the only sounds that of the crinkle of muffin paper as she helps herself to breakfast. Even though there are freshly baked goods on the counter, I can't eat a bite. I'm too full of frustration.

Moments tick past. It's utterly silent. Finally, I hear the sound of Reggie's chair being shoved back, and I turn to look at her. She has a muffin shoved into her mouth, her cheeks bulging. "This is ridiculous," she says, her mouth full of crumbs. "I'm going to find Dru and get this over with."

She rushes out of the kitchen, as if she's afraid I'll stop her, and now that I'm alone again, I just feel hollow. Cold. If I'd have known four hundred years ago that this would haunt me . . . No, I'd still have done it. I didn't trust anyone else to do it. They deserved for it to be me. I can't change the past, but it's no wonder that I can't keep a familiar.

No one wants to serve a monster.

Certainly no one wants to kiss one. I press my hand to the hidden pocket inside the front of my jacket. Tucked in there is Reggie's Sun-Phoenix card. She forgot all about it last night after we kissed, and I'm not ready to give it back. I might never give it back. I think about familiars and Reggie and my parents, and my mood is dark and bleak. I could approach the Society of Familiars. Put my name on the list again. It's just, they wouldn't be Reggie. I don't want a familiar. I've managed without one for decades, draining my own strength and being judicious with my casting.

I want a companion. A lover.

I've fallen hard for someone that loathes the sight of me. My jaw clenches at the thought.

"BEN!" Reggie's scream cuts through the silence in the large house.

My blood turns to ice. I've heard that kind of panic in Reggie's voice only once before.

I race across the house and up the stairs. I can hear Reggie weeping, her voice frantic as she calls my aunt's name over and over again. I skid down the hall, barreling through the door to my aunt's suite of rooms. Everything looks in order, the rooms neat and tidy enough, despite Dru's usual clutter atop every surface. In the center of the bed, though, my aunt lies on her back, her eyes closed. Reggie's seated on the edge of the bed. She shakes Dru hard, weeping, and then turns to me. "I can't wake her up, Ben. Something's wrong."

I can scarcely breathe. I know Aunt Dru is old—beyond old—but she's been such a fixture for the last five hundred years that I've always assumed she'd be around. That she'd somehow outlive me, just endlessly smiling and saying inane things and being Dru until the end of time. It's never occurred to me that she could be weak . . . or that she'd die. My tongue feels as if it's glued to the roof of my mouth as I move to Reggie's side and kneel next to my aunt's bed.

Aunt Drusilla's chest moves, her breathing easy. Her face looks peaceful, serene, her hair in curlers, as she always sleeps. Her cheeks are pink with health, and she looks happy, strangely enough.

"She's breathing," Reggie chokes out, tears rolling down her face. Dru's hand is clenched tight in her grasp. "But I can't get her to wake. Should we call an ambulance?"

I touch my aunt's neck, feeling for her pulse. It's there, beating strongly under her papery, delicate skin. An ambulance or a healing potion? I get to my feet—and my skin prickles with awareness. Stale magic hangs in the air. Quick as I can, I pull out a knife and slash through my palm, letting my blood splatter on the floor as I hold my fist out. Reggie squeals a protest, but I ignore her. Closing my eyes, I call out to any of the gods that might be listening.

"Show me what this is," I murmur. "Please." I put all the emotion and feeling I have inside me into that one word, that single plea.

"Don't we need spell components?" Reggie murmurs at my side. "You can't just cut your hand open and expect the gods to answer, can you?"

Maybe most can't, but the blood of my ancestors, the "ambrosia" that gives us our magic, flows heavy in my veins. I've had five hundred years to hone my power. I squeeze my fist tighter, making the wound hurt, letting anyone that might be listening know that I mean business. All I need is a hint, a sign—

On the bed, Dru snores loudly.

Reggie gasps, her hand touching my clothing. "Ben—"

"Thank you," I say quietly before I open my eyes. I know without looking that my request has been answered, and I make a mental note to do a large offering of thanks once things have calmed down. Once my aunt is awake and healthy. I lower my fist and look over at Reggie, and I can feel the magic in the room, like the heaviness of the weather before a storm.

Wordless, Reggie points at my aunt.

Dru has turned her head to the side, exposing more of her neck. A word is written there in charcoal, near her collarbone.

SOPOR

"Sleep," I murmur. "Someone's cursed her."

"What the fuck?" Reggie weeps, swiping at her tears with the backs of her hands. "Someone got into the house? While we were sleeping?"

I brush the word off my aunt's neck to see if that will break the curse, but it doesn't. That would be far too easy. "Not necessarily.

Some curses can be cast from a distance. A sleep curse is an ancient one. You've read the fairy tales, yes? Simple, but effective." I tuck the blankets under Aunt Dru's chin, as if I can somehow make her comfortable. For some reason, this makes me less frantic than a heart attack or a stroke. I don't know how to deal with those. But curses and magic? Those are a warlock's repertoire. I can fix this. "It's going to be all right, Reggie."

"You're bleeding all over the blankets," she tells me accusingly, then sniffs. "You're not going to be much help to anyone if you bleed out from a stupid cut in your hand."

"I'm not going to bleed out." Exasperated, I look over at her. I'm about to make a cutting comment, but the look on her face stops me. Reggie's expression is devastated. I know she's attached to my aunt but she also looks incredibly fragile, and I remember how frightened she was last night. That she was going to end up cursed. Now Aunt Dru can't protect her. "You can't leave now, Reggie."

She gives me a horrified look. "Of course I'm not going to leave, you idiot. Dru needs help—"

"No, you don't understand." I shake my head, resisting the urge to touch her, because blood and . . . well, because I'm a murderer in her eyes. "Remember last night when I said you need to stay close by me? I mean it. Don't leave the room unless I know where you are. If you're with me at all times, I can protect you."

A wariness enters her eyes. "How? If someone can cast on me from afar, how can you possibly protect me?"

"Obfuscation spells." It's not the best answer, but it's an immediate one. "No one can curse you if they can't find you. They have to be able to locate you, even if it's just with a scrying spell, to be able to attach the curse to you. I can obfuscate my general area, but it'll require help from you."

"You mean you need me to be your battery," Reggie states bluntly.

"Partly," I agree. "But we'll also have to stay in the same room at all times. No more than a few feet apart."

Her nostrils flare, and her back stiffens ever so slightly. I can see her considering my offer, can see the hesitation and worry in her eyes that wasn't there last night. Now that I'm a murderer in her eyes, I'm suddenly terrifying. I pull out my sacrificial knife again and brandish it over my throbbing, blood-covered palm. "I will make a blood promise to you that you're safe with me."

"Oh my god, you are so dramatic." Reggie grabs my wrist before I can cut. "What am I supposed to do with you if your hand looks like sushi?" She frowns, staring down at where she grabbed my wrist. "I know you won't hurt me, okay? I trust you, even though it's incredibly stupid for me to say that."

I shake my head. "I might have done bad things in my past, Reggie, but that doesn't mean I'd harm you. Ever. I'd sooner cut off my own hand."

"Obviously." She gives me a faint smile. It fades quickly as she looks over at Dru. "I just . . . I trust you, okay? Please don't betray that trust."

I nod, my throat thick. For some reason, having her trust means a lot to me.

"But I also need to establish boundaries," Reggie continues. "We're not—the kissing. We're not doing that again." She grows flustered. "This is just about saving Dru, all right? So if I have to stay in the same room as you and wear your familiar bracelet, I will. But it's only for Dru."

"I understand." And I'll take whatever I can get, because I'm pathetic when it comes to Reggie.

Reggie looks up at me, her dark eyes full of worry and trust. "So how do we do this? Where do we start?"

I think for a moment, though it's difficult to do. My hand throbs, blood still dripping on the carpet. Aunt Dru snores. And Reggie . . . she stands so close to me that it's distracting. Her fingers are still on my wrist. "I need components."

To my surprise, her expression turns determined. "I know just the person."

REGGIE

"Oh em gee," Penny hiss-whispers as she pulls me aside a few hours later. "You told me you were bringing someone, but I didn't realize it would be *that* someone!" She clutches the sleeve of my hoodie even as she looks over at Ben Magnus, who's studying the CBD products on the near-empty shelving at the front of the store.

"It is absolutely a long story, and I will give it to you, but we need your help." I give her a tight smile. "It's kind of an emergency, actually."

Her eyes widen. "I am so good in an emergency. Tell me what you need!"

I squeeze Penny's hand, because I know she is. Penny is nothing if not enthusiastic and knows a lot about familiars and witchcraft, and she's my friend. We need all the help we can get. Quickly, I brief Penny on everything that's happened in the last few hours—Dru's Sleeping Beauty curse, the additional curses on Lisa and all the familiars, and that Ben and I are now working together. I skip the part where I practically shoved myself in his face, asking for a kiss, because, well, it feels weird.

I keep waiting for the loathing for Ben to kick in, and it hasn't happened. He's always so protective. Kind. Him being a murderer doesn't fit, but then again, nice-seeming people can also be serial killers, so maybe I can't trust my instincts. Because my stupid instincts are to stare at his mouth and wonder about that kiss, and that makes me think there's something wrong with my head.

"Who's with Drusilla right now?" Penny asks.

"Lisa is. She's there with her husband, since she can't open any doors for herself and she's a million years pregnant. They're moving into the house temporarily to help out until we get things figured out." I've given them my room and relegated myself to the sofa. "It'll give me and Ben time to look for a solution, but for starters, we need these spell components to cast some obfuscation spells so no one curses me while we're working on saving Dru." I hold the list out to her. It's one that Ben hastily dictated to me this morning before we rushed over here, full of all kinds of bizarre things in large quantities. "Can you help us?"

Penny's eyes light up with pure joy. "It would be my pleasure!" She practically snatches the list from me. "If you guys need a familiar for Caliban, maybe I could fill in . . . ? It would be good practice for me. I know he's evil, but they're the best spellcasters. Think of how good that'd look on my résumé. And when a position from the society comes open—"

"It's okay," I say quickly. "I'm helping him since Dru doesn't need me right now."

Penny beams. "Of course. That makes sense. I'll be right back!" She races off with the list, thrilled to be of assistance. I feel oddly guilty. Penny has been such a good friend and is always willing to help, but the moment she mentioned being Ben's familiar, even temporarily, some ugly part of me reared up.

I didn't like it. One bit.

I'm not jealous. I'm not. Ben's a murderer and a warlock and a bad guy, and I shouldn't give a crap—but I do. For some reason, I don't like the thought of someone else spending those intimate moments with Ben. Maybe it's because my brain is still messed up over him and considers him mine even though it shouldn't.

My phone pings with an incoming text, and I bite back a groan. It could be Lisa or Nick or any number of terrible things. I'm starting to dread when my phone goes off, because it never brings good news. Instead of checking it, I look over at Ben. He's staring at some of the CBD posters on the walls, his brows knit together as if he's trying to grasp why someone would drink a CBD-infused sports drink. As I look over, a stream of blood drips down one of his fingers and onto the floor.

Something in my heart clenches. I move to his side. "Ben, you're bleeding."

He lifts his hand, adjusts the loose, soaked bandage there, and shrugs. "It'll heal."

I don't like how blasé he is about the wound. He's been quiet all morning, and I know he has to be worried about Dru. I remind myself that no matter how much affection I feel for her, she's ten times more important to Ben. She's his blood aunt, his sole living relative, and they've known each other for centuries. He has to be torn up inside. Aching for him, I reach out and touch his shoulder. "Come sit down in Penny's break room and let me look after you."

Ben turns and gives me a wary look, like a wounded animal. "I'm fine."

"You're not fine. Let me take care of you."

"Why?"

Because I want to. "Because you're making a mess."

He glances down at the floor, where he's leaving a tiny puddle of red. "I see."

I tug on his sleeve and he lets me pull him along. "We're going to the break room, Penny," I call out. "I'll watch the front for you."

"Sounds good," Penny chirps back, her voice muffled. "I'm

just going to pull some full-moon-gathered sphagnum moss from deep storage! Be back in a jiffy!"

I steer Ben toward the only seat in the tiny break room. There's a small fridge next to the sink, a wall is covered with Occupational Safety and Health Administration posters hastily tacked up, and the shelves are absolutely laden with boxes of CBD supplements and samples of all kinds in no particular order, shoved together and overflowing. It's a cluttery mess that makes my teeth ache at the sight of it, but I don't have time to get Penny all straightened out right now. I fix a stern glare on Ben. "Don't move from this spot."

After I clean up the blood spilled in the store with a few wads of Kleenex and paper towels, I grab a bottle of water from the mini-fridge and head into the bathroom of the small store, opening cabinets and looking for a first aid kit. Oh god, the small bathroom is worse than the break room, but I clench my jaw, determined to ignore it, even though my skin practically crawls with how disorganized this all is. I fetch the first aid kit quickly. When I step back into the break room, Ben gives me an odd look.

"What?" I ask.

"This girl." He nods at Penny. "How is she your friend with this disaster on her hands?" He gestures with his good hand at the clutter of boxes, and I can't help but notice there are several boxes in the corner stacked atop one another—crushing one another—with no labels on them. The sight makes my hands itch. "How do you let this go on under your nose without trying to go Marie Kondo on her?"

Is he teasing me? I give him my very best scowl, fighting back the urge to laugh. "I don't organize everyone, thank you."

He snorts. "Yes, you do."

I glare at him. "I should ask how a five-hundred-year-old warlock knows about Marie Kondo." I don't point out that *Tidying Up with Marie Kondo* is my favorite show or that the reveals always bring me to tears. Confessing that might be a little too on-brand, even for me.

"I'm not a mummy, Reggie. I'm just long-lived."

My lips twitch. "I actually haven't had a chance to help Penny straighten up in here. It's on my list of things to do after I finish the library." I take his hand in mine and gently pull the soaked bandages free. They're sticking to his wound in one spot and completely loose in another. "And I do like a tidy workspace."

"You'd like her show." When I give him a look, he lifts one shoulder in a shrug. "You know I don't have a lot of friends. I spend most nights either reading or watching TV."

Oddly enough, I know how that is. Other than Nick and now Penny, I tend to rub people the wrong way. Most don't get my obsessive need to control the space around me, my hunger for tidiness and organization. Most friendly working relationships sour quickly once people find me in their closets, sorting their shirts by color. It does make me sad for Ben, though. Five hundred years is an awful long time to be lonely. It's his own fault, though, but I don't point that out. Instead, I say, "You didn't bind your hand very well."

"We were in a hurry. It's fine."

It's not, but I suspect Ben has never had anyone beyond Aunt Dru to fuss over him, and it makes me sad all over again. Not just for Dru, but for him. "Do you think we'll be able to help Dru, Ben?"

"I do," he says firmly. "Simply because I won't allow myself to think of the alternative."

I nod. I know that feeling. I open a packet of antiseptic gel and dab it on his cut. "Did you have to slash your entire hand open? I get that it's dramatic, but now you've got this massive gash in the center of your palm. It seems more than a little ridiculous."

"The gods like a good show" is all he says.

I purse my lips, but I guess he knows more about that sort of thing than I do. He didn't think twice when it came to Dru, either. Just boom, hack the hand open to try to help her. I could say a lot of things about Ben, but he's definitely devoted. I dab the gel into the wound, wincing in sympathy when he tenses. Touching him like this, with my fingers on his, and me seated so close to him, reminds me of last night, when I was practically sprawled in his lap while we kissed. I'm just as much to blame for what happened between us as he is. I was the one that pushed into his space, and when it became obvious that he wasn't thinking about the card anymore, I encouraged more between us.

I wanted him to kiss me.

We were friends, and now I feel like I've ruined it for both of us. Ben's pretty much just confessed he doesn't have many friends, and I love playing cards with him and just hanging out together. All worries over Dru aside, I feel like I've lost something precious, and I'm full of regret. "Ben . . ."

"Mmm?" He's deliberately not looking at me.

"Do you think it's Livia? Remember, they fought at the restaurant. And Dru threw a sandwich at her mole."

"Not Livia," he says. "They've been friends since ancient Rome. I believe Livia helped Dru get rid of her first husband. They're contentious and fight like cats and dogs, but they're more sisters than friends. Livia wouldn't do it." He shakes his head. "I know Livia. She's harmless."

She didn't seem so harmless when Dru smacked her with a sandwich. "You're positive? It seems like an obvious sort of thing that it would be her."

"Livia wouldn't hide her spell," he explains. "She'd want Dru to know it was her."

Oh. I guess that makes sense in a weird sort of way. If it's not

Livia, then who? Dru's a harmless, sweet old lady. She's a Rose. No one ever wants to harm a Rose . . . except a Dorothy. I frown at that. The only Dorothy is Ben, but he adores his aunt. He would never.

And speaking of Ben . . . I lick my lips, deciding to broach the topic I truly want to talk about. "I'm sorry about last night. We really shouldn't have kissed, you know? And it's my fault for getting carried away and encouraging you." He probably thinks I'm no more than a baby, at twenty-five years old to his five hundred. I probably embarrassed him with my attention, and what guy wouldn't be interested in a girl throwing herself in his lap?

"It's fine." His voice is hard, and he still won't look at me. "We won't speak of it again."

"Great," I say brightly, wishing it felt as great. "And since we're going to be working together to help Dru, I feel like we should talk about . . . the whole parents thing."

Ben looks at me warily, like a cornered animal. His eyes are so dark and full of emotion. "I don't want to talk about it, Reggie."

"I just—" I swallow hard. "I'm going to take you at face value, Ben. You're my friend, and you say you won't hurt me, and I believe you. If you, ah, killed them, you must have had a reason." I pause, then add, "Please tell me you had a reason."

His throat works, and he stares at me with those dark, dark eyes. "I said I don't want to talk about it, Reggie."

"Right. Okay." I guess if I murdered my parents, I wouldn't feel chatty about it, either. I study his face as I pull out a fresh strip of bandages. Ben's expression is tight and unpleasant, but I could swear there's that wounded emotion in his eyes. Something in all this doesn't fit. Or maybe I'm just trying to make sense of a handsome, lonely five-hundred-year-old warlock that I had a crush on.

Still have a crush on, which really says something about me, doesn't it?

I wrap the bandages around his wound after packing it with a bit of absorbent padding. I give it a little pat once I'm done, pleased at the tidiness of my work. "I'll check it for you again later tonight."

Ben says nothing. His expression is unreadable, and he just flexes his hand and stares down at it.

I get to my feet, turning away. "Maybe I should see if Penny needs help."

"Reggie—"

I glance back at him. Our eyes meet. His jaw moves, as if he's considering words he wants to say to me, and I wait, hoping.

After a long, tense moment, he reaches into his pocket and pulls out a heavy silver cuff identical to the one on my left wrist. He says nothing, simply holds it out to me.

Right. Because I'm going to be temporarily filling in as his familiar—his battery—to help cure Dru.

I reach out for it and our fingers brush. Startled, I glance up at him, and the heat and intensity in his gaze steal the breath from my lungs. My eyes remain locked to his even as I put the bracelet on. It feels heavy on my wrist, but comfortable and warm, as if it belongs there.

Before I can say anything I might regret later—or kiss him until that hot yearning disappears from his eyes—I race out of the room to find Penny.

A SHORT TIME later, Penny has all the spell components bagged up for us and is chatting to fill the silence. Ben and I haven't spoken to each other since I put on his cuff, and the uncomfortable feeling in the room is palpable. "So," Penny says cheerily. "I'll charge this to Drusilla's account since it's for her, and we'll settle up some other time. I've also packed a few other common components that you might be low on, just in case, and threw in a reorder sheet in case you want to sign up for automatic re-ups every month." Penny beams at us. "Can I do anything else to help? You guys want some coffee? Or some CBD? There's a great one for helping you sleep at night—"

"You really are the best, Penny," I tell my friend, smiling. "I'm sorry this ruined our coffee date for this morning."

She waves a hand, her eyes shining with excitement. "This is way more thrilling than coffee! Please call me if you need anything. I will be there in two shakes of a lamb's tail. I promise!"

I have no doubt she would. Penny so desperately wants to be an apprentice that it practically oozes from her pores. Whoever gets her as a familiar is going to be the luckiest person alive, because she's going to give 110 percent at all times. I take the bag and glance over at Ben. "Shall we go?"

He shrugs, looking moody and unreadable. So basically typical Ben.

"Oh!" Penny cries out. "I almost forgot. Do you want Gwen's contact info?"

That makes Ben stiffen, his eyes going wide.

I turn back to Penny, frowning. "Who's Gwen?"

She blinks at me. "Another one of Dru's old familiars? She's a client. I figured you'd want to contact her prior familiars and see if they had any ideas as to who would be throwing out curses. Is that not part of your plan?"

"No," Ben says quickly. "We're not contacting Gwen."

I cast a frown at him over my shoulder. "Actually, I think that's a great idea. Can we have her info?"

"No," Ben says again.

I ignore him and put my hand out. Penny's eyes are wide, but she quickly prints out a sheet from the computer and hands it over to me.

"I'll call you," I promise her. "Thanks again."

"Tell me all the details!" Penny calls after us as we leave. "I want to hear everything!"

We get into the car, and Ben's jaw is clenched tight. I'm about to comment on it when my phone pings with a text again. Shit. This time, I suppose I can't avoid it. Juggling the bag of components in my arms, I pull out my phone and flick the screen. I've missed three calls, and a line of texts pops up on my screen.

NICK: Bad news, my friend.

NICK: Okay, I wanted you to call me, but since you must be busy, I'll just let you know over text. Today a bunch of new credit card statements came in with your name on them. I didn't open them, but you and I both know what that means.

NICK: I'll hold onto them for you. Call me when you get a chance.

Shit. Shit, shit, shit. I close my eyes, biting back a groan of pure frustration, and lean against the seat. Could today get any worse? Maybe I'm already cursed, and that's why I'm stuck in the car with my murderous crush while my boss is hexed into permanent sleep and my parents are running credit cards up in my name again.

"What is it?" Ben asks quietly.

I try to be casual about it, but tears threaten behind my eyes. Not just because it's a ton of work to get the cards closed and the charges disputed before my credit is ruined (well, more ruined), but because every time it happens, it feels like a fresh betrayal. To them, I'm just another person to grift from, not a daughter that should be loved and cherished. I love how they never remembered my birthday when I was growing up, but they apparently have my Social Security number memorized, because this happens all the fucking time. Swallowing hard, I compose myself. "My crappy parents opened a bunch of credit cards in my name. Again."

Ben grunts. After a moment, he looks over at me. "Want me to kill them?"

I slap his arm. "That's not funny!"

He smirks, just a little. "You already think I'm a heartless murderer. What's one more? Two more?"

I scowl. "I asked you if you killed your parents, and you said yes!"

Ben nods, slowly. "And I did. And I'd do it again."

"So what am I supposed to think when you joke about shit like that?"

He's quiet for a moment and then shrugs. "I suppose you either think the worst of me, or you think I have a bad sense of humor."

I shake my head, not wanting to answer that. Honestly. "Look. My parents are not good people. That doesn't mean I want them dead. I just want them to be . . ." I pause, thinking.

"Not them," he answers flatly. "Good luck with that." Ben pauses, staring at the steering wheel, and then glances over at me. "I know what it's like to want better for someone than what they want for themselves. But sometimes you have to accept that some people are just the way they are and there's no saving them."

"Is that what happened with your parents?" I ask.

"Does it matter?"

I guess it doesn't, since his solution was to murder them. I shake my head. "No. Forget I asked." I pull out the printout that

Penny gave me. "So should we talk to this Gwen person after you cast the obfuscation spell?"

"No."

"But Lisa didn't know anything. Maybe this Gwen person might?" I gesture at the paper. "And she's a few hours away—"

Ben looks mulish. "No, Reggie."

I turn to face him. "Why not? Is she dangerous? Horrible? Will she hurt us?"

He shakes his head, then rubs a hand down his face. "Gwen is just . . . We don't get along."

That's why he doesn't want to go visit her? "Ben Magnus, the list of people you get along with isn't exactly going to stun anyone with its length. Are you really going to be a stubborn ass about this when we should be taking every opportunity to find out what happened to your aunt and who's behind this? Maybe Gwen will have some insight into things you haven't thought about. Maybe—"

He groans. "Fine. You win, Reggie. We'll go visit Gwen."

25

BEN

The car ride out of the city and into the countryside is uncomfortable. There's a faint feeling of magic in the air, the weight of the obfuscation spell pressing onto us like a gentle blanket. Reggie's in the passenger seat, phone in hand and her feet up on the dashboard as she goes through another customer-service chat with the bank, typing furiously. She's been on the phone for the entire drive, her expression growing more drawn and tense as the details of the fraud her parents committed are made more evident. Six cards in her name, three of them linked to her account, and her savings has been drained away.

I try not to stare as her throat works and she sniffles. She doesn't want to cry in front of me, and even though I ache to comfort her, I focus on driving. I know how she feels, though. That soul-deep betrayal. That hurt that goes far, far deeper than anything monetary. It's the realization that how you feel doesn't matter to the people that should love you most. That they can't—won't—change, no matter how much it hurts you.

Yeah, I know just how that fucking feels, and four hundred

years isn't enough to dull the ache. But vomiting out my sad past will feel too convenient right now when Reggie's got enough shit on her plate.

"How are you feeling?" I ask once she puts her phone down.

"Fine." Her voice is tight.

I pull a sports drink out of one of the cup holders. "You should drink this. Get some electrolytes back into you. The obfuscation spell is going to be a slow drain on your energy. And you might want to eat something. A pack of those nuts, or some crackers—"

"I'm fine, Ben." Reggie hugs her knees to her chest and stares moodily out the window. "Are we almost there?"

"Almost." I don't tell her that we've been in Gwen's vicinity for fifteen minutes and that I've been driving in circles around the small town so Reggie could finish her business with the bank. "She knows we're coming? You texted her?"

Reggie nods. "She said that we're welcome."

I'm not sure if that'll be the case, since she and I weren't the most comfortable with each other. Or rather, I was never comfortable with her after a while. I swallow hard. This is going to be more awkward than I could have imagined. I can't believe I'm driving the woman I'm in love with to my former lover's farm.

But like Reggie said, what other options do we have? We need to find out what's going on with Aunt Dru. She can't sleep forever. She'll wither away and starve to death in a *sopor* spell. Just because it makes you sleep, it doesn't stop the rest of the body's needs. If Gwen doesn't prove useful—and something tells me she won't—I'll have to contact some of the warlocks I know, feel around for information. I won't give up. Even if I have to bribe every warlock on the Eastern Seaboard to help me, I'll find a way to fix this for Aunt Dru, because I know she'd do the same for me.

We turn down a country road, and Reggie perks up. She peers out the window. "Is this a farm?"

"No, lots of corporate buildings have gravel roads leading up to them."

She looks over at me, and a snort-giggle escapes her. "You asshole."

I smile a bit at that. "I should probably tell you a bit about Gwen. She's very much the crunchy-vegan type and has been for the last two hundred years. She's going to give you this whole Earth Mother song and dance, but she'd also happily sacrifice one of her beloved chickens for a spell, so don't let it fool you."

"Yikes."

"She's also, ah . . ." I try to think of the most delicate way to put it. "A very specialized sort of witch."

Reggie looks over at me, her beautiful dark eyes full of questions. "How so?"

I shrug, trying not to focus too hard on her or else I'll moon like a schoolboy rejected by his crush. I keep my gaze on the road as we pass lines of trees and pastures with goats. "So back in ancient Rome, a lot of witches and warlocks specialized in a particular kind of magic. Back then, it was common to set up a business where you cast spells for those that needed it. So you had the local haruspex, who would sacrifice an animal and read what the entrails told you."

"Ew!"

I flash a grin over at her. "The ancestors were big on entrails. It's a practice that's fallen out of popularity, thank goodness." Well, mostly. Aunt Dru still likes to do it every now and then, but she's avoided it lately since Reggie is so new. "And then you have your augurs, who specialized in interpreting the patterns and flights of birds. They were also government officials, by the way.

Magic was very respected in Rome." I run my hand over the steering wheel as I pull up to the charming white farmhouse with the wraparound porch. "You have your oracles, too, and then you have people like Gwen."

"And what does Gwen specialize in?" Reggie asks innocently.

I bite back a sigh. "Sex magic."

REGGIE

Sex . . . magic.

Ben says it like it's actually a thing. Like that's a job that people have. *Here's Bob, who watches birds migrate, and here's Jimmy, who shoves his hands into cow intestines and reads your future. And then there's Gwen, who . . . I don't know, orgasms to get her magic motoring.*

It's just downright bizarre.

Ben parks the car in front of the farmhouse—which looks like something out of a *Better Homes and Gardens* magazine. There are flowers everywhere, neatly trimmed hedges, and an arching, vine-covered trellis over the sidewalk. Cute little garden-gnome statues peek out of the flower beds, the porch has a cozy swing on it, and chimes tinkle somewhere nearby. This does not look like the home of a sex witch, not even slightly.

The screen door opens and a woman steps out. "Well, my goodness. Look at you, Ben Magnus. As sexy as the day I last saw you."

Ben flushes beet red. I stiffen, glancing over at him, because apparently she finds Ben sexy, and for some reason, it gets me hot under the collar. Like, that's not how you greet an old buddy. That's how you greet a former fuck buddy.

To my dismay, I realize Gwen is totally a Blanche in every sense of the word. Damn it.

Gwen steps down the front porch, holding her arms out. "And you must be Reggie. Look at how young you are. Gracious! You've even got freckles. Such a little baby. My goodness, I can't remember the last time I was that young." She beams at me, clearly heading in for a bear hug.

I take it awkwardly, sending Ben a plea for help with my eyes, because what else can I do? We need Gwen's assistance.

She immediately moves over to Ben and grabs him in a hug, but she lingers over him, her arms moving up and down his back. Ben is clearly uncomfortable, not hugging her back, and it'd be funny if I wasn't so damn mixed up over him myself.

It'd be even funnier if Gwen wasn't so stinking gorgeous.

Ben was right when he said she'd have an Earth Mother vibe. She's dressed in a long, flowing sundress of pale pink-and-white ombré, and she has a crown of freshly picked flowers in her long, wavy blond hair. She wears no bra under the spaghetti straps of her dress, and her ample breasts shiver and shake with every movement. I'm not wearing a bra, either, but the only time my microscopic tits shook like that was probably in an earthquake. I resist the urge to cross my arms over my chest.

Gwen finally lets Ben go, and then she beams at the two of us. "Why don't you two come inside? We'll have some lemonade and get acquainted."

"We're actually in a bit of a hurry—" I begin.

Gwen heads inside, all swaying, lush hips and bare feet. When she lifts her skirt to go up the steps, I see pretty, slinky anklets that chime and clang on her ankles. I hate that she's so perfect, and I shouldn't. But I can't stop thinking about her long, extremely familiar hug with Ben. I glance over at him as we follow her inside, and he still looks incredibly uncomfortable.

I move over to his side and touch his arm. "Hey, sexy Ben Magnus, is there something I should know about you and our friend here?"

He leans over slightly toward me as we go up the stairs. "It's been over for almost two hundred years."

Well, that's not a fucking answer. I swallow back my outrage and remind myself that I was the one that pushed to visit Gwen. Ben didn't want to, and now I'm starting to see why.

The inside of the farmhouse is just as cute and Martha Stewart as the outside. There's no sex dungeon, no orgy to step over, nothing weird at all. I relax a bit at that. Maybe Gwen's turned to green magic instead of sex magic in the last two hundred years or so. "Your house is lovely," I offer, determined not to be a jealous turd when she's going to help us out. "It feels so calm and peaceful."

"Oh, thank you!" Gwen beams at us, leading us to the large white-painted wooden table with benches in the center of her kitchen. Fresh flowers are in a vase here, too, and everything smells like honeysuckle and summer. I sit on one bench, and to my surprise, Ben immediately slides in right next to me. Gwen continues brightly. "Farming's a bit of a hobby of mine. More than a hobby now, since witchcraft can't exactly pay the bills. I find it soothing, though. If you like, later I can show you my bees? I'm very proud of my hives."

"That sounds awesome, actually," I say. Ben reaches over and touches my leg under the table, a silent warning. Okay, no bees, then. "But we are in a hurry."

"Of course, of course." Gwen pours three lemonades as Ben quickly fills her in on the situation. She says nothing, just nodding as he goes into detail, and when he's done, she sits down and doles out the drinks. I pick up my lemonade and take a sip, since I was being petty and didn't drink my sports drink earlier. I'm parched. As I drink, Gwen's gaze drops to the cuffs on both of my wrists. "Oh, double penetration. Nice."

I immediately spray lemonade all over the table, coughing.

Gwen just chuckles and gets up, retrieving a towel. She mops up the table and gives me a wistful look. "Gosh, it's been forever since I was as young and innocent as you. It's so charming." She looks over at Ben. "They get younger every year, don't they?" Before he can answer, she leans over, her chin on her hand, and flutters her lashes. "And I swear, you get handsomer every year, Ben. Though it's been a while since I've seen you with clothes on."

"Gwen," Ben says sharply. "Enough. All right? You're making Reggie uncomfortable."

Gwen just chuckles, leaning back and stretching, no doubt a deliberate move to show off her amazing cleavage. "I'm just having a little fun. I mean, what's the point in living for hundreds of years if you can't enjoy yourself? And you do know I love to enjoy myself," she purrs at Ben.

Now I'm the one that's flushing. "Can we just talk about Dru, please?"

"You don't want relationship advice?"

"No." Ben's voice is flat and cold. "When I want help coordinating an orgy, I'll reach out to you. Otherwise, we just want to ask you about Aunt Dru. We're trying to determine who cursed her."

Gwen thinks for a moment, the comment about orgies apparently not offensive in the slightest. "You tried scrying? Yes, of course you did. It must be blocked." She taps a finger on her chin, considering. "I can attempt a commune with Venus, but it'll require a few orgasms, and I'm guessing neither of you wants to assist me with that."

I clutch at Ben's leg, because he seems like he's ready to snap again. "Dru mentioned all her familiars have been cursed," I blurt out. "Can you tell us more about that? Were you ever cursed?"

"Me? Oh yes." Gwen shrugs. "It was a very, very long time ago, though. Luckily, the tablet wasn't hidden very well, so I found it and destroyed it. I'm guessing that whoever is responsible has probably gotten better at hiding these sorts of things."

"Who was it?"

Gwen tosses her hair. "I don't know. It was a rather nasty sort of curse, too. Made me repulsed by tongues." She shivers. "I was glad to get rid of it. It positively put a pall on my casting, as you can imagine."

"Where was the tablet hidden, then?" Ben seems frustrated with Gwen and her unhelpful answers.

"I don't remember. Some old bank that burned down in the fifties. Or was it the twenties, during the stock-market crash?" She pauses, thinking, then shrugs. "Doesn't matter. It's long gone now." She reaches across the table and brushes her hand over Ben's large one. "You could help me cast a memory spell. Help me recall."

She flutters her lashes at him in an extremely obvious way that makes me, well, steamed. We're trying to find who cursed her old mentor, and she's hitting on my temporary boss? What the fuck? I should have listened to Ben when he said he didn't want to visit her. But then I wouldn't have found out that they were lovers, and that's a tidbit I feel I should be aware of.

Not that I'm going to be his lover. Just . . . because.

Ben carefully extracts his hand from Gwen's clinging grasp. "You know I'm not a fan of the type of magic you cast, Gwen."

She tsks, undeterred. "Such a traditionalist." Her smile is undaunted as she looks over at me. "No, I can't really help you with that particular curse situation. I actually thought both of you were coming to take a peek at Dru's old hiding place."

"Hiding place for what?" I ask.

Gwen gives me a patronizing look. "Aren't you precious. Her hiding spot for her old curse tablets, of course. She used to hide them here on my property after I left her service. You might get an idea for who cursed her by seeing who she cursed in the past, perhaps? It's clear someone has a vendetta against her."

That sounds like an excellent lead, and my heart thumps with hope. "Wonderful. Where is it?"

Gwen rises to her feet, every inch the sultry goddess. "An old dry well in one of the back pastures. I'll show you."

BEN

I want to choke Gwen. Not in a murderous sort of way. Just in a why-won't-you-shut-the-hell-up sort of way. She natters on to Reggie as she leads us out into her fields, talking about a fertility ceremony she's going to be holding tonight, and inquiring about Reggie's "moon cycles." Reggie answers her politely enough, but I can tell she's more than ready to leave Gwen's company.

"Well, here's the well." Gwen giggles at her own joke and tosses her hair. "Now, I have to get ready for my party tonight. You two are welcome to join our drawing-down-the-moon ceremony. The more the merrier, I always say—"

"No," I butt in before Reggie can answer.

"But—" Gwen begins.

"No," I say again. And just to emphasize the situation, I pick up Reggie's hand and indicate her wrist. "See this? You know what it means. She's working for me, and you know I don't like to share."

Gwen affects a pout. "Fine, fine." She gives Reggie an interested look, me a lascivious one, and then heads back toward her house. "Have fun playing with the well. I need to make my canapés."

Reggie gently draws her hand out of my grasp as Gwen leaves, and sidles toward me. "Do I want to know what a drawing-down-the-moon ceremony is?"

I lean in toward Reggie, resisting the urge to bury my face in her soft brown hair. "Let's just say it involves fertility and a lot of fluids."

"Ah." She wrinkles her freckled nose. "I should have guessed that one." Taking a step away from me, she approaches the well. "So Dru hid her tablets here? Why a well?"

I follow after Reggie as she circles the thing. As wells go, it's a fairly large one, with an old rock lip that reaches my waist, and a diameter of about ten feet. The size of it makes me wonder if there was some sort of machinery attached to it long ago, but now the lip is old and weathered, and vines grow over the sides. There's an old wooden pulley on one side with a bucket and rope, and they look as old as the rest of it. As I watch, Reggie moves to the well and pulls the wooden lid off it, pushing it over to one side and peering over the edge.

"Wells were a traditional hiding spot of curse tablets, as I've told you before," I say, trying not to stare as Reggie leans over the well and her perfect ass goes up in the air. "You're not a very good listener, are you?"

"I tune out when you lecture me, if that's what you're asking." She braces her hands on the rock lip and stares into the darkness.

I clear my throat. "I don't lecture. I'm just trying to help you understand. As for why a well, no one ever climbed down a well, so it was a good spot to easily hide a tablet and have it disappear for good."

Reggie leans over the edge. "Hellooooo down there. Are

there any tablets? Hello? Tablets?" She looks over at me, that impish smirk wreathing her face. "No answer." She widens her eyes as her gaze sweeps the old well. "The entire thing looks rather ominous, doesn't it?"

"You wouldn't want to hide a tablet someplace clean, obvious, and easily accessible."

"Fair point." Reggie leans over and pulls off one of her shoes. "At least it doesn't look that deep."

I frown as she plucks off the other shoe, too. "What are you doing?"

"I'm going into the well," she tells me, then goes over to the bucket and the rope pulley, giving it a tug. The wood groans, but she seems satisfied with it. "Think it'll hold?"

Is she insane? She's insane. "You're not going into a well."

"Yes, I am."

"No, you are not, Reggie. I forbid it."

"Well," she says brightly, looking over at me. "It's a good thing you're not my boss. Besides, if one of those tablets holds the information we need, we have to get to them. I'm not a huge fan of Gwen, but she's right—if Dru cursed someone and they're getting revenge, we might find the answer we need down there. How else do you propose we retrieve the tablets?"

"No." Just the thought of Reggie—fragile, headstrong Reggie—lowering herself into the bottom of a well fills me with all kinds of terror. "People threw things down these kinds of wells because they didn't want them to ever be found again, Reggie. You are not going down there."

She ignores me, untying the rope from the bucket and looping it around her waist. "It can't be that deep. Maybe fifty feet? When I called out, I could hear my echo bounce off something. I think." She wrinkles her nose and looks up at me. "Actually I don't know all that much about wells. But it doesn't seem that deep."

She's going to give me gray hair.

I reach for the rope, determined to pull it away from her. Instead, she pats me on the arm. "You're going to need to lower me slowly, Ben."

"You're not going down, Reggie."

"Yes, I am. We're going to save your aunt, and this is the first step toward it."

She's not listening. "It's dangerous."

But Reggie only beams up at me and slings one leg over the lip of the well. "Then it's a good thing you're a warlock with magic potions, or we'd really be fucked, huh?"

"Reggie." I grab her shoulders before she can leap over the edge. "At least let me go down there."

"Ben," she says, ever so reasonable as she gazes up at me. Her eyes are clear and unafraid. "You're bigger than me, so you're going to have to pull me up. And besides, you dramatically sliced your hand to ribbons earlier, remember?"

I hate that she's right about those things. "I don't like this."

"I don't, either, but it needs to get done." She shrugs, smiling. "But if you don't want to watch, go back to the house and let Gwen bounce her boobs in front of your face a little longer. Now, lower me in?"

REGGIE

Climbing down into a really old well is not high on the list of smart things I could do. I know that, but we're low on options. What are we supposed to do—make an appointment with well diggers and see if they can dig up some tablets that might or might not be here and that might or might not be helpful? This is the only answer I have, so down the well I go.

At least the well is wide, so claustrophobia isn't an issue. Instead, it's just dark and damp and terrifying. I close my eyes, trying to calm myself, as Ben lowers me. It's deeper than I thought it would be, and with every grunt he makes as he lowers me in, I start to have regrets. Dangling in midair in an old well? Pretty typical Regina Johnson move. It's just like me to be pigheaded and stubborn to the point of idiocy. Nick could tell a dozen stories off the top of his head.

I bite back a sigh. Probably should have thought this through before I was halfway down the well. Too late now.

After what seems like forever, my feet touch something wet and cold. I squeal in surprise, and the rope jerks. "Reggie?" Ben sounds frantic. "What is it?"

"It's not a dry well," I call back up. "There's water down here!"

"Are you all right? I'm pulling you back up—"

"I'm okay," I yell up at him. "Don't pull me up! I'm down here, might as well see what we have."

"Has anyone ever told you that you're a stubborn ass?" Ben calls back down.

"Nearly everyone!"

"Good!"

I can't help but smile a little at that. Ben sounds downright protective, which makes me feel . . . things. Things I absolutely do not want to feel, given the situation. I'm just working for him to help out Dru. That's all. But his cuff feels heavy and good on my wrist, and I can't help but think about how Gwen blatantly hit on him and how it made me feel.

I didn't like it. Not one bit. And if I'm determined not to get involved with Ben Magnus, I shouldn't care. Let him fuck Gwen (again). Let him help her with her moon ceremony and all the damn fluids. I'm sure they'd be very happy together and make cute little immortal warlock babies. It's just, the thought of that makes me grit my teeth.

I finally meet a guy that's everything I want, and he's a centuries-old evil warlock. Except the evil part doesn't fit so well. He looked at me earlier in the car with such sympathy—like he knew what it was like to have parents that were absolute dickbags. There's more to that story. I trust Ben, even though the world keeps giving me reasons not to trust him. But here I am, dangling down a well in a witch's field, my fate solely in Ben's hands, and the biggest thing I'm worried about is if there are snakes down here.

There had better not be snakes down here, damn it.

Ben lowers me a little more, and then my feet hit bottom. "It's not very deep," I call back. "Just a foot or two." I stand upright and wriggle my toes in the mud, trying to focus on the task at hand

and not Gwen's beautiful hair and her big glorious braless boobs. I mean, if my boobs looked that good, I'd probably show them off, too. I can't hate her for being sexy.

I decide I can hate her for hitting on Ben, though.

A shadow moves above—probably Ben, trying to see me down here. "Any tablets?"

"Give me a moment to look around."

"I can't see you down there, Reggie." There's a worried tone in his voice. "Be careful."

For a murderous warlock, he sure is a mother hen. It's completely dark down here, which is unnerving, but the circle of light up above is comforting. If I stand still, I don't hear anything at all, which is good. No slithering or well-monster noises or whatever else might be down here. I'm pretty sure it's just me. I shuffle my feet in the muck, feeling around with my toes, but all it feels like is more mud. There are no tablets, no rock, no anything. "Would they be hidden?" I call back up to Ben. "In addition to being down a well?"

"It's possible?" he yells back. "This is my aunt we're talking about."

Excellent point. Dru's mind is twisty at best. She might look like a Rose on the outside, but she's definitely got a Sophia soul. I touch the wall of the well, and it's cold and slick. Stone? Brick? Who the hell knows. I feel around, looking for gaps in the rock. To my surprise, I find one about waist high. Excited, I kneel in the water and probe the crack with my fingers. It's about the size of a tablet, now that I think about it, if the tablet was on its side. "I think I found something!"

"What is it?"

"I don't know yet!" My voice echoes loudly at the bottom of the well, making me wince, and I push my fingers in a little farther. I don't feel anything yet, but I also can't quite reach far enough. My wrist keeps getting in the way. I think for a moment, then pull my hand out, grease my wrist up with the mud from the bottom of the well, and then try the secret chamber again. I still can't reach quite far enough, so I push harder, until it feels as if my bones are going to crack. Something pops, and then my hand pushes through to the other side—

To encounter nothing at all. It's just a crack in the rock that I've jammed my hand into.

With a frustrated sigh, I try to pull my hand back out . . . and I can't.

Frantic, I jerk on my wrist. It's like I'm held fast now, and no matter how much I twist and turn and writhe, I can't get my wrist free. The more I struggle, the more it hurts, and it feels like my wrist is swelling after minutes of terrified jerking on it. I'm . . . stuck.

I'm stuck, and there's not even a curse tablet in this hole. It's just a hole.

"Reggie?" Ben calls out above. "I hear splashing. What's going on?"

"Um. Small problem?" I give my hand another yank, and my eyes nearly cross at the pain that shoots up my arm. "I think I'm stuck."

"What do you mean, you're stuck?"

"I mean I'm fucking stuck!"

"Explain to me how you get stuck at the bottom of a well?" He's shouting. I can tell he's shouting. He's mad.

"I might have shoved my hand into a spot that it didn't fit? And now I can't get it back out."

Silence. Then "I'm coming down after you."

"Well, I'd love to come up to you," I bellow, "but I can't!"

Honestly, he acts like this is my fault.

REGGIE

I continue to jerk on my hand, but it's stuck fast. No matter how I twist and turn, my wrist isn't coming free. It just shoots with pain the more I try, to the point that I give up and crouch in the waist-high water, panting in frustration.

I can't stay here forever, so I need to think.

Maybe Ben could toss down a crowbar. Or something to grease my hand, maybe, since the mud isn't doing it any longer. "Hey, Ben?" I call up to the shadows that are moving around frantically at the top of the well. "You got any butter on you? Or lube?"

"Why the fuck would I carry those with me?"

"I don't know! You're the warlock that plays with entrails and candles. Maybe you've got a butter fetish." I give my hand another half-hearted yank. "Maybe go and run down Gwen and see if she has some lube? She's definitely the type that would have lube. Like, gallons of it."

"Reggie," Ben calls out from above. "I am about to lose my shit, so do me a favor and stop talking."

I scowl up at him. Is it me, or does his shadow look closer? I glare at the blinding circle of light and tug on my hand again, then look around at the bottom of the well, searching. I can't see anything—not only is the sunlight above rather blinding, but I'm pretty sure there's nothing down here except . . . well, me.

This is my new home, apparently. Maybe I'll be here for the rest of my days, just like Gollum, screaming about my precious and rocking some seriously lank hair. With a frustrated whimper, I tug on my hand again. And again.

I'm so busy tugging that I don't notice Ben until he swears directly above and then crashes into the water next to me. I bite back a small scream of terror and surprise as he sits up, wiping muddy water from his face. There's a necklace under his long tunic shirt that's glowing, providing just enough light for me to see the murderous expression on his face.

"What the fuck, Ben! You can't come down here! Who's going to pull me up?"

He sits in the water, his black hair plastered to his face, and scowls at me. "No one, since you've gotten stuck somehow."

I splash at him, furious. "I'm trying to find the tablets, idiot. Now we're both stuck down here! Why didn't you go get Gwen?"

"Why'd you shove your hand someplace it doesn't belong?" he retorts, glaring at me. "Why'd you insist on jumping down here? Are you trying to get killed, Reggie?"

"Of course not."

"You don't listen," he rages as he gets to his feet, sopping wet. Between the shadows and the water dripping down him, it only emphasizes how big he is as I crouch in the water nearby. With the light under his chin, Ben should look ghoulish and menacing, but his eyes are blazing with anger over my safety, and I find that . . .

Hot.

Sexy.

"When are you going to learn that you're not always right?"

he snarls at me as he moves to my side and studies the crack that I've shoved my hand into. Now that there's a bit of light on the situation, I can see where I actually pushed my hand in—part of the crack is bigger at the top, and Ben quickly guides my hand up to the larger part of the gap, and then I'm free. "When are you going to ever *listen*, Reggie?"

"I listen," I hiss back at him, rubbing my aching wrist. "What makes you think I don't listen?"

"Because I tell you things that are for your own good, and you just charge ahead and do them anyhow," he bellows in my face. "You're going to get killed!"

"It's a well, not a pool of lava, Ben Magnus. Don't be so damn dramatic."

His nostrils flare dangerously as he glares at me. Don't stare at his mouth, Reggie. Don't stare at his kissable pink mouth, Reggie. Don't—

I glance at his mouth. Shit. It is very kissable and full, and the wet hair slicking his face is only adding to how it stands out against his pale skin. Why am I all turned on right now? We're both at the bottom of a well on a sex witch's property, and Ben is raging at me for no reason at all.

"I was trying to help your aunt," I point out. "And speaking of pigheaded moves, why didn't you go and get Gwen like I told you to?"

Ben's eyes flare with anger. He leans into my face, trying to intimidate me. "Because we have to stay together. The obfuscation spell would follow me and leave you open if I went to get her."

"It would only take five minutes," I yell back at him, standing taller as he gets in my face. I'm not afraid of him. I'm horny. He's so big and beautiful and protective. God, I love that he's so protective. He cares about what happens to me. He doesn't want to lose me. That's as heady and appealing as his sexy exterior.

"Five minutes could be the difference between life and death, Reggie," he snarls, looming over me. "And I'm not going to fucking lose you like I'm losing Aunt Dru—"

I grab his face between my hands and kiss him.

Ben stiffens against me for a moment, taken by surprise. I kiss him again so he doesn't mistake what I want. My blood is singing in my veins, and it doesn't matter that we're down a well, or that we're supposed to be enemies, or that I'm working as his familiar as we try to help his aunt. All I know is that after the kiss we had last night, I want more from him.

I want to kiss him all over. I want to devour him whole. I want to see every inch of his pale skin and watch his eyes widen with arousal when I touch him.

I open my mouth to tell him these things, but then Ben springs into action. With a groan, he drags me against him and turns us. My back hits the stone wall of the well, and then I'm pinned between his big body and the well and Ben kisses me back. His mouth is hot and hard and questing against my own, his tongue plunging into my mouth in a silent claim.

I moan, hiking one leg up around his hips as he takes over the kiss, his mouth slanting over mine. Ben kisses like a demon, his mouth and tongue frantic against mine. His hand skates up and down my side as I cling to him, and then he palms one of my small breasts. I cry out against his mouth, arching against his hand.

"Mine," he growls into my ear like some sort of animal, and it makes me instantly wet.

His urgent mouth kisses down my jaw as I claw at his back, my fingers tearing at his soaked clothing. He pinches my nipple, sending a needy whimper through me, and then his hand slides lower, to between my thighs. My jeans are heavy and thick with water, and I can't feel him the way I want to. Frustrated, I capture his mouth in another rough kiss even as I reach between us and undo the snap on my jeans.

Ben's big, warm hand immediately slides inside.

"Mine," he whispers again, the word against my skin. His thick fingers move down into my panties. "You headstrong, insane, gorgeous creature."

I find his mouth again, hungry for more, and when his fingers slide through the cleft of my pussy and find my clit, I cry out against his mouth. He starts to rub me in just the perfect way, small, light circles around that sensitive spot, completely at odds with the wild kissing we've been doing. I rock against his hand, desperate. "Ben," I pant. "Oh god, Ben. Please. More."

"You want to come on my hand?" he purrs, all dark and sexy and gorgeous. "You want me to make you feel good, Reggie?"

Do I ever. I ride his grip, lost in pleasure as his mouth moves over my neck, kissing and licking everywhere, nipping at my skin as he works my clit like an absolute maestro, his touch going from gentle and slow to faster and more urgent along with my need. When I come, it's explosive. I shudder against his hand, rocking against his grasp as he pleasures me and whispers dark things against my skin.

When I finally come down, I let out one last whimper as he kisses my lips, his movements gentle now. "Reggie," he murmurs. "Headstrong, wild Reggie. You're going to make me lose my mind."

I slide my arms around his neck and snuggle against him as he presses a kiss to my cheek, his nose brushing against my skin. His hand is still firmly entrenched in my panties, and he absently caresses my skin, as if he doesn't want to let me go. Like Gollum with his precious, I think, and chuckle to myself.

"What was all that for?" he asks, voice soft and husky. "You thought you were going to die down here and decided to have one last hurrah with a murdering warlock?"

I smack his shoulder. "Don't kill my post-orgasm buzz." He rubs his nose against mine, still lost in a haze of need, and I nuzzle up against him, kissing that sinful lower lip of his. "I don't know. I just . . . Maybe I still like you despite everything. Maybe I wanted to touch you." I smooth a hand down the front of his wet chest. "Maybe I didn't like the way Gwen was looking at you, and it made me want to claim you."

He stiffens a little and pulls back to look at me. "You didn't like the way Gwen was looking at me?"

"No," I say stubbornly. "All that calling me a child while she was hitting on you? I wanted to claw her eyes out. Still do."

Ben groans, and then he's kissing me frantically again. "You're jealous."

I wriggle against him, because his hand is skimming spots a little too sensitive now. "So? What's wrong with jealous?"

"No one's ever jealous over me." The thought seems to turn him on like crazy. His hands are all over me again, his hips driving the bulge in his pants between my thighs to press against my pussy and . . . damn. Ben Magnus is packing some intense heat under all that dark, moody clothing.

He loves my jealousy. Loves that I'm possessive of him. And even though this is absolutely the worst time and place, I can't seem to stop touching him. I slip my feet to the muddy ground and slide out from under him, then press my hands to his chest, backing him against the wall. Ben watches me as I run my hands over his damp sweater, my thumbs moving over his nipples. His eyes are like hot coals, and I love the intensity on his face.

I grab the front of his jeans and undo the buttons there, then shove my hand into the space I've made, searching for his cock. He made me feel good, and I want to do the same for him.

The hard, cloth-covered bulge I uncover is even more impressive under my hand than it felt through his jeans. I saw a lot of him in the crystal ball, but like in my rearview mirrors, objects are apparently larger than they appear. "Good lord, you've got quite the equipment," I whisper, even as I drag my palm down the length of him. "So big. I should have known that you'd be size appropriate, but no wonder Gwen's chasing you."

"Reggie," he pants, tilting his head back against the rock, his gaze locked on me.

"I don't want you to start with that whole white-knight 'you don't have to touch me' thing," I tell him as I rub up and down his serious length. "I want to do it."

"Not gonna say anything like that." His hips twitch, as if he wants to jerk up against my pressing hand.

For some reason, that makes me smile. No, my Ben isn't a white knight at all, is he? He's someone with dark secrets, but I feel like I know him. I trust him. He might be older than I am, with a different story, but we're the same people inside—lonely and looking for that right person.

And with him, I never feel lonely anymore. I feel seen. I feel cherished. Important.

So I lean forward, getting in his face as much as I can as I stroke his cock through the wet fabric. I put a hand behind his neck and pull him down for a kiss, our tongues touching as I curl my hand around his shaft and pump.

We're still kissing when he comes in my hand a brief time later, and I love the way he sags against me, the groan of my name on his lips as the heat of his release gets all over both of us. He kisses me again, but this time our kisses are soft and sweet, as if all the edge has been taken off. I love when he puts his arms around me and holds me tight, cuddling me against his chest as if he never wants to let me go.

"That was lovely," I whisper. "But I'm afraid we're still down a well."

"Gwen will show up when we don't leave," he points out, his hand moving up and down my back in sensual strokes. "I'm parked directly in front of her house."

"And no tablets, either," I say mournfully. I'm trying to be sad and frustrated, but really, I'm rather distracted. Ben feels good against me, and my body's throbbing with the best orgasm it's had ever since I bought a bullet vibe. I haven't used it since I moved in with Nick, because I didn't want to get caught working myself with a toy, but now I can't help but wonder if Ben might be interested in watching that.

"This was a long shot anyhow," Ben says. "Which I tried to tell you. And you didn't listen."

"I'm not a very good listener," I agree. "That's something you're just going to have to get used to." I've always been the one that had to be responsible, to take charge of things. Even when I lived with my parents, I was the one that paid the bills, the one that made sure the rent was taken care of, that the water wouldn't get turned off. I was the one that cleaned up the apartment and took out the garbage. It's made me controlling and stubborn, sure, but I also like to think it's made me strong. "Everyone has flaws. So mine is tidying and taking charge. So what." I poke him in the gut. "I could name a few of yours."

"I have no flaws," he says in a lofty voice.

I snort at that.

His arms tighten around me. "Reggie . . . I . . ." He pauses, and when I look up at him, there are a million things in his gaze, as if he wants to tell me something important. "I . . ."

"Are both of you down there?" calls out a sweet voice from above. Gwen. "My goodness! Don't you know that's dangerous?"

Ben glances up at the light, his hands tightening on me. Whatever he wanted to say is gone, I imagine. Thwarted by Gwen, though I'm not super upset to see her here, since we need a rescue. I just wish she'd have waited maybe five more minutes so Ben would spit out whatever it was he was going to say.

I grimace. "You talk to her," I whisper to Ben. "I still want to claw her eyes out."

He chuckles, still holding me close. "We had a mishap," he calls up. "I don't suppose you have a really long ladder?"

"You're lucky I know the local fire department," Gwen calls down. "Give me time to make a few calls. You just stay right there."

Like we're going to go anywhere? But Ben's thumb slides under my wet shirt and rubs against my bare side, and I think, maybe, that I don't mind being down here a little longer.

29

BEN

A few hours later, Reggie and I check into a hotel. It's dark, and we've made no progress on helping Aunt Dru, and yet . . . I find that I'm not full of despair. I'm actually in a good mood.

For one, I'm not in this alone. Reggie's right by my side, just as determined to help Aunt Dru as I am. Gwen has promised additional help if we need her, as well. Lisa is at my aunt's side and reports no changes one way or another. I've got people I can call, with Willem at the top of that list, for ideas and suggestions.

In the bathroom of the hotel room, Reggie sings in the shower, her voice charmingly off-key. I sit on a chair near the bed, my clothes still dripping wet, a towel underneath me. I let Reggie have the shower first, because it's the polite thing to do. And because I wanted time to think.

What happened in the well was a little insane. I'm still not entirely sure why I climbed down after Reggie instead of calling the local fire department. Maybe it was the fact that she was down there alone and scared that ate at me. Maybe I was frustrated with her hot-and-cold mentality after last night. We'd kissed passionately, she'd decided that I was too scary for her, and then this morning Dru was cursed, and now it's almost midnight and Reggie and I kissed and made each other come at the bottom of a well.

If she tells me that she wants to be just friends again after that, I think I'm going to lose my mind. I know there are a million reasons not to touch her, but Aunt Dru's curse has taught me that if you care about someone, you need to say something or you might lose them. And when Reggie grabbed me and kissed me—and then confessed she was jealous of Gwen—it made me realize how much I didn't want to let her go. I don't care if she's younger. I don't care if she's my aunt's familiar. We'll figure out a way to make it work.

I feel like Reggie's the only person other than Aunt Dru who has ever bothered to see the real me. Maybe she doesn't know all my secrets, but Reggie knows that I was responsible for my parents' deaths, and she kissed me anyhow. She worked me with her hand and made me come, all the while gazing up at me, our eyes locked.

It was the most erotic experience I've had in five hundred years, and it was all because Reggie was right there with me, the look in her eyes confident and full of affection, as if to say that she had me just as much as I had her. I didn't realize I needed that until that moment.

The shower shuts off and so do my thoughts. I should be reaching out to contacts, working my network of warlocks and Aunt Dru's acquaintances to see if anyone knows anything. Warlocks love to gossip as much as witches do, and it's entirely possible that someone's blabbed about what they've done to my aunt.

But tonight . . . tonight I'm just tired, and I want to see where this thing is going with Reggie, or if we're at an impasse again.

A few moments later, Reggie comes out of the bathroom with wet hair falling around her shoulders, her skin freshly scrubbed, and she clutches the neck of the oversized robe to her collarbone.

"Shower's all yours," she calls out cheerfully. "I even saved you hot water."

I stare at her, because she's beautiful, and all the things I want to tell her stick in my throat, because I'm not good enough for her. So I just get to my feet and push past her without a word, closing the bathroom door behind me and shutting her out. I wash quickly but not so quickly that I don't stroke out another quick release, thinking about the way her eyes shone as she rubbed me, or the way she rode my hand as I made her come.

I suspect I'm going to be thinking about those moments a lot for the next, oh, five hundred years.

When I emerge from the bathroom, my hair slicked back and wearing a robe that fits me a lot better than hers fits her, I find Reggie on the lone bed in our hotel room, seated upright against the headboard, her legs crisscrossed under the robe. She has a small bag of pretzels in her hand and the wrapper of a bag of M&M's on the nightstand next to her. She looks over at me, then pats the spot next to her invitingly. "Get yourself a snack from the minibar and let's talk."

"Everything in the minibar is exorbitantly priced," I say, but I pluck a couple of packets of peanut butter crackers and a bottle of water out of there anyhow.

"Then it's a good thing you're a rich old warlock," Reggie tells me in a bright voice. "Now come sit, because you and I have a lot to discuss."

I sit on the bed next to her, my legs stretching out in front of me. Compared to her, I'm a tall, pale giant with dark hairy legs and a weird face. She's so delicate and beautiful and . . . sunny. Determination and happiness personified. The thought of that makes my chest tighten all over again, because I suspect she's going to tell me once more that we should be nothing but friends.

"You're probably tired," I say, because I feel I should say something. "Maybe we should just call it a day."

She turns toward me on the bed, and her nearness hits me like a fist. I know we have to share a hotel room because of the obfuscation spell that protects her, but I thought it would be easier than this. Right now, all I want to do is grab her and throw her down onto the mattress and push her legs into the air so I can tongue her for hours. To taste her and claim her and make her so giddy with lust that she'll fall in love with me no matter how awful my past is.

That's . . . actually not a bad plan. I glance over at her to see how receptive she might be to having her pussy licked.

Reggie leans forward, her expression gentle even as the robe gapes, showing more freckled skin. "Ben, you and I need to talk. I know you like to keep things bottled up, but if we're going to have a hope of this working out, we need to clear the air. I'm not here to judge anything, just to understand. I know you're old as the hills and a warlock, and that makes your perception of things different than mine. This is why we need to talk things through."

I narrow my eyes at her. When she says "this working out," does she mean rescuing Aunt Dru? Or something else? She brought up my age, which isn't a good sign. Of course she thinks she's too young for me. Of course. My jaw clenches, and I'm tempted to skip the talking and just go straight to the pussy-licking. Get her so dazed with pleasure it won't occur to her that I'm five hundred years old. Plan decided, I reach for the ties of her robe.

Reggie immediately smacks my hand away. "You are not avoiding another conversation with me, Ben Magnus." Her cheeks flush bright. "Don't think that just because you made me come hard earlier, it means we shouldn't talk like adults."

"I could make you come hard again," I offer. "Many, many times."

She shivers, her eyes slightly glassy, as if considering that. Then she shakes her head. "I have too many questions that need to be answered first."

"Who says I want to answer you?"

Her nostrils flare and she gives me a stubborn look. "Are you going to pout because I won't let you distract me? Fine." She reaches for her bag of pretzels and offers me one. "You can have a pretzel for each answer you give me." She flutters her lashes. "Sound good?"

"I want a kiss," I demand. I take the pretzel from her hand and toss it over the side of the bed, onto the floor. "You, in my lap. One answer for every kiss I get."

She pauses, her lips parting, and then that determined Reggie look crosses her face. "As if that's a hardship," she mutters, and then climbs the distance between us in the bed. She tosses a leg over my hips and then settles herself atop me, her robe gaping at the top and not nearly enough at the bottom. Her weight is light over mine, but she feels so good. Perfect. She smells like soap and she has freckles everywhere, and this is the best idea I've ever had.

Reggie puts a hand on my cheek, her thumb skating over my jaw as she gazes down at me. She thinks for a moment more, then carefully brushes her lips over mine. The kiss is gentle, a mere promise. She presses her mouth softly to mine, lingering on my upper lip before pulling back. "Since we're on the subject of kisses . . . I want to know about your relationship with Gwen."

This is what she wants to start with? Of all the things we have going on, she's asking about *Gwen*? I study her face. "Are you still jealous?"

"Me?" She snorts. "No, of course not."

"You are."

Reggie shrugs, averting her eyes. She stares at my mouth. "Does it matter? I just want to know what the situation is there, all right?"

She's jealous. Incredulous, I stroke my hands up and down her sides. Reggie's jealous over me. It's hard to believe that someone as perfect as Reggie even wants me, much less is jealous of someone from my distant past. "When Gwen was a familiar for my aunt, she wanted to practice her sex magic. She'd sneak into my room at night and seduce me. I was just convenient."

Reggie frowns at me. "The looks she was giving you were not the looks of a woman who finds you just convenient. She was acting like she wanted to devour you whole." She brushes a wet lock of hair back from my face. "Have I mentioned I didn't like it?"

It amazes me that she's even feeling threatened. "Three hundred years ago, I thought Gwen was special. I thought what we had was special. I was flattered that she'd chosen me out of everyone she could have. Then I found out she was practicing on everyone in the house." I shrug. "After that, my affection for her died. It's been two hundred years since I've even thought of her."

"Oh." Reggie bites her lower lip. "I see."

I squeeze her waist with my hand. "I should also remind you that I didn't want to come see Gwen. In addition to her being self-absorbed, she's also a terrible gossip and very indiscreet. If she knew anything about my aunt, we'd already know it."

"She told us about the well."

"And you saw how useful that was," I point out. "My aunt might have hidden her tablets there long ago, but it's clear she's moved them. Or they're so buried with mud that we'd never be able to find them anyhow. Either way, it's a dead end."

"I see." Her fingers move against my nape, twining in my hair. She looks at my mouth again and then lowers her lips to mine. "I have more questions," she tells me between kisses. "So get ready."

I groan, holding her tightly against me. I love the way Reggie fits in my arms, the scent of her, the way she sighs when our lips meet, even the feel of her breath against my skin, warm and slightly ragged, as if she's affected greatly by our kissing, too. This time, I don't wait passively for her to kiss me. I kiss her back, stroking my tongue against hers when she parts her lips. My cock is hard and aching all over again, which isn't surprising, given that Reggie's straddling me, her smaller body covering mine. We kiss for what feels like hours, and I'm lost in Reggie's soft, giving mouth and the little noises she makes.

When she finally pulls back from me, she's dazed.

"I want to kiss you all over," I tell her, rubbing a hand up and down her spine. Her robe is gaping even more, exposing her freckled collarbone and an expanse of soft skin with just a hint of cleavage. I want to jerk that stupid covering off her so I can feast on the sight of her naked body, but I need her to give me permission first. "Let's forget about the questions. You can lie back in the bed, and I'll lick every inch of your skin."

The needy sound Reggie makes is incredibly erotic. She leans in and kisses me again, her mouth hot and urgent, and then just as quickly pulls back. "Talking. We have to talk." She pants. "Those are the rules, Ben."

"We can make our own rules—"

"Talk," she repeats, a stubborn note creeping into her voice.

I groan. "Fine, then."

Her hand slides down the front of my robe, touching the amulet I'm wearing around my neck. "What's this? It was glowing in the well."

That's what she wants to ask me about? "It's just a light pendant. I was scared of the dark when I was a boy. The person that gave this to me bespelled it so it'd light up whenever there was darkness."

Her gaze flicks up to mine. "Did Dru make this for you?"

"No. And I don't want to talk about it." Because I don't like to think about who did make it for me.

That steely expression crosses her face. "Tell me about your parents, Ben. They made you that amulet, didn't they?"

I glare at her. "Reggie, I really don't want to talk about it."

"And I"—she grinds down against me suggestively, riding me—"want my answers in exchange for my kiss. Or should I get off you and we end this?"

"Unfair," I rasp, torn. She rocks her hips over my aching cock again, and I am utterly aware of just how little separates our bodies. I could shove open her robe and mine, and then she'd be rocking against my shaft directly, rubbing her slick pussy up and down my length. Instead, she wants to talk about my parents. "Besides, I thought you had all the answers. I'm a murderer, remember?"

Reggie leans forward and brushes a kiss over my mouth, her hand trailing inside the front of my robe to my chest hair. "It doesn't fit you, Ben," she says softly. "It scared me at first, because I didn't know what to think. But you're so patient and kind with Dru. And with me. You never lose your temper, unless one of us is trapped inside a well." She gives me an impish look and then leans in and presses her lips to my jaw. "But I know you. You're like me. I know you could never kill your parents, or anyone else, in cold blood. That's not who you are. You might practice magic and do things that some people frown on, but you're never cruel. So I want you to tell me the real story behind it." She lifts her lips and gazes up at me with those big, dark eyes. "Please?"

There's an enormous knot in my throat. A knot that feels as if it's been there hundreds of years. "You truly think I'm not a murderer?"

"I know you're not." She takes my hand in hers and raises it to her cheek, all gentleness. "Like I said, you're like me. And whenever I mention my parents, you have this look on your face that I recognize so much. It's the look that tells me you know just what I'm going through when they hurt me. You know what it's like to feel that ache." She nips gently at my thumb. "So I want you to tell me your story."

My jaw works as I'm overcome with emotion. How many hundreds of years have I had the worst reputation of any warlock? How long have I brought down House Magnus with my actions? And yet this simple, beautiful woman believes the best of me. Believes there's more to the story.

It's humbling and it makes me love her all the more.

Love.

I'm in love with Reggie Johnson.

REGGIE

Ben looks as if I've asked him to describe his own funeral. There's so much blatant emotion on his face, and I know this is something that hurts him. So I keep petting him and touching him, letting him know that I'm here for him, that I believe in him. I don't think many people do. There's something in him so very raw and full of hurt, and it needs to come to the surface between us if we ever hope to get past it.

Because I don't believe that he's a cold-blooded murderer. He wouldn't look so wounded and shut down every time a parent is brought up if he truly was.

It occurs to me that I'm manipulating him, just a little, with kisses and cuddles. But the way I see it, Ben's not good at sharing, and he likes my kisses. This makes it easier for both of us. I'm not going to use him like Gwen did, either. This thing between us, this connection, it's real and I intend to pursue it. But I need answers first.

Ben's mouth works for a moment, as if he wants to swallow back any words that threaten to escape. "What have I told you about my past?"

"Just that you were born in England about five hundred years ago?"

He nods, his expression growing distant. "Henry the Eighth's reign. My mother was a courtier of his. She loved political games and intrigue. And clothes." He thinks for a moment. "My father was a warlock who she'd been obsessed with for centuries. My mother was nearly a thousand years old when she had me and very set in her ways. She was a beautiful, bright thing but very selfish. I think she had me to keep my father anchored to her side. They stayed together after I was born, but they fought a lot. And neither one of them wanted anything in particular to do with a child, so I was left alone at the country manor while they were at court. I'd see them maybe once, twice a year, and never for very long. I bothered them." His mouth twists. "Imagine that, a child wanting to spend time with his parents."

"It sounds lonely," I say softly.

"It was." His expression is shuttered. "Aunt Drusilla would come around when she could, but my mother didn't like her much, so she tried to keep Dru away from me. She was very angry when I apprenticed with Dru. Said that I had betrayed her. Never mind that I offered to apprentice with her or my father first. They had no time for that." He shrugs. "Anyway, I grew up and became a warlock of my own power." Ben gets thoughtful. "And then 1665 happened."

"What happened in 1665?"

"A lot of things. But mostly, the bubonic plague broke out again. That was entirely due to my mother."

I gasp. "What?"

Ben nods. "It was a curse gone wrong. She visited some little hamlet outside of London—the name escapes me—and felt that the local shopkeepers didn't pay her the proper deference or some bullshit. She ended up cursing the local butcher with plague, but he gave it to his family, and then some of the people in town fled to London, and from there, it became a full-blown pandemic." He shakes his head. "My parents were not good people. My mother was very selfish and cruel and didn't care about anyone other than herself. Word had gotten out that my mother had started the plague and refused to put an end to it. It went on for over a year and a hundred thousand people died, and my mother still didn't care. The council decided that since my mother—and my father with her—would accept no responsibility, that they would take them out for the good of mankind." His mouth curves in a faint smile. "Even though my parents were terrible people, I still loved them. Still sought their approval. I found out what was going to happen, and I approached them in London, determined to make them see the error of their ways. It turned out that my father had just contracted the plague and was dying, and my mother still didn't believe it was a problem." He shakes his head. "When they wouldn't listen to reason, I had to take them out myself."

I gasp, aching for him. "You had to?"

He nods, emotion stark on his face. "If I hadn't, they would have met a worse fate. The plan was to point out that my parents were witches and let an angry mob take care of them. After they'd have been tortured, they would have been burned at the stake. I poisoned them." His throat works. "It seemed . . . easier."

"Oh, Ben." I'm horrified at the trauma he's gone through. I wrap my arms around him and hold him tight. His arms are like a vise around me, and he holds me like a man drowning. I let him, because I understand. I can't imagine being in the same place and having my parents do such awful things. Having to take action like that. "And because you tried to give them a kinder way out, now everyone thinks you're a murderer?"

"For a long time, it was good for my reputation," he says, voice low. "I let it carry on, because why not? But now I'm the monster everyone tells their children to hide from. I'm tired of it. I just want to be left alone."

I press my nose against the crook of his neck, breathing in his scent. "Should I leave you alone, too, then?"

"Gods, no." He holds me tighter. "You stay. Stay forever."

Hearing that makes me feel so good. I wrap myself around him, just to comfort him. Just to let him know that I'm here, and I understand.

"What's worse . . . ," he begins, and I feel him tense under me. As if he has more to confess and doesn't want to. He pauses and then continues on. "What's worse is that I leaned into that bad reputation. I let it carry me for ages. And after a while, I think I became that person. I told you that I do investment jobs, cursing competitors for clients and tinkering with the stock market, right?" When I nod, he continues. "And I thought that was okay, since I figured it wasn't hurting anyone. It's just business, right? Doesn't matter how ruthless I am, because it's all business. But I had a client . . ."

His voice trails off again. I stroke his neck, silently encouraging him.

He clears his throat. "I had a client that was a regular of mine. Hired me to screw over product launches of some of his competitors. I thought he was happy with my work, but he killed himself." Ben's voice grows rough. "I guess being responsible for driving some of his competitors out of business got to him. And I told myself it wasn't my fault. That I don't deal with mental health, and that I couldn't have known. It's just, at what point do I become my parents? I didn't care whose lives I destroyed, because it was just business. My mother didn't care about anyone but herself, and I don't want to go down that path."

"The very fact that you worry about it means that you won't,"

I tell him, soothing. He seems so vulnerable in this moment, it makes me ache to help him.

He swallows hard, his Adam's apple working. "I guess that's one reason why I've been here instead of back in Boston. That, and freckles."

I look up at him and smile. "Aha. I knew you had the hots for me." I wiggle atop him. "Was it my fiendish charm? My sexy outfits?"

Ben arches an eyebrow. "Do you even own a sexy outfit?"

"All of my outfits are sexy because I'm in them."

"I really can't disagree with that." A hint of a smile curves his mouth as he studies my face. "Now that you know all of my awful secrets, do you still want to kiss me? Knowing what I did? Who I am? Because I'm sure I've cast other questionable things in my lifetime. Five hundred years is a long time. I worry if I start working privately again, I'll go down that path once more . . ."

"Are you rich?" I ask bluntly. I've seen him and Dru toss around all kinds of money, and I suspect I know the answer already.

He frowns down at me. "I'm not sure I understand the question."

"Are you rich? Are you wealthy? Are you balling? Do you have bling? Are you—"

Ben covers my mouth. "Please never utter the word 'bling' again." His mouth quirks at me, and he lowers his fingers when I mock-bite them. "I guess I'm well off. I have a couple hundred here and there."

"Thousand?"

"Million, Reggie. I'd be a terrible businessman if in five hundred years, I only managed to get a few hundred thousand."

I feel faint at the thought. A couple hundred million? "You're good, then. Don't work anymore."

"Then what do I do with myself?"

I shrug, propping an elbow up on his shoulder to regard him. "Whatever you want to? Buy a private island and lord over it? Write a memoir? Teach?"

His eyes grow vague. "Teach. I wouldn't mind that. Except I'd need to get a familiar—"

"No, not like that." I shake my head at him, deliberately avoiding the fact that I'm a little jealous at the thought of him taking a familiar. "Teach people like Penny. People that want desperately to learn but have to wait to apprentice. Teach them basic, small things that will get them prepped to be better familiars, but it'll give them something to work on while they wait. Penny told me some apprentices wait decades and never get a chance."

Ben looks thoughtful. "That would be useful. The council would hate it, though. They don't like change." He grunts, tilting his head. "Then again, the council doesn't like me much, either, so I guess it doesn't matter if I have their approval."

"See?" I say happily. "There are things you can do without feeling as if you're going to compromise yourself."

"Thank you." The look he gives me is full of gravitas. "I mean that, Reggie. Thank you for talking this through with me. I've never really talked to anyone about this kind of thing."

I nod in understanding. "Because you'd get judged."

"That, and I don't want my aunt to know how bad it was for me growing up. And what happened recently . . . She's the only person that's ever had an unwavering good opinion of me, and I guess I've always protected that."

I suspect Dru knows more about Ben than she lets on. She's a sharp cookie, for all that she likes to play dumb at times. She'd adore Ben no matter what he told her. I bite my lip, thinking about poor Dru. "Do you think she's all right?"

"I called Lisa while you were in the shower. There's been no change. She's been working on some scrying spells, too, but she and Jim can't do much with her being pregnant. Not that they'd be able to tell who cast, because it's been shielded." Ben's expression grows distant.

"What?" I ask, poking his chest. "What is it? What did you just think about?"

"Willem."

"Who?"

Ben blinks, then focuses on me. "My friend Willem. Well . . . not friend. Acquaintance. Warlock. He apprenticed under Louis Abernathy." He presses a kiss to my cheek and then gently pulls me off his lap, distracted. He gets to his feet, crossing the room, and pulls out his phone.

I almost want to be hurt that he's ignoring my very sexy attempts to seduce him, but if we can save Dru, I can seduce him some other time. "Am I supposed to know who Louis Abernathy is?"

"He's a very old recluse," Ben tells me, flicking his phone's screen. He sits on the edge of the bed, and I sling my arms over his shoulders, peeking over him as he moves through his contact list. "Was a monk in the Middle Ages."

"A monk?"

"Said they had the best books, yeah. Anyway, Abernathy is also the only person alive that's so good at scrying he can crack any spell and tell you who cast it and when."

I gasp, squeezing Ben's neck with excitement. "Call him! Call him right now!"

"I don't have his phone number. Only Willem knows how to get in touch with him." He pulls up a name—Willem's—and begins to text. I rumple his hair and move away, not wanting to bother him while he texts his friend, and lean back in the bed again. My stomach growls, and I reach over to snag Ben's peanut butter crackers.

As I pick up a package, I see a card on the nightstand. It's soggy and smeared with mud, the edges warped. But there's no mistaking that card. I'd know it anywhere.

It's my Sun-Phoenix. He's kept it with him? I touch the edge, and the smear of mud on my fingers looks just like the mud from the well. My heart squeezes as I look over at Ben, the man willing to let all the people he knows think terrible things about him for centuries because he didn't want his parents to suffer. Because he didn't want them to be tortured and burned at the stake.

I can't imagine the trauma he went through, and my heart aches for him all over again. I curl up in bed, watching him as he types, worrying about Dru and about myself. If we can find out who cast this spell, maybe we can stop them before they get to me.

I don't want Ben to lose anyone else he cares for.

I mean, I don't want to get cursed, that's for sure. I'm worried about it happening and totally fucking me over like it has Dru. But I also recognize that it won't affect just me. Ben will be affected, because he cares for me. It's a strange, humbling feeling, different from my friendship with Nick. Nick is a wonderful friend, but he's also a Blanche at heart. He exists in a state of pleasure-seeking and enjoyment, and if something happened to me, he'd be hurt and upset, but it wouldn't destroy his world.

Ben—my precious, darling Dorothy of a man—would be destroyed. It's so odd that I've fallen for a man that's everything I always told myself to look out for. Haven't I always avoided the Dorothys of the world? But there's no doubt that Ben is a Dorothy in my mind. He tends toward sourness and looks down on others. His mind is always working with some sort of hidden machination. Whereas Nick is all surface, Ben has depths that go beyond anything I could imagine. Those are also the things that give him strength.

I eat Ben's peanut butter crackers as he types, hunched over his phone. When he finally lets out a sigh and rubs his brow, I suspect the conversation is done. "How'd it go?" I ask. "Is he going to help us?"

"Willem is incredibly unhelpful," Ben says, glancing over at me briefly before turning back to his phone and typing one more thing. "He's agreed to meet us for coffee in the morning. No more, no less. I'm sure he's got an angle."

I brush crumbs off my chest, accidentally getting them all over the bed. Whoops. "Doesn't he know that Dru's life is in danger?"

"He doesn't care. To him it'd be one less witch to worry about." Ben shrugs and tosses his phone to the end of the bed. "He's meeting us a few hours from here, so we'll have to wake up early." He glances over at me again and his eyes narrow. "Did you just eat my food?"

"You're rich—get yourself something else out of the minibar."

He grabs my ankle and yanks me down the bed, toward him. I yelp, surprised at how strong he is. Of course he's strong. He's bulging out of the same bathrobe I'm swimming in. But his strength always surprises me. When I'm flat on my back on the bed, my robe shoved up under my butt, Ben prowls over me like a predator, and I shiver with anticipation. He gazes down at me, his eyes devouring, and I can tell he's no longer thinking about Dru or Willem or anyone at all other than me.

My mouth is dry, and I lick my lips. Sure enough, his gaze follows the tip of my tongue. "You kept my Sun-Phoenix."

"I think I ruined it in the well," he admits, then leans down to press a light kiss to my mouth. "I'll buy you another. That one's mine, though."

I like that he wants to keep something of mine so badly. I like that when he cages me here on the bed, I feel tiny and helpless and yet utterly protected by his sheer size. "It's not yours. We never even played cards for it."

That makes Ben pause. "Are you asking to play cards right now?"

The look of confusion on his handsome face is so damned cute. I chuckle, deliberately stretching and making the robe gape in interesting ways. His gaze goes there, where my small breasts are practically popping out of the loose neckline of the robe. "I had other things in mind, actually. I was thinking you could entice me into giving it to you."

"I'm thinking about enticing you into giving me a lot of things," he murmurs, voice husky with lust. He leans over and I lift my chin for him to kiss me, but he fakes me out, instead moving to my neck and kissing me there, on the spot I'm learning is ultrasensitive. My hands go to his damp hair, and I gasp as his tongue flicks at my pulse point. He sucks on my throat a moment later, his teeth scraping, and I feel as if I'm about to come out of my skin.

And then Ben pauses over me. "Can I—"

"Yes," I blurt out. "Yes to everything."

"Greedy little thing," he whispers, but he sounds so pleased. He moves lower, nuzzling at my neck and then my collarbone. With one hand, he brushes aside the robe, exposing one of my breasts to his gaze. On a good day, my build would be described as "athletic." On a bad day, I'd probably be described as "flat as a board." When I'm on my back, my breasts are nothing more than nipple, but he gazes at me with sheer reverence. "Look at how beautiful you are."

It makes me want to preen with pleasure. I wasn't sure what he'd think after being reminded about Gwen's gorgeous, ample body, but hearing his approval takes all the uncertainty away. "I am pretty amazing," I agree, making my tone lofty. I reach down and brush my own aching nipple, flicking it with my thumb. It's already tight and pointing, but I love the way Ben's fascinated gaze can't look away. I touch myself a little more, performing for him, until he pushes my hand away and lowers his mouth to capture one peak between his lips. "Oh! That feels good, Ben."

He groans, rubbing his mouth against my breast before capturing my nipple again. He rolls it with his tongue and lips and then sucks on the tip until I'm squirming and panting. When he lifts his head to look at me again, his eyes are dark with need. "You have no idea how long I've wanted to touch you like this."

"Sometime between when you met me and when you stopped hating me?" My goodness, it's hard to think when his wicked tongue is teasing the underside of my nipple in a way that makes me want to crawl up the blankets and mount his face.

Ben moves to my other breast, giving the tip a pinch that makes me gasp and sends heat rocketing straight through my body. I jerk, my legs automatically opening in silent encouragement for him to go lower. When he finally looks up, he gives one of my pebbled nipples one last wet, openmouthed kiss before answering me. "You think I didn't want to touch you when you were driving me crazy? I can't tell you how many times I jerked off to the thought of coming all over those freckles of yours."

Filthy, filthy man. I love it. I wriggle underneath him. "Tonight's your night, then."

"I want to make you come first," he tells me, giving my breasts one last affectionate squeeze before kissing his way down my belly.

I moan, practically shoving my hips in his face. "Tonight's my night, then, too." I'm panting with eagerness as he kisses my navel and moves lower, heading for my favorite territory. He takes his sweet time, though, nipping and kissing every inch of skin on my abdomen, until I'm primed and so turned on that just the slightest touch is going to make me detonate like a firecracker. "Please, Ben. Please."

"Shhh. Let me enjoy the moment." He moves to my hip—my hip, of all places—and presses a gentle kiss there.

"Enjoy a little faster, maybe? With more tongue? In a certain spot?"

"My ravenous, ravenous Reggie," he chuckles. "Will you flip over for me?"

I practically pout. "Why?"

The look he gives me is warm and fascinated. He traces a finger down my belly. "I want to see if you have freckles there, too."

"Ugh. You're lucky you're so damned cute." Grumpy, I sit up as he moves off me and pull my now-loose robe off and toss it to the floor. I turn over and flop onto my belly. I've never both loved and hated tender foreplay so damn much.

His big hand skims down my spine in an almost reverent fashion. "Look at you. So damned beautiful."

The compliments take some of the edge off my frustration. I close my eyes, resting my cheek on my hands, and decide I'm going to enjoy the impromptu massage. "Are there many freckles back there?"

"Mostly on your shoulders." His palm feels warm as he runs it over my skin. "You're beautiful everywhere, though."

I smile at that. "Just for the record, I am not immune to compliments."

Ben chuckles. "I'll keep that in mind." The bed sinks down as he moves over me again, and then I feel his mouth on my shoulder, even as his hand rubs over my back. "I want to kiss every freckle."

"Oh boy. We're going to be here a while, then."

"Hush. I'll make you feel good."

I know he will. I smile again, relaxing under his touch. True to his word, Ben seems to kiss every freckle on my shoulders, then moves to my mid back, his mouth pressing on each spot with reverent appreciation. I let out a soft sound of pleasure as Ben moves along my spine again, then kisses the top of one of my buttocks.

"More freckles," he promises me.

"Mmm," I respond, drowsy with bliss. "They're everywhere."

"They are," he agrees, and kisses another spot on my buttock. His teeth graze my skin and I bite back a moan. His hands grip both rounded curves of my bottom, kneading them, and then he kisses another spot. And another. His tongue flicks out over my skin, as if he can't resist tasting me with every brush of his mouth, and my arousal surges. By the time he reaches the spot where my butt cheek joins with my thigh, I'm squirming with heat.

And still Ben moves his mouth over me. He palms my ass again and then whispers over my skin, "Raise your hips for me, Reggie. I've got more places to check for freckles."

I moan. Loud. My fingers tangle in the sheets, gripping desperately, even as I rise up on my knees and lower my head again, my ass in the air.

"Ahhhh," Ben murmurs, his hands skimming over my hips possessively. "I definitely need to check for more freckles."

And before I can respond to that, he pushes my legs apart just a little more, and then his mouth is between my thighs.

I cry out. I've had boyfriends go down on me in the past, but never from this angle. There's an entirely new intensity to things, and Ben seems like he's in so very deep as he tongues me, learning the folds of my pussy. I quiver every time he strokes his tongue over my skin, and my hips push higher into the air, as if that can somehow assist the situation.

"Still checking," he murmurs, and then his tongue teases a circle around my clit.

A sob breaks in my throat and I bite down on my fingers, because it's either that or I'm going to start screaming for an orgasm. Nothing has ever felt as good as Ben Magnus's mouth between my legs, and he seems determined to take just as much time there as he did worshipping each freckle.

He licks me endlessly. Slow licks. Fast licks. Teasing licks. Exploring licks. Licks that go from clit to backside and then up again. There's no inch of skin he leaves unattended to, and he's shameless in his tonguing. He pushes his tongue inside me, tasting me, but never stays in one spot long enough to let my orgasm build. I writhe up against his mouth, frantic, as he continues to fuck me with his tongue, and he still won't let me come. Not yet.

"Please, Ben," I pant, my toes permanently curled. "Please, please. Need you."

"I know you do, Freckles." His voice is like liquid against my skin, smoky and erotic. "Don't worry. I'll make you come."

And he strokes a finger deep inside me.

The caw I make is one of both pleasure and frustration, and I shamelessly grind against his hand as he drives his finger into me. It feels so good, especially when paired with the flicking of his tongue, but it's not enough. It's never enough, and it's making me absolutely crazed with need. "Don't . . ." I pant. "Don't call me Freckles."

"But I love your freckles," he tells me in a sultry tone, and then gives me another intense lick. "They're beautiful and unique, just like you." He flicks his tongue in an utterly ticklish way that makes me squirm anew. "But if you don't like it, I'll call you something else."

"Ben," I plead, desperate to come.

"Not that. It'll get too confusing."

I grind my fist into the blankets even as he drags that finger inside me. "You. Stop talking. Fuck me."

Ben chuckles, and his mouth rubs against my backside. Then he sighs. "I don't have protection, Reggie. We can't do everything tonight."

A whiny sound of protest escapes me. "What about . . . magic? A potion?"

One hand strokes my ass while his fingers work my pussy. "Can't. That sort of magic won't get answered. The gods are big enthusiasts of surprise pregnancies, which, given mythology, isn't exactly surprising. We'll have to save the rest for some other time."

I can't believe I'm being cock-blocked by millennia-old Roman deities.

"But don't worry," Ben continues. "I'll make you feel good, sweetheart."

"Yes! Yes. Now." I'm so hungry for it. I want more and more and more.

Ben's hands leave my body, and I make a growl of frustration. In the next moment, though, his head appears between my legs. He grabs me by the backs of my thighs and pulls me down, and I realize he's on his back on the bed, and he wants me to sit on his face. With a little cry, I do as he demands, and his mouth is everywhere, devouring me. He settles on my clit, sucking and tonguing, and one of his fingers steals into my core once more. Using mouth and hand, he works me hard, his tempo increasing until the orgasm he's been teasing finally crashes through me, drawing another undignified cry out of my throat and a full-body shudder out of the rest of me.

I collapse over him, and Ben keeps kissing my thighs, my pussy, everywhere he can reach. "So beautiful," he murmurs. "Love touching you, sweetheart."

When my brain finally feels like it's stuffed back into my head again, I roll off him and flop onto my back on the bed. "Good lord."

Ben moves up next to me on the bed, on his belly, and takes my hand, kissing the palm.

I give him a dazed look. "You're really good at that."

"I know."

I push my palm against his face, smirking. "I take it back. No one needs to feed that ego of yours. It's plenty healthy already."

He grins against my hand and then presses a kiss to each of my fingertips, all boyish pleasure and flushed face. I roll onto my side, facing him and studying his expression. There's an odd sort of peace on his features I haven't seen before. Like he's vomited out all of his past, expecting me to hate him. Now that it's no longer hanging over him like a dark cloud, he's calm. Happy.

I snuggle closer and give him a kiss. Just a light one, but Ben holds me against him, his lips hungry, and I'm reminded that only one of us came. "What about you?"

Ben nips on my lower lip. "What do you mean? I enjoyed that, too." His eyes are hazy, and he can't stop kissing me. "I love touching you, Reggie. I want to touch you all night long. I want to touch you until the sun rises. Until the next full moon, and the one after that." He grins. "And the one after that . . . and the one after that . . ."

It fills me with a strange, unholy sort of joy that someone could want me that much. Me, who's always been the after-thought, the roommate, the one left behind, the one not quite right for the job. Ben sees me as whole, complete, and desirable. He hasn't left my side in all this mess, even when he was mad at me. It just makes me want him all the more.

I push him onto his back and lean over him, kissing his face. "Is it going to bother you if I clean up this room after we're done?"

"Depends." The heat is still there in his eyes, and I can feel the hardness of his length against my thigh. "Will you be naked?"

"So naked cleaning is acceptable to you?" I pretend to consider this. "What if I offer to clean you?"

"Will you be naked?" he asks again.

I chuckle, smacking his chest lightly. "You're obsessed with my nudity."

"It's because you look so good like this." His eyes are dark with both lust and approval.

I slide my hand down to his cock, very aware of how hard he is, how he made the pleasure all about me. "And what do we do about this?"

"What do you want to do about it?"

He feels like a shaft of pure heat in my hand, and I can't resist stroking him. All the romance novels describe a cock as velvet-wrapped steel, and they're not actually wrong. He's all hot, soft skin over a rigid length, and I love touching him and exploring him with my fingers, even though I know I'm making him crazy. As I skim the heel of my palm down his length, he kisses me again, his mouth more urgent this time.

"I think I want to touch you," I whisper to him, smiling. "But I never finished asking my questions earlier. You distracted me."

Ben pants, a hint of frustration on his features. "I can't even remember what we were talking about five minutes ago," he confesses. "So you'll have to ask it again."

I curl my fingers around him, my fingertips not quite touching as I squeeze the base of his cock. I haven't forgotten that I wanted to ask about his age. I'm still stinging from Gwen's remarks about how young I am, what a baby I am, and I worry I'm too young for Ben. That horse might have already left the barn, so to speak, but the thought of him seeing me as just some idiot youngster won't stop nagging me.

Of course, he's going to say whatever I want to hear as long as my hand is on his cock. So I reluctantly let go, sit up, and gaze down at him. "Does my age bother you?"

His dark brows knit together. "Where'd this come from?"

"I know you're like a million years old—"

"Ouch." Ben sits up, a frown on his face. "I'm five hundred, but we age differently, Reggie. You'll see that age matters very little after the first hundred years or so."

"First hundred years?" I echo, surprised.

"Well, yes. You have the same ambrosia in your blood that I do—the bloodline of magic. If you start practicing on your own, you'll be just as long lived as the rest of us."

"I . . . Oh." It's not something I considered before now. "Then you don't mind that I'm young? Gwen said—"

He rolls his eyes, reaching for me. Ben grabs me around the waist and drops onto his back again, pulling me back down with him. "When will you realize Gwen was pricking at you? She was bringing you down to make herself look good. As if I'd be swayed by that. I know how Gwen is, trust me." He buries his face against my neck. "And you have nothing to worry about when it comes to her."

The nagging worry eats at me. Ben might look like he's only a few years my senior, but he's got centuries on me. If people get hung up on age differences between normal couples, what are we going to seem like? "I just worry the age difference is going to be too much for you. Like you won't have anything in common with me—"

"Like magic? Like the card games? Like our parents?" He arches an eyebrow at me. "How many things do we need to have in common before you decide we're good together?"

I bite my lip. "I don't want you to feel like being with me is a mistake—"

He cups my jaw, pressing a soft, reverent kiss on my mouth. It might be the sweetest kiss yet, and the most erotic, because he still tastes like my body. "Reggie. When you get as old as I am, you learn pretty quickly to recognize the people in your life that feel fleeting and the people in your life that feel right, deep in your soul. And you feel right to me. Perfect." He slides his hand to his chest and makes a fist over his heart. "Like you've always been right here. I love you."

I go still. A vague sense of dread washes through me, even though the look on Ben's face is utterly earnest and full of emotion. I . . . don't know what to say. Love is terrifying to me. My parents said they loved me, and they treated me like I was there only for them to use and abuse. I've had ex-boyfriends who said they loved me and showed it with their fists. I'm not good with love. But Ben stares at me, waiting, and I know I should say something.

I lick my dry lips. "Ben . . ."

"It's all right," he murmurs, reaching out to tenderly brush a lock of hair back from my face. "I know what you're thinking. You think I can't understand you, because of our age differences, but you and I are very similar, Reggie. You're thinking that people use the word 'love' as a tool against you. That just because they say they love you, it somehow gives them permission to do awful things."

Oh god, he does know me, so very well. It makes me ache deep inside. "Everyone I've loved has used me. Except Nick." I manage a watery chuckle. "It took me a long time to trust him, and even now, I still sometimes think he just used me for free housekeeping."

Ben shakes his head. "Don't doubt that people love you, Reggie. You're an amazing person. Nick loves you because you're his friend. Penny loves you, too. I was expecting her to attack me on your behalf at any time." His mouth crooks up in a half smile. "I know me saying this makes you nervous, but don't be. You don't have to say it back, Reggie. I know how I feel, and that's all that matters. I'll prove it to you. Just give me time."

I feel shy and full of hope but still scared. "I would love that."

He gives me a beautiful smile and leans in to kiss the tip of my nose. He's so damned tender and sweet that it makes me ache . . . and then I want to make him ache. "Do you have more questions for me?" he asks.

"Just one."

"Mmm?"

I reach between us and grip his cock again. "Did you still want to come on my freckles?"

Ben's eyes flare with heat, and then neither of us speaks again for a very long time.

31

BEN

When Willem meets us at the coffee shop, his gaze immediately goes to the twin bracelets Reggie wears, one on each wrist. His mouth thins with disapproval, and I know what he's thinking. He thinks I'm stealing my aunt's familiar while she's under a curse. Or he thinks that I cursed her myself.

I'm not surprised. Others have taken out rivals just to steal their familiars. Finding one that can handle all the casting a warlock wants to do is a tall order. Finding one you don't want to strangle is a difficult task, too. That Reggie is both makes her priceless in my eyes. Plus the fact that I'm in love with her. But I wouldn't steal her away from my aunt. I'd just monopolize her time a little.

I wait for Willem to comment on the bracelets, though, and I'm not disappointed. He lifts his cup to his lips, arching a brow at me. "Determined to ruin any shreds of reputation you have left, Magnus?"

"I don't give a damn about my reputation."

"Obviously." He stares pointedly at Reggie's neck, where I've left multiple love bites all over her skin. It was on accident, but I don't regret them. I like seeing her wear the evidence of my touch.

Reggie gives me a worried look. "What's he talking about? What's wrong?"

I don't want her to worry. "It's nothing."

"It's not nothing," Willem corrects, giving me a thin frown. "Reputation is everything among the warlock community. You're already on thin ice as it is. The only reason you haven't had sanctions put on you is because they shit their pants at the thought of angering you. But if you push too far . . ." Willem shrugs. "You don't want to end up like me."

The look on Reggie's face becomes even more distraught. She looks to me for reassurance, and I lean over, sliding my arm around her shoulders. "It's frowned upon to make advances on another's familiar. Since my aunt is currently under a spell, there are those that would assume I'm responsible for it."

She looks down at the bracelet on her arm, realization dawning on her face. "Oh god. No, it's not like that. Ben hasn't done anything wrong." She shakes her head at Willem. "He's just borrowing me for a spell to protect me, and we're trying to figure out how to save Dru. He's going to release me the moment she's awake again."

"Mmm" is all Willem says.

I say nothing, too. The truth is, I like Reggie wearing my cuff. I like having that part of her that belongs to me. Warlocks (and witches) as a rule tend to be possessive and secretive, and we're bad at sharing. I would never steal her from Aunt Dru, but the thought crosses my mind at least once an hour. Maybe twice an hour.

"Just because it looks bad doesn't mean that it is," Reggie says defiantly. "Ben has been working tirelessly to save Dru, and he deserves your respect. And as for what the other warlocks think of him, I agree that it doesn't matter. Ben's retiring. He's going to teach."

"Is he, now? Gods help those baby warlocks he decides to unleash himself upon." Willem smirks.

"He's going to teach familiars," Reggie continues, defending me. Her expression is fierce. "And you need to stop disparaging him in front of me, because I won't sit here and listen to it. You either talk to him like a respected ally and a friend, or you fucking leave."

Willem stares at Reggie. I do, too. No one has ever defended me like that. Aunt Dru has always been a big believer in fighting your own battles, but for someone to stand up to Willem because he was making mild comments about me? I'm filled with a rush of awed affection. She's defending *me*, and I love her even more for that simple gesture.

"Yes, well, did you want my assistance or not?" Willem gives me a dismissive look. "Because I have other things to do with my time."

"Apparently not if you're going out of your way to meet us first thing this morning," Reggie retorts, practically bristling.

I slide my hand into her lap and take her hand, squeezing it. "It's all right. We do want his help." I glance over at Willem, who is flushed almost as red as his hair. Reggie's sharp, though. Willem is rather eager to help us. "But I suppose that begs the question, what do you want?"

Willem just picks up his coffee and sips it again, as if considering how much information to expose to us. "I know exactly where Abernathy is. You can talk to him tomorrow, if needed. I'll arrange the meeting. I know you're in a time crunch. But yes, I suppose I do want something."

Of course he does. Everyone always wants something. "And?" I prompt.

His gaze falls back to Reggie's braceleted wrist, the one still on the table. Her other hand is in her lap, tightly clenched in mine. "I need a familiar," Willem admits. "I still have ten years to go on my ban, and I'm tired of it. I need help finding a familiar that won't mind working . . . under the table, so to speak. Outside of the Society of Familiars. And since you found your rogue familiar through unconventional means, I thought you could help me find one, as well."

I stiffen the moment he mentions that he wants a familiar. For a brief, ugly moment, I imagine a third bracelet on Reggie's slender wrists, and hot jealousy roars through me. It takes a moment for the rest of Willem's words to sink in—that he wants help finding a familiar of his own, not that he wants Reggie. I breathe after that.

No one gets Reggie but me.

Reggie leans over to me, her expression neutral. She indicates I should lean over, and when I do, she whispers in my ear, her breath ticklish. "I bet Penny would do it."

"She's in the society," I remind her.

She shakes her head. "She's also been waiting a very long time and is eager to get started. She might be waiting another ten years if she goes by the society's rules. I'll talk to her, but I bet she'd do it."

I remember the excitable, friendly woman at the component shop. Willem would absolutely loathe her. Which means it's perfect. "Reggie has someone in mind," I tell Willem. "We'll speak with her once Aunt Dru is recovered."

Willem's face reveals a hint of surprise, quickly masked. "Is that so? Fascinating." He pulls a slip of paper out of his pocket. "There's a party at this house tomorrow night. A celebration of scholars, if you will. Abernathy is going to be there."

Reggie snatches the piece of paper and then hands it to me. I don't recognize the address, but I can guess what a "celebration of scholars" entails. Group casting. Everyone brings their familiar, and together they cast a powerful spell of some kind. It's both dinner party and business, all in one, and I should be surprised that the reclusive Abernathy is going to take part in it . . . but Abernathy does love to learn new spells.

If we're going, we're going to have to dress the part. I resist the urge to groan in frustration, because this is helpful—it's just not exactly what I wanted.

"Are you going to this party?" Reggie asks, glancing at me before looking back at Willem.

His smile is tight and slightly unpleasant. "No familiar, so I'm not invited."

"Oh." Reggie looks over at me, and I can practically read her thoughts. "Then we—"

"We're going," I say firmly. They'll judge my relationship with her, but I don't care. They'll think I'm making designs on stealing my aunt's familiar, but if it means saving my aunt's life, I'll take another hit to my already tattered reputation. It doesn't matter. Aunt Dru would do the same for me, so I'll do it for her, no question. "It'll be fine."

"Perfect," Willem says. "I look forward to hearing from you two about the status of my future familiar." And he takes another elegant sip of his coffee, the arrogant prick. "Do tell my old master I said hello."

REGGIE

I'm a little worried about all of this. We know where to find this Abernathy guy, but it's not his particular contact information, just the address of a party he'll be at. It means Ben and I have to go to that party. It means everyone's going to see that I'm wearing his bracelet, just like Willem did, and they're all going to think bad things about Ben. That he's stealing me. That he's responsible for his aunt's curse.

I don't like it, but what other choice do we have?

I stew on this even as we take the long drive back to Aunt Dru's house. Lisa's been there at Dru's side ever since we left, and even though we've been checking in with her via texts and phone calls, it'll still be good for us to go to the house and see if we can help out in any way. Ben's going to try casting a few more spells to see if he can determine anything. And I'm going to find a dress for the party. Somehow. "I'm not sure if I have anything appropriate," I tell Ben for probably the third time today. "I'm not a very dressy girl."

"Don't you have a black dress?" He shrugs. "It's fine. You'll look beautiful in anything."

I guess it doesn't matter, but I also don't want to be an embarrassment for him. "Maybe I can run to the store," I say as we pull toward Aunt Dru's house. "See if I can find something appropriate for . . ." I trail off as a familiar Volkswagen van comes into sight. It's parked on the curb in front of Dru's house, and my heart starts to pound at the sight of it.

"For?" Ben prompts.

I'm not listening. I'm staring in horror at the beat-up old van. I recognize the foil over the back window, the faded pink dye job, the junk shoved into the back since it serves as a mobile home as well as a van. Oh god. Oh god.

Ben parks in the driveway, and the moment the car stops, I launch myself out of it, racing toward the van—and my parents. It doesn't matter that I'm wearing damp, slightly muddy clothing from yesterday's well incident. It doesn't matter that I have half a dozen hickeys on my neck and that they're sure to comment on it.

I have to stop them. I have to get rid of them. Now.

As I fly toward their van, my parents emerge from inside. Mom slinks out of the passenger side, and Dad steps out from behind the wheel. They look the same as they ever did. Mom's got her long hair pulled back into loose blond dreads held back by a scarf, and Dad's salt-and-pepper beard is long and bushy. They both wear flowing clothing, and the stink of patchouli and incense wafts toward me. "What are you doing here?"

"Regina," my mother cries, extending her arms out. "It's been so long since we've seen you!"

I come to an abrupt halt a few feet away from them, because I'm torn between wanting to shove my mother right back into that van and falling into her arms, like the lonely child I was. "How did you find out where I am?"

"Your boyfriend, Nick, gave us your new address. Said you were living here?" My father's voice is jovial. "Looks like you're doing quite well for yourself, Little Button. Good to see. Good to see."

"Nick wouldn't do that," I say, hands clenched. "And he's not my boyfriend."

I can feel Ben come to stand behind me, and my mother's gaze moves over him. "Of course not," she soothes, an exaggerated wink on her face. She holds a braceleted hand out to Ben. "You must be the boyfriend, then."

He stares at her hand, cold as ice. "Reggie asked what you're doing here."

I'm oddly glad that he's not warm to them. Part of me cringes inside when my mother's face shows blatant hurt, but I take a step closer to Ben, drawing from his strength. I'm torn. Torn because they look good and they're being so warm and friendly, and torn because I know it's all an act.

"We just worried about our little girl," my father says, smiling so brightly. "Being protective parents and all."

"And we were drifting through town and thought we'd say hello, but you weren't there." My mother pouts. "Do you know how hard it's been to chase you down? We've gone to such effort."

They have? They wanted to find me? That stupid, awful hope bubbles in my chest. "You did?"

"Of course we did." My mother gives me that motherly, inviting, confusing smile. "Look at how good you look. You're doing so well for yourself. Are you hungry? We'd love to take you out for lunch."

I hesitate, weak. Maybe this time it's different. Maybe they don't really need money. Maybe—

"Reggie's busy," Ben says harshly, and I wince at his tone. He puts a hand on my shoulder, possessive and supportive all at once, and I don't know how I feel about it. "Come on, Reggie. Let's go inside and check on my aunt."

"Can we come in?" my mother asks. "I want to see where my daughter is living, to make sure it's safe for her." That mama-bear look is all over her face.

"No," Ben says flatly. "And if you don't remove your van from the premises, I'm going to call the police."

My mother recoils, clearly hurt, and my father's expression goes from jovial to displeased. They both look at me, and I feel frozen, on the spot. "Reggie, baby," my mother coos. "Say the word. You're the one in charge here. Don't let a man tell you how to think."

I feel as if I'm being forced to choose between my parents and Ben.

"Reggie," Ben says, voice soft. "It's okay."

I look up at him, at his dark eyes full of understanding. He knows what it's like. He knows how it feels to be so torn, to hope that there's more to someone than what you know, than what your instincts tell you. Because my parents are here, looking for me, and I want desperately for them to be for real this time, to just honestly care about me . . . but my instincts are telling me otherwise.

I swallow hard, and I can't answer. So I turn and march toward the house.

"An hour," I hear Ben tell them. "I want you gone within an hour."

"We're not leaving until we talk to our daughter," my mother claims. "Don't let him brainwash you, Button! We're your parents!"

I head inside and close the door. The interior of Dru's house is cool and tidy, no sign of the destruction I've wrought on her poor library at this end of the house. Fresh flowers are in a nearby vase—Lisa's work. The ugly Roman bust in the entryway stares at me, and I stumble my way through the downstairs, toward the living room, and fling myself down on the couch. I curl my legs against me, hugging my knees, as my heart aches and aches.

Lisa thumps down the stairs, her pregnant belly bigger than ever. "I thought I heard someone. Glad to see you're back." She smiles at me, but that smile fades when she sees my face. "Is . . . is everything okay?"

"Just give us a minute, please, Lisa. How is my aunt?" Ben's voice is smooth and calm.

"More of the same," Lisa says. "She hasn't woken up." She looks between us, a million questions on her face, and then gestures at the stairs she just descended. "I'll, uh, just go back up."

"Thank you," Ben says.

"Don't close any of the doors in the house," she warns us. "I have them all open, even the back door. Did you close the front door?"

"I'll handle it."

"But—"

"I'll *handle* it," Ben says firmly.

Lisa doesn't protest again. She leaves us alone, and Ben comes and sits next to me, stroking my hair. I want to bury myself in his arms as much as I want to push him away. I'm all torn up where my parents are concerned. He just continues to stroke my hair, his presence quiet and calm, and it helps.

There's a noise toward the back of the house, like someone crashing through Dru's hedges. My heart sinks as Maurice races through the living room, a black streak of terror.

Ben sighs, getting to his feet. "I'll handle it."

I nod, hugging my knees as Ben leaves the room. Sure enough, I hear the sound of an argument and my mother's voice raising. "You're not going to keep me from my daughter!" she shouts, loud for my benefit. Ben's voice is softer, and all I can make out is the deep tone of it, not what he's saying.

It gets quiet, and that makes my stomach ache more than before. Because I know my parents won't just leave. They see an opportunity here, and they're not about to waste it. It means that Ben either threatened them—or bribed them to leave.

Both thoughts make me sick. Not because of Ben—I know he's protecting me—but because of my parents. They know how to make such nuisances of themselves that someone will pay for them to just go away. I think of the time they—we—squatted in a house when I was a child. How the law wouldn't allow anyone to kick us out, because we were occupying the home. I didn't understand why we had no power, no water, and why we had to hide inside. Didn't understand until the teary-eyed homeowners showed up and wrote my parents a check. We were gone the next day, and six months later, my parents tried to go back, only to find the couple had installed an alarm system. My father spent a few nights in jail while my mother and I slept under a bridge, hiding in the van.

I remember that moment clearly, and I remember how I'd

make myself a tidy little nest that I could control, just so I could feel better. I remember my parents tossing their garbage on the floor and smearing food on the walls just to be jerks. I hadn't grasped that as a child, so I'd gone back behind them and cleaned up. Always cleaning up after them.

Ben returns to the living room and sits down next to me. He tugs me into his arms, pulling me against him until I fall into his lap. I wrap myself around him, determined not to cry. I just feel hollow inside. "How much?" I finally ask.

He tenses and then says, "Two thousand."

I nod. That sounds about right. "You're not the first to bribe them to leave."

He rubs my back, trying to comfort me. "I'm sure Nick didn't give them this address."

"I know. He wouldn't. He knows how awful they are. They must have gotten it some other way." I wouldn't be surprised if they were stealing the mail—it would explain how they got the credit cards in my name. "They've always been like this. Always."

"I understand," he says softly. And I know he does. He holds me close, letting me press against him, letting me choke on the tears I refuse to let fall. "They're why you're so controlling of your environment, aren't they? Why you're always tidying and organizing."

"It was something I could control. Everything else was a mess, but at least I could control that."

"Because you never feel safe." He holds me tighter.

It's funny, because I feel safe right now. I'm sad and miserable because my parents showing up dredges up all kinds of terrible feelings, but I feel less alone than I have in the past. I know that no matter what happens, Ben understands. He has my back. "They're probably going to come back," I whisper. "Once they smell money, they won't leave."

"We'll handle it," he promises.

"Maybe we could curse them to forget this address," I say, and then gasp, sitting up. "Ben! What if . . . what if they've been cursed all this time? What if they're not really like that? They've just been cursed to want money more than anything else? What if—"

"Reggie," Ben says calmly, and there's such sympathy in his eyes. "Reggie, sweetheart, you know that's not the case."

This time, the tears fall. "But what if—"

He shakes his head, his expression sad. "Sometimes people just aren't good people, sweetheart. We can't make them be better just because we want them to be."

I press my face to his neck, dripping tears all over his black clothing. I know he's right. I know he is. Even so . . . "Can we . . ."

"Cast a spell to check? Of course, love. You know I'd do anything for you."

I hold him tighter, because he really does understand.

And when, hours later, the scrying spells we cast show there's nothing lingering on my parents, no evil eye, no curse, no affliction other than pure selfishness, I cry all over his shoulder again, and he lets me.

BEN

We should have gone straight to Abernathy's party. Just skip from the meeting with Willem and head right to Abernathy's door to wait. Coming home was clearly a mistake, because Reggie is miserable. Her parents showing up was the icing on the shit cake she didn't need, and for the rest of the day, she mopes, her eyes broken inside even though she tries to hide it.

I know how that feels, and I want to give her space as much as I want to carry her up to my room and kiss her until she forgets everything else.

Having Reggie's parents lurking around is almost as bad as having to be in the house with Aunt Dru sleeping upstairs. It feels odd to not have her walking around, saying inane things and smiling cheerfully for no reason at all. Aunt Dru is a lot like Reggie, I think—as determined as she is cheerful—and not having her warm presence feels like there's a gaping hole in the house. Lisa is exhausted from watching over Dru, so Reggie and I take over for the night and stay at my aunt's side. I cast spell after spell, trying to find something to break the curse on her. A spell for waking. A spell for hiccups in the hope of rousing her. A spell to break an existing spell. A spell to obfuscate her location so it could potentially "unhook" an existing curse on her. I try spell reversals. Crystals. Offerings.

Nothing works, and the only thing I succeed in is wearing out Reggie, who bears the brunt of my spellcasting.

"It's all right," she tells me, her eyes drooping as she struggles to stay awake. "We have to try everything." She weaves in her seat, and I move to her side and scoop her up into my arms.

I contemplate setting her down next to Dru again, but what if Dru's curse somehow latches onto Reggie? She's been so worried that she'll be the next to be hit with a curse, and after the day we've had, I really just want to hold her close for a while. To my relief, Lisa enters the room, yawning. She wears a big floral zip-up muumuu, stretched tight over her belly, and her hair is pulled up into a messy bun. She gives a tired smile at the sight of us. "She's worn out?"

"Spellcasting," I say. "We tried a few things."

Lisa nods. "Nothing works. My husband, Jim, has been trying a few things, and nada." She shrugs. "You and Reggie should rest. I can't sleep anyhow. My back's killing me." She rubs her lower back and grimaces. "Can't wait for this baby to be out."

"We'll be down the hall," I tell her. "Come knock if you need anything. I probably won't be sleeping much, either."

She waves us off, and I carry Reggie away. I have a new, grudging respect for Lisa. I've never been a huge fan of hers because there's always been something a little too lackadaisical in her for my tastes, but her loyalty to Aunt Dru is unwavering. I make a mental note to insist that Aunt Dru give her a bonus payment if she wakes up.

When she wakes up, I amend. I'm not going to lose Aunt Dru, too.

With Reggie in my arms, I don't even stop to consider where to take her. I take her straight to my room, where the bed is large and soft, and settle her in gently. She reaches for me, her eyes closed, and clings to my hand. As if I'd leave her. I kick my shoes off and study her clothes. We both changed out of our mud-crusted clothes earlier, and Reggie's in a pair of pajama pants and an old, faded T-shirt. She looks comfortable enough fully dressed, and I pull her slippers off, wincing at how worn out they are. We'll have to have a talk about Reggie's cheapness when she wakes up.

Some other time, though. I tuck the blankets around her, then crawl into bed next to her. Reggie immediately turns toward me, snuggling up against my chest. "Tired," she murmurs.

"I know." I slide my arms around her, holding her close. She's perfect like this, in my arms, the right height for me to breathe in the scent of her freshly washed hair and tuck her under my chin. It's only because of Reggie's steadfast presence that I haven't lost my shit about Aunt Dru being cursed. If I were going through this alone . . .

I cut the thought off, because I don't want to entertain it. I'm just glad Reggie's at my side.

✶ ✶ ✶

THE NEXT DAY, we wake up early. While we slept, Lisa and her husband made the final preparations for our flight out to Abernathy's location. He's in remote Pennsylvania, the address popping up in Amish country, so it'll be fastest for us to take a quick plane trip out and then rent a car to drive the rest of the distance. Reggie wears a long coat over her clothes, and Lisa gives her a pair of black strappy heels to put on at the last minute. She's borrowed something to wear from Lisa, but I don't get a chance to see it just yet. I'm sure it's fine. I dress in my favorite designer black suit, the tie chokingly tight around my neck.

Tonight, everyone's going to see Reggie with me, wearing my cuff and my aunt's cuff, and they're going to judge. Rumors will fly, and before the end of the week, everyone with a drop of ambrosia in their blood will think I've stolen my aunt's familiar. It doesn't matter. If this is what it takes to rescue Aunt Dru, I'll tarnish my reputation a thousand times over.

I just don't want Reggie—or Aunt Dru—to suffer.

As if we're on the same wavelength, Reggie touches the cuff on her wrist—my aunt's cuff. "Should I take this off?"

I shake my head. "If you do, it can't ever be put back on again." I turn her wrist over, showing the symbol etched on the underside. "Because familiars are so important to a witch or a warlock, loyalty is valued above all else. To take off a cuff is stating that you're done with that person."

Reggie swallows hard, lifting her other wrist. "Then . . . you and I . . . Your cuff . . ."

It means I can't take another familiar while Reggie wears it. It means if she takes it off, I can never claim her as my familiar again. "I know," I say softly, running my thumb over her lower lip. "Worry about it another time."

"I worry about everything. That's what I do." But she smiles up at me. "One problem at a time, right? We rescue Dru, and then we figure out the rest."

"This might be just the first step," I warn her. "Abernathy can't break the spell, but he can tell us who put it on her. We handle it from there."

Because I'm going to kill whatever bastard cursed an elderly woman. I haven't mentioned that part to Reggie yet, but it lurks in the back of my mind, deadly. They're not going to get away with this, whoever it was. I don't care if I have to go into hiding for the rest of my days; whoever hurt my aunt—my family—is going to pay for it with blood.

REGGIE

I'm full of worry on the plane ride to our destination. I think Ben is, too. We're both silent, the only sound that of the plane engine. Ben looks uncomfortable in his suit, which is fair. It doesn't look like a very relaxing getup. Dashing, yes. Comfy, no. I wiggle my feet in my sneakers, trying not to panic about the upcoming party we're going to. A party full of witches and warlocks that are all going to judge Ben and find him lacking.

I touch the cuffs on my arms, thinking about all the strange, archaic rules that his kind have. My kind, too, I guess, if I have this ambrosia in my blood as well. But I can't help but think about the fact that if I take Ben's cuff off, I'll never be able to put it on again. I should take it off so no one will think terrible things about him or assume he's stealing me from Dru.

I just don't want to. I like belonging to Ben, which sounds crazy and needy, but it's true.

I fight back a small yawn, and Ben touches my hand. "Tired? Is the obfuscation spell wearing on you?"

I guess it is? I shrug. I didn't think about it much. I'm no more tired than if I'd missed a few hours of sleep. I don't feel like I'm about to pass out, though. Just a little more low energy than usual. "I'm fine. You?"

"Worried about Aunt Dru. Dreading this party. I don't know if you know this about me, but I'm not exactly a people person."

I chuckle at that. "Ben Magnus, if I was thinking of words to describe you, 'people person' would be the very last two words on that list."

His mouth lifts in a faint smile that quickly disappears. He studies me again.

"I can take the bracelet off," I offer, even though I don't want to. I also don't want him destroying his already tattered reputation for me.

"No. Absolutely not. It's the only thing keeping you from being cursed. If I lose you, too . . ." His mouth flattens and his expression grows hard. "No, Reggie. Don't even consider it."

"Okay," I say softly. I want to reach out and squeeze his hand, but I'm not sure how he'd take me comforting him. He's wound up tight right now, and I feel like one wrong move—or word—and he'll snap in half. "So, what should I expect at this party? I've never been to any sort of witch or warlock function."

Ben grows thoughtful. "That's right. You didn't come from the Society of Familiars. This is new to you." When I nod, he continues. "I imagine this will probably be a fairly small gathering, maybe no more than ten or twelve. Abernathy is rumored to be a hermit, so I would be very surprised if it's more people than that." He thinks for a moment longer. "Most of these get-togethers are to brag about spells or castings, or to share information, so I imagine there will be a faint bit of magic hanging in the air at all times."

"That doesn't sound too horrible."

He nods. "If it feels thicker in certain areas than others, though, maybe avoid them. Actually, avoid anyone that looks at your bracelets for too long or asks too many questions." Ben frowns. "Actually, don't leave my side."

"I wasn't planning on it."

"And if anyone touches you, deck them."

I swallow hard. "Is someone going to try to touch me, then?"

"They shouldn't, no, but I have to remind myself that most of these men aren't exactly modern thinkers. Some warlocks are older than Aunt Dru. They've owned people in their pasts. They think women aren't equals. Just be on your guard."

Charming group I'm getting involved with. Something tells me that I'm going to have more than one old coot tell me to smile tonight. "Got it. So if anyone thinks I'm less than a person because I'm a girl, I get to kick them in the 'nads." When he nods, I ask, "Are they going to say bad things about you in front of me?"

"Probably."

"I'll kick them in the 'nads for that, too."

Ben smiles over at me, but it doesn't reach his eyes, and I know he's stressed. I know he says he doesn't care what they think, but considering it affects not only him but me and his aunt, he has to be a little worried. I guess if you live for two thousand years, you run into the same people over and over again, and pissing them off (especially when they're curse-happy) is not a good thing.

The stressed-out tension remains between us as we land at the airport and rent a car. Using the map app, we follow the address out into the countryside, and Ben's frowns grow increasingly more intense as the sun goes down and we approach our destination. It's just after dark, the skies hazy and purple, when we first start to see the cars lining the side of the road. "Someone else is having a party, too," I joke, because there really are a lot of them. We're out in the middle of nowhere, with trees all around us and the roads deserted, nary a streetlight to be seen, but there are cars up and down the side streets, packed bumper to bumper.

Those warlocks are going to be super annoyed when someone throws a rave just down the street.

Ben turns down a side street, and not only do the woods grow denser, but the line of cars continues. I begin to get a weird, prickling sensation on my skin. "Are all these people going to the warlock party?"

"I hope not," Ben says grimly. "I thought Abernathy was the type to enjoy solitude."

Apparently not. Because as we turn down the driveway to the address in the GPS, it becomes very obvious that all these people are attending the same party we are. I give Ben a worried look and notice his hands are tight on the steering wheel. It's one thing to be showing off your sins in front of ten people, another to be showing off your aunt's familiar in front of a couple hundred.

I didn't even know this many witches existed. Not only that, but it's a party that everyone seems to have been invited to except Ben. My heart squeezes for him. "Did . . . Do you think Willem knew it would be this many people?" I ask, whispering. "Because—"

"He knew," Ben says flatly. "I wouldn't be surprised if he's here tonight himself, even without a familiar. He's not one to be left out."

"Good. If he's here, I'm going to add him to the list of people to punch in the balls."

He gives me a ghost of a smile and then parks deliberately in front of the house, blocking the driveway. A few people standing on the steps of the enormous house pause to frown at us, but no one comes out to demand we move. I imagine this is Ben's way of doubling down on his bad-boy reputation. If they expect him to be a dick, he'll be a dick. And I'll stand by his side every step of the way.

I take a brief moment to stare up at the house. It's something.

It looks like the hideous offspring of a hunting lodge and a castle. There are gables upon gables, and windows everywhere. The roof looks like an endless series of high, tight pyramids that lead down to walls with so many windows that they seem made entirely of glass. Inside I can see chandeliers filled with yellow light, animal heads mounted on the walls, and decorative antlers everywhere. So many antlers. I can also see a red-carpeted staircase, and the interior walls look to be made entirely of more shiny, glossy wood.

It's a little bit country and a lot upper class, and I'm glad I dressed up.

Ben gets out of the car and moves around to my side, intending to get the door for me. As he does, I hastily kick off my sneakers and switch to the strappy heels Lisa lent me. I tear my coat off, too, since it's now party-dress time, and I want to look good in front of everyone else. Witch and warlock society seems to involve a lot of pissing contests, and I didn't want to embarrass Ben by showing up in my old plain dress, so I borrowed a gown from Lisa, too. I've kept it carefully covered up until now, and when I step out of the car, Ben sees me in it for the first time.

His eyes widen and he stares at me. Hard.

I touch the low neckline and then sling the strap of the slim black purse I've also borrowed over my shoulder. "Too much?"

As I look at him for approval, Ben's nostrils flare. He puts a hand on the small of my back and leans in protectively. "I can't decide if I want to kill you for wearing something that provocative or find a dark corner and strip it off of you."

"Well, I know which one I vote for," I say breathlessly. And I smooth a hand down the tight bodice. Lisa's built differently than me, so the dress doesn't fit quite as it should. It's a fitted dress in dark, deep gray with paler gray piping to set off the tight bodice. It's sleeveless and the straps tie behind my neck, the front of the dress a loose gather that implies more cleavage than I actually have. Because I have less cleavage than Lisa, I have to remember not to lean over, or else I'm going to give everyone some full-frontal action. The back is entirely open and swoops down to the curve of my spine, and the skirt flares out ever so slightly at the knees so I can walk. It's pretty and flirty, and I've never worn anything like it. Even though it shows off the dual bracelets I'm wearing, I also feel powerful and sexy in this, which I figured I'd desperately need if the rest of this witchy crew are anything like Gwen.

Ben's hand is massive on the small of my back, and I can feel his fingers twitch as he escorts me toward the house. He shifts as if to move away, and I immediately snag his hand, nervous. I smile brightly at the people staring at us and try not to gawk at the house we're about to go into. I want to touch my hair to make sure no strands have gotten loose from the tight bun I've worked my brown waves into, but I don't want to fidget. So I just smile as if this is the greatest, clutch the strap of my purse in one hand and Ben's fingers in the other, and do my best to look thrilled even as I lurk as close as possible to Ben.

The inside of the house is an absolute sea of people. The moment we step inside, the temperature seems to rise by about ten degrees due to body heat, and the stink of a hundred perfumes and the flowers in vases on every surface fills the air. It's overwhelming. I wondered why people were standing outside of the party, and now I know—it's impossible to breathe in this crush. I've never seen so many people converging on a single house. There must be hundreds here.

And my temper flares, because Ben apparently wasn't invited. Neither was Dru.

Someone moves past us with a pair of champagne flutes, glancing in our direction as we make our way inside. It feels like everyone is eyeballing us, and I wish my dress had sleeves to cover the too-obvious and too-large familiar cuffs on my arms. I look for the same cuffs on other people and spot a few in the crowd, usually on the arm of a much younger woman who's leaning on a gray-haired man in a suit. Lovely.

Actually, now that I look around, the average age in the room seems to be wildly skewed. Most of the men are gray haired, their faces lined. Most of the women look to be close to my age, though a few pass by that could be age-mates of Dru. Every woman's wearing a fancy cocktail dress and high heels, and I can't help but notice that most of the younger women are wearing the familiar bracelets.

Yay, patriarchy.

I think of Penny, who's been waiting a long time for her chance. She's small and excitable and not slinky and seductive like the women here. I suspect that's a reason why she's been left on the shelf, and it makes me ache for her. I lean in close to Ben to share my observations. "So far I'm seeing a lot of old men with all the power."

"An accurate assessment," he murmurs against my ear. "Let's just find Abernathy and get the fuck out of here."

"What's he look like?" It occurs to me I probably should have asked this earlier.

"Small, tanned. Bald, with just a hint of white fringe above the ears. Favors wire-rimmed glasses. Usually hunched over a book."

I glance around at the partygoers. They look like they should be in Hollywood rather than at a witchcraft party, and I bite my lip, because the man Ben is describing doesn't seem like he would fit in with this crew. But we wasted all this time and money, so he has to be here . . . right?

As Ben leads me in, the uncomfortable staring continues. Every time I look around, I notice someone's watching us. People whisper, too. They smirk as we walk past, and someone stares pointedly at my dual bracelets. I feel like we're stomping all over everything these people—who are *our* people, I guess—hold sacred. We head down a hall that's just as crowded as the main foyer, and the rooms have the doors closed. Each one is labeled, though, and someone with a cuff like mine stands outside, guarding.

Bloodletting Required, reads one.

Do Not Enter Unless You Bring Your Own Fluids!!, reads another.

Orgy Room, reads a third. I lean over toward Ben at the sight of that one. "Um, is that for sex magic?"

"I'm not going to go in and ask," he murmurs. "Come on."

Before we can round the corner, a man approaches us. He doesn't match the description that Ben gave me. He's got a full head of hair, his skin is pasty white, and he's rotund. He's also got a furious look on his face as he storms toward us.

"You have some nerve, Magnus," the man says, and our surroundings go quiet. My skin prickles, and I realize everyone's listening in.

The look on Ben's face is cool and remote. Deadly. "Is there a problem, Tiberius?"

Tiberius curls his lip as he looks at me. "It isn't enough that you poisoned your aunt, but you have to steal her familiar out from under her nose? Your mother would—"

"I killed my mother," Ben says flatly. "So I don't know why you assume that I care what she thought."

The silence is deafening. Somewhere out in the party, a glass clinks. A giggle is stifled.

Tiberius glares at both of us. "You—"

"Excuse me," I say quickly, and step in front of Ben. He tries to pull me behind him, but I hold both his hands in mine and pin them at my back, as if we're just a lovey-dovey couple that can't keep their hands off each other. "But I don't appreciate your tone."

"Reggie," Ben begins.

"I don't appreciate your tone," I say a little louder, repeating myself. I decide to lie my ass off. "Ben was invited to this party, as was I. Now unless you have business with the two of us, we'd like to be on our way."

Tiberius looks astonished, as if no one's ever talked to him like I have. Maybe no one does. But I'm tired of all this shit. I'm tired of everyone looking at Ben like he's a piece of garbage, and I'm tired of him having to fall back on his parents' deaths—something that hurts him—to defend himself. "You, a mongrel—"

"Me, a mongrel," I say sharply. "Yes, that's right. I didn't come up in your little familiar society. I don't care. You're letting plenty of good familiars wither on the vine with that little society of yours, so I'm glad I didn't—"

"You should be at Drusilla's side—" Tiberius raises his voice, trying to get one up on me.

I just speak even louder. "Drusilla is the one that brought us together," I bellow. At Tiberius's astonishment, I continue to talk, because I'm angry and no one is on Ben's side but me. "Ben and I are *dating*. What part of that is hard for you to understand? Drusilla set us up. She likes that I'm wearing his bracelet. She encouraged it." It's a *tiny* bit of a lie, but I suspect Dru wouldn't mind it. She did hint that she wanted me with Ben, but that's all she mentioned. Still, I continue on, because I want to put this asshole in his place. "Now, if you're going to tell me that you've never fucked anyone that wore your bracelet, I'm going to call you a damn liar. Can we enjoy the party now, or is there some other make-believe issue you want to take up with my boyfriend?"

I'm panting from stress, and my head feels as if it's an orange that's been squeezed dry of all its juice. I hate standing up to people. Hate this party. Hate this asshole in front of me. But I hate that he's disparaging Ben more. I hate that he's trying to humiliate him in front of his peers just to get a leg up on him, and I won't stand by and let it happen.

Somewhere in the distance, amid the crowd, I catch a glimpse of bright red hair—Willem. He smiles approvingly in our direction and disappears into the crowd once more.

"It's not proper for her to speak to me in that kind of tone," Tiberius blusters, shocked by my vehement defense of Ben. "Where are her manners?"

I open my mouth to point out that I can speak for myself, but Ben detangles his hands from mine and puts them on my shoulders in a possessive gesture. He leans over me, getting in Tiberius's face. "You'll have to forgive her. She's a mongrel without any training, remember?"

And he quickly steers me away before I—or Tiberius—can say anything more.

I bite back the response brimming inside me, because everyone's still staring. My cheeks flush with anger and embarrassment both, and I let Ben tug me down a side hall at breakneck speed, my shoes clattering. After a too-long moment, the murmur of the party returns, and I'm able to breathe a little easier.

I just told off a warlock who'll probably curse me with eternal hiccups the moment we get out of this party, but I can't be sorry about it. Ben deserves better than that idiot's scorn. No wonder Ben doesn't like to spend time with his fellow warlocks. No wonder he feels alone. If they're all like that guy, I get it.

Ben speeds up, and I nearly lose one of Lisa's shoes as he drags me toward a pair of double doors down another hall. I totter after him as quickly as I can. The air is slightly cooler here, the crush of bodies less pressing, and the moment Ben reaches the doors, he pushes them open. I catch the barest glimpse of neat, organized bookshelves before Ben hauls me inside.

"Are we hiding?" I ask, confused. "Because—"

Ben shuts the door, and in the next moment, he presses my back to it, his hands cupping my face as he kisses the hell out of me.

I bite back a moan, my hands curling against the chest of his jacket as his tongue teases mine, his lips devouring. All the air in the room is suddenly gone, because Ben's stealing it from my lungs with his intense, hungry kisses. His hands are all over my torso, his thumbs working my nipples through the slinky fabric, and I'm writhing with anticipation when he slips a hand into the loose front of my dress, cupping my breast even as he devours me with hungry kiss after hungry kiss. When he finally comes up for air, I let out a dazed whimper of protest.

"No one," he murmurs, kissing me one more time, "has ever done that for me."

"N-not even Dru?" Oh god, he's kissed me so hard I'm stuttering. I stare at his mouth, wondering if maybe he'd kiss me again. I think I'm addicted to his mouth.

Ben shakes his head and presses his mouth to mine again, but it's a short, hard kiss. "That's different. Right now, I'm not sure if I should kill you for looking so fucking sexy in that dress and standing up for me, or if I should eat you alive. You—"

Someone clears their throat behind us.

We both go still. Ben suddenly grins down at me, boyish delight on his face, and I fight the urge to giggle. This is the happiest I've seen him all day, and it makes me want to wrap my arms around him and squeeze him tight. If everyone saw this man smile, his fearsome reputation would be gone in an instant. It just lights up his whole face, that wide, goofy, radiant smile.

"Are we interrupting something?" Ben calls over his shoulder. I peek over, too . . . and then I pinch Ben, because that's the guy we're looking for.

That's Abernathy, standing right by the bookshelves. His little wire-rimmed glasses are perched on the end of a long, thin nose, his white hair circles the lower half of his head like a fuzzy collar, and he gives us a look of pure disapproval as he flips through an old leather-bound book the size of a wallet. "This area is off-limits."

Ben turns, his expression serious. "Abernathy? Louis Abernathy?"

"What of it?" The man turns away, his back to us, and returns his book. He picks up another and peers at the pages. I frown because the tidy, straight lines of his coat are suddenly pulling to one side as if weighted down. When he immediately turns away again, I realize he's not putting the books back. He's stealing them and shoving them into his jacket.

Holy shit, is everyone at this party absolutely out of their damn minds? I give Ben an incredulous look, but I don't know if he's noticed Abernathy's light-fingered actions. He strides toward him, grabbing my hand again as he does. "Willem told us you'd be here tonight. We need your assistance with something."

Abernathy lifts his head. "Oh?" His gaze falls to my front and he frowns, then looks over at Ben.

Ben looks at me and then shifts his weight, leaning in front of me and blocking me from Abernathy's view as he discreetly tucks my roving tit back into the front of my dress. Whoops.

"We need your help breaking down a spell," Ben tells him. "Is it true that you can tear apart a spell and see who's cast it, even without the original components?"

Abernathy nods. "Yes, that's true."

Ben sags with relief. "Good. Someone's cursed my aunt, and if we can find out who did it, we can fix it."

"Cursed? Drusilla?" Abernathy looks surprised. He glances up from his book. "That is too bad. What kind of curse?"

"*Sopor.*" Ben's hand tightens on mine. "She won't wake up. She also says her familiars have been cursed, all of them. Clearly someone has an ongoing feud with her."

Abernathy's gaze moves toward my wrists, both of which are covered in familiar cuffs. "Is that why you're . . . sharing her familiar?"

"I volunteered," I say before Ben can respond. "I want to find who's doing this to Dru, and Ben needed my help."

Abernathy just nods and goes back to reading his book.

I can feel Ben tense. He glances back at me, then watches Abernathy. The man continues to read, licking a fingertip and flipping a page before setting the book down on the shelf once more. He picks up a new one, and Ben's hand clenches mine.

"Well?" Ben says after another tense moment. "Will you help us?"

Abernathy looks up, as if just now remembering we're still in the room. "Oh. No. Good evening to you both."

"Why not?" Ben's voice is full of anger and frustration.

"Because I am retired," Abernathy says, looking back down at the book. He flicks through a few more pages, then turns his back to us, and I'm almost positive he shoves the book into his jacket instead of putting it back on the shelf.

"What do you want to help us?" I suggest, because I can feel Ben tensing, like a volcano about to blow its top. "We have money. We'll get you whatever components you need. We'll pay you whatever you want. We just need to help Dru. She doesn't have much time left."

"No thank you."

"Please," I beg. "It would mean so much to us."

"I don't need money." Abernathy sounds bored.

I'm starting to tense as much as Ben is. "Then what?"

"Silence would be nice. A quiet place to study would be nice."

"We'll leave you alone if you cast this spell for us," I say quickly. "The moment we get the answer we need, we'll leave this party and leave you alone. We won't ever bother you again."

Abernathy smirks, running a finger along the spine of another book. "Tempting, but no."

Nothing we offer works, either. We try money, jewels, cars. Ben suggests a house. A private island. Rare components. That makes Abernathy pause, but he only shakes his head and does his best to ignore us. All the while, he fingers the books on the shelf, flicking through them as if they're so much more important than a woman that's dying, withering away under a spell.

And Ben just looks . . . furious. Defeated, but furious. As if he wants to wring Abernathy's neck but he can't, because we need him.

I'm so frustrated that I'm tempted to rip the next book out of Abernathy's hands when he hesitates, then turns his back again. "We know you're stealing those books," I snap. "How would it look if I went and found the host and told him all about how you're here at this party just to steal from him?"

That gets a response. Abernathy stiffens, then straightens to his full height. "Or how would you like it if I cast a spell that put your fingerprints all over these books instead?"

"Or," I retort, trying a different tactic, "how would you like it if I smuggled those books out for you in exchange for our help?"

That makes him pause. "You . . . what?"

Ben looks at me, a hint of a smile playing at his hard mouth. He's been so frustrated that I love the look of approval he gives me. It makes me feel good, like we really are a team.

"Yup." I gesture at Abernathy's jacket. "It's obvious that you're stuffing the books inside your coat. The outlines press through the material, and it makes your clothing hang funny. The moment you leave this room, it's going to be incredibly obvious what you're doing. You're going to piss off your host."

Abernathy adjusts his glasses, peering at me. The stubbornness is gone from his face, replaced by mild interest. "What do you suggest, then?"

I hold up my purse.

"You suggest I carry a purse?"

No, you idiot, I want to say, but I bite it back and keep my voice sweet. "No, I'm saying girls carry purses so we can smuggle tampons and other things with us. I could slide a book or two into my purse and carry them out for you. No one would be the wiser. We could meet up, you could cast the spell for us, and I'd give you the books."

Abernathy considers. He looks at Ben, then at me. He clutches a book to his chest and sighs. "I truly would like to help you both, but . . . I shouldn't."

"Why not?" Ben's frustration is evident in his tone, in the tightness of his shoulders. "We're running out of options. You're our best hope for figuring this out."

Abernathy shakes his head. "No one likes the answers. Every time I dissect a spell, someone gets mad, so I've stopped doing it." He shrugs, running a hand over a leather-bound book. "It's just easier."

"Please," I whisper. "Please help us. We won't get mad. We just want answers so we can save Drusilla."

He stares down at the book in his hands, and Ben reaches for mine. I clutch him tight, feeling as if I'm going to shatter if Abernathy says no again. Shatter . . . or fling myself at him in a rage.

The elderly warlock sighs. Fingers the book in his hands some more. Then he looks over at me. "How many books will your purse hold?"

REGGIE

It turns out my purse holds only two slim volumes, and Abernathy wants six books smuggled out. We figure out a compromise, and I put two books in my purse at a time, then find a bathroom with a window. We mingle for a bit, pretending to enjoy the party. Ben talks to Willem for a while, or another warlock, and then I make excuses and head to the restroom. I drop the books out the window, and when all six are deposited in the yard, it's near the end of the night, and my shoulders are screaming with tension and my head is throbbing.

We leave the party, circle around to the back of the house, and, thanks to the already-existing obfuscate spell, don't set off any alarms or trip any magical traps. We collect the books and then head to the hotel that Abernathy said to meet him at.

It's three in the morning before we get to his hotel room, but when he sees us, his eyes light up with greed. He clutches the books to his chest and sighs with bliss. "Perfection. I shall have to get a handbag of my own for the future."

"Or just bring a familiar that has one," I point out.

He wags a finger at me. "Genius. Now, come on. If you really want this spell cast, follow me."

Ben escorts me inside, his hand on my shoulder. I can feel the tension brimming through him, and I feel the same. We so desperately need answers for poor Dru, and Abernathy is our best hope. If he can't help us, we have to start over again.

The hotel room is an utter mess, so much so that it makes me twitch. There are books of every kind stacked all over the generic hotel dresser and tables, and dirty clothes strewn on the floor that Abernathy kicks aside. I see a blanket and pillow are on the sofa, as if he's been sleeping there instead of in the bed. As we get farther into the room, though, I catch sight of the bed, and I'm right—he's not sleeping on it. Instead, it's been set up as a table of some kind, I think. A sheet covers the bed itself, and underneath the sheet, I can make out a variety of shapes that look like bowls and unlit candles and a few other things. He's set this up as his spellcasting station.

I move to the bed and touch one corner of the sheet, curious to see what's underneath. Immediately, Abernathy rushes to my side and slaps my hand. "It's covered for a reason, little girl!"

I scowl at him, rubbing my fingers. Ben moves to my side, his hand rubbing my shoulder. "If the components are secret, we won't look," Ben promises.

"Very secret," Abernathy says, shooting me another displeased look. "You're going to have to turn your backs as I cast. I won't do it otherwise."

I don't care if I see him casting or not. "That's fine. Whatever you want to do. Let's just get it done."

We stand aside, watching as Abernathy rolls the two chairs in the room to the far side of the bed, making them face the wall instead of the spread he has atop the mattress. He indicates that we should sit, and so Ben and I do, and I stare at the ugly, generic pink-and-brown abstract on the hotel room's wall as Abernathy makes noise behind us, the clinking of glass and the rustle of dried leaves making my ears prick. I rest one hand on the arm of my chair, a foot away from Ben's chair, and when Ben touches my hand with his pinky, I link mine with his.

It's a small touch, but we're in this together and it's comforting. Linking pinkies with him gets rid of some of my anxiety. Just knowing that Ben's right there with me as we try to fix this . . . It's everything. With him at my side, I feel like it's all going to be okay. We'll save Dru, figure out who's behind this, and get them before they can curse me, too. Once all that's been handled, we'll figure out the two of us.

"I'm going to need a few components from the two of you," Abernathy says. "Are you averse to kissing?"

"Not at all," Ben murmurs, and his pinky strokes mine, ever so lightly.

"Excellent," Abernathy says, and then he pushes a bowl between us. "Both of you chew these leaves and then kiss. Make it good and wet, or the spell won't be as potent."

I give Ben an odd look, but he only shrugs and tugs my chair closer to his. I pop a leaf into my mouth, crunch down, and wrinkle my nose at the acrid taste. Horrid.

Ben leans toward me, cupping my cheek, and I can't help but ask a question. "Is this sex magic?" I whisper, curious. "Or do a lot of spells require kissing?"

"Does it matter?" Ben smiles, then leans in and brushes his lips against mine. He tastes like peppermint. No fair. I clearly got the short end of the leaf stick, and as we kiss, I'm torn between wanting to lose myself in his soft mouth and wanting to pull the leaves out of mine. But then Ben does this thing with his tongue, and I forget all about the spell. I wrap my arms around his neck, hungrily kissing him back—

"That's plenty," Abernathy snaps. "I just need a kiss for this to work, not coitus."

Ben smirks at me and pulls a leaf out of his mouth. *My* leaf. I can't decide if that's sexy or gross. Probably a little of both. I brush my lips with my fingers, flustered.

"Now, I need a secret from each of you." He hands us each a pen and a long strip of a thick, strange-feeling paper. "Write it down, curl up the paper, and then hand it to me. It must be secret or this won't work. Minerva requires your knowledge."

I blink, trying to think of something. I've never had to offer a secret before. He didn't say it had to be weighty, so I try to think of something that no one else would know but me. Ben knows about my parents. Nick, too. I consider for a moment longer and then write down:

Maurice doesn't want to be changed
back from a cat. He likes it.

It's something I learned one night while playing "blink for yes" with Maurice. He has his perverted moments, but he also really enjoys being a cat. I asked him if he wanted to be changed back, and he assured me that he did not, which made me feel a little less guilty about his curse.

I fold my secret up and hold it out to Abernathy, and Ben has one written, too.

"All right. You can look over. I have everything prepared."

We get up from our chairs, and I look over. Abernathy sits on the corner of the bed, his legs crossed, his small form hunched over a series of covered bowls. One of them smokes, and the faint scent of incense fills the room. As I watch, he takes a small silver blade, runs the knife over the back of his hand, and lets it bleed into another bowl. I nudge Ben, thinking about the fresh Band-Aids I put on his palm wound earlier today.

He just smirks at me, arching a brow.

Abernathy bleeds into the bowl, and the feeling of magic slides through the air, making it heavy. He sprinkles a bit of blood into each bowl, and they all begin to steam, as if suddenly activated. I watch as he waves a hand in the air, calling out names and invoking different gods. Some I recognize—Minerva, Jupiter—and some I don't. He mumbles under his breath, his eyes closed. He raises a hand into the air, gesturing toward me. My bracelet—Ben's bracelet—grows hot. I touch it, worried.

"Just borrowing," Abernathy says without opening his eyes. "If it bothers you, you and Mr. Magnus can perform a sexual act to supply the power I require—"

"Borrow away," I yelp before he can finish the sentence.

Ben just arches a brow at me, but I ignore it. He thinks it's cute that I'm so flustered, but I'm not about to perform some sex-magic nonsense with this Abernathy guy around. He can have a secret about Maurice and a leafy-tasting kiss, but that's it.

Abernathy pulls on the magic again, and I feel energy drain out of me as if I'm a tire with a slow air leak. My head grows heavy, and then I sag against Ben as Abernathy continues to cast. Ben wraps a strong arm around my waist and presses a kiss to my temple, holding me up.

"Sorry," I whisper.

"Don't be." He rubs his lips against my hair. "I've got you."

Abernathy picks up the bowl with the wadded-up secrets and sprinkles a bit of his blood on them. One catches on fire, but the other remains paper. He frowns at us. "Which one of you gave me a dud?"

Ben nudges me. "I think it's you. I'm a hundred percent positive mine's secret."

Oh. I blink heavily, trying to concentrate. It's late and I'm sapped, though, and I nod as Abernathy hands me another piece of paper and a pen. I move across the room to write it, hiding my paper from both Ben and Abernathy. I try to think of something no one knows but me. One thing immediately pops into my mind, and even though it feels dangerous to write it down and acknowledge it, I do.

I'm in love with Ben Magnus.

I fold it up tight and hand it back to Abernathy. The moment he sets it in the bowl, it goes up in smoke. Abernathy nods. "Minerva is pleased now." He gestures at Ben. "Do you have something of your aunt's I can use to focus my casting on?"

Ben pulls out a fat, ugly ring from his pocket. He holds it out to Abernathy. "Her first wedding band."

I didn't even know he had it with him. Then again, of course Ben would. He's always prepared. He knows how this stuff works. Me, I'm just the battery.

The sleepy, sleepy battery.

I don't protest when Ben moves back to my side and wraps his arms around me, tucking me against him. I can feel Abernathy pulling more magic, and I nearly groan aloud when he uncovers a bowl full of bones and chicken feet. In my experience with Dru, the spells that take the most out of you are the ones with the animal parts. I wonder if it's too late to ask Ben to fuck me atop the table instead.

"We're going to toss the bones," Abernathy says, raking the used components aside with one arm and clearing off a spot on the bedsheets. "And they will spell out the name of the person that cast the spell upon your aunt." He drops the ring into the bowl full of bones and shakes it like a Christmas present. Then he takes a handful of bones, closes his eyes, and casts them on the mattress.

I peer down, both worried and excited to find this out. Is it Livia? I still have my money on Livia.

It looks like nothing more than a scatter of debris in front of Abernathy, though. He doesn't look worried, however. He runs his hand lightly over the bed, and as he does, the bones seem to jump and move, forming a letter.

M

My lips part in surprise. Oh. It's working. I'm always shocked when magic works. Some part of me keeps expecting to wake up and realize that everyone's been faking, but there's no mistaking that *M* spelled out in chicken feet and wishbones.

Abernathy grabs another handful of bones and tosses it down next to the first pile. This time, the bones move into place as if drawn by magnets.

A

An uneasy feeling starts in the pit of my stomach. That's . . . awfully coincidental.

When Abernathy tosses out another handful, the *G* that shows up is stark and obvious. I swallow hard.

"I don't understand," Ben says, voice low.

Abernathy ignores him, tossing another handful onto the bed.

N

I slide out of Ben's grasp, feeling sick. Ben killed his parents, sure, but he said it had to be done. It was to save them. But . . . what if he's been lying to me this whole time? Using me? Just like my parents always say whatever is necessary to get what they want? I think back to Dru's words, about how all her familiars get cursed.

Of course they would, if Ben doesn't like them. He's the only person other than Dru that's been around every single one of them over decades and decades.

Abernathy casts again, and my vision hazes, the power drain taking its toll on me.

U

I sway, but when Ben reaches for me again, I shake my head and push him aside. I don't want him to touch me. Not if he's the one that cursed his aunt. He knew I was going to quit . . . What if he did this just to make me stay?

I was leaving that night, and then the next morning, Dru was cursed.

I swallow hard. It's not coincidence. It's not.

I turn to him, utterly shattered. "Was this all just to get me to stay?" I whisper, beyond hurt. I'm numb (though that might be the casting). "You couldn't just let me leave?"

"Reggie," Ben says, shaking his head. "I didn't. I would never—"

There's one final draw of power that drags me under, and I collapse before I even see the bones spell out the *S* in Magnus. I don't need to see it.

I already know the answer.

BEN

I carry Reggie to our hotel room. It's late, and luckily I had the forethought to get us a room in the same hotel as Abernathy just in case we were both too tired to leave after the casting was done.

Abernathy had no explanations for me, just a sad shake of his head. "I told you. No one ever likes the answer."

"It's wrong," I snarled at him, furious. "I didn't do it."

He shrugged. "Whatever. I told you you wouldn't like it."

"It must have read the ring wrong," I stammered, trying to understand why the spell would firmly point the finger at me. "I held on to it for too long. It targeted me instead of my aunt. It must have—"

The look Abernathy gave me was pitying.

Fuck him. Fuck all of this.

I settle Reggie into the bed. She's pale and wan, her freckles standing out on her skin. Abernathy pulled too hard from her, drained too much. He doesn't care if he pushes her beyond her limits, but I fucking care. The thought of Reggie hurting because a too-powerful spell drained her wrecks me.

The thought of Reggie hating me because she thinks I did this wrecks me even more.

There was no mistaking the look of betrayal on her face as Abernathy cast. As she realized it was going to spell out my name.

I don't understand it, but I need to make her realize it wasn't me. That I'd never injure my aunt like that. That Dru's the only family that's ever stood by my side. I might have some dark spots on my soul, but not that. Never that.

But I don't expect Reggie to believe that. We've known each other for months, not centuries. She doesn't believe me when I say it's not me. And I get it. I understand why she can't quite trust . . . even if it still makes me ache.

I watch her as she sleeps. I don't get into bed with her, because I suspect I'm not welcome. Reggie loves and cares for people openly, giving them everything she can of herself, but when she feels betrayed, it goes deep. I understand that, and it's why I need to talk to her, just to explain myself to her so she'll understand it wasn't me. So she'll give me another chance to prove to her that I'm trustworthy. That I'm not the monster she thinks I am.

I doze in a chair fitfully, watching as she sleeps.

My phone rings just after dawn and I jump to my feet. Clutching it to my chest, I glance over to see if it's awoken Reggie, but she still sleeps. I answer the call and step out of the room, heading down the hotel hallway as I do so I won't accidentally wake her. "Hello?"

"It's Lisa. How did it go?"

I shake my head in frustration. "Not good. We found Abernathy, but he miscast the spell. Pointed the finger at me."

"Oh no." Lisa sounds upset. "You would never, Caliban."

I know that. Of course I know that. "Like I said, it misfired. We'll have to figure something else out. How's Aunt Dru?"

Lisa sighs, her tone more annoyed than sad. "The same as always. Are you guys returning soon? I could use a break, and I have a doctor's appointment tomorrow. Jim's warlock is getting a little impatient, too."

I want to snap that Jim's warlock can fuck right off, but I don't. Lisa has been helpful, and she doesn't deserve my wrath. However, if I see Abernathy again . . . "We'll catch a flight back today."

"Super. We'll be waiting. Safe travels!"

I hang up and shove my phone into my pocket, and my hands into my pockets, too. I want to grab my phone and fling it down the hall, to watch it smash into a million pieces against the wall, but I don't dare. I need to stay in contact for Lisa and for Aunt Dru, just in case my aunt takes a turn for the worse . . . or she magically wakes up.

I don't know what to do. I pace down the hall, lost and frustrated, and when I finally return to my room, I'm not entirely surprised to see that it's empty. While I was gone, Reggie snuck out. She must have been faking sleeping and decided to flee me when the moment arose.

She thinks I'm guilty.

She's left. She's done with me.

This time, I don't resist the urge to throw my phone. I fling it from me and let it crash into the wall, watching as it shatters into a hundred pieces. Instead of making me feel better, I just feel worse. Hollow. Angry.

Defeated.

I shouldn't be surprised. Reggie has trust issues, and I have a long and ugly past and a bad reputation. It's obvious that she shouldn't trust me. Yet I'm still disappointed that she doesn't.

I shouldn't have gotten my hopes up. Shouldn't have hoped that someone would see me for me, and not just the reputation. I stare at the empty hotel room and feel completely, utterly alone.

REGGIE

I've made a huge mistake.

The words echo in my mind over and over again as the Uber takes me to Nick's apartment, the one I used to share with him.

I've made a huge mistake.

Hot tears roll down my face, and I bite back a sob of misery, because the driver's already giving me weird looks. It's just . . . I've fucked up so badly. I look at the time on my phone. How long has it been since I left Ben and ran out of the hotel? Nearly a full day. I've spent the last twenty-four hours taking planes and cars back toward Dru's house, only to realize that I can't go there.

Not right away.

I need Nick's help because I have to somehow fix this.

More tears roll down my face, and I swipe them away, furious with myself. It's my own fault. I stare down at the twin cuffs on my wrists, and I touch Ben's over and over again.

Ben.

I'm so damn stupid. I take another shuddering breath. I was so tired and loopy from Abernathy's spell that I immediately thought he'd betrayed me. It didn't matter that he's never done anything to indicate he would do so. I just assumed Ben was like my parents, only using me for his own ends. I let that hot panic sweep over me, and I ran away. I got a car to the airport and booked a flight with a stupidly long layover on a commercial airline, just because I didn't want to meet up with Ben again on the private flight.

When I got on the first plane, I was convinced he was guilty and that he'd simply manipulated me. That he'd put his own aunt at risk to get me to stay.

But then small things didn't add up. The ugly wound he sliced into the center of his palm because he was so rattled about Dru's curse. Climbing down in the well after me and kissing me silly. Showing up at the party even though it would destroy what little he had left of his reputation. His confessions about his parents. If he'd wanted to keep me at his side, he wouldn't have said anything about them. He wouldn't have me wearing his bracelet and angering every warlock on the continent.

He wouldn't have looked so completely and utterly betrayed when I pushed him away.

I made a knee-jerk reaction and panicked. By the time my second flight landed, I'd worked through my thoughts and realized it wasn't Ben. The spell *had* misfired, like he'd said. Dru is his only family. Ben would never harm her.

After my plane landed, I called Ben.

No answer.

I texted him.

Nothing.

I waited at the airport for an hour, not sure if I could go back home to Dru's house. I wasn't sure if I'd be welcome. After all, Ben's had centuries of people abandoning him and thinking the worst. It probably cut him deeply when I didn't trust him.

But Ben didn't answer my calls. He made it clear he wanted nothing to do with me.

So I'm panicking and utterly distraught. I'm on my way to talk to Nick. He's better with people than I am. He'll know what to do.

The moment the Uber pulls up to Nick's apartment building, though, I bite back a groan of dismay at the sight of my parents' van. Of course they'd be here on the worst day of my life. They're like sharks that can smell blood in the water. I yank the hood of my sweatshirt over my head to hide my face, and make for the front door of the building. Maybe they won't see me—

"Reggie!" My mother's voice is like nails on a chalkboard. "There you are!"

I do not have time for this shit today. I don't stop walking, increasing my speed as I race for the door.

"Reggie! Stop right now! We need to talk!" My father, too. Footsteps sound on the pavement behind me, and when a hand touches my arm, trying to stop me, I lose it.

"I DO NOT HAVE TIME FOR THIS SHIT TODAY," I bellow in my mother's face, repeating my inner monologue for their benefit.

My mother flinches back, wearing a wounded expression on her face. My father moves to her side, his disapproval obvious. This is how it always goes with them. I try to be strong, but they act like their misfortune is somehow my fault. Like they're just trying to love me and I'm the one that's hurtful. Like I'm the one in the wrong. Like Mom has medical issues and Dad has had yet another employer that didn't understand him. Then they make me feel so guilty for accusing them of manipulation. They deflect when I ask about stealing my money, my mail, my identity, and say that it was all necessary because Mom needed money for some sort of treatment that never has receipts or an office that exists, and it's just never-ending and I am tired of it.

So damned tired of it. I'm tired of them making me the bad guy and gaslighting me when I try to stay strong. I'm tired of them stealing from me and acting like I'm the unreasonable one. I'm tired of them stalking me.

I am *done.*

I shake off my mother's hands, determined not to feel more guilt. "I am not doing this today," I tell them in a loud, warning voice. "I am not. I am going up to visit my friend, and you are not going to follow me. You are not going to steal his mail. You are not going to open more credit cards in my name. And you are not going to keep showing up on my doorstep, hoping for handouts." I raise my voice. "I have never sought a restraining order or sent your information over to the police, but so help me, if you don't leave me alone this instant, I will have your asses thrown in jail before the week is out. Do you understand?"

I might be yelling. I don't even know anymore. All I know is that I need them to understand that I have just destroyed the heart of the love of my life and I am not in the mood for their bullshit.

"But—" my mother begins.

"Restraining," I snarl. "Order!" And before they can say anything else, I storm inside the building. I stomp to the elevator, half daring them to follow behind me, and I'm a little surprised when they don't. Full of righteous indignation, I glare at the elevator walls as it takes me up to the third floor, where Nick's apartment is. I draw myself up, clutching my overnight bag in one hand and my useless phone in the other, just in case Ben texts me, and march to Nick's door. I knock hard. Twice, just in case he didn't hear it the first time.

Nick comes to the door and opens it a crack, a confused expression on his face. "Reggie? What—"

All my bluster disappears and I burst into tears again. "I've ruined everything, Nick. You have to help me."

He looks wary. "Ruined how?" Nick's gaze moves up and down my party dress and sneakers, my tangled hair and the makeup that's probably under my eyes instead of on my eyelids at this point. "You look like shit."

"I . . . ruined . . . *everything*," I sob again. "Everything! Ben hates me!"

Nick glances behind him, where no doubt Diego is waiting for him to come back into the apartment. "You should probably come in—"

"We tried to find out who was casting spells on Dru," I babble, tears gushing from my eyes. "And we went and found a warlock to help us figure it out, and we went to a party and everyone was so mean to him there, Nick. It was awful. I wanted to show him just how amazing he is, and I might have yelled at some of his friends, and then Abernathy said it was him and I know it's not Ben, but I was tired and confused and I thought I was being used again, because my parents make me distrust everyone, you know? And so I freaked out and ran away without talking to him, and now he won't return my phone calls, and how can I tell him that I love him and I believe him if he hates my guts?" My wail echoes in the hall. "He doesn't know I love him, Nick! That was my stupid secret for stupid Abernathy, and I didn't even get a chance to tell him! I was too afraid, and now he thinks I hate him."

Nick listens to me blurt out my misery, a weird look on his face.

"And I don't," I continue, sniffling. "I love him. So much. And that scares me and I don't know what to do. And you . . ." I wipe at my nose, which is running with snot at this point, since I'm not a pretty crier. "Why aren't you saying anything?"

Nick continues his silence. He simply opens the door to the

apartment wider, and instead of Diego, I see Ben Magnus on the other side of the door.

"Oh fuck," I breathe, clutching my phone to my chest. "Ben—"

"It's okay," he says, and they're the two most beautiful words in the world.

"It's not okay." My face crumples and I start to cry all over again. "I didn't trust you, and I should be the one person that always trusts you and—"

"Hey, hey," Ben says softly, pushing past Nick to gather me in his arms. "Reggie. It's all right."

I sob against his chest, curling my hands against his soft, soft sweater over his big, broad chest. "I wasn't thinking straight," I tell him. "My parents—"

"Are outside," he agrees, stroking my hair.

"And I thought for a moment you were like them, because I always think no one can really love me. That they're just using me and I'm too stupid to figure it out."

"You're not stupid—"

"I yelled at them," I tell him, sniffing. "I threatened to get a restraining order."

"You did?" Ben sounds delighted. "I'm so proud of you, sweetheart—"

"And I wanted to come to you, but I wasn't sure if you'd want me there—"

"I'd always want you there—"

"Your phone—"

"Broke it," he says quickly. "That's why I'm here. I wasn't sure where you'd go, and I was worried sick about you—"

"I love you," I say again, frantic he didn't hear me the first time. We keep talking over each other, desperate to get it all out. I pull back, still clutching a handful of his sweater, searching his face to see if I'm forgiven for hurting him. "I love you. That was my secret for Minerva—at first it was about Maurice, but my real secret was that I love you, and I didn't tell you—"

He silences me with a kiss. I choke back a sob of pure happiness, clinging to his mouth. This has been the worst day of my life, but it's getting better by the moment.

"I am really, really confused," Nick says somewhere behind us as we kiss. Ben strokes my face, his eyes full of emotion as he wipes away my tears.

I swipe at my nose, because I know I'm a mess, but god, the way Ben looks at me, I know it doesn't matter. He stares at me as if he wants to devour me, his gaze intense, and it's like there's no one in the world but the two of us.

"I love you," I say again, just because I know I hurt him and I'm desperate to make it better. "Once I realized I'd made such a mistake—"

He shakes his head. "It's okay. You panicked."

"It's not okay, but I hope you'll give me the chance to make it up to you."

Ben's eyes gleam. "Did you have something in particular in mind?"

"A lot of things," I confess. "Most of them filthy—"

"Ew?" Nick breaks in. "Can you two save that for the bedroom instead of my hall?"

Ben grins down at me, still cupping my face, as if we're sharing a secret. "Later?" he whispers.

"Later," I agree, and glance over his shoulder to give my friend a sheepish look. "Sorry. Was I interrupting?"

Nick gives us both an incredulous look. "I'm still trying to figure out all this babble about spells. What the hell are you two going on about?"

I exchange a look with Ben, biting my lip. I haven't really updated Nick on the whole witchcraft-is-real situation. "Oops."

Ben just laughs, and the sound fills me with sunshine and joy. Leaning over me, he whispers again. "We'll worry about that later, too."

"How's Dru?" I ask.

"The same." He shakes his head. "There's no change. Lisa's still with her."

Thinking about Dru triggers another confession from me, because I desperately need Ben to understand why I panicked. "That's one reason why I suspected you, you know."

"Reggie, it's okay." The look in Ben's eyes is soft. Loving. Forgiving.

But it's not okay. Not to me. It won't be okay for a long, long time. And if I can make him understand that I didn't panic blindly, all the better. "After we kissed on the couch, I tried to quit. Remember? I told myself I couldn't stay, because you were my boss's nephew and I couldn't work every day knowing I wanted to kiss you and touch you."

Nick makes another sound of disgust. "Can we please not talk about this in my hall?"

"So I was going to quit, but then Dru got cursed and the timing was just fucked and . . ." I trail off.

Of course.

The timing of everything.

I'm an *idiot.*

"I told you, Reggie, it's fine." Ben's voice is gentle as he takes the box of tissues that Nick extends toward us. He pulls one free and mops my tear-swollen face tenderly. "We won't give up. We'll figure it out—"

I clutch his hand, my eyes wild. "I already did."

BEN

I can hardly believe she's here.

My Reggie.

Even though she stands at my side, it's difficult for me to grasp that she really, truly is here with me. No, not just *standing* at my side. She clings to me as if she never wants me to leave her sight again. Her hand is tight in mine, and even though her eyes are swollen with tears, there's a look of determination on her face.

The last day has been rough. My protective instincts wouldn't let me forget about her. The moment I got home, I looked for Reggie. When I saw she wasn't in her room and Lisa said she hadn't stopped by the house, I was worried. I hunted down Nick's address and showed up at his place to ask if he'd seen her. When he said he hadn't, I demanded to stay and wait, and a frantic Reggie showed up hours later, tearful and distraught that she'd somehow lost me.

It would take a lot more than one small argument for me to stop loving her. And because I know Reggie's past, I immediately knew why she panicked. We're alike, she and I, and I understand her far better than she thinks.

Except I don't know what she's thinking now, as we return to

Aunt Dru's house. She said she'd figured out who cursed my aunt, and though I've told her a dozen times that the spell misfired, she wants to talk to Lisa. Reggie thinks there's a clue we've missed, and since I can deny her nothing, I drive us both back to my aunt's.

Reggie's hand is on my leg the entire time, as if she's afraid to let me go. It's the best feeling in the universe.

When we return to Aunt Dru's house, everything is quiet. We head up to her room, and Lisa is seated by the bed, a paperback romance open over her belly as she dozes.

For a woman that's been in a coma for five days, my aunt actually looks surprisingly good. Her cheeks are rosy and full, and Lisa has her dressed in clean clothing. Poor Lisa looks more tired than Aunt Dru, actually. The pregnant woman opens her eyes and gives us a weary look, dark circles hollowing her face.

"No change," Lisa tells us as we head into Aunt Dru's room. "I'm sorry to say that we haven't seen her wake up at all. No one's come by to visit, either."

"You can tell us the truth, Lisa," Reggie says, her voice surprisingly hard. "We've figured it out."

Lisa looks confused. She turns to me, and when I shrug, she gives Reggie a puzzled look. "I'm sorry?"

Reggie squeezes my hand, shooting me a confident look. "Where is it?" she demands boldly as she strides into the room. "Did she hide it somewhere in here?"

"Hide what?" Lisa asks.

"The tablet. You cursed her. Or she cursed herself." Reggie feels along the edge of the bed, flipping up the corners of the blankets as if hunting for something. "It's all in the timing."

Lisa shoots me another helpless, confused look. I have to admit that I'm confused, too. "Reggie, sweetheart. My aunt is a little eccentric, but this curse is dangerous to her. She could starve to death and never wake up. Aunt Dru wouldn't put herself in danger like this."

Reggie just shakes her head, that expression of determination written all over her pretty, freckled face. "It's the timing," she says again. "Every time you and I got close, Ben, and I tried to run, something happened. Lisa got cursed, so Dru suggested you stay by my side, remember?"

I frown, because I distinctly remember my aunt pulling me aside and having a conversation with me. Insisting I stay in the area to help her watch over Reggie, to keep her safe. That I stay at Reggie's side at all times to protect her. And that suited me just fine, because I was fascinated with Reggie already . . .

"And the night we kissed, Dru kept asking if we were going to get together," Reggie says, dropping to her knees by the bed and flipping the bedskirt up. "And I told her I was quitting, and she asked me to wait until morning and—aha!" Reggie's head pops up over the side of the mattress, a wild-eyed and triumphant look on her face.

She tosses an empty potato chip bag onto the mattress, directly onto Dru's sleeping form.

"I was looking for that!" Lisa exclaims. "My snacks have been disappearing."

Reggie disappears under the bed again, and a moment later, she tosses a drained soda bottle next to the chip bag, followed by an empty cookie container. "She doesn't look thin for someone that's been unconscious and unable to eat for several days, does she? She cursed herself," Reggie says again, triumphant. "There's a mess of empty snack bags and drink bottles under here. She's cursed herself somehow, but there's a loophole. But because she cursed herself, that's why Abernathy's scrying spelled out 'Magnus.' She's doing this to force me and Ben together. She's playing matchmaker."

I stare down at my aunt's peacefully sleeping, cursed form. "No . . ." I breathe. It's insane, even for Aunt Dru.

"I thought Lisa was in on it at first," Reggie admits, getting back to her feet. When Lisa makes a sound of protest, Reggie nods. "I know. But you're so tired and pregnant that it doesn't make sense. I bet if we checked on your curse, though, it was probably cast by Dru. It's not a very harmful curse, after all. It's just inconvenient."

Lisa's mouth opens. She stares at me, then back at Reggie. She stares down at her arm and then slowly pulls her sleeve up to reveal that she's still wearing Dru's familiar cuff. "She asked me not to take it off," Lisa says. "I thought it was just her being, well, Dru. But she asked me to hide it from Reggie. Didn't want to hurt her feelings. Said once the baby was weaned, we'd pull me back into service. Do you think this is all some weird game of hers?"

I bend over and gaze down at the empty chip bags and soda bottles underneath the bed. I think of all the times Aunt Dru brought up Reggie to me, insisted I spend more time with her. Nudged her in my direction. I was all too happy to do so, because I was fascinated by Reggie. And that fascination distracted me from the fact that perhaps Aunt Dru was being a little pointed in her enthusiasm. Scheming machinations are definitely an Aunt Dru thing. She's sweet when she wants to be, but she's also a two-thousand-year-old witch who insists on getting her way.

I put my hands on my hips, thinking. "She's definitely cursed to sleep, but she also seems to be waking up at some point to eat."

"I don't understand," Lisa says. "I never saw her wake up, much less eat anything."

Reggie snaps her fingers. "Maybe she can't do it when someone else is in the room."

"Now that sounds more like Aunt Dru," I say with a rueful shake of my head. "Shall we exit the room and see if Sleeping

Beauty awakens, then?" And if she does, I just might strangle her for scaring the life out of me.

We usher Lisa out of the room and shut the door behind us. Reggie presses her ear to the door, frowning, and then shakes her head. "Nothing. Maybe we have to be farther away?"

"Let's go to my room," I suggest. "We can scry to watch her."

The three of us head into my room, and instead of going into my hidden study, I pull out the emergency components I keep handy, and make a quick offering to Mercury. "Can I borrow your phone, Reggie?"

She immediately hands it over, no questions asked, and it makes me want to kiss her that she trusts me so much.

I turn the cell phone on, the passcode showing on the screen. I ignore it, swiping my finger down the left side to keep the surface active. "Show me Aunt Dru."

Reggie presses her chin to my arm, leaning over me to watch the screen, and I love the way she casually drapes herself on me, freely touching me as if I belong to her. I like the thought of belonging to her. A lot.

The phone's screen goes black, and then a picture begins to slowly form once more. It focuses in on Aunt Dru's bed, and I watch in disbelief as she yawns and slowly rises, rubbing her eyes. She smacks her lips and then frowns down at the chip bags on her blankets. She gets up from the bed, stretching, then checks under the bed, disappearing for a moment. When she resurfaces, she has a bag of chips and starts to eat again, shoving them into her mouth quickly.

"I'll be damned," I say softly.

Aunt Dru's fooled us all.

REGGIE

In a way, I'm relieved Dru cursed herself.

Even though I want to kill her (cheerfully) for deceiving us all, I'm glad it's going to be easy to resolve and Dru's not in danger of dying. Ben's expression is utter relief, and when he hugs me close, I know he was worried. He's more relieved than I am. Dru is my friend and employer, but she's Ben's family.

Lisa is pissed, though. Really pissed. "Not only has she been stealing my snacks for days, but I have spent hours in that fucking uncomfortable chair with my bladder being kicked by my baby, and she has the nerve to play these games?" She rubs her distended belly, teeth bared in a snarl. "Do you know how pissed Jim's warlock is at how much time he's taken off? Oh my god." She shakes her head. "Unbelievable. I love how this is all a joke to her."

"She must have her reasons," I say softly. "At least, I would hope so."

I suspect she does, though. Dru strikes me as a little manipulative, but her heart is in the right place. She adores Ben, and this scheming seems to be centered around him.

"Whatever you say," Lisa says with a shake of her head, writing the last of the note we've decided to leave in Dru's room. It seems the easiest way to communicate with her—let her know that we're aware of the curse, demand to know where the tablet is so we can destroy it and break it, and then have a nice, long talk with her after the fact and find out what the hell she was thinking for scaring Ben like that.

I wrap my arms around him a little tighter, fighting back resentment. All the hours of worry, all the stress . . . and Dru was never in danger. If I'm feeling a little worn out and used, I can't imagine how hurt Ben is, how utterly frustrated. I'm draped over him as we sit on the couch, while Lisa composes the note. When she gets up, Ben gets to his feet, too, taking it from her. "You sit. I'm going to be the one to deliver this, right on her forehead so she can't say she didn't see it."

Oh yeah, he's a little mad.

Lisa sits down again gratefully, rubbing her belly. "I think we're all going to have a few things to say to her when she wakes up."

I BITE MY nails, waiting, while Ben is upstairs. He doesn't come back down to join us, and I suspect everything he's feeling is bubbling over. When he does stalk through the living room, he pauses by my seat on the couch, touches my cheek tenderly, and then hands me the two broken halves of a tablet. "I need some time alone."

He heads outside to Dru's gardens, and my heart squeezes. I feel bad for him, because I know he's frustrated and hurt. Lisa gives me a curious look, but I just shrug. It's between him and his aunt. I can't interfere in it; I can only be there for him if he needs me.

Dru comes down the stairs in her favorite fluffy pink robe, giving us a wobbly smile. "Surprise."

Lisa immediately gets to her feet, waddling over to hug Dru. She embraces her tightly despite her enormous belly and wiggles back and forth. "Do not ever scare us again like that, Drusilla, or I'll murder you myself."

Dru just chuckles, and the sound is weary, as if she's the one that's been put through the wringer for the last several days. "No you won't. You're too softhearted." She touches Lisa's belly. "How's my baby doing?"

"She's tired," Lisa says. "We both are. And we have a doctor's appointment this afternoon. Jim's going to pick me up any minute now. Now that you're awake, can you break my curse, please? I'm getting really tired of having to pee with the bathroom door open, and I suspect the doctor isn't going to be a fan of that, either."

"Oh yes, your tablet is between the mattresses upstairs. I should go get it—"

"I'll get it," Lisa says, a warning note in her voice. "You have a lot of explaining to do."

Dru looks over at me, uncomfortable. "I'm not sure anything I say will do any good."

"Try?" I say. "How about you try and explain why you put us through hell for the last five days?"

"'Hell' might be a little bit of an exaggeration," Dru begins, shuffling over to where I'm seated on the couch. "Perhaps 'mild strain' would be better?"

"No," I say firmly. "It was hell. It was hell watching Ben slice open his palm because he was frantic to help. It was hell going to that house party. It was hell having to chase down Gwen and dealing with her. Ben's reputation is fucked all over again because of what you did. He's upset. He's angry. And I need to understand why. Just . . . *why*, Dru?"

She beams at me, all white curls and sweet smile. "It makes me so happy to hear you defend him like this, dear. You have no idea how badly I've wanted this for both of you."

I raise a finger. "Don't change the subject. You're still not telling me why you cursed Lisa, threatened me with a curse, and cursed yourself! Was this all some ridiculous matchmaking scheme? You couldn't have thought of *any* other way to get us to talk to each other? Because that's what this is, isn't it? Some matchmaking scheme?"

Dru sighs heavily. She puts her hands in her lap, and they're nearly buried in the folds of her pink robe. "It's hard for me to watch my dear Caliban be so sad and lonely."

I spread a hand. "So you cursed yourself? I'm not seeing the reasoning behind it, Dru."

She taps my leg. "Quit interrupting and I'll tell you." Dru ignores my scowl and straightens her shoulders, tossing her head back and sitting as regally as a queen next to me on the sofa. "I'm two thousand years old. I've outlived six husbands . . . though I did get rid of a few of them," she admits with a wink. "But I like being ancient. I like near immortality. It means people flit in and out of my life before I can grow tired of them. It means that when I have a friend—like Livia—they're a friend for hundreds and hundreds of years. It allows us to be very close. Now and then, when we get tired of witch society, and who wouldn't, we take a sabbatical. We disappear for years at a time and avoid casting. I've had several sabbaticals in my years. Normally when I get tired of people, I just pack up my things and head off to explore some new place. I'd retreat from society for a few years, and when I got the itch to cast again, I'd return to society and pick right up where I left off." She shrugs. "It works very well for me because I don't mind solitude. Even when I'm alone, I'm not *lonely*. I like who I am and the choices I've made."

I curl up on the couch, following along. I'm not entirely sure what this has to do with her curse, but I listen anyhow.

She looks over at me and her expression grows soft. "Caliban isn't like me. He's not suited for endless years of solitude. He doesn't have anyone to fall back upon. He's always been an island alone, even surrounded by people. I blame his parents for that." She sighs. "I never had children of my own, but my sister did. Caliban's mother was my great-grandniece, and the moment he was born, she abandoned him. He grew up unloved and forgotten. I did my best to step in, but I feel as if that loneliness has just covered him like a cloak, always. He doesn't get along with others in witch society, you know. After growing up half-feral, I suppose the boy got used to doing as he liked, and now he doesn't appreciate it when others tell him what to do." She chuckles and leans toward me. "I think he gets that from my side of the family."

I say nothing, but my heart squeezes. Ben is alone. Always has been. I think of five hundred years of his loneliness, and it makes me hurt for him.

"He's always been an outcast," Dru says softly. "And sad. So very sad. I'm getting old, you know. And I thought about what would happen to my poor Caliban if I eventually die and rejoin the gods in their heavens. Even those of us with ambrosia in our veins don't live forever. And it hurt me to think of Caliban just drifting along, forever alone, when he is so smart and thoughtful and loving." She looks over at me. "He has so much love to give, Reggie."

There's a knot in my throat. "I know."

Her gaze grows distant. "So I made plans. I always wanted Lisa to come back after the baby. We talked about it a little—she loves magic and loves apprenticing. I don't think she dreams of becoming some great caster on her own. There's no ambition in her. She likes helping, loves assisting. It's the mark of a fantastic familiar—that eagerness to please. And so I figured while she raises the baby, I'd take a little vacation, you know? Visit some old friends, see some tropical islands, maybe tour Australia and get myself a pet kangaroo."

"I'm not sure you can keep them as pets—"

She waves a hand. "Don't ruin my fantasy. Anyhow, I was getting everything prepared to leave, and then Ben came to visit me. And I knew something was wrong. He's always a little sad and remote, but lately he's just looked . . . lost. Something's happened to make him retreat within himself, and I knew then I couldn't leave him. I wasn't sure if he'd be there when I came back."

I think about Ben, about the client that killed himself and how much it made him question whether he was on the right path. Dru was right that something was bothering him.

"So I thought, well, what my Caliban needs is someone to love. And that's where you come in." She beams at me. "I spent days casting spells, looking to find the perfect person for him. Someone that would be able to see through all the prickly layers he puts over himself, someone that could understand where he comes from. Someone smart and brave and just as loving as him. I told Caliban that I needed a familiar while Lisa was unavailable, put an ad in the paper, and enchanted it to draw you toward it. Did you know you had the job before you ever stepped foot inside this house?"

I don't know if I should be flattered or offended. "So you hired me to be Ben's girlfriend."

"Oh no. I simply hoped for the best." She smiles sweetly. "I merely put you two in proximity to one another and let the sparks fly. Venus is never wrong, you know. When she suggests a pairing, I always listen."

"And when I tried to leave, you pulled a stunt to force me to stay. To force me to Ben's side, because I was afraid I'd be cursed. You knew that he'd protect me."

Her chin lifts. "It worked, didn't it?

"It worked, all right. And now Ben's furious with you and he's ruined his reputation with the other warlocks, so I'm not sure if that was what you wanted to achieve."

Dru waves a hand. "Oh, Caliban doesn't care about any of that. All those warlocks could fall off a cliff for all that he cares. He could stop casting tomorrow, and I think it wouldn't bother him. He needs someone that sees him, though. Someone that understands him and loves him and supports him despite all the terrible things in his past. There's no warlock or witch that doesn't have a terrible history, myself included, but Caliban carries it heavier than most of us." She shakes her head. "He thinks he's fine alone, but I know he's not. And my time here on Earth is limited, you know. I'm not going to be around forever."

Oh. Is Dru . . . dying? That adds a horrifying angle to everything we've been through. Her machinations make sense, her scheming to secure Ben's happiness. "How much longer do you have?"

She reaches over and takes my hand, her expression tragic. "Maybe another hundred years, max."

I snatch my hand out of hers. "You are the fucking worst, you know that?"

Dru blinks at me in surprise. "What did I say?"

I rub a hand down my face, shaking my head. Dru's actions make me want to strangle her, but she's not wrong about Ben. He's been lonely and alone, and I can't be mad that she dragged us together. If she hadn't, I might have left that night and never returned, and then I wouldn't have the man I love. The man who clutches a muddy, waterlogged card because it's my favorite, the man who looks at me like he wants to devour me, the man who tells me he's proud of me when I yell at my parents. It's all so very complicated. "Dru, I know you mean well, but you need to talk to Ben. He needs to hear all of this from you."

She sighs heavily, dramatically. "Oh, I know. It's just easier to run it past you first. I know you won't give me those wounded eyes like he does. He's really, really good at wounded eyes, you know."

Oh, I know.

39

BEN

I'm going to wear a fucking groove into Aunt Dru's garden with my pacing. My arms crossed tightly over my chest—it's either that or I start throwing things—I walk back and forth, back and forth, past the fountain and the rosebushes in the backyard. My aunt has never been much of a gardener, but she keeps a garden for herbal spell components, and roses just so the gardeners don't think she's weird, she always says. I suspect she has tablets buried under each rosebush, and I'm tempted to yank each one up just to see what sorts of things my aunt has been up to.

Apparently I don't know her as well as I thought. It was Reggie who realized that Dru had cursed herself. Reggie that pulled all the pieces together, and I'm both awed at how clever and fucking brilliant she is and chagrined that I didn't figure it out myself. I've always had blinders on when it comes to my aunt, but this has really made me take a long, hard look at her.

Reggie would call her a Dorothy for sure. I always thought she was more of a Rose—to quote Reggie—but I see now I've been wrong all along.

Just thinking about Reggie settles me. I pause in my frustrated pacing, imagining how much she's going to tease me when we can finally laugh about this. For some reason, instead of pissing me off, the thought makes me smile. I hate being teased . . . unless it's Reggie, because then I can see that radiant, delighted smile of hers, and her eyes crinkle at the corners and then I have to kiss the hell out of her. I'm smiling to myself as I turn to pace the garden again.

And my aunt stands there in her fuzzy slippers and pink robe. Her snow-white curls are flattened on one side from sleeping, but her cheeks are full of color, her skin as golden with health as ever.

I stop smiling immediately.

Aunt Dru sighs at the change that comes over my expression. "I'm so very sorry, Caliban. I had no idea you'd worry so much."

I arch a brow, trying to hold back my frustration. "You thought I wouldn't worry, then? My aunt falls over from a curse, and I wouldn't worry? Her familiars all get hit with curses, and you think I'm not going to fucking *worry*?"

"Well, when you put it that way, it does sound rather optimistic, doesn't it?"

"No, why would you?" I snap, and all the pent-up fear and frustration spills out of me. "All you think about is yourself. Do you have any idea of how much danger Reggie was in while you were unconscious? I was worried I'd lose you both—" I stop abruptly, because it feels too vulnerable to say it aloud.

Aunt Dru's look is soft. She pads forward, her slippers scuffing on the ground. "Oh, Caliban. I really, truly am sorry."

"Was there ever a curse on your familiars? Or was that just more bullshit you were selling to make Reggie think she was in danger?"

Aunt Dru pauses. "Well, yes and no." At my glare, she continues. "You know as well as I do that most people only get cursed because they've done something obnoxious. Maurice got turned into a cat because he can't keep his willy in his pants." She taps her chin. "Though I really should work harder at finding that poor man's tablet—"

"Don't bother. Apparently he likes being a cat."

"Oh? Well, that's lovely." She smiles. "Solves all kinds of problems. As for the others, Gwen ended up sleeping with the wrong man. You know how that sort of thing is."

I don't, actually, since I've never been in that particular situation. Most of my relationships have been . . . particularly detached before Reggie, and I don't plan on there being an "after Reggie." She's it for me.

"And Lisa, well, I'm afraid that was all me, but it was really just a harmless little curse. Doors are a simple enough thing to get around. I truly didn't mean to scare you so badly, though." She approaches me and puts her hand on my sleeve. "I'm sorry, Caliban. I never had children, so I guess I don't stop to think about how my actions affect others. I've always been a solo operator, much like yourself."

She doesn't get it. I shake my head. "I don't care if you weren't my real parent, Aunt Dru. You were the one that taught me magic. You were the one I went to when I was sad or afraid. You were the one that looked after me, the one that sent presents on holidays. My real parents were never there for me, but I could always count on you." My voice grows ragged. "I didn't like the thought of you being hurt . . . or gone."

"Oh, Caliban." Aunt Dru sniffs and then flings her arms around me. "My sweet little boy."

Ugh. "Ben, Aunt Dru. It's been Ben for forever and a day."

"You're always going to be my sweet little Caliban with the runny nose and running around naked in the gardens with your winky hanging out." She sniffs. "You really were the cutest little thing."

Great. Now she's talking about my winky and how cute and

small I was. I really hope Reggie isn't listening in on this part of the conversation. I pat Aunt Dru's back awkwardly. "It's forgiven."

She looks up at me, her expression sly once more. "But I did pretty good bringing Reggie to you, didn't I—"

I scowl. "Don't push it."

She giggles, all mischief once more, and I know my aunt has learned nothing from this. She's had two thousand years to become set in her ways. She'll never, ever change.

I hug her anyhow, because we're family.

A FEW HOURS later, I'm alone in the house with Reggie.

Lisa and her husband, Jim, are off for a doctor's appointment, and they're not coming back until tomorrow. Aunt Dru insisted on meeting up with Livia, who she hasn't seen "in positively ages," so they can go to bingo together. I think Reggie would have gone, too, just to fuss over Dru, but my aunt insisted she stay home and rest after all her "trials."

And then Dru gave me an obvious, obvious wink, which means our alone time is more of my aunt's machinations.

I'm not all that upset about it, either. The last time I was alone in a room with Reggie, we were in the hotel together, and I was mourning the lack of a condom. I have some upstairs, though I admit the ones I had were expired by about a decade. Luckily, Nick's boyfriend, Diego, came to my rescue. As Reggie clung to me back at Nick's apartment, Diego walked up to me, slapped me on the shoulder, and then shoved a fistful of condoms into my other hand.

I don't think Reggie noticed.

But now I'm alone with her again, and the condoms are burning a hole in my pocket. I'm exhausted—we both are—but I'm not ready to lie down and go to sleep. I want to touch her. Gods, do I want to touch her. My hands itch with the need to caress her skin, to hear the little gasps she makes when she's being pleasured. My cock tightens in my pants, and my favorite heavy black sweater becomes too hot, too itchy, and I'm tempted to take it off and see if Reggie runs her hands over my chest like she did earlier.

That might be too obvious, though.

I saunter into the kitchen, where Reggie is seated atop the counter next to the coffeepot. She yawns, and her hair has strayed out of the tight bun from the party and straggles all over her neck and sticks up in random brown tufts. Her eyes are still red and swollen, and her makeup has gathered in the corners of her eyes.

She's damned beautiful.

Reggie looks up and tilts her head toward the coffee maker, which is brewing a fresh cup. "You want some? I'm going to need some major caffeine to prop me up if I'm going to make it through the night."

"Why do you need to make it through the night?" I ask, all casual. I should have definitely taken off my sweater, I decide. Reggie's texting on her phone, her thumbs flying over the screen's keyboard, and she has a look of concentration on her face.

She doesn't look up as she types. "Because we'll want to check on Dru when she gets home, just in case. Don't you think?"

"Of course." I lean over the counter, watching her. I don't have to rush things, I remind myself. I want Reggie to feel comfortable being with me, and we've had a tumultuous last few days. The last thing I need is to push her into something she's not ready for. I'm five hundred years old. I can wait a few months. Or a few weeks. Or . . . days. Or whatever she needs.

"You look really tired," I point out. "Who are you texting?" Fuck, I feel obvious.

"Nick," Reggie says, yawning. "And Penny. It's a group chat.

You want to be in on it? Penny wants to learn how to play Spellcraft, and I just talked you up." She glances up at me, mischievous. "I told them your technomancer deck is impossible to beat, and Nick says that's bullshit and to bring it next Friday." She pauses. "I might have said I was bringing you over to Nick's for Friday-night cards next time."

"Ah." I'm actually rather pleased that she's being so commandeering of my time. I like that she wants to monopolize me. "That's fine." I lean against her side, watching her text, and when she continues, I slip one of her shoes off. "Want a foot rub?"

She obligingly sticks one foot out and keeps typing. "Everyone wanted to know how things ended up with Dru, also, so I'm updating them. I'm also telling Penny that Nick doesn't know magic is real, so there's a lot of back-and-forth." She makes a face that I find utterly enchanting. "I can already tell this is going to get wildly complicated."

"It'll be fine." I rub her toes, massaging, and I can't help but notice that she's still wearing my bracelet. I haven't asked her to take it off yet, and I don't know how I'm going to handle that. I kind of want her to wear it forever. Well, maybe not forever. Just until she becomes a full-fledged witch in her own right. I like the thought of that almost as much as I like her wearing my familiar bracelet.

Reggie whimpers as I rub her arch, and she leans back against the cabinets, eyes closed. "Oh, fuck."

"Ticklish?"

She makes a little sound in her throat. "If I didn't know better, I'd swear you were trying to get laid."

"Mmm."

Reggie chuckles. "Come to think of it, Ben Magnus, are you trying to get laid?"

"I'm not sure what the right answer is here," I say, voice low and even as I rub my fingers over the ticklish spot on her foot. "If I say no, then I don't get laid. If I say yes, I sound too eager."

She giggles and pulls her foot out of my grasp. In the next moment, Reggie launches herself at me, her arms going around my neck and her legs locking around my waist. "You idiot. Why didn't you say something? I've been wanting to jump your bones all day long."

"You have?"

Reggie nods, and when my hands go to her ass, she wriggles against them, burying her face in my neck and kissing me. "Didn't want to seem too greedy, though. I thought I'd let you set the pace."

"Here I've been waiting for you to notice me. I almost came in here without my shirt."

She giggles, and the sound is like pure sunshine in my veins. "I wouldn't have minded that. I do like touching you."

"Fuck, I like touching you, too." I look around the kitchen for a suitable surface to set her down on. "Where do we do this?"

"Five hundred years and this is the experience you have?" She teases me, her teeth scraping on my neck. "Should I be worried?"

She wiggles against me, and that decides the matter. "Fuck it, we're going to my room." When she licks my throat, I hold her tighter, determined not to lose control before I have her on my bed.

I've never gone up the stairs so damn fast in my life. Reggie's slight weight gets heavy, however, and by the time I get to the top of the stairs, I'm panting. This just makes her laugh even more, and if it was any other woman, it'd probably piss me off. But because it's Reggie, I just laugh with her. I'm still laughing when I kick my door open, and Maurice tries to saunter in after us.

"Oh no you don't, you pervert," Reggie calls out. "Stop him, Ben. I'm not having sex with Maurice under the bed!"

I toss her down on the bed. She sprawls, all legs and smile, and she's never been more beautiful. I'm utterly entranced, and the breath catches in my throat. Reggie. Incredibly beautiful, twice as stubborn as anyone I've ever met. I love the combination. I love how she never backs down when she wants something. I love how she tries to organize everything and everyone she comes across. I glance down at Maurice, who is watching us with interested golden eyes. "If you don't get out of here, I'm going to make you into a spell component," I warn him. "You have three seconds."

The cat yowls and races out of the room, prompting another peal of laughter from Reggie. I shut the door after the cat and kick off my shoes. I pull my sweater off and toss it to the floor, and I'm rewarded with Reggie's wince. She jumps to her feet, picking the sweater up off the ground. "Ben, you really should be more careful with your clothing—"

I scoop her into my arms again, hauling her back onto the bed. "You can fuss at me later, when I'm balls deep inside you."

"Ben!" she squeals, but there's a delighted note in her voice. "You dirty thing."

"Filthy," I agree. "Especially filthy when it comes to you. Should I be quiet?"

"No." Reggie gives me a scorching look and holds her arms up. "You should help me undress."

"Gods, I love you," I groan. I lean over her and cage her with my arms, and I love that she reaches for me and raises her mouth to mine. Her lips brush over mine and she bites down on my lower lip, then soothes it with her tongue. My cock twitches in response, and I claim her mouth with the kiss. It becomes a tug-of-war between us, trying to get the upper hand on the other via kissing.

I grab her sweatshirt and drag it over her head—or I try to, at least. The collar gets stuck on her nose and suddenly her face and arms are trapped, and the only part of her free from the tangle of her shirt is her chin. Reggie sputters, giggling, and mock-bites at the air. "You're supposed to help me get undressed, not trap me."

"I think I like you like this," I admit. "Helpless and freckled and sexy."

She squirms against the shirt. "Those words don't go together, you ding-dong."

"I disagree." I lean in, my hands holding her arms pinned, and kiss her neck. I love that her breath catches and her body quivers under me. "I think they perfectly encapsulate just how amazing you are."

Reggie makes a soft sound in her throat, and I slide a little bit lower, fascinated by her breasts. She's wearing some small, pale pink scrap of material that barely passes as a bra. It's sheer and dainty and such a fucking tease that I reach down and lick her pretty little nipple right through the material.

She arches off the bed, moaning. "Ben. Fuck, yes. Ben."

"You like that, Reggie?" I lick her nipple again, then move to the other, not bothering to move the bra. There's something sinful about tonguing her through the material, and I suspect she likes the naughtiness of it as much as I do. I don't think I've ever heard anything better than how she says my name. Like it's both pleasure and wonder when I touch her like this, and it makes me want to do more, endlessly. I don't think I'll ever get tired of hearing her call for me.

Ever.

I nuzzle at her pretty, pretty breasts until she's going wild on the bed under me, panting my name over and over again. She bucks her hips in silent demand, and I raise up to kiss her again, to plunder that soft, pretty mouth that just says my name over and over again like a prayer. I finally help her out of the sweatshirt, and then she's looking at me, flushed and eager. She lies back on the bed again, stretching out in silent invitation.

One I take her up on.

"Beautiful, perfect Reggie," I breathe, showering her torso with kisses. Her nipples are tight and pointing, and I can't resist tonguing them over and over again. "Tell me that you're mine."

"I'm wearing your bracelet, aren't I?" she retorts, her frantic hands going to the waistband of her pajama pants.

Hearing that reminder makes me go still. "Did you want to take it off?"

She shakes her head, her gaze meeting mine. "I kind of wish I was just yours. Only yours."

My heart swells and that fierce, possessive feeling returns. No one has ever wanted to be purely mine. Even my earlier familiars couldn't wait to finish their time with me. They considered me a necessary evil, a means to an end. With Reggie, though, it's all different. I feel wanted. Seen. Understood.

It's the most enticing aphrodisiac ever.

I lean over her and give her one more hungry kiss, then stand up. I rip at my clothes, and Reggie grins feverishly, tearing at her pants. Her panties are plain, floral cotton, but for some reason, I find that incredibly arousing. Like she knows she doesn't have to pretend with me. She can just be herself. I kick off the last of my clothes and then grab her hips, pressing my mouth all over those damned panties. "Look at you. So fucking pretty."

"I wasn't . . . I didn't think we'd be doing this today, so I didn't prepare." Her voice catches. "I didn't think we'd ever do this again. I thought I lost you, Ben, because I panicked." She touches my face, caressing. "Promise me if I ever freak out on you, you'll give me time to let me work through it."

I kiss her palm, awed that she's actually worried she might

have lost me. As if I'd ever let that happen. "I promise as long as you promise me that we talk things through, no matter what they are."

"Deal." She lifts her chin. "Seal with a kiss?"

Sounds like a good idea to me. "Seal with a kiss," I agree, and press my mouth directly over her clit.

Reggie moans, her thighs going wide. "Oh god, I like your idea so much better."

I lick her through the gusset of her panties, my tongue stroking her soft flesh through the now-damp material. She rocks against my mouth, her hands in my hair, clinging to me. When she begins to shudder with every drag of my tongue, my own need starts to get the better of me. My cock throbs with the need to be inside her. I close my mouth over her pussy, pushing hard with my tongue, and then I lift my head. "I have condoms."

"Oh, thank fuck." Reggie's hands tighten in my hair. "Get one before I lose my mind. Quick."

I certainly don't need to be told twice. I press one last open-mouthed kiss to her pussy, then get to my feet and hunt the condoms out of my jeans pocket. I rip one open with my teeth as Reggie squirms on the bed, wriggling out of her panties and shucking her bra. She sits back down on the edge, her elbows propping her up, and watches me as I roll the condom down my length. I love how greedy her eyes are, how she's just as possessive as I am. She watches me as if I'm something she can't wait to get her hands on, and she's just as needy as I am.

"I can't help but think electric purple is an odd choice for a man like you," Reggie murmurs as I step forward.

"Diego."

"Say no more," she tells me with a grin, reaching for me. "I'm just glad you came prepared."

I kiss her again, covering her smaller form with mine. Her

skin is so warm and soft, and I love the freckles on her shoulders. After I kiss her mouth thoroughly, I move to those freckles and nip at them until her nails dig into my back. "Ben," she whimpers. "Are you just going to rub that big purple cock against me, or are you going to do something with it?"

"So bossy, even in bed." I love it. I drag her hips to the edge of the bed, then take my cock in hand. Instead of pushing into her, though, I press it against her folds and rock against her, still teasing. "Is this what you wanted?"

Reggie growls, rubbing against me with frantic, needy motions. Her hands dig at the blankets on the bed, and her legs twitch, spread wide in silent anticipation. "Wasn't . . . what I had . . . in mind."

"Something more, then?" I put a hand on one of her hips, anchoring her, and then rub the head at the entrance to her body. Just a tease. Just enough to make us both insane with sensation. My breath catches when she arches, the movement pushing the tip into her body.

"Oh, fuck, yes," Reggie says, her eyes fluttering closed. "Give me that big, thick cock, Ben."

Her blatant demand takes me by surprise—I should have known that Reggie wouldn't be a shy, sweet partner in bed. She's always been demanding and slightly pushy, and it's one of the things I adore about her—that she doesn't let the world happen around her; she changes her environment to be how she wants it. She demands things of it.

Just like she's demanding things from me. With a groan, I push into her, because I can't deny her anything.

Reggie makes a soft noise in her throat as I stroke into her. I go slowly, because she's tight and slick and oh so sweet, and I don't want to hurt her. I also want to savor this moment, and so I drag it out, taking my time as I ease into her body. I tell her how good she feels, how pretty she is when she squirms on my length, how wet she is, how much I love her, and Reggie's whimpers grow louder.

When I'm finally fully in her, I close my eyes and drink in the moment. I'm deep inside the woman I love, the woman who's wearing my bracelet. The woman who gets me. The woman who . . . begins to impatiently rock under me, demanding that I move.

Well, I can do that.

I put both hands on Reggie's hips, locking her in place, and then I begin a slow, steady rhythm. She moans, her head going back, and gives herself over to me. She's so fucking beautiful, her small, perfect tits jiggling with my movements, her hands twisting in the blankets as if she doesn't quite know what to do with them. Being inside her like this fuels my possessiveness as well as my need, and my pace increases. I move faster, stroking harder into her, and when Reggie cries out words of encouragement, it only adds to my hunger. Before I realize what I'm doing, I'm pounding into her, claiming her so hard that the bed is shaking, and she arches her hips with every thrust, forcing me deeper, making each plunge into her body as intense as possible.

Even though I've imagined this particular moment a thousand times since meeting her, I lose all semblance of control. I take her over and over again, wild with need, and Reggie just encourages it with demands like "harder" and "faster" and "deeper" and "more." When her body tightens around me and her legs jerk, tightening with her release, she cries out my name—*Ben*. Not Caliban. Not "god" or "please" or anything but "Ben."

It shatters my control. I hammer into her soft, welcoming body until I crest, the climax ripping through me with such force that stars dance behind my eyes. I rock into her as the release racks through my system, filling the condom and leaving me boneless and utterly sated. I sag against her on the bed, covering her with my larger frame as she wraps her arms and legs around me and kisses my neck and my cheek, everywhere she can reach.

"Ben," she whispers, stroking my hair. "My Ben."

It's the perfect thing to say. I'm hers, and she's mine, and I think it's all I've ever wanted.

She nips at my ear with small teeth. "Can I ask you something?"

I can barely think straight, but I can also refuse her nothing. "Anything."

"What was your secret?" Her hand trails over my spine. "The one you gave Abernathy?"

I chuckle. She wants that, does she? Reggie doesn't like anything being kept from her. "I told him that I was moving books in the library at night so you wouldn't quite finish your organizing. Ever."

She gasps, and I feel it all the way down to my cock, still deep inside her. "You *what*?"

"I wanted you to stay." I bury my face against her hair. "Forever. And I figured if you didn't finish the library, it'd encourage you to stay. And it kept you out of my rooms if you were working on it."

Reggie giggles, her arms tightening around my neck. "You are a wretched man, and that might be the sweetest thing anyone's ever done for me."

Only Reggie would find my manipulation sweet, because she knows how important it is to be wanted. In that way, we're perfectly alike. She doesn't have to worry about anything like that anymore, though. I couldn't stop wanting her if I tried. I'm going to want her for the next thousand years or more.

"I didn't know hiding books would make you so happy. I should tell you about all the other things I'm hiding." I lean in and nip at her ear, because it's soft and delicious looking and right there.

"Mmm, is one of them bright purple?"

She's far too good at this game already.

Epilogue

REGGIE

Six Months Later

"Mercury, show me Ben," I say, trailing a finger over the crystal ball. "Please," I add, remembering to be polite.

My offering—high-end olives with just a touch of caviar, along with a few pricks of blood from my finger—smokes in the offering bowl. The globe fills with fog, and I trace my fingertips over it again and again, willing the picture to come into focus. Ben uses his phone for scrying, but I'm still not quite good enough to do that, so I use what he calls "training wheels"—namely Dru's favorite crystal ball, now mine.

Just thinking about Ben makes the picture focus, and the crystal ball shows me a big, strong, pale back, dripping with water. Ben is naked, his hand on the shower tiles, his head bent under the spray. I grin, full of mischief, and watch him, wondering if he's going to touch himself while I'm creeping on him this time.

Ben tilts his head under the water. "I know you're watching, you pervert," he says. "I can feel the magic."

I let out a huff and tap the crystal ball to end the vision. "Thank you, Mercury." I try to be polite to the gods, even if I'm not entirely sure I believe in them. But you never know, and someone's answering the spells, so . . . yeah. I toss a cloth back over the crystal ball and saunter up the stairs to the bathroom I share with Ben on the second floor of Aunt Dru's house. Maurice rubs against my leg, so I scoop him up as I head toward the bathroom, rubbing his soft, furry head.

Ben didn't lock the door, so I let myself in and lean against the sink as he showers. "You told me to practice," I remind him. "You didn't say when."

"You're an absolute deviant, woman."

"A mongrel deviant," I correct. "Which means I'm perfect for you."

Ben just turns in the spray, giving me full frontal. Maurice makes a pained cat sound and squirms out of my arms, running back down the hall. He's not a big fan of Ben's nudity, which is hilarious since he constantly tries to sneak into the bathroom to watch *me* shower. I appreciate the sight of my lover, his bracelet warm on my wrist. I never get tired of looking at his big, naked body. He's got such broad, delicious shoulders and long, muscular legs that it's hard for me to remember sometimes that he spends most of his days hunched over books or working on scrolls. Though since he sold his brownstone in Boston and moved in permanently with me and Dru, he's joined a local gym, and we go running together in the mornings.

"Did Aunt Dru call?" he asks, turning off the water.

I automatically hand him a towel. "Yup. Fiji is beautiful, blah, blah, blah, she's not coming home anytime soon. The usual."

"She didn't want to talk to me?" He looks surprised.

I smile, because it's adorable how much Ben loves his aunt. "She found a bingo place even in Fiji. Promised to call once she's out, and I'm sure she'll talk your ear off then." I touch Dru's cuff as he towel-dries his hair, the one I'm still wearing just because. After the big scare—which is what we're politely calling Dru's coma—Dru decided it was time for a sabbatical. She and Livia are visiting several islands in the Pacific and have been gone for several months. My job title has changed from "familiar" to "housekeeper" since I'm watching over things while she's gone, and Lisa is currently tending to her newborn. Lisa swears she'll be back next spring, so I don't expect to see Dru return to the States before then. Which is fine. Ben keeps me happily busy. He's taken over my familiar training and says in a hundred years or two, I'll be ready to cast on my own. I personally plan on surprising him with it much sooner than that. Maybe fifty years, though I'm in no rush to stop being his familiar. I like being his.

Ben finishes toweling his hair and moves toward me, looming as I lean against the edge of the sink. He presses a light kiss to my lips, then begins to make his way along my jaw, toward my ear. I helpfully tilt my head to give him access, winding my arms around his damp neck. "You're in a frisky mood."

"Willem texted me this morning," he tells me between kisses.

"Oh?" That makes me pause. Penny started working for him as his familiar a month ago, and from what I've heard, things have been rocky.

"Yep." He sucks on my earlobe, sending shivers up my spine. "If I recall, it said, 'Fuck you, you cold-blooded Magnus asshole.'"

"So it's going well," I breathe. "Poor Penny."

Ben chuckles. "Poor Willem. Penny's probably so enthusiastic it wears him out."

Penny is a happy, excited sort. I still don't know why she agreed to work with grumpy, unpleasant Willem, but she's more than happy to finally be a familiar. She'd barely started her classes with Ben when she took on Willem's bracelet. I personally worry my sweet friend is in over her head, but Ben assures me Willem is all bark and no bite.

Ben's mouth moves to my neck, licking my pulse point and nearly making my eyes roll back in my head with how good it feels. I can't let him distract me from my news, though. "I followed up with the police this morning," I mention as he tugs on the thin strap of my tiny, summery top, easing it down over my shoulder. "Restraining order is in place, finally."

He lifts his head to gaze down at me. It's something we've talked about for the last week, ever since my parents resurfaced yet again and attempted to guilt me into giving them more money. Ben said he'd support me no matter what I chose, because he knows it's hard for me to be firm with them. The restraining order was my idea, and quiet approval shines in his eyes. "I'm proud of you."

"It was hard," I say softly.

"It'll always be hard, but I'll be right here with you." He kisses the tip of my nose.

"You're always hard, too," I joke, even as I ease backward onto the counter so I can wrap my legs around him. He's still gloriously naked, and I can feel his cock against my thigh, making my insides turn to liquid.

"Can you blame me? My girlfriend is the sexiest thing I've ever seen." He bends over to kiss my shoulder again. "Just look at all these glorious freckles."

I squirm against him, aroused and yet still obligated to point out, "Your students will be here soon."

"They can wait." His hand steals to the front of my shorts. "I'll tell them I'm giving my familiar a very important lesson."

"We were late last time," I pant as his fingers dance over the fabric and ease into my panties. "Same reason."

"Consistency is very important for warlocks," he tells me,

claiming my mouth with another kiss. "Something else they'll need to learn."

I can't argue with that. Nor do I want to. I'm too happy to be in his arms, always. It's where I belong, where I'm safe and loved and always, always needed.

Ben's my home. My wonderful, grumpy Dorothy home.

Acknowledgments

The idea for this particular storyline came about several years ago, when I ran across an article online about Roman curse tablets, and the hundreds that were found in an old well in Britain. This inspired me to go down a research rabbit hole and find out everything I could about Roman magic practices. I've wanted to write a novel about a regular woman who apprentices with a bunch of ridiculous witches, but it wasn't until I added the element of the Roman magic that it really came together for me.

While I'd like to say that this book includes legit Roman magic, I'd be lying. I started authentic and then took a right straight into fantasyland for the purposes of the story. That being said, if you'd like to find out more about Roman witchcraft and rituals, I have a few books to recommend. I used these as reference and inspiration, but at the end of the day, this is definitely a work of fiction.

- *Magic, Witchcraft and Ghosts in the Greek and Roman Worlds: A Sourcebook* by Daniel Ogden
- *Magic in Ancient Greece and Rome* by Lindsay C. Watson
- *Drawing Down the Moon: Magic in the Ancient Greco-Roman World* by Radcliffe G. Edmonds III
- *Curse Tablets and Binding Spells from the Ancient World* by John G. Gager

No book is written in a vacuum, of course, so I have the following people to thank for inspiring me along the way—Mick and Jen and Daphne, for being my longtime besties. Alicia, La-Donna, and Caye of Team Velociraptor—long may we send weird text messages to one another about nothing at all. Thank you to my husband, who is unwavering in his support, encourages me when I'm behind, and insists on me taking "big writing days" for myself so I can feel better about deadlines. Thank you to Kristine Swartz and Holly Root for the endless cheerleading and guidance. Thank you to Ana Hard, who came up with the delightfully fun cover.

I'm sure there are a dozen other people I'm forgetting, and that's why acknowledgments make me so nervous! Please know that I love and appreciate you even if I've forgotten to include your name here. Like Reggie, I don't do well under pressure.

New York Times and *USA Today* bestselling author **Jessica Clare** writes under three pen names. As Jessica Clare, she writes contemporary romance. As Jessica Sims, she writes fun, sexy shifter paranormals. Finally, as Jill Myles, she writes a little bit of everything, from sexy, comedic urban fantasy to zombie fairy tales. She lives in Texas with her husband, cats, and too many dust bunnies.

CONNECT ONLINE

Jessica-Clare.com
AuthorJessicaClare
_JessicaClare